Praise for Darien Gee's

Friendship Bread

"An engrossing story about a small town and lives transformed."
—*Miami Herald*

"Charming." —*Ladies' Home Journal*

"*Friendship Bread* is a poignant, utterly compelling read—a novel you won't soon forget. Darien Gee has deftly created a small town so endearing, you won't want to leave."
—PATRICIA WOOD, nationally bestselling author of *Lottery*

"*Friendship Bread* is a heartwarming novel that celebrates small-town life, good friends, and the healing power of bread. Like the bread of the title, read this then pass it on to someone you love!"
—ANN HOOD, nationally bestselling author of *The Red Thread*

"An utterly heartwarming tale of sisterhood and forgiveness."
—ModernMom

"The wonderful characters in *Friendship Bread* face life-changing adversity of the sort that either brings us down or transforms us into better people. Darien Gee has a writer's heart and a baker's sense of mixing it all just right. The result is a book you will read over and over."
—NANCY PICKARD, *New York Times* bestselling author of *The Scent of Rain and Lightning*

"This entertaining series debut by Gee . . . will appeal to fans of tear-jerkers like Kristin Hannah's *Winter Garden* or novels dealing with the loss of a family member, such as Lolly Winston's *Good Grief*. It's also ideal for book clubs and readers who like stories about small-town life; it expertly weaves together numerous characters and narratives and even includes recipes and directions for making friendship bread."
—*Library Journal*

"Gee has created a wonderful cast of characters (and there are quite a few) to populate this story, and she creatively includes a bit of romance, a bit of mystery (where did that first starter come from?) and a lesson or two about the value of friendship in a delightful tale that is sure to have readers clamoring for more."
—Wichita Falls *Times-Record News*

"A satisfying first novel by Gee; perfect for the book-club circuit and beyond."
—*Kirkus Reviews*

"A multi-layered tale rich in friendships and personal growth."
—*Grand Rapids Press*

FRIENDSHIP BREAD

BALLANTINE BOOKS TRADE PAPERBACKS

NEW YORK

Friendship Bread

A Novel

DARIEN GEE

Copyright © 2011 by Gee & Co., LLC
Reading group guide copyright © 2012 by Random House, Inc.
Excerpt from *Memory Keeping* © 2013 by Gee & Co., LLC

All rights reserved.

Published in the United States by Ballantine Books, an imprint of The Random House Publishing Group, a division of Random House, Inc., New York.

BALLANTINE and colophon are registered trademarks of Random House, Inc. RANDOM HOUSE READER'S CIRCLE & Design is a registered trademark of Random House, Inc.

Originally published in hardcover in the United States by Ballantine Books, an imprint of The Random House Publishing Group, a division of Random House, Inc., in 2011.

This book contains an excerpt from the forthcoming book *Memory Keeping* by Darien Gee. This excerpt has been set for this edition only and may not reflect the final content of the forthcoming edition.

LIBRARY OF CONGRESS CATALOGING-IN-PUBLICATION DATA
Gee, Darien.
Friendship bread : a novel / Darien Gee.
p. cm.
ISBN 978-0-345-52535-2—ISBN 978-0-345-52536-9 (eBook)
1. Sisters—Fiction. 2. Female friendship—Fiction. I. Title.
PS3611.I5834F75 2011
813'.6—dc22   2010048268

Printed in the United States of America
www.randomhousereaderscircle.com

2 4 6 8 9 7 5 3 1

Book design by Dana Leigh Blanchette

Dedicated to the mothers

Acknowledgments

The following people have helped make the town of Avalon and its wonderful residents a reality:

Patricia Wood, a good friend and fellow author who was so enthusiastic about *Friendship Bread* that she introduced me to her agent; her husband and first mate, Gordon Wood, who read the novel and (very neatly, in Adobe) annotated pages with useful comments; the Wirth family (Greg, Tina, Amelia, Eli, Maisie), who gave us our first bag of Amish Friendship Bread starter and later read Leon's passage to make sure I didn't mess up the heavens or at least how one would view them; artist Mary Spears, whose friendship (and cooking) have been a true gift, for which I am very thankful, and her hubby, Phil Slott, who always knows the right thing to say. My dear friend Nancy Martin's friendship is the basis of my books and this one especially—we are blessed when people whom we least expect become good friends. Her keen eye and honest emotional response to my novels have helped me become a better writer. Mary Embry, Esther and Jerry Hicks, and Abraham keep me grounded so I can do what I love, never doubting for a second that I can do it.

Darien Gee/Mia King friends and fans stepped up to help with reading an early draft of the novel, providing lots of helpful feedback: Anne Alesauskas, Kari Andersen, Linda Bass, RoxAnn Batovsky, Robin Blankenship, Susan Buetow, Linda Buron, Philip Carmichael, Kelli Jo Calvert, Bertha Chang, Traci Clark, Maria Cogar, Kelli Curtin, Jacqueline Graves, Elaine Huntzinger, Chris Hijirida, Marcia Hodge, Patricia Hopkins, Layla Johnston, Gaby Lapus, Wilma Lee, John Martin, Shannon Martin, Sharon McNally, Megan McNealy, Rose Milligan, Elaine Monteleone, Becky Muehling, Holly Nakfoor, Melissa Nichols, Kari Noel, Vanessa Primer, Vickie Sheridan, Val Stark, Jan Terry, Amanda Villagomez, Kathryn Wilkie, Philip Yau.

Writing a novel, of course, is only half the battle. Publication is another matter, the not-so-simple act of putting all the pieces together so that readers may have another good book to savor and keep on their shelves. Big hugs to Dorian Karchmar and her wonderful team at William Morris Endeavor who have championed the book here, there, and around the world: Rayhané Sanders, Laura Bonner, Raffaella De Angelis, Michelle Feehan, Tracy Fisher, Rachel McGhee, Margaret Riley.

At Ballantine/Random House, my heartfelt thanks to publisher Libby McGuire and my lovely editor, Linda Marrow. I know the sales and marketing teams worked hard to share their enthusiasm for this book, and I'm grateful for the many reads and editorial suggestions by Linda and senior editor Dana Isaacson. Junessa Viloria makes sure we're all connected (since I am literally an ocean away) and the copy editorial team including Penelope Haynes and Angela Pica have cast a careful eye over the manuscript. Thank you all.

My appreciation to Lawrence Hsu, Monika Wiatr Kwon, Neil Morris, and Matthew Pearce, who have helped in countless ways.

My never-ending gratitude to Mia King readers who told me to keep writing so they could keep reading.

I'm lucky to be surrounded by a supportive family—the Hsus and the Gees—and my own little clan: my husband, Darrin Gee, and our three kids—Maya, Eric, and Luke. I love you all, and yes, this is what Mama was spending all her time doing ("You're writing *again*? Are you ever going to be done?"). To answer that, I hope not. I love what I do, and it's my wish that we all find—and do—the things that make our hearts sing.

Friendship is precious, not only in the shade,
but in the sunshine of life.

THOMAS JEFFERSON

FRIENDSHIP BREAD

❀

Leon Ydara, 81
Amateur Astronomer

Leon adjusts the 25mm Plossl eyepiece and swings his scope toward the heavens. It's a clear night, perfect for stargazing, with a moon so bright it's actually interfering with his night vision. He slips in the moon filter at 9mm and takes another look. Mare Crisium is simply beautiful.

Next he turns the scope toward the horizon, toward the crescent-shaped face of Venus. Then Mars in the southern sky. He can see the Cassini division between the rings of Saturn. Pleiades, the Orion Nebula. A satellite blinks across his field of view, typical at this time of year.

Leon stands back to change the eyepieces, taking his time to put everything back in its proper box. That's the problem with beginning astronomers. They get so excited by what's in the sky that they shove spare filters into their pockets, not wanting to lose a minute of time at the risk of missing something. But it can damage the lenses, and then what have you got?

There's a chill in the air. He buttons up his coat slowly, his fingers stiff. Old age is hard on the joints. Standing over his homemade Dobsonian telescope makes his back hurt, so when Leon gets tired he simply sits down on the lawn chair and takes out his binoculars.

Most people don't realize that you don't need an expensive telescope to see the night sky. A lot of backyard astronomers rely on only two things: a dark night and their eyes. You don't need much else to see the best show in the world.

It was Marta who first turned him on to stargazing. They were at a party, each with different dates, each bored out of their mind. He found her outside, down the lawn from the party, staring up at the sky. Her russet-red hair tumbled down her back as she tipped back her head, her lips slightly parted as she breathed in the night air. Even in the waning night Leon could see her skin, clear and pale as moonlight.

"The Milky Way," she said softly, pointing. He didn't know her name, but looked up anyway. "Ursa Major—the Big Dipper. Ursa Minor—the Little Dipper." Her finger trailed across the sky. "Orion's Belt." Three stars in a row.

It was winter 1962. Six months later they were married, her ring a constellation of three diamonds. Their only child, a girl they named Rosa, came one year later. She had her father's dark hair and her mother's fine features, their pride and joy.

Leon lifts the binoculars to his eyes. He should probably invest in a 10 x 50 pair, something with a broader angle of view and better optics, but he can't let this pair go. Marta gave it to him for their first anniversary, and it means something to him to know that she held and looked through these very same lenses.

Over the years they've seen a lot. Planets, stars, comets, meteor shows, star clusters, galaxies, nebulae. The birth of their daughter, three miscarriages, four moves, numerous job promotions, the loss of both sets of parents.

His daughter, Rosa, and her husband, Jack, visit when they can. They live in Grand Rapids. Rosa will cook for days and then they'll pack up the car with ice coolers and drive the five hours from Michigan to Illinois, arriving with enough food to feed Leon for a month. He tries to tell his daughter that he doesn't need so much, but she doesn't listen. Food has always been a comfort in their home, and it's what Rosa does best. Just like her mother.

Rosa came for a visit last month. She and Jack are trying to have a baby, but can't, and it makes Leon sad to see her sad. He tries to tell her that these things sometimes just happen, but he knows that's a flimsy excuse. He's an engineer by training, a scientist at the end of the day. He looks for the reason behind everything. When he and Marta were first together, she couldn't believe that he didn't believe in God.

"How can you not?" she'd asked, surprised.

Leon shrugged. "I just don't." The truth was, he didn't really need God. He had all the answers he needed and didn't think any more of it. Marta wasn't religious, but she had a spiritual outlook on life that was contagious to anyone who came in contact with her. Even when she was sick, she held on to her beliefs. When Leon tried to contact every doctor, every specialist, anyone who could give her a different diagnosis, Marta had simply smiled, almost amused. She was too weak to argue with him, but her eyes were still bright and full of life.

In the end, she'd had enough of the doctors, enough of the hospitals, enough of the heavy medications that made her sick. She was okay with dying, even though Leon implored her to live.

"Oh, Leon," she said. "I am so tired. My body is tired. Can you let me go?" She placed her hand against his cheek while he cried.

So they stopped the chemo and moved her home so she could be in her own bed and see the stars. She slipped away two weeks later.

On her tombstone he wrote MARTA YDARA, BELOVED WIFE, 1935–1995. And beneath it, her favorite quote, which he reads aloud every time he visits her grave.

THE TRUE HARVEST OF MY LIFE IS INTANGIBLE—
A LITTLE STAR DUST CAUGHT,
A PORTION OF THE RAINBOW I HAVE CLUTCHED.
Henry David Thoreau

Leon lowers his binoculars. The lenses are fogging up. It happens. Some nights the equipment won't work right, or the weather won't cooperate. The night sky teaches you patience.

He turns to cast an eye over his neighborhood. At this hour families are tucking their children into bed, ready for the quiet relief that graciously accompanies a long day even though there will be dishes to wash, toys to pick up, lunches to be made. This is part of what keeps Leon here in Avalon, in this house. The house itself is much too big for an old man like himself, but he has secretly fallen in love with the people who surround him, their familiar faces, their history now a part of his own. They remember Marta, her laugh that put everyone at ease, made everyone smile. There are still so many wonderful Marta stories they share—every now and then he is reminded of a memory long forgotten—and it fills his heart with unexpected joy, like a child discovering a silver dollar beneath his pillow the morning after losing a tooth.

He imagines Marta watching over them, over the sadness that hangs over one house that used to be filled with laughter, and he wishes she could tell him how he can offer comfort, if such a thing were possible. There are so many unspeakable tragedies, things that are over in a moment but leave so much unhappiness in their wake, lives put on hold, families torn apart.

What do you think, Marta? What is there left to do?

He feels her warm breath on his neck, a tickle, a hint of a smile.

Oh Leon.

He feels her chiding him, or is it his own foolish mind beginning to fail? Leon is practical about this. He has seen death take the people he loves as it will one day take him. There is no use in arguing . . . or is there?

He reaches for his mug of hot water, picks at the crumbs of the cake he's been making since Rosa's last visit. Now that he is in the dusk of his life, Leon has time to indulge in such thoughts. After everything that has happened, does he believe in God? That is the question, perhaps the only one that really matters. How can anyone be absolutely positive that God exists? Is there a God, yes or no?

He feels his head tip back as he is startled by a sudden realization. He wants to burst out in laughter.

The answer is there—in the stars, in the universe, in the galaxies. You just need to look up.

AMISH FRIENDSHIP BREAD

NOTE: Do not refrigerate the starter. It is normal for the batter to rise and ferment. If air gets in the bag, let it out. DO NOT use a metal spoon or bowl for mixing as it will interfere with the fermenting process.

Day 1:   DO NOTHING
Day 2:   Mash the bag
Day 3:   Mash the bag
Day 4:   Mash the bag
Day 5:   Mash the bag
Day 6:   ADD to the bag: 1 cup flour, 1 cup sugar, 1 cup milk. Mash the bag.
Day 7:   Mash the bag
Day 8:   Mash the bag
Day 9:   Mash the bag
Day 10: Follow the directions below

1. Pour the entire bag into a nonmetal bowl.
2. Add: 1½ cups flour, 1½ cups sugar, 1½ cups milk.
3. Measure out four separate batters of 1 cup each into four one-gallon Ziploc bags.
4. Keep one of the bags for yourself, and give the other bags to three friends along with the recipe.

REMEMBER: If you keep a starter for yourself, you will be baking in 10 days. The bread is very good and makes a great gift.

CHAPTER 1

❀

I HOPE YOU ENJOY IT.

Julia Evarts looks up from the paper in her hand and studies the gallon-size Ziploc bag. Inside is a substance that reminds her of drywall compound, except it's much pastier and filled with tiny air bubbles. It would have gone straight into the trash had Gracie not been standing beside her, eyes wide with curiosity.

"Mama, can I try one?" Gracie asks. She holds up a china plate decorated with pansies and roses. Several slices of what looks like banana bread are fanned out on the plate and covered with plastic wrap. Gracie was the first to spot it when they pulled up to the house—the plate, the Ziploc, and the accompanying instructions for "Amish Friendship Bread" sitting on their front porch. There was no card, only a yellow sticky note with the five words written in shaky cursive.

For a moment Julia was confused—had the weekly meals started up again? Not that she'd mind having a casserole to serve for dinner tonight, but this? This smelled suspiciously like a chain letter, with the added headache of having to bake something. Julia can't remember the last time she'd baked something.

Gracie tears off the plastic wrap before Julia can stop her. "This looks good!"

Julia has to admit that it *does* look good. It's coming up on 3:00 P.M., time for an afternoon snack anyway, and as usual she hasn't thought this far ahead. She has no idea how other mothers do it, or how she managed to pull it off before.

"Gracie, hold on. Let's get inside first." Julia unlocks the front door and ushers her five-year-old daughter inside.

She puts their things on the kitchen island and then opens the fridge. It's pretty bare because Julia has forgotten to go grocery shopping, and there's no milk. She doesn't want to have to go out again, so she pours Gracie a glass of water from the tap and heats up the remains of this morning's coffee for herself.

"Now?" Gracie is practically bouncing in place.

They eat straight off the plate, using their fingers. It's not banana bread or like anything Julia's ever tasted before. It's moist and sweet with a hint of cinnamon. It hits the spot, as unexpected kindness always does, and soon there is only one slice left.

"I bet Daddy would like it," Gracie says. Her fingers have crumbs on them, and she licks each one.

Julia bets he would, too. Mark has a sweet tooth, even though he's been on a bit of a health kick lately. She tucks a stray strand of Gracie's mousy brown hair behind her ear, so different from Julia's flyaway strawberry-blond curls. "We'll put it aside for him," Julia says, even though she was hoping to have the last piece for herself. She reaches for the used plastic wrap but Gracie gets to it first.

Julia watches as Gracie tries to extricate the wrap from itself. She waits for the tantrum, for the meltdown that sometimes happens at this time of day, but Gracie manages to pull the plastic wrap apart and lay it over the single slice of bread, carefully tucking it under the scalloped edges of the plate.

"I did it!" Gracie looks at her handiwork, proud. "So now what?"

Julia notices a blue streak of dried paint on the back of Gracie's hand and gives it a rub. "What do you mean, now what?"

Gracie holds up the note and the instructions. "Is this a recipe? It looks like a recipe. Are we supposed to do something? I can mix. I'm great at mixing!" The sugar from the bread has clearly entered Gracie's bloodstream.

Julia turns to look at the Ziploc bag slouching on the counter. She has figured out that it's basically fermenting batter, but the mere thought of baking and what it entails exhausts her. "Yes, you are great at mixing, Gracie," Julia concedes. "It's just that . . . well, someone gave this to us to be nice. They don't expect us to actually do it. I'm not sure I even have the ingredients."

"We could buy them."

Julia gives her daughter a small smile. "I don't think so, Gracie girl." Her voice is apologetic but firm. "Would you like to watch a little television while I get dinner ready?"

Gracie slides off the stool. "I think Clifford is on," she tells Julia, then runs off.

The microwave dings. It's a reminder ding, a clever feature the manufacturer came up with. Or maybe all microwaves have reminder dings now—Julia has no idea. Their previous microwave caught fire when she placed a box of dry macaroni and cheese inside and set the cook time for an hour. Black smoke billowed out and the fire alarm shrieked. Gracie was barely a month old. She was startled but didn't cry, even when Julia broke down and Mark frantically ran about, fire extinguisher in hand as he tried to air out the house.

The microwave dings again. Julia opens the door and sees her cup of coffee. She takes a sip and finds that it's lukewarm and stale. She puts it back in for another minute then stares at the last piece of bread, wondering if Mark will care if she eats it.

He probably won't. He's deferred to her for the past five years, too tired to argue, too tired to try. She can't say she blames him. She doesn't know what to do to make things better, either.

Her coffee is now hot and she pulls back the plastic wrap to finish off the last piece. The evidence is still between her fingers when Gracie walks in holding a piece of pink construction paper.

Her daughter looks shocked, as if Julia has just committed a cardinal sin. "Mama! That was for Daddy!"

Julia feels guilty, and then defensive, but it's pointless either way. First, Gracie is five. She has the clear advantage in this situation, as Julia can't bear to see her daughter distraught. Second, Gracie was born after everything happened. She doesn't know a life other than the one she's living now, where the worst thing that can happen is Julia eating the last piece of Amish Friendship Bread.

Julia tries for an apology. "I'm sorry, Gracie. I was just really hungry."

"But I wanted Daddy to try it." Gracie is near tears.

"Well, we could make him a smoothie or maybe some fruit salad . . ." She has none of these ingredients but offers it up anyway.

"No, I know he'd like this best. I even made a card for him." Gracie holds up the paper in her hand. On it she's laboriously copied the five words from the yellow sticky note.

I HOPE YOU ENJOY IT.

Julia feels a lump in her throat. Her daughter's neat, careful handwriting looks like that of an eight-year-old. Julia knows this because that's how long it took for Josh, a leftie, to master printing. His teacher had suspected developmental dyslexia, and Julia had to fight to keep him out of special ed, not wanting him to be labeled for life. In the end, she had been right. While Josh's handwriting would never be called a thing of beauty—his letters were always sloped, almost kissing the line—he had ended up one of the brightest kids in his class.

As Julia gazes at Gracie's tear-stained face, she knows there's only one solution. She reaches for the instructions for Amish Friendship Bread and sticks it on the refrigerator with a magnet. She steps back, resigned, then puts the Ziploc bag safely to one side as she pulls her daughter into her arms for a tight hug.

"Hold on to your note, Gracie. We'll be baking in ten days."

. . .

Mark doesn't want to go home.

That's not entirely true, actually. He wants to go home, but he doesn't want to get into another fight with Julia or hear about what an awful day she's had. Sometimes she'll just look at him in stony silence, indifferent to his questions, a wall.

But it's the sighs that get to him the most. He'll take silence over sighs any day. The sun can be shining, the house spic-and-span (seeing how he stays up late every night cleaning it), Gracie healthy and full of joy, and still it's not enough.

He sits in his car in the parking lot, unsure of what to do. He doubts Julia has come up with a game plan for dinner. She'll probably ask him to get some takeout or heat up leftovers while she goes into the bedroom for a rest.

A rest from what? Gracie's in kindergarten at the Montessori school, gone for a seven-hour stretch of time. Julia doesn't work anymore, doesn't have to do anything. She picks up Gracie from school and that's pretty much it. Mark does everything else, filling in the gaps wherever he can.

There's a rap on his window and he jumps. The smiling face of Vivian McNeilly is looking at him. Vivian is an interior designer with Gunther & Evarts Architects, in charge of all their high-end commercial and residential projects. She motions for him to lower his window.

Mark presses the button but nothing happens. It takes him a second to realize that the engine's not on. He fumbles for his keys and turns the ignition, feeling like an idiot when the window finally descends with a hum.

"Am I interrupting anything?" Vivian is all smiles. She has a lilting voice, something Mark has always noticed and appreciated for its ability to charm a client. "You look like you're deep in thought."

"What? No. I'm just debating whether or not to go to the gym." What a dumb thing to say, especially since he already worked out before going to the office this morning. Mark wishes he could take it back.

But Vivian nods solemnly as if this is the most intriguing thing she's heard all day. She's worked for them for a year and he's never felt uncomfortable around her, but suddenly he's picking up a vibe he hasn't felt in months.

Years.

"Where do you work out? I ask because I usually run through Avalon Park after work, but I was thinking about picking up a gym membership somewhere." She leans forward, just a bit, and he catches a whiff of perfume.

Mark knows where this is going and that he should just nip it in the bud, but he finds himself contemplating Vivian instead. She makes it look effortless—the wavy auburn locks that fall just past her shoulders, her fitted suit and heels, the way she leans comfortably against the door of his car. She can't be a day over thirty but she holds herself like a woman who's seen the world. She's bright and single, much too young to be living in a small town like Avalon. Before he can stop himself, Mark says, "I go to a gym in Freeport. Fitness Lifestyles. It's a really great facility—they've got an indoor pool and everything."

Why is he telling her this?

"That sounds great," Vivian says. She is beaming and Mark's not sure what just happened. "So I'll follow you there? I have my running gear with me. Maybe we could grab a quick workout after I sign up?"

He's in dangerous waters. Sink or swim.

"Maybe some other time," he says, and offers a conciliatory smile. His palms are sweating as he grips the steering wheel. "See you tomorrow." He manages a wave before putting the car into drive and gunning it out of the parking lot.

Julia stands over the kitchen sink, her hands soapy as she washes each dish and puts it onto the wooden rack to dry. Mark is getting Gracie ready for bed.

This time, the evening time, is the only time Julia feels sane. Safe. She can finally breathe, can finally let herself exhale without fear that the ax is going to fall and destroy what's left of her life. Whatever has happened during the day is over, gone and done with. Her husband is here, her daughter is here. They are all in the same house, under the same roof. Even if they pass each other silently in the hallway, at least they are together.

All that's left to do is finish washing the dishes, then she'll wipe down the table, shower, and crawl into bed. She won't bother with a book or television, as Mark likes to do, but fall straight into a dreamless sleep, her mind and heart finally at rest.

Julia reaches for the next dish. The unfamiliar weight in her hand makes her look down and she sees that it's the scalloped plate that was left on their porch, a few crumbs still on it. She takes a moment to admire the red roses, the pale blue and violet pansies dotting the dish. When she and Mark had married, they were poor and young. It seemed like a waste to register for china, an extravagance. Plus, they had joked, the children would probably break it. They rolled their eyes, imagining the messes to be made by their future progeny. Already Mark and Julia were making plans for these children, letting their decisions revolve around these little beings that had yet to be conceived.

"Can we register for Tupperware?" Mark had asked, and Julia had only giggled.

Julia runs a soapy hand over the smooth plate, wistful and sad for what could have been. When she turns the plate over in her hand, she sees a printed stamp on the back side.

FINE BONE CHINA

SHELLEY

ENGLAND

But that's not what makes her suck in her breath, almost drop the plate into the water. There's a pattern number, and then the name of the pattern right above it.

Rose . . . Pansy . . .

And then the last one, on a line of its own.

Forget-Me-Not.

CHAPTER 2

"Heads, it's a girl. Tails, it's a boy." A shiny quarter sails through the sky and Livvy catches it with a laugh. She gives her coworker a nudge. "Come on. Guess!"

Edie takes a bite of her sandwich. "While I appreciate your highly scientific method for determining the sex of my unborn child, I think I'll pass. Besides, I don't know for sure that I'm even pregnant. I'm just late."

"Edie, come on! I don't know what you're waiting for."

Edie's blue eyes sparkle behind a pair of rectangular glasses. "My period, maybe?"

Livvy slaps the quarter onto the table. "Heads. You're having a girl." She reaches for her own lunch, a cold pasta salad tossed in a low-fat Italian dressing. She can't understand Edie's nonchalance about this. If Livvy were late, she'd be in the drugstore buying every pregnancy kit available to man. Or, in this case, woman.

She hasn't told anyone that she and Tom have started trying, just in case it doesn't happen. Livvy's thirty-seven, not exactly over the hill, but Tom is convinced that the longer they wait, the greater the chance that something could go wrong. He knows two people who know other people who have children with Down syndrome. Livvy feels her indignation rise. You can't really control these things, and even though she's not a religious person she believes all things happen for a reason. Even the unthinkable, which she's witnessed firsthand. She just nods her head when Tom suggests forgoing birth control to "see what happens."

Now, six months into it, she's warming up to the idea of getting pregnant and becoming a mother—more than she's willing to admit. She doesn't want to jinx it, but her thoughts always go to Josh, her nephew, when the pregnancy test reveals a single, sad line. She tries to cheer herself by remembering how he used to say that she was fun to be with, that she was a cool aunt. Does that mean she'd make a cool mom, too? Livvy hopes so.

"Why don't you get a test and find out?" she presses Edie. Her excitement grows as she considers the possibilities on Edie's behalf. Maybe Edie is worried that her boyfriend, the town's new GP, will freak out or break up with her. "I'm happy to go with you to buy a test," Livvy offers.

Edie shakes her head. "Thanks, but I prefer to keep my ten dollars where it belongs."

"In your wallet?" Livvy guesses.

"In my bank account. Earning interest." Edie finishes her sandwich and crumples up the wax paper, tossing it into the trash can a few feet away. She misses. "I need to go back inside. I have to finish a story on another shared water well that's run dry." She gets up to retrieve her trash.

"Am I going to hear about this on the six o'clock news?" Livvy teases.

"No, but it'll be in the *Gazette* tomorrow. Front page. Six homes are affected, Livvy. Not everyone is on county water, you know."

Livvy is sensing that Edie doesn't think she knows any better, and she hates that. Why do some people look at her and assume one thing about her when the opposite is true? She was just joking, for God's sake. "Edie, I was born and raised in Avalon. I think I know about these things." *Thank you very much.*

Edie frowns. "Then you know how expensive it will be for these families to tap into the county line. Plus some of them are without running water as we speak."

The last thing Livvy needs is a lecture. In fact, Edie is acting a bit like Julia right now, and Livvy definitely doesn't need another older sister in her life. She stares down at her pasta salad, her appetite lost.

Edie can tell by the way Livvy is suddenly engrossed in her lunch that she's been too critical. Livvy's not a reporter, she's in advertising sales, and Edie needs to give her a break if she expects to have any friends in this town of 4,243 people. Her boyfriend, Richard aka Dr. Richard, really wants Edie to give Avalon a chance and Edie wants to, but it's not easy. That's the part Richard doesn't understand, because he gets along with everyone and everyone gets along with him. But Edie isn't Richard, and she knows she can come off a bit prickly sometimes. Okay, a lot of the time. It's just that some of the things that people like to talk about seem pointless and frivolous to Edie. How can hair coloring or the price of pork compare to the fact that there is so much poverty and disease in the world?

Edie's not a bleeding heart liberal by definition (well, by her definition, at least). Others, she knows, may disagree. She just knows from having lived overseas that it doesn't take much to make a big difference, and she wants to be a part of that change. The lightweight conversations of everyday life often drive Edie to distraction and, try as she might, it's only a matter of time before her polite head-nodding becomes tiresome and she says what's on her mind. A few seconds after that, the room will empty as people suddenly remember they have some place to be, or, like Livvy, clam up and stop talking altogether.

"Look," Richard told her one night when she suggested they finagle their way out of yet another dinner at the home of one of his

grateful patients. Patients were always inviting them over, in part because they were still new in town and in part because Everybody
Loves Richard. "I know it's painful, but it doesn't have to be. These
are good people and this is how they show their gratitude. And," he
continued firmly as Edie opened her mouth in response, "they are not
going to box up this food and ship it to Africa to feed people in need,
so don't go there."

"I wasn't going to suggest *that*," she had retorted, a little stung.

"Of course you weren't," Richard said with a grin. They both
knew it would have been something else, like cutting a household
food budget in half and donating the difference, or volunteering their
time in a soup kitchen instead of spending two or three hours in their
own. "But these people are now our neighbors, and if you give them
a chance, they might even become good friends."

Good friends. Edie somehow doubts this, but there's no question
that coming to Avalon was a smart move, if for the cost of living
alone. Chain restaurants and fast-food joints don't bother with a
market this size, and there are no large shopping malls. There is a
movie theater, a bowling alley, a park, a handful of restaurants, a couple of bars. Even if you wanted to spend some money there's nowhere
to spend it. Housing prices are insanely low. Unlike other parts of
America, Avalon is a place where you can actually afford to raise a
family.

Longtime residents, or Avalonians, don't use street names but refer
to places by how they're situated to other places. "Over by the bank,"
"next to the library," or "behind the Pick and Save." Edie likes this
sort of navigation, of how each place seems to point to another, like
clues in a treasure hunt. Her stories for the *Gazette* have evolved in
this way—the women of the local sewing circle heaped praises on the
local butcher who was also the star of two stage productions by the
Avalon Theatre Company (*Hairspray* and *You're a Good Man, Char-
lie Brown*). A small theater is home to the robotics club run by two
fifth graders. One of the fifth graders was musing aloud as to the un-
canny lucky streak of longtime bingo champion Harold Sibley whom,
Edie discovered, was winning all the bingo games on Thursday nights

at St. Mary's because his mistress was calling out the winning numbers. Lead after lead, almost seventy stories in total. Not exactly hard-hitting news. At first Edie figured she just hadn't found the "real" stories of Avalon, but it's becoming clear to her that maybe this is as good as it's going to get, that Avalon isn't more than what it seems to be—a small, simple river town in northern Illinois.

Still, Richard is becoming a permanent fixture in town, and Edie is pretty permanently attached to Richard. So even though she's worked at the paper for almost three months and was doing fine with a simple nod to people here and there, she pushed herself beyond her comfort zone to actually exchange a few superfluous words with Livvy when the opportunity arose.

Edie likes Livvy, but she's fairly confident that if they had gone to the same high school, Livvy wouldn't have given her the time of day. Olivia "Livvy" Scott has cheerleader written all over her. Shoulder-length straight blond hair, thin, exuberant, suspiciously perky. Livvy always looks good in her coordinated outfits and flawless, dewy skin. Standing next to Livvy brings up every insecurity Edie has ever had about her looks. Even with a trendy pair of glasses and a new haircut, Edie Gallagher still feels like she has CLASS GEEK stamped on her forehead.

But Livvy is always delighted to see Edie, wanting to spend as much time together as possible. It's a bit puzzling, actually. She has the odd thought of Livvy sitting on her bed, writing in her diary about their escapades as if they were teenagers. BFF. *Best friends forever.* It's a concept completely foreign to Edie, who has never really had many female friends, much less a best friend.

So she pushes herself again.

"If I don't get my period by next Friday, then we'll take a trip over to the Avalon Pharmacy, okay?" Edie doesn't bother to mention that her period is perpetually late and totally erratic, and that the likelihood that she is pregnant is pretty low. She also doesn't bother to point out that she can get a urine test for free at Richard's office. She can see how peeing on a stick in the bathrooms of the *Avalon Gazette* with your coworker standing outside the stall might be fun (not). But it's what girls do, right? Bonding time. Maybe this was the part Edie missed out on when she was in the library browsing through volumes of the *Encyclopedia Britannica.*

Livvy gives a half nod but looks appeased. "Okay. Hey, do you want to meet later for coffee?"

Not really, but Edie gives Livvy a thumbs-up. "You know where to find me."

Livvy flips through her checkbook, looking for the missing entry. It's been months since she balanced her checkbook and to be honest she's not great at it, but the last bank statement showed an automatic withdrawal in the amount of $500 to CMFTP.

Livvy has no idea what that is. She ticks through the obvious big-ticket items—the mortgage, the car loans, the membership fee for the golf club Tom belongs to—but those are all accounted for. She decides to call the bank.

Tracy, the *Gazette*'s business manager and Livvy's boss, pops her head into Livvy's office. Livvy pushes her checkbook to the side and pretends to be looking at something on her computer.

"Livvy, where are you with that web-based advertising proposal? I want to show it to Patrick." Patrick Chapman is the publisher and editor in chief, a hands-on sort of guy who really doesn't know much about the newspaper business but has the money to keep the small paper from floundering into oblivion.

Livvy had been hoping to show the proposal to Patrick herself, especially seeing how she was the one who came up with the idea in the first place. "It's not ready yet. I should have it later this afternoon."

"Great. I'll be by at three to pick it up. Can you make four copies? Collated, with a binder clip. No staples. Thanks." Tracy gives her an obnoxious wink and hurries away.

Since when did Livvy become the copy girl? She opens the file on her computer and hits PRINT. As her clunky old laser printer churns out each page, she finds she's seething. The only reason Tracy is the business manager is because she walked through the door one week before Livvy did. Livvy could easily do Tracy's job managing the display and classified advertising. In fact, it was Livvy's idea that they catch up with the rest of the world and go online, if only for the simple reason of being able to sell some web advertising in addition to their meager print advertising. She should just march into Patrick's office and give him the proposal herself. She should pitch the idea to him in person, let him see that she knows what she's doing, that she's worth more to the *Gazette* than he realizes.

But she won't. Despite all of Livvy's big talk and her reputation for fearlessness, she doesn't want to risk Tracy's wrath or Patrick's disapproval. She needs this job, she needs the money, and if she has any hope of getting a raise or being promoted, she needs to stay in both of their good graces.

The thought of money reminds her to call the bank. She punches in the number. She'll deny the charge, whatever it is, and demand they credit her account. She'll call it fraud if she has to, make them initiate an investigation, and in the meantime she can use the money to pay the loans on their cars.

"Avalon State Bank. How may I help you?"

It's Charlotte Snyder, one of the head tellers. "Hello, Mrs. Snyder. It's Livvy Scott."

"Who? I'm sorry, the connection is terrible. Can you speak up?" The connection is fine—it's Charlotte Snyder who is going deaf.

"Olivia Scott. Frederick and Rebecca Townsend's daughter."

"Olivia!" Mrs. Snyder exclaims. "How are your parents? Enjoying Florida? Tell your mother to write more—the time difference just never works out for us to talk."

"I'll tell her," Livvy says, but she knows her parents have a new life, one that doesn't hold painful or sad memories of Avalon. They moved two years ago, saying they needed a change of pace. It was supposed to be a temporary thing, for six months or so, but it's clear they have no intention of returning. Their flamingo-pink condo in Boca Raton is a huge change from the neat but somber house they had in Avalon. Now they play bingo on the weekends and take salsa dance lessons. Her mother paints watercolors and her father has taken up deep-sea fishing. Florida is the last place Livvy envisions her parents, but she can see how all that carefully planned living has its appeal. Everything in its own time slot, with no surprises—dinner at five, canasta at seven, chicken on Mondays, Wednesdays, and Fridays. Livvy yearns for that kind of certainty right now. Maybe she should move down there, too.

"And how is Julia? I never see you girls anymore. Everyone is on-line banking these days or going through the drive-through. You know we're offering free doughnuts if you get here before ten. Sweet on the lips, but straight to the hips!" Mrs. Snyder chortles.

Livvy ducks the question about Julia and gets straight to the point. "Mrs. Snyder, I think there's a mistake on my last statement. There was five hundred dollars taken directly from our checking account and neither Tom nor I authorized it."

"Oh dear." Mrs. Snyder is serious now. "Let me pull up your account. Five hundred, five hundred . . . oh yes, there it is. To CMFTP. You say you didn't authorize it?"

"No, I did not." Livvy is firm.

"Well, it's already been paid out. I can go ahead and file a dispute and the bank will look into it." Mrs. Snyder is typing something into the computer. "There's a phone number here associated with the transaction. The area code is 773. That's Chicago, isn't it? Do you want to call them first?"

Livvy tries to remember the last time they were in the city—it's been at least a year. Possibly Tom made another whimsical purchase— a new golf club or something like that—and then forgot all about it. When they were first dating Livvy loved that about him, that he was a guy who didn't obsess about the details, that he was spontaneous and would surprise her with an expensive treat here and there. She didn't realize until later that they were living beyond their means. By then it was already too late—she liked having nice things and had figured out how to float from one month to the next, how to get a late charge waived, assuming all the while that they'd eventually get caught up. Then the economy slowed to a stop and credit card rates rocketed, raises put on hold. They're feeling the pinch now, and Livvy wishes she could turn back the clock, but of course that's impossible.

Livvy takes the number from Mrs. Snyder and promises to call her back if she wants to file a dispute. She punches in the number, a barrage of questions at the ready. What is the amount for? Who authorized it? What does CMFTP stand for?

A pleasant voice answers right away.

"Children's Memorial Hospital, Foundation Office."

Livvy sucks in her breath, then quietly places the receiver back in the cradle. She closes her eyes.

She won't be calling Mrs. Snyder back after all.

Tom is hitting golf balls in the front yard when Livvy pulls up. She doesn't want to ask why he's already home. His commute from work is an unfortunate forty-five minutes one way, and he usually doesn't make it back to Avalon until right before dinnertime.

"Hey, good lookin'!" he calls out, then chips a shot into the old dog bowl.

Why can't he do this in the backyard, where there's plenty of room, instead of in their front yard for the world to see? She sees some movement from a window across the street. It's Mrs. Lowry, the neighborhood watchdog, peeking through her lace curtains.

"Tom," Livvy hisses as she walks up to him. "Can you please keep your voice down?"

"Why? That old bat can't hear us." He gives a laugh, and Livvy smells alcohol on his breath.

"God, have you been drinking?"

"I've been *celebrating*." He hits another shot and it bounces out of the dog bowl. "Damn."

"Can you tell me why you're celebrating? *Inside* the house?" She nods to the house and walks up the steps.

He tosses his pitching wedge onto the grass and follows her, catching her in an amorous hug from behind. He rains kisses on her neck, making Livvy protest and laugh at the same time.

"Stop!" Livvy knows Mrs. Lowry just got an eyeful.

Once they're inside, Tom's bluster disappears.

"What's wrong?" Livvy asks. She sees a stack of mail and is about to reach for it, but the top two envelopes have OVERDUE and FINAL NOTICE stamped on the front in big letters. She decides it can wait.

Tom sits down on the bench in the hallway. "They took my car."

She looks at him in alarm. "Who? Who took your car?"

"The bank. They sent a repo guy to my office. My office! Kurt saw the tow truck and told me, but it was too late. Guy was gone by the time I got downstairs." He bangs his fist on the wall behind him.

"Can they do that? Aren't they supposed to give us notice or . . ."

"They did give us notice. We were late on three payments, and I didn't pay the last one."

Livvy bites her lip. "Why not?"

"Why not? Because we don't have any money, that's why not!"

Livvy tries to think. "So what does this mean? That we don't owe anything more on the BMW?" This could actually be a good thing. The BMW was such a temperamental car, always breaking down. Now they can get a cheaper car and have a little more cash each month.

"We might. It depends on how much they can get when they sell it. If they sell it for less than what we owe, then we still owe them the difference."

"What?" This doesn't seem fair to Livvy. "Why? We gave back the car."

"They *took* back the car. I don't want to talk about this anymore." Tom stands up and heads for the kitchen.

Livvy's mind is spinning. She follows him. "But I thought you said you were celebrating, Tom."

"It's called sarcasm, Livvy."

"So how did you get home?"

"As soon as that guy took the car, I called a taxi to take me to the bank. It cost me seventy-five bucks."

Ouch. "Did you tip the driver?"

"What do you think?" Tom glares at her as he opens the fridge and takes out a beer. Livvy sees three bottle caps already discarded on the counter.

"So they'll let us know if we owe anything?"

Tom takes a long draw on his beer. "Who the hell knows."

Livvy hesitates. "Well, we just paid our annual donation to the Children's Memorial Hospital for Josh. Five hundred dollars."

Tom swears. Then he looks at Livvy. "Do you think we still need to do that?"

"Tom!"

"Livvy, it's been six years."

"It's been five, Tom, and we talked about this. I want to do this. It's important to me."

"Forever?" He looks cross.

God, he doesn't remember anything. He had been equally distraught by Josh's death, and when she proposed an annual donation to the allergy and immunology department of Children's Memorial Hospital in Chicago, he had readily agreed. They never really discussed how long it would go on for. It's a small gesture, she knows, but it's the only one she's able to make and she doesn't want to stop.

"So how are you going to get to work?" she asks, changing the subject.

"I guess I'll have to take the Pilot."

Livvy's mouth drops. "Tom, the Pilot is my car." She had it before she even met him.

"It's *our* car, Livvy, and what do you expect me to do? Take the bus all the way to Dixon? We can't afford another car and I can't go around in some beater."

Livvy feels her throat tighten. There's no point in arguing. Tom's a pharmaceutical rep and needs to always look his best, not just what he wears, but also what he drives.

"Besides, the *Gazette* is practically within walking distance." He adds this last part flippantly.

"Tom, it's not within walking distance. You're just going to have to give me a ride in the mornings and pick me up on your way home."

"Liv, I'm driving all over the place for my sales calls. You can't count on me to take you to work." Tom takes his beer and goes to the living room. Livvy trails after him and tries not to lose it when he picks up the remote and settles himself onto the couch with a sigh.

Get up! She wants to yell. *Hold me! Tell me it's going to be all right!*

Tom notices her standing there and gives her a pained look. "It's been a bad day, Livvy. I just need to detox. Can you make dinner tonight? You're a doll." He turns back to the TV and flips to the Golf Channel.

She hears him cajoling some golfer to make the shot. Livvy turns on her heel and heads back to the kitchen, wishing desperately that she had someone to call, someone to talk to. She doesn't want Edie to know about their financial troubles, and all of her other friends just wouldn't understand. She could call her parents in Florida but she knows her father will be disappointed and probably think them completely irresponsible, which wouldn't be far from the truth. The only person who would understand is Julia. She'd be critical at first, but then she'd help Livvy figure out what to do. Julia has always pulled through for her.

But Julia won't take her calls.

CHAPTER 3

"Please sign here." The UPS deliveryman points to the dotted line, and Hannah scrawls her name with the electronic pen. He hands her the long, slim package, glancing briefly at the sender's address: "Delivery from Hans . . ." He stumbles, unable to pronounce the last name.

". . . Weishaar." Hannah accepts the package, pleased to see that the wrapping, the corners, everything looks good. Intact.

The deliveryman smiles sheepishly, but it's a great smile. He's tall, with sandy-blond hair and classic good looks, the kind of guy most girls fall head over heels in love with. Her parents used to have heart attacks over guys like this, worried that Hannah would want to date one of them, but they were being ridiculous. Hannah goes for the moody, brooding type, not the ones who look like they'd be happy sitting on the beach with a cheap bottle of beer and a surfboard nearby.

"I'm usually really good with names," he continues apologetically, and Hannah wants to tell him that he doesn't need to apologize, that she didn't get it right the first time, either.

Instead, she simply says, "It's a German name. German names are tricky."

"You're new to Avalon?"

She nods. "Just moved here from New York three months ago."

His smile broadens. "Then welcome to Avalon"—he checks his handheld computer—"Hannah. Is that you? Hannah de Brisay?" He glances back down uncertainly.

Hannah is used to this, to the double check that often happens when you are Asian with a Caucasian last name. She explains, "It's my married name." She resists the impulse to add any other commentary but her mind does it for her, flashing automatically to the headlines of her tumultuous relationship with Philippe.

A Meeting of the Prodigies—Cello and Violin Darlings Engaged!

Rising Cellist Hannah Wang and Violinist Philippe de Brisay
Wed in New York

Classical Musicians No Longer Living in Harmony?

"It's French. My last name is French." Is she so desperate for conversation that she's chatting up the UPS man? "My husband is French," she adds lamely. *Stop talking, Hannah!*

"Oh." The smile doesn't leave his face but she sees him straighten up, his body language the equivalent to a tip of the hat. "Well, it was nice meeting you. Have a nice day, ma'am."

Ma'am. The word makes her cringe. She's twenty-eight years old, but because she's married, she's *ma'am.*

She doesn't watch him walk away, but smiles politely and closes the door. The house is suddenly silent again, the white wainscoting standing at attention as she walks down the hallway toward the music room.

The music room is a sunroom that doesn't get much sun because of the looming oak tree out back, but it's better this way. The small room has expansive glass windowpanes that overlook the modest backyard, and it's Hannah's favorite view. Her cello rests against the stand and framed photographs of concerts and glowing reviews are hung symmetrically on the walls.

In fact, everything is symmetrical in their house. Philippe has a need for things to be placed exactly so, even the mail when it's placed on the console in the hallway. Utensils lie patiently in the drawer, spoons spooning, fork tines shined, knives with their edges pointed down, perfectly fanned and separated. The canned goods in the pantry with their labels facing out, the stockpiles of boxed risotto in various flavors stacked alphabetically. One thing Philippe can't buy enough of is nesting mixing bowls, of which they have almost ten sets. He loves how they are made to fit together, one inside the other.

"It's like us," he used to say. She knows that he has always been attracted to what he refers to as "her natural precision"—her body, her talent, even the way she walks. "You glide," he would say, his accent thick with desire as he tugged at her clothes, impatiently fingering the buttons on her blouse. Nothing gets Philippe more excited than perfection, or at least the illusion of it.

And now . . . what? Hannah stares at herself in the antique silver leaf mirror on the wall, one of her favorite finds from a second-hand store in Brooklyn. Philippe never let her put it up in their apartments in New York and Chicago, but was more than pleased to let her hang it in their house in Avalon. At first she had felt a surge of hope that their four-year marriage wasn't over, that Philippe wanted to include the parts of Hannah that weren't just about music and beauty. But as soon as Christmas had passed, he was gone again.

She tugs at her straight shoulder-length hair. *Boring,* her reflection seems to tell her. Other musicians tell her they're envious of its dark sleekness, of how smooth and perfectly straight her hair seems to be, of how elegant it looks when pulled back in a tight chignon while she's performing. How easy it must be to have such obedient hair! They chalk it up to her Chinese genes, but Hannah knows better. Her hair actually has a natural wave to it, one with no rhyme or reason that looks terrible if left alone. She used to go to a salon in New Jersey and then found another in Chicago's Chinatown where she pays to have her hair straightened on the sly. Even Philippe doesn't know. She always meant to tell him but now it's too late—it'll just give him another reason not to love her anymore.

The phone rings. Hannah anxiously waits for the third ring before answering, another Philippe decree.

"Hello?"

"Hello, Hannah."

At the sound of his voice, she feels her heart clench. She grips the phone tightly with both hands. "Philippe, where are you? Are you at the apartment?"

"It doesn't matter." His French accent makes everything sound intelligent and romantic, regardless of what he's saying. "I'm just calling to tell you that I am sending a truck over for my things. They'll have a key. You don't have to be there, in fact it'll probably be better if you're not." He goes on, talking about some list they'll have indicating exactly what to pack and take, but Hannah's mind is swimming in shock.

"Philippe, just come home and we can talk," she begs.

There's a labored sigh on the other end, as if he's speaking to a child, as if the whole conversation is too tiresome for words. "There is nothing to talk about, Hannah."

Nothing to talk about? They've been together for seven years, married for four, and there's nothing to talk about? They used to spend hours in bed doing nothing but talking. Well, making love and talking, and they haven't done that in a long time, either. Still, Hannah doesn't know how—or when—everything started to fall apart. Why can't he tell her and give her a chance to make things better? She knows Philippe, knows that he doesn't do well on his own. Unlike most men, he likes being a couple. He likes the coziness, the intimacy. He loves being in love, but how can he be in love if he's not with her?

Because he's in love with someone else, dummy!

This realization hits her square between the eyes. *Of course.* Even when they first met in New York he was seeing someone else, a concert pianist whom he dumped to be with Hannah. Hannah had felt bad, but not *that* bad—after all, how could you control matters of the heart? Plus he told her that things were miserable and about to end anyway. And she believed him, ignoring the pianist's pained look when they bumped into her at a mutual friend's birthday party on Park Avenue.

"Is there someone else?" The question sticks in Hannah's throat. There is an interminable pause.

Then he says, "Hannah . . ." and nothing more.

In that single word, her own name, she hears his defensiveness, his irritation, his relieved unspoken confession. But it's also clear that he's not going to tell her anything more, and he's sure as hell not going to apologize.

She buries her face in her hands. How can she have been so clueless? She thinks of her friends who play with Philippe, advising her to keep an eye on him. She had laughed, and then she had panicked, unsure of what to do. So she did nothing.

"Look," Philippe continues, "just go get a cup of coffee or something. They'll be quick, in and out. They know what to get, they have a list, they'll pack everything up. After that's all done we'll talk, figure out what to do next."

Next? Is there a next? There is only one "next" that she knows of.

Oh God. She's shaking as Philippe calls her name, impatient. "Hannah, are you listening? The moving company is on the other line and I need to confirm this." He says something about the day after tomorrow.

Hannah is numb. The phone drops out of her hand and the plastic cracks when it hits the hardwood floor. She walks back to the music room, where she finally opens up the package that's been delivered. Tucked amid all the foam packaging is her bow case.

She opens the case and pulls out her bow, rehaired and ready to go. She turns the tension screw slightly, pulling the hairs taut. She picks up a small cake of rosin lying nearby and runs it across the full length of her bow in short circular motions, feeling her breath return to her, the familiarity of this simple act restoring her.

The day after tomorrow. Not if she can help it.

She settles into the chair, then draws her legs apart as she slips the cello between her knees. She takes a deep breath then slowly draws the bow over the strings. Instantly the room is filled with a deep, rich resonance that sends shivers up her spine. She closes her eyes. The music lifts her, carrying her out of her own body until she expands like smoke from a chimney, pouring into an open sky. Her thoughts are moved to silence as she feels herself dissipating into everything and nothing.

Hannah has never quite understood this, but she accepts it graciously and thankfully, even beckoning it. She doesn't have to ask it to take away the pain because the pain is no longer there. It's only the music that remains. The music, and nothing else.

The day after tomorrow comes. At daybreak, Hannah wakes up feeling achy and terrible. Then she remembers that the movers will be here at 10:00 A.M. She only has a few hours left.

She works steadily, building up a decent sweat, her dark hair pulled away from her face with a bandanna. Her mind is admittedly blank, unable to process anything more than it already has, but fortunately her body is trained to work even when her mind cannot.

At 9:45 A.M., Hannah pulls the bandanna from her head and takes a deep breath. She grabs her purse and slings it across her body, then walks outside, closing the front door behind her. She takes out her new key and inserts it into the new lock she had installed yesterday. Then she gingerly steps over Philippe's things, packed neatly in boxes, and makes her way down the walkway.

CHAPTER 4

Madeline Davis doesn't know what it is that draws her to the small town of Avalon. After all these years it's apparent that Chicago is too cold for her old bones, and not the temperature so much as the people. She never considered herself a Chicagoan anyway, and once Steven was gone, Madeline suddenly felt like the transplant she really was.

She hadn't meant to come here originally—that wasn't the plan. But when she saw the sign welcoming her to Avalon and the canopy of dogwood and buckeye trees shading the wide streets, she thought, *I could live here.* The next thing she knew, she was signing papers.

Madeline arranges some lemon scones on a porcelain cake stand then covers it with the fitted glass dome. Steven loved her scones, especially the ones made with chocolate chips. It's been over twenty years, but she still misses him terribly.

She wipes her hands on her apron then looks around her empty tea salon with longing, wishing she had more customers, more traffic. *Madeline's Tea Salon.* That was certainly ambitious. She didn't have a business plan, hadn't really a clue as to what she was doing. The whole business had been born more from what she was given, a six-bedroom, yellow-and-white stick-style Victorian that had been built in 1886 by a wealthy egg merchant. In its last incarnation it had been a bed-and-breakfast. The grounds were well-maintained and the previous owners avid gardeners. There was a vegetable patch; several rows of basil, rosemary, thyme, and mint; and lots of colorful flowers and shady trees.

Madeline loves the spacious rooms, each with its own sweet name and personality, the generous kitchen and sunroom, the full basement and large living and dining area. There were a few surprises, too—a china closet and a root cellar out back—making the home a bit too eclectic for the average buyer but perfect for someone like Madeline. It was more house, more yard, more everything than she could possibly ever need, but it was so full of possibilities that Madeline used what was left of her savings and bought it.

Now it's been six months, with only a trickle of business from tourists who happen to drive by. The locals regard her with guarded suspicion, holding tight to their wallets with the national economy in the pits. Despite her best efforts, she's still an outsider in this small town. Who is she kidding? Why would a small town like Avalon need a tea salon?

Madeline shakes her head as she wipes down the teacups for the umpteenth time. Why can't she be like other people her age who seem content to kick back and play bridge or watch daytime television? The more active ones volunteer or lunch or take in a show, talking endlessly about grandkids, which Madeline doesn't have. It seems, in fact, that she has no one. It isn't entirely true, but feels that way nevertheless. And it's been that way for a long, long time.

She tries not to look surprised when the little bell above the door tinkles and a woman with curly strawberry-blond hair walks in carrying a large tote bag.

"Do you serve food here?" the woman asks.

Madeline nods, remembering the portobello-mushroom-and-spinach quiche that will be ready any minute. She should push the lunch special. Then again, it's not quite eleven, so maybe talking up a mid-morning snack would be more appropriate. She's been meaning to put up a sign for tea and crumpets. It's a great deal at $5.99—a fresh pot of tea, two small crumpets, one scone, and a side of home-made raspberry preserves and lavender butter. She has such a fabulous selection of herbal teas, black teas, green teas, white teas, fruit teas . . .

There's an awkward pause as Madeline realizes that the woman is staring at her. She's done it again, her mind wandering off into la-la-land. She wishes she could say old age is to blame but it's not—it's just part of who Madeline is. She gives the woman a bright smile. "I'm sorry, I got lost there for a minute. Would you like a table?"

The woman shakes her head. "I just wanted to get something to go." Her eyes scan the buffet of baked goods hungrily. "Maybe a scone or muffin."

"Or both," Madeline says. It's a bold suggestion, but it does the trick. The woman lets out a small laugh, as if she's been holding it in.

"Or both," she agrees.

The bell over the door tinkles again. Two in one day? Madeline looks over and sees a slender young Asian woman walking in uncertainly. She's wearing a work shirt and dungarees. There's a refined elegance about her, the way her hand flutters to her neck nervously. "Are you open?" Her voice is soft, a hint of sophistication.

"I certainly am. Come on in." Madeline watches the young woman choose a table by one of the large picture windows.

The woman with the strawberry-blond hair is hovering between the pecan sticky buns and toffee chip bars. She suddenly seems anxious to leave, her eyes darting to the door as if she's afraid someone else might come in. "I'm not sure what to get . . ."

Madeline gives her a reassuring pat on the arm. "Take your time." The oven timer dings. "That'll be my quiche." She's about to head into the kitchen when she adds, "Portobello mushroom and spinach. Side salad of organic greens with sliced strawberries, walnuts, and shaved Parmesan, tossed in a homemade balsamic vinaigrette. Eight dollars and ninety-nine cents. Comes with your choice of tea afterward." She hurries off, hoping she hasn't scared anyone away with her impromptu sales pitch.

When Madeline returns, quiche in hand, she's surprised to see that the woman with the tote bag is still there, standing by an empty table. "You're welcome to sit if you'd like to get off your feet," Madeline offers.

"What? Oh no, I'm just . . ." She eyes the quiche in Madeline's hands, fragrant with herbs, the caramelized mushrooms gently browned, the spinach a dark, delicious green. "That smells wonderful." Her voice is hesitant.

"It tastes wonderful," Madeline says. She isn't boasting. Madeline knows she's an excellent cook and she's not afraid to own it. She begins to cut the quiche, six fat wedges instead of eight.

The woman looks at her, blinking, then to Madeline's delight she drops her bag onto a chair and sits down. "Okay," she says. Her voice is agreeable but cautious. "I'll try the special."

"Me, too." The young woman is staring out the window at a moving van making its way down the street. She turns to look at Madeline, a mix of uncertainty and determination on her face. "Do you by chance have anything chocolaty for dessert?"

The smell of quiche catches Julia by surprise. Even though it's only 10:30 A.M., she's starving.

The woman behind the counter introduces herself as Madeline, which Julia should have figured out seeing how the place is called Madeline's Tea Salon. Madeline looks to be in her seventies, friendly and vibrant, wearing a clean apron over her slacks. She's clearly a masterful baker given the delectable spread of baked goods on the antique buffet. Scones, cookies, cakes. Shelves are filled with teapots, tea cups, tea saucers, tea cozies. And then there's the vast selection of every tea imaginable, loose and bagged, tin after tin after tin.

"This used to be a B and B," Julia says, more to herself than anyone, but Madeline overhears her and smiles. "The Belleweather. Frank and Jan Morgan used to own it. But you probably already know that."

"That's pretty much all I know, too," Madeline says. "I stumbled onto this place. I was actually on my way back to Chicago after twenty years in California. Berkley." She serves the women their quiches then sits down at an empty table with a pot of tea. "I pulled over on the side of the road to take a little break and stretch my legs, and that's when I saw the FOR SALE sign. The minute I stepped inside I knew I was home." She stirs some milk into her tea.

"Really?" For Julia Avalon has always been home, even when she went away for school, and that was what kept her grounded when everything fell apart. Change—a new location, a new job, *a new life*—never held much appeal for Julia the way it had for others, so she's surprised by an unexpected stab of envy at hearing Madeline's words. What would it be like to stumble onto your future and recognize it so clearly? Was it really as simple as opening a door and seeing it before you? Then what?

The Asian woman is listening intently, too, her fork poised in midair. "But how did you *know*?" she asks. Julia has never seen her before, so she's either new or just passing through. Julia can see that her arms are toned, her posture tall and erect. She's slender and willowy, but not weak. If she were taller Julia imagines she'd be a ballet dancer.

Madeline shrugs, stirring some milk into her tea. "I just had that feeling of certainty. You know how there's that moment when you're sure of something? Even if it makes no sense?" She gives a commanding wave of her teaspoon.

"No." Julia and the other woman say this simultaneously, then stare at each other for a moment.

"Jinx," the other woman says, and Julia finds herself grinning. There has to be at least ten years between them, maybe more, but she feels a dangling thread of possibility and reaches for it. "I'm Julia," she says.

"Hannah." There's a pause as the women consider each other politely. "Are you from Avalon?"

Julia nods as she spears a strawberry with her fork. She remembers moments like this, though barely. It hasn't appealed to her in a long time, this meeting new people or talking about herself. She knows almost everyone in this town, but for the first time in a long time the feeling of claustrophobia, of being under the magnifying glass, is gone. "Yes. I was born and raised here. I went to college at UIC. Went back for graduate school, too." She doesn't mention that she never had a chance to finish her master's degree. She's always been okay with that decision, because something bigger and better had come up—she was pregnant. "What about you?"

"I moved here with my husband three months ago," Hannah says. "From New York by way of Chicago."

"I love New York," Madeline says with a sigh. Julia wishes she could say the same, but she's never been. "The shows, the shopping . . . although, to look at me now, you'd think I do nothing but spend all day in the kitchen. Which I suppose is actually true." Madeline rubs a spot of flour from her hand.

But Hannah doesn't respond, her attention taken by something down the street. Unease crosses her face and then gives way to a look Julia recognizes and is unfortunately all too familiar with.

Regret.

This is a mistake.

The table by the window gives Hannah a view of her home, a sweet bungalow with a white porch swing out front. The driver of the truck looks perplexed at seeing Philippe's possessions already stacked on the porch. His attempts to unlock the front door obviously fail. He looks at his work order again and then gives a shrug as he motions to his crew to start loading up the truck.

After Philippe's phone call and two hours of playing Prokofiev,

Hannah found the reserve of strength she'd been looking for. She changed the locks and packed up his belongings, unwilling to let a bunch of strangers into her house to pick through their things while she was out getting "coffee." Where did Philippe think she was? Starbucks hadn't found Avalon yet, and the thought of being in a busy diner or getting something from the grocery store was overwhelming. And then she remembered the tea salon that always seemed empty, an elderly woman behind the counter, always dusting, always moving about in a no-nonsense sort of way.

This will show him not to mess with me, had been her triumphant thought an hour ago as she headed toward Madeline's. But now Hannah contemplates running into the street and telling the movers to stop so she can unlock the house and put everything back in its proper place. To be honest, she probably would have done it if Madeline and Julia hadn't engaged her in conversation. By the time Hannah looks out the window again, Philippe's possessions and the truck are gone.

Hannah suddenly feels sick to her stomach.

"Hannah? Are you all right?" Madeline is standing by her table, clearing her empty plate.

Hannah can't speak. *What was she thinking?* Madeline and Julia are staring at her, a look of concern on their faces. Hannah tries to force a smile, but instead realizes that she's going to throw up. She puts her hand to her mouth. "I think I'm going to be sick."

Madeline puts down the plate and rushes Hannah to the bathroom where she promptly vomits into the toilet. Madeline's hand is warm on her back, steadying her, her voice soothing.

When it's over, Madeline brings out a fresh hand towel and places it on the side of the basin. "Take your time," she says kindly. She offers a smile before closing the door behind her.

Hannah stares at herself in the mirror, horrified, and closes her eyes. He'll never forgive her. He'll never come home now.

What had she done?

When Hannah finally emerges from the bathroom, Julia and

Madeline are speaking in low whispers. They straighten up when they see her. Madeline guides Hannah back to her table, and there's a slice of white toast, no crust, and a cup of tea waiting.

"Only if you want it," Madeline says. "I thought it might settle your stomach."

Hannah wipes her eyes. Growing up, she and her older brother would get spanked *and* grounded if they so much as shed a tear, which of course only prompted more tears, at least in the beginning. Albert ended up as stony-faced as her father while Hannah seems to cry at the drop of a hat, especially these days. "*Yǒng zhě wú wèi,*" her father would snap, the Chinese equivalent to, *Suck it up.*

"I'm sorry. It's not your food—it was really delicious." Hannah reaches for the toast and breaks off a piece. She tries to smile, but can't. She's scared she's going to cry again, make a fool of herself in front of these women. "I'm just not having a good day, I guess."

Julia has come to the side of her table. "I can understand that." She gives Hannah's hand a squeeze and when Hannah looks up, she sees something in Julia's eyes that's both sad and haunted. "I can definitely understand that."

Madeline's not quite sure what to do about these two women gathered in her house. Yes, it's a tea salon, but it's first and foremost her house, her home, and Julia and Hannah are essentially in her dining room, both looking tearful. She doesn't know what has happened to these two women, but something has.

What a life, she thinks as she hovers over a plate of double chocolate chip cookies before selecting a few and putting them into a paper bag. She takes another bag and puts in several muffins, her special blend of raspberries, blackberries, and gooseberries with a maple crumble topping. She's about to fold down the tops of the bags when she decides to fill them with whatever else she can fit. She knows it's unlikely that anyone else will come in today and she doesn't want it to go to waste.

She hands a bag to Hannah. "Here's your something chocolaty for dessert," she tells her. "For when you feel up to it." Hannah is about to protest but Madeline holds up a hand, stopping her. "It's on the house. You're my one millionth customer today." She hands the other bag to Julia, who looks equally stunned but grateful. "You, too."

"We're both your one millionth customer?" Julia smiles, and Madeline is struck by how beautiful this woman is.

"I know. Can you believe it?" Madeline feigns disbelief. "What a day. In fact, I'm not sure it can get any better." And she means that. This is one of the best days she's had since moving to Avalon, and the company of these women has lifted her spirits considerably. Maybe if she hangs in there long enough, something will eventually come to pass.

Hannah sniffs, manages a small smile. "It can get better for me. I have nowhere to go but up."

Julia is digging through her tote bag and Madeline tries to keep her curiosity in check. Call her nosy, but she can always tell when something interesting is about to happen.

"I know you don't really know me," Julia says to them, her voice dubious. "But I don't suppose either of you might be interested in some Amish Friendship Bread by chance?"

Julia feels ridiculous even asking the question. But she was trying to make room in her cluttered bag for Madeline's generosity when she sees the extra Ziploc baggies. She pulls them out and Hannah's eyes widen in confusion. Or, possibly, revulsion.

"This isn't the bread exactly," Julia explains. "It's just the starter. You let it ferment on your counter for ten days and then you can make the most wonderful bread with it. My daughter and I got it last week and we baked yesterday. I'm keeping one so we can bake again next week but I don't know what to do with these extra bags." She brings out a couple of Xeroxed sheets of paper. "I have instructions and everything. I know it seems silly, but it was actually a lot of fun.

The bread is delicious." She thinks of Mark's delight when he tried a slice, catching Gracie in a hug after reading her note. Julia was on the outside, watching this happy moment, wanting to fit in but not sure how.

Madeline is the first to hold out her hand. "I'd love a bag," she says. She takes it and gives it a squeeze. "Lots of bubbles. It looks like a good, healthy starter."

Julia is surprised. "You've done this before?"

Madeline nods as she gives the bag a poke. "Let's see—the first time was back in 1996, I think. I got mine in a lovely porcelain container—kept it for years. I tried all sorts of variations but eventually ran out of people to give it to. Friends and neighbors would run in the opposite direction when they saw me coming." Madeline laughs at the memory.

"It's Amish?" Hannah asks, tentatively accepting a bag and glancing at the instructions. She looks at the page, perplexed. "Jell-O instant pudding? The Amish eat instant pudding?"

The women look at one another before bursting out in laughter.

"I did look it up," Julia admits. "It seemed odd to me, too. Apparently it was started by a Girl Scout troop in Buffalo, New York, in 1990. I doubt it originated with the Amish, but who knows?"

"It seems a bit like a chain letter," Hannah says. She looks ready to hand the bag back to Julia.

"I didn't want to do it at first, either," Julia tells her. "I haven't baked in years and it just seemed like so much work. But we had fun squeezing the bag every day and adding ingredients on the sixth day. By the time the tenth day rolled around, my entire family—" Julia stumbles here for a moment, but keeps talking. "I mean my husband, daughter, and I, we were actually looking forward to it. We baked two loaves and ate most of one in ten minutes." Maybe it was even five minutes, and Julia can't help but smile. "Gracie took the other loaf and one bag of starter to school today."

Hannah is finally persuaded. "I'm a terrible cook, but I need something to take my mind off things. This seems like a nice distraction."

There's the now-familiar tinkle of the bell and an elderly couple walks in, arguing and clutching a map. They seat themselves without a glance at the women and the husband orders a pot of Earl Grey.

"Well, back to work for me," Madeline says cheerfully, pushing herself up from the table. She tucks a tea towel into her apron.

Julia checks her watch—it's time to pick up Gracie. She pays the bill, leaving a healthy tip that still doesn't equal Madeline's generosity.

It's awkward saying goodbye after their unexpected camaraderie for the past hour. Julia lingers, trying to think of an appropriate farewell, when Madeline breaks through the awkwardness by catching Julia in a surprise bear hug. Madeline's much stronger than her slender frame would have you think, and she smells wonderful— clean and fresh. Julia wishes she could stay in her arms forever.

Madeline does the same for Hannah, who is blinking back tears and smiling bravely at the same time. Then she gives the women a wave and shoos them out the door.

CHAPTER 5

Mark hasn't seen his wife like this in a long time. The Julia of the past five years has been withdrawn, uninterested in holding on to old friends or making new ones. The Julia of the past five years was combative with him, shutting down for long stretches of time, sometimes refusing to talk to anyone other than Gracie. The Julia of the past five years hardly ever smiled, not even when Gracie learned to crawl, then walk, then ride a bicycle. And laughter? Forget about it.

Mark saw in the handful of grief support groups he went to that marriages didn't always weather the death of a child. At first Mark hadn't been worried, because they weren't just husband and wife but best friends before Josh's death—they understood everything about each other. Nobody else knew what they were going through, not even other grieving parents, because there was always something different about *their* loss—no family out there had the same set of circumstances, their exact situation, their children. Because of this,

Mark and Julia only had each other. They were the only two people who knew what this really meant.

Then somewhere along the way the grief evolved. It was no longer their tragedy, their grief—it all became Julia's. Mark understood this somewhat—after all, she and Josh had been close, almost quiet echoes of each other. The same wild and curly hair, the same mischievous grin. But Mark also gets that he's the father, not the mother. While it does not take away from his grief, he knows it's not quite the same.

Julia had carried Josh for nine months, then endured almost thirty-six hours of hard labor before he was born. She was the one staying up nights when Josh had colic. She nursed him for over a year. Mark understands the mother-child bond, that it's a complex, primal relationship, so of course it makes sense that Julia's loss would be different from Mark's.

Still, he hadn't counted on her drifting away, of letting go of the buoy they held on to together. She retreated and left him behind. He doesn't love her any less for it, but he's starting to wonder if the same can be said for Julia.

Can you love someone but not want to be with them anymore? That's the question he doesn't want to ask himself, but it lingers nonetheless. Mark is a patient man, but he's no longer sure of what he's waiting for or if the person in question even wants him anymore. He feels like he's in the way, an inconvenient remnant of a life they once shared. He watches his wife wistfully, sadly, and it's been dawning on him that the Julia of his memory no longer exists.

Or does she? Twice this week—twice!—he caught her smiling. *Smiling!* It wasn't at him, which would have been nice, but that's okay. And yesterday when he came home to find the kitchen a mess and both Julia and Gracie covered with flour, he actually heard her laugh. Mark wanted to join in, to hear what was so funny, but Julia stopped when she saw him, suddenly engrossed in checking the oven timer.

Mark punches in a higher elevation on the treadmill, then adjusts his speed so he doesn't have to slow down. He's still not sure what to think, but he's feeling hopeful. At long last. The first few years had been the worst—the shock, the walking around in inconsolable disbelief, the pain in his heart so sharp he couldn't breathe. Twice he thought he was having a heart attack. The first time it happened he didn't care. He was almost relieved. It seemed appropriate, and he waited to die. But he didn't.

The second time was different. It was four months after Josh's death and Mark was in his office, trying to work and failing miserably, when he knocked over the ceramic pencil holder Josh had made one year at summer camp. It didn't break, but part of it chipped off, and Mark felt a searing pain across his chest as he gripped the broken piece. He fumbled to reattach it, desperate for the pencil holder to be whole again. Then his lungs gave a squeeze. The pain was excruciating.

He managed to buzz his secretary who called 911. She gave him an aspirin and sat with him on the floor as he struggled to breathe, clutching the broken piece in one hand, waiting for the medics to arrive.

They took him to the hospital in Freeport where Julia met him, only days away from her due date. She looked terrified, her eyes wide, her lips white. It was at that moment Mark realized that he didn't have the luxury to grieve for his son. Julia needed him. Their unborn child needed him. His business was floundering and it was his responsibility to keep it afloat, because that's what fed his family and paid for the house.

"I'm okay," he told the doctor who was reading the printout from the EKG.

"You're not having a heart attack," the doctor confirmed. "But I definitely don't think you're okay."

Mark ignored him, accepted a prescription for sleeping pills, and got back to his life.

Keeping busy is the thing that saves him from losing it altogether. That, and Gracie, whom he calls his little spark plug because she's so full of life and can change his mood in an instant. Gracie, who was born to grieving parents a week after Mark's trip to the ER, four and a half months after Josh's death. Gracie, who came into the world joyful despite all the sadness surrounding her. Gracie, who is okay with the pictures of Josh on the wall even though she's not in them, who isn't surprised to see her mother crying throughout the day. He knows from talking to therapists that the day may come when Gracie has questions or there may be a sudden explosion of emotion—resentment, possibly competitive behavior, or even the not-so-simple question if she is loved as much as Josh. Mark doesn't dare say this aloud, but he is so grateful that Gracie was already on her way when Josh died. He wouldn't want her to think for a second that she was a replacement child. He cherishes her, his little spark plug.

The machine beeps and the elevation starts to flatten. He slows his pace, cooling down, debating whether or not to do a few minutes on the rowing machine. He has some time before he's due in the office for an eight-thirty meeting.

"Wow, it looks like the early bird gets the worm," says a voice from behind him. The conveyor belt rolls to a stop.

Mark turns to see Vivian decked out in full workout regalia. Her hair is pulled back in a sleek ponytail, and he can tell she's wearing a hint of makeup. He knows it makes zero sense to wear makeup to the gym, but at the same time, she looks good. Julia hasn't worn makeup in years, but she doesn't need it. Whenever he tells her that, even now, she just gets angry.

"Turns out I'm not much of a morning person," Vivian jokes. "I just got here. If I'm lucky, I can squeeze in a five-minute workout."

Mark is still a bit out of breath as he reaches for his water bottle. "Hey, it's better than nothing." He's determined to keep things amicable, friendly. He doesn't want weirdness even though it's already weird to be standing there in their workout clothes. It feels odd, almost intimate, and he doesn't like it. He wipes down the machine with his towel and steps off, heading toward the rowing machine.

"I've been meaning to talk to you about the Cherry Hill project," Vivian says, following him. "I think I found a way to maintain the openness of the house so it can still have those fabulous views. I also think we can upgrade some of the antiquated materials that were used in the kitchen by adjusting the color palette rather than replacing all of the . . ."

"Vivian." He interrupts her, turning around. *Be firm.* "That all sounds great and I want to hear about it, but not now."

She tilts her head to the side. "So when? I'll be at appointments all day in Rockford. I promised the client I'd give them some recommendations by tomorrow."

Mark drops his things onto a bench, irritated. Why did she wait until the last minute to tell him?

"I didn't wait until the last minute," she says, reading his mind. She straightens up looking mildly irritated herself. "I sent you three emails and a couple of voice-mail messages."

He remembers now, but he didn't know she needed a response before tomorrow.

"I've got to go," he says, glancing at the clock. His fifteen minutes have just evaporated and he needs to head to the showers if he's going to make his meeting on time. "We'll have to talk about this later."

"My day's already pretty full," she says. "And I'm sure yours is, too. What about discussing this over an early dinner? I've always wanted to try that new restaurant, Roux."

Mark knows Roux, because it was written up as one of the hottest new French fusion restaurants to watch. He's been wanting to go there himself to check out the architecture and decor, but Julia hates going out. Plus Roux is forty minutes away.

"It's halfway between Rockford and Avalon," she continues. "This way you'll still have the rest of the evening to spend with Julia and Gracie." The smile on Vivian's face doesn't waver. "We can meet at five and you'll be home by seven."

If he stands here any longer, he's going to be late. "Fine," he says. "Roux it is. Five o'clock."

When Mark walks into Roux, an apologetic Vivian is waiting by the bar, drink already in hand.

"This is what small town life does to you," she says mournfully.

She looks dazzling in a tailored wraparound dress and heels. It's professional yet soft and feminine. "I forgot that most restaurants don't start serving until five-thirty. They'll seat us at the bar, though, until a table is ready."

Mark is about to suggest that they just stay at the bar and get this over with, but at that moment a young man dressed in black walks over. Mark recognizes him as Bruno Lemelin, owner of Roux and two other award-winning restaurants in the state of Illinois.

"Mark Evarts," Lemelin says, shaking his hand. They've never met, but Lemelin is all smiles, as if they're old friends. "It's a pleasure to meet you. When Vivian called and I heard the two of you were coming in, I couldn't believe my good fortune. I saw the work you did on Bacchanali in Chicago. Nicely done."

"Thank you." They exchange cards.

"I'd love to talk with you about a couple of projects I have going on, maybe see if there's a fit." Lemelin claps him on the shoulder and gives Vivian a smile, his eyes flicking up and down the length of her body. "The hostess will seat you in a little bit, but I'll send some apps to tide you over in the meantime. I'm going to have our chef pull together some of his favorite dishes for your dinner."

Mark doesn't know what to say. He'd heard rumors that Lemelin wanted to open another place, a high-concept restaurant that would combine stunning interiors with his signature dishes. He also knows Lemelin has a reputation for hiring and firing his architects at the drop of a hat, and it's clear that he's shopping now.

Lemelin gives Mark a wink. "I'll tell the bartender to fix you up with our house martini. It was featured in *Food & Wine* last year. You'll love it." He turns and strides into the kitchen with a wave.

Mark is flattered to be getting the royal treatment. He's forgotten this feeling, this thrill of being noticed, this cutting to the front of the line. Since Josh's death he's passed on travel and evening meetings, and he knows his business has suffered for it. His partner, Victor Gunther, has been socializing and hobnobbing on his behalf, but it's not his forte. It's Mark's. He's forgotten how much fun it can be, and how much he really misses it.

He excuses himself to step outside and call Julia. It's a courtesy call because she probably won't answer the phone. Sure enough, the answering machine comes on, his own voice asking him to leave a message. Suddenly Mark is tired of talking to himself. He disconnects the call before the beep and slips his phone into his pocket.

Back inside, Vivian holds up a martini and gives Mark a conspiratorial grin. "Cheers," she says.

He picks up his glass from the table and holds the thin stem between his fingers. "Cheers." They clink glasses and take a sip, their eyes meeting over the rims.

It's a damn good martini, and Mark would ask for another if they weren't here on business. "Tell me again how you pulled this off. How do you know Bruno Lemelin?"

Vivian shakes her head. "I don't," she says. "Just call me lucky. I called to make a reservation and he picked up. Said he was waiting for a call and the hostess was on break. I talked him up, of course, once I realized it was him."

"Of course," Mark says with a grin. Vivian only offers a nonchalant shrug in response, confirming what Mark already knows. However lucky Vivian may be, she knows how to spot an opportunity and is not the kind of girl to let it pass her by.

A waiter brings out a full tray of appetizers: foie-gras-and-onion soufflé with Armagnac-soaked prunes, ravioli stuffed with braised celery root and goat cheese, a marvelous crispy soft-shell-crab tempura. Mark orders a bottle of chardonnay. Vivian starts telling him about her suggestions for the Cherry Hill project, and Mark finds himself enthralled by her ideas, by her use of found objects coupled with new materials, the overall depth of her knowledge. She confesses she had been looking for opportunities in Chicago or New York when she stumbled across their website, saw Mark and Victor grinning at her from cyberspace, and thought, Why not?

"Why not?" Mark repeats as he watches her cut a sliver of ravioli and slip it into her mouth. He finds himself staring at her lips, still glossy with color, and he forces himself to think of other things. Bruno. Gracie. Architecture. The balding guy in the corner who's obviously on a blind date. "Because we probably don't pay as well. And we don't have any of the glitz or glamour."

Vivian gives a gentle shake of the head. "Trust me—been there, done that. That's not what I'm looking for."

He wants to ask her more, ask her how it is that she's been there and done that, whatever that means. What exactly is she looking for? He wants to know even though he knows he might regret it later. But before he can say anything Vivian changes the subject and he finds himself regaled by her tales of travel and misadventure, marveling at how tenacious and smart a woman she is.

When they're brought to a table, the food starts coming out almost immediately: roast breast of duck with more foie gras, hazelnut risotto with sweetbreads, quail with a yellow-raisin sabayon and semolina gnocchi. It's a far cry from takeout pizza and Chef Boyardee.

By the time they're finished with dinner, Mark feels alive. He has just eaten one of the best meals of his entire life. And then Lemelin is there and they're discussing a time to meet—will next Thursday work? They'll meet here, at the restaurant. Mark can't wait to come back.

"Wow," says Vivian as they walk to the parking lot. "That was certainly productive. Business meeting, amazing meal, new client."

"He's not a client yet," Mark corrects, laughing. The food and alcohol have made him giddy, but he's also just happy.

"He will be," Vivian says confidently. She reaches into her purse and pulls out a small key fob with the unmistakable Porsche insignia.

"You drive a Porsche?" Mark stares at the 911 coupe in front of them, cherry red with glossy black detailing and alloy wheels. How much are they paying her?

"I lease," she says. She points the key fob at the car and the doors instantly unlock. Mark's not sure if he's filled with admiration or envy. "I trade up every five years. Everything seems to break down the minute the warranty expires, so I prefer to play it safe." She dangles the keys in front of him. "You're welcome to take it for a drive if you like."

Part of his brain is telling him to get his ass home and the other part is figuring out how long it would take to circle the block. Just once. Maybe twice. It's a Porsche, for God's sake.

Instead he holds the door open and waits for Vivian to get in, choosing to change the subject. "Why don't you enlighten me as to why you think Lemelin will be a client?"

Vivian slides into the driver's seat and then pauses, one long leg remaining on the pavement.

"Because," she says, her eyes locking on his. "Some things are just meant to be."

She drives away, the most perfect exit in a beautiful piece of well-crafted German automobile machinery. The red glow of the taillights stare back at him, taunting him, daring him to follow.

The upstairs bedroom light is on, the door slightly ajar. Mark stands in the strip of light, briefcase still in hand. He sees Julia sitting on their bed, cross-legged, already dressed in pajamas. She's reading a magazine. He edges the door open a little wider and clears his throat, worried that he's interrupting her but wanting her to know that he's there. "Hey."

Julia looks up. Her hair is twisted up in a simple knot, a few loose tendrils framing her face. Her face looks shiny and clean, as if she just washed it. "Hi."

"Sorry I'm late. I had an unexpected dinner meeting and it just got later and later . . ."

"That's fine." Julia looks back down at her magazine. She reaches for a pen, clicking it several times before circling something.

Mark loosens his tie but doesn't step into the room. His room is down the hall, the room formerly known as the guest room. It wasn't anything they planned. It came about because Julia was having so much difficulty sleeping after Josh's death and Gracie's birth. She couldn't fall into a deep sleep and Mark's tossing and turning would wake her up. And then there was his snoring. He tried everything—chin straps, nasal strips, spray, even hypnosis. Nothing helped. He would find Julia sleeping on the floor of Gracie's nursery or on the couch downstairs.

He puts down his briefcase, not ready to leave but unsure of what to say. He opts for something basic. "Did you and Gracie have dinner?"

She gives a small nod. "Leftover meatloaf. Did you eat?"

The question catches him by surprise. It's been a long time since Julia asked about him or his day, about the business or anything other than Gracie. He decides to confess everything. "I did. I went to Roux, that new restaurant in the valley, with someone from work. The owner wants to talk next week, possibly about getting us involved in his next project."

"That's great." Julia doesn't look up.

"The food's amazing," he continues, encouraged. "Maybe we could go sometime."

Julia doesn't say anything, but gives a halfhearted shrug.

Mark wishes he thought to bring home a dessert for her. He used to do that all the time, take one more look at the dessert cart and order something to go. His clients were charmed by this gesture and his colleagues would chide him ceaselessly, but he didn't care—he wasn't doing it for them, he was doing it for Julia. It pains him that he didn't remember to do that. How could he forget?

"That Amish Friendship Bread was really good," he says instead, determined to keep the conversation going. Gracie and Julia made the bread yesterday and they had it for dessert and then again for breakfast this morning.

"Thanks." She looks up and smiles.

It's the most beautiful thing he's ever seen. He's about to step into the room when she says, "It's late. I should get some sleep."

"Oh. Right."

Julia puts her magazine and pen onto the nightstand and burrows under the covers. She pulls the comforter up to her shoulders and turns on her side, reaching up to turn off the light. "Good night."

The room is suddenly bathed in darkness. "Good night," he says. He steps back into the hallway, closing the door behind him.

Clinton Becker, 36
Copy Machine Technician

"It's what?" Clinton Becker frowns at the bag. He's convinced it's some kind of art or science project, but his daughter, Juniper, is insisting it's bread.

"We can make it at home and share it," she tells him from her car seat in the backseat. "I got it from Gracie Evarts at school. And I got instructions, too."

Clinton keeps one hand on the wheel as he lifts the Ziploc bag for closer inspection. There's a red light up ahead and he slows to a stop. It looks a bit like watery hummus. He tried hummus once and it wasn't so bad. Clinton opens the bag and sticks his head in for a sniff, then makes a face. It's definitely not hummus.

The car behind him lays on the horn and Clinton sees that the light has turned green. He tries to reseal the bag but can't get the plastic ridges to line up. He carefully props up the bag in the passenger seat next to him. He's not one for these crafty school projects. Juniper can do this with her mother, though he doubts Angie can be bothered. She's too busy with her new boyfriend, some stupid accountant.

"What's for dinner?" Juniper wants to know.

"McDonald's," he says, and smiles when he hears a cheer from the backseat. He glances in the rearview mirror at his daughter who's happily kicking her heels and humming some song he doesn't know. Thank God he fought for joint custody. He's made a lot of stupid mistakes in his time, but Juniper wasn't one of them.

At the drive-thru, Clinton orders a hamburger Happy Meal with apple slices and chocolate milk for Juniper and a Big Mac meal for himself. When he pulls around to the window, he spots a familiar face.

"Hi, Clinton." Debbie Reynolds gives him a shy smile. Debbie was a class behind him at Avalon High but had skipped a few grades, so she's actually a few years younger. Debbie had gone on to some fancy college, then some fancy business school, and then came back to Avalon to care for her mom. He used to think it was a shame such a smart girl ended up flipping burgers in a fast-food joint, but then he read an article in the *Avalon Gazette* that said she and a couple business partners owned all the McDonald's franchises in Avalon and a few of the neighboring towns, a total of five or six in all. There aren't many girls like Debbie Reynolds, that's for sure.

"Hey, Debbie. What's cookin'?" Clinton gives her a grin.

She smiles. "That'll be nine dollars and eleven cents."

He hands her a ten-dollar bill and waits while she makes change. "So how come you're always working if you own the place?" He knows it's probably not nice to ask, but he also doesn't think Debbie minds. Plus he's curious.

Debbie hands him his receipt and a handful of coins. "Oh, I don't know. I rotate around to all of the restaurants. I like to see how things are going. Anyway, it's not like I have a whole lot else to do."

"Really?" He's genuinely surprised. She's smarter than anybody he knows, and nice-looking in a quiet, understated sort of way. "I can't believe that!" He's not hitting on her, just telling the truth.

Debbie reddens, a shy smile on her lips. Then her expression changes as she squints at something just beyond him. "I think you spilled something on your seat," she says. "Would you like some extra napkins?"

Clinton turns to see that the Ziploc bag has tipped over and the starter has oozed onto his seat. "Dammit!" He grabs the bag and gets a handful of goop.

Debbie quickly passes him several napkins. Clinton tries to mop up the mess while holding the plastic bag, which he still hasn't managed to seal. "What is that?" Debbie asks, trying not to laugh.

"Something Juniper got at school," he says, disgusted. His car has cloth upholstery. Now he'll have to pay to have it steam cleaned. Great.

"It's Amish Friendship Bread!" comes a cry from the backseat. Juniper is waving a piece of paper. "We squish the bag every day and then we get to make cake next week!"

"That sounds like fun," Debbie says to Juniper, a sincere look on her face.

Clinton is about to ask Debbie to throw the Ziploc away when another idea comes to him. He grabs the paper from Juniper and skims the instructions, then looks at Debbie who is holding out their bags of food. "If you're free next week, you can come over and help us make it," he says.

"Me?"

"Sure? Why not?" Clinton grins as he takes the bags from her and puts them on the floor of the passenger seat. He tosses the soggy napkins into one of the bags.

"It's so yummy!" Juniper adds.

Clinton doesn't consider himself a fast thinker, but he's able to count ahead ten days and is pleased to discover that it's a day that Juniper is with him. "Are you free next Saturday? Around ten? We can do lunch after." The car behind him honks a few times. Clinton sticks his head out of the window and yells, "One minute!" Idiot. What is it with people today?

"Okay," Debbie says, her eyes shining. She glances apologetically at the car behind him. "Sorry, but I kind of have to keep everything

going. Here's my number." She looks around for something to write
on. Flustered, she grabs an apple pie from the warming rack and
writes her number on the sleeve with a Sharpie. She hands it to him.

Clinton fumbles for his wallet again, not wanting to take advantage. "Let me pay . . ."

"No, no," she says hastily. "It's on the house."

Clinton grins. "Okay, great. So, next Saturday, then."

"Next Saturday." She waves goodbye and Clinton notices for the
first time that her eyes are a lovely clear blue. He pulls carefully out
of the drive thru and tries to seal the Ziploc one more time.

This time it works.

CHAPTER 6

"Oh, bother." Edie lets out a sigh of defeat.

Richard looks up from the medical journal he's reading. "What's wrong?" he asks. A smile tugs at the corners of his mouth as he watches Edie bend over a square piece of paper. "Look at you— you're just so crafty, honey. I'm proud of you."

Alphabet stickers are stuck to her fingers, bits of patterned paper and embellishments everywhere. She's already spilled glitter on the floor and there's a smudge of it on her cheek. She's burned herself twice with the hot glue gun. Edie considers herself a competent person but at the moment feels completely helpless and inept.

"This is why people spend so much time scrapbooking," she tells him. She tries to hold the scrapbook page in place as she pulls the stickers from her fingertips. Part of the letter "E" rips and an "A" folds on itself. "It takes forever to get anything done!" She manages to spell out her name then sits back to survey her work.

It looks terrible. It took her a full thirty minutes, and now she has to do Richard's name, too.

Why she agreed to this, she has no idea, but one of the women she recently interviewed, Bettie Shelton, is an avid scrapbooker with a home-based scrapbooking business on the side. She gave Edie a small starter packet to thank her for spreading the word about the smattering of break-ins over the past year, including her own in which two garden gnomes, a rusty rake ("Though I was happy to be rid of it, I have to say"), and a potted begonia were taken. Edie isn't a hobbyist of any kind and tried to protest, but Bettie insisted, pressing the sealed packet into Edie's hands. Then, to make matters worse, she invited Edie to attend the next scrapbooking meeting. There, Bettie promised, Edie would get an earful from other concerned citizens.

"The things I do for a good story," Edie sighs. She can dig trenches, build a schoolhouse, teach basic English to someone who's never spoken it before, but she can't develop a "Passion for Paisley" or figure out how to stamp a piece of vellum with embossing ink.

"Hey, is that my name?" Richard asks. He puts down his reading and comes over to where Edie's sitting. She decided to cheat and just put down "Dr. Richard" instead of "Richard Johnson" since it spares her the extra letters.

"The ladies of the Avalon Scrapbooking Society have a meeting next week and the theme is romance."

"Hence me."

"Hence you." Edie glues a picture onto the page at an angle, thinking it looks more artistic. Or amateurish. She can't decide, but it's too late anyway.

Richard points to the picture of the two of them in Benin, West Africa. "You were out of cooking propane the day we met," he reminds her affectionately.

"Yes." Edie gives him a playful swat. "And you were too busy getting ready to play basketball to help me."

"It was the ribbon-cutting ceremony," he protests. "I spent two years raising the funds to build that basketball court. It was a big deal for the community—of course I had to be there."

She does an eye roll. "My first day on site and you leave me to fend for myself."

"Hey, it's the toughest job you'll ever love," he says, repeating the Peace Corps motto. And it's true, she did love it.

Edie rummages through the paper scraps and finds a piece of brown corrugated paper. She begins to cut out an outline of Benin, which always reminds her of a torch.

"It's nice to see you're becoming a part of the community." Richard finds a die cut of a heart and glues it onto the page.

"I'm not sure that going to a couple of scrapbooking meetings qualifies, but it's okay. Oh, and I've been having lunch with a girl from work."

Richard looks impressed.

"Livvy Scott. Blond, bouncy. Tall." Edie wishes Livvy weren't so pretty. She's seen pictures of Richard's exes, girls much more glamorous than she, girls who know how to style their hair and put on makeup, who know how to work their femininity to their advantage. People have called Edie pretty before, but it's usually in the context of smart pretty, not turn-heads kind of pretty. Edie didn't know the difference until the seventh grade, when Missy Davidson made fun of the way she was dancing during the Fall Fling.

"Is this how you do it?" Missy had asked innocently, mimicking Edie's middle school MTV move. Laughter erupted around them. It took Edie a minute to register that Missy was making fun of her. She suddenly felt clumsy and self-conscious, saw how the same turquoise blouse hung on her like a bedsheet while it hugged Missy's body and breasts like a second skin. She watched Missy laugh, passing around her Bonne Bell lip gloss to girlfriends while Edie fingered the hard round tin of Carmex in her pocket. She forced a smile, pretending that she was in on the joke and not the joke itself, but the moment had done its job. After that, she let herself fall into the smart-girl category, the girl with a cause, the girl who didn't have time for frivolous things like makeup and boy talk. She even boycotted her senior prom—the thought of having to find a suitable dress, much less a date, terrified her.

Edie can't help adding, "She's totally your type, I think. Maybe I should introduce you."

Richard doesn't bite. "Nice try, honey, but you're not getting rid of me that easily." He knits his eyebrows as he pushes some scattered sequins into a pile. "Livvy Scott . . . why do I know that name? What does she do?"

"She manages our display and classified advertising. She acts like a bubblehead sometimes, which I just don't get. Maybe she thinks she has to play up to the stereotype." Edie glues Benin onto the page. *There.* She's done. It's actually not half bad, now that everything is on the page together. She wishes she had some mementos from Benin, but she's made it her practice to live light. She begins to clean up. "Maybe she came into the clinic for something."

Richard shakes his head, frowning. "How well do you know her?" he asks.

"Not very. Her husband is in pharmaceutical sales."

"She mention any other family?"

"It hasn't come up. Why?"

"Because," Richard says, "I think there's something you should know about your friend."

Livvy balances herself on the step stool and peers at a stack of boxes on the top shelf of the closet. It's that time of year again, when the baby shower invitations start flooding the mailboxes in earnest. Chalk it up to the cold Illinois winters, she supposes. Carol Doyle and Jo Kay Buckley are both expecting in August and they each already have three children. It annoys Livvy that some people have babies so easily, Carol and Jo Kay especially. ("We weren't even trying!" Jo Kay confided to Livvy on the phone, a fact Livvy finds hard to believe. For as long as she's known her, Jo Kay has always been trying for something.)

It doesn't seem fair somehow. Livvy recalls numerous conversations where all Carol and Jo Kay seem to do is complain: they're so tired, their husbands don't help, they don't have enough time to do the things that *they* want to do. Livvy doesn't understand why they want more children. *I'll take one,* she wants to say. *And I won't complain.*

Livvy picks a box at random and turns off the closet light. Maybe it's just sour grapes. She and Tom haven't been trying that long, and it probably doesn't help that she's stressed out about the whole thing, wondering if they'll have any problems, which is probably why they *are* having problems. It's just that she never expected she wouldn't be able to get pregnant right away if she wanted to. Livvy wonders if maybe, possibly, it's some sort of divine punishment for what happened. She hopes not, but she doesn't know.

She sits on her bed and opens the box. Inside is a mishmash of photos and other childhood memorabilia—a homemade pot holder, one too many God's Eyes made from Popsicle sticks and yarn. Carol had asked Livvy if she would go through her old pictures to see if she could find any of Carol or Jo Kay "back in the day." Both women have decided that the only gift they want are photo quilts for their babies with pictures of them and their husbands from birth to present.

"It's *so* important to give children a sense of history," Carol had informed her. "To let them see where they came from. Who needs more diaper rash cream or another stuffed animal?"

Livvy had cringed—she'd bought stuffed animals for all of their previous baby showers and had planned on doing it again. "Some of them are kind of cute," she ventured.

Carol snorted. "Most of them are surface wash only. How can you really get them clean? It's no wonder Ruben has asthma." Ruben is Carol's youngest, an overweight six-year-old who always has a fat-free licorice whip in hand. "Can you see if you have any pictures from cheerleading camp after sophomore year? I remember you took really good pictures and they turned out pretty cute." Meaning that Carol looked pretty cute.

Livvy put it off for a couple of weeks, but now both Carol and Jo Kay are breathing down her neck, leaving voice messages and emails that border on harassment. Livvy reminds herself that they're hormonal, that Julia had once warned her that pregnant women were not to be reckoned with. That was a long time ago, when Julia was pregnant with Josh and had just passed her first trimester. They were getting pedicures, a birthday present from Julia for Livvy's twenty-first birthday. Julia was always good about things like that, and it's one of the many things that Livvy misses.

But now birthdays aren't the same anymore because Julia's absence is so noticeable Livvy would rather not celebrate them. Tom isn't much for sentimentality—he barely remembers her birthday or even their anniversary. Livvy doesn't fault him, though, because he's always been that way. He's the kind of guy who picks up a card from the drugstore on his way home from work or takes advice from a female salesclerk about what to buy his wife, even if the salesclerk knows nothing about Livvy.

But it's not just the special days that Livvy misses—it's every day. Every day used to be dotted with Julia, with visits, combined errand runs, last-minute babysitting requests. It wasn't unusual to have two, three, even four phone calls exchanged between them in a single afternoon. It was Julia who remembered to pick up flowers for their mother on Mother's Day and add Livvy's name on the card, who cooked extra servings so Livvy wouldn't have to figure out dinner on her own. It was always like that, and Livvy misses it.

Livvy continues to burrow through the box, wading through keychains, matchboxes, pressed pennies, old report cards. No negatives. There are a few more boxes in the closet and then they multiply as you look in the other rooms or go up in the attic. Livvy hits the side of the box in disgust—this is going to take forever.

Under a red handkerchief she spots something familiar. She pulls out a picture frame and turns it over, wiping the glass with the sleeve of her shirt.

The faded photograph shows Livvy and Julia, eight and thirteen respectively, sitting side by side in a bumper car. They're grinning as they hold on to the steering wheel. It was 1979, the year Julia got to decide where they'd spend their family vacation. The choice was hers because she had not only officially become a teenager, but had ended the school year with a straight-A report card.

Livvy was used to the look of pride her parents would exchange when talking about Julia, a huge contrast to how they'd cast their eyes to the ceiling when talking about Livvy. Julia was their pride and joy while Livvy was their "handful." She remembers Julia announcing her decision in their kitchen, the sudden realization that Livvy's turn might never come, that she would never be as smart as Julia. They would never spend one week doing whatever Livvy wanted.

Julia chose Hershey Park in Pennsylvania. Their father had groaned about the drive, but finally agreed. Livvy felt a wave of panic once she realized what this meant—*her* dream place to go was Dutch Wonderland, not even an hour away from Hershey Park—her classmates said it was a million times more fun. But what were the chances her parents would take them back to Pennsylvania? Zero, that's what.

The long car ride had been the worst—she got carsick and threw up twice. When they crossed the state line into Pennsylvania, Livvy saw a sign for Dutch Wonderland and felt the tears coming. She squeezed her eyes shut. One tear leaked out anyway and she quickly brushed it away with the back of her hand. *Don't cry,* she told herself fiercely. So she didn't.

That night at the EconoLodge, Julia suddenly announced, "If it's not too late, I think I'd like to go to Dutch Wonderland instead." Livvy held her breath as their father groaned and their mother gave in. Julia quickly shot Livvy a warning look and whispered, "I'm not doing this for you. I'm doing this for me." She had looked her sister in the eye, serious, and Livvy had nodded, her lips obediently sealed tight, even though she knew better.

Because doing things for other people, for Livvy especially, is how Julia does things for herself. Despite their fights, their arguments, and their disagreements, Julia has Livvy's back. Or used to. Every childhood memory includes Julia, which would make sense since Julia has been there since the beginning—Livvy's beginning. It's unfathomable to think of what her life would have been like without Julia. Julia was the one who took care of her, who thought of her, who included her. It was Julia who saved the day at Livvy's wedding, when the photographer failed to show up, her gown had ripped, and the flower girls were refusing to walk down the aisle. Julia could fix any problem, get total strangers to work together. Gazing at this picture sadly, Livvy feels the pang of a loss so deep she feels broken in two.

Anything, she thinks desperately as she touches their faces in the picture. *I'll do anything, Julia. Just ask me.*

The girls just stare back at her happily from that sunny day at Dutch Wonderland, unaware that a day will come when everything will end, when two sisters will cease to talk, unwilling to touch or see each other, unable to offer or accept a helping hand.

The *Avalon Gazette* is published on Tuesdays and Fridays. It's a small paper with a circulation of 2,500, which means that the pay is essentially crap, but Edie isn't in it for the money. Her boss, Patrick, wanted her to come on board as a full-time staff reporter, but Edie pushed to maintain her freelance status. She covers the community beat and pitches in as needed, which leaves her with enough flexibility to think about other writing projects.

What Edie is hoping for is an opportunity to string for some of the larger regional papers like the *Chicago Tribune* or the *Chicago Sun-Times,* writing special features from the small-town front. She's overqualified for this tiny paper, but it's the best she can do under the circumstances. Richard pointed out that Patrick might step down from his editorial responsibilities at some point, in which case Edie would be in a position to become editor.

But Edie has since realized that Patrick is the kind of guy—and this is the kind of town—that likes to be a part of everyone's business. He's not going anywhere anytime soon, and that's fine by Edie. It's one reason she chose journalism—she loves writing and interviewing people, hearing about their lives, about what works and what doesn't. She doesn't want to be a glad-hander like Patrick, someone who's at ease with the politics of business, something Edie is terrible at. She prefers to be in the background, quietly going about her work, mind-ing her own business. Having coffee and doughnuts with the Avalon Chamber of Commerce or local Elks Club isn't really up her alley.

When the opportunity came up for Richard to take over as the town's GP, it seemed like the right thing to do. Having grown up in Springfield, gone to school in Chicago, and then traveled the world, Edie was curious to see what living in a small town would be like. When she and Richard traveled in Africa and Asia after their Peace Corps tour, they lived for weeks in small villages here and there, villages with a fraction of the population of Avalon. They fixed huts, carried water, helped with meals, offered rudimentary health care when asked. They spent hours listening to stories from the village elders or playing games with children who needed nothing more than rocks, sticks, and their imagination. A leaf was a bird, a pile of dirt a mountain. There was always something to do and they were always on the go. Edie could always find something to be intrigued by, which is why she finds herself a bit at a loss in Avalon. She hadn't expected it to be so, well, *quiet.*

But now, as she peruses the past bound editions of the *Gazette,* she feels that familiar stirring of excitement, the small rush you get when you've had too much caffeine or stumbled onto something you know you shouldn't have. Then again, it's not as if this is a secret. Here it is in black-and-white. The papers for the last week of May in 2003.

There's not a lot—the paper has always been a modest sixteen-page spread with a page for classified ads, and the story is only a few paragraphs. But it's enough. As Edie reads the story, she knows now that Livvy is harboring a painful memory, a guilty secret she's chosen not to share with Edie.

And Edie can't say she blames her.

CHAPTER 7

Mornings used to be Julia's favorite time of day. She's an early bird by nature, up with the sun, ready to tackle whatever's ahead. The rest of the house was slower to move—it took a little more work to rouse them, one too many snooze buttons, feeble protests from beneath the blankets. They'd brush their teeth in a half daze, possibly still dreaming, not quite awake and back in the world as they knew it.

But now it's Julia who stays buried under the covers, feigning sleep until Mark and Gracie have left the house. She'll lie in bed, staring at the ceiling, not wanting to think about laundry or lunch, the inevitable drive in the afternoon to pick up Gracie from school. It seems so futile, so unimportant, these demands of the day. Is this really what they were put on the earth to do? To wipe down counters and sweep away stray crumbs?

She thinks back to conversations with her mother, who used to keep a constant vigil over Julia in the early days following Josh's death. Her mother read every book on grief, compiled lists, talked about stages, explained how the grief response for the sudden death of a child is vastly different from other sorts of loss. As if Julia hadn't figured that out.

But—and there was always a but—she insisted that Julia would eventually find life worth living again. It wouldn't be easy, her mother warned, but it would happen. Julia would be able to create a new reality, a new life. Not just for Gracie, but for Josh. In his spirit, his memory. When she heard this, Julia turned on her heel and went into her room, refusing to talk to her mother or anyone else for the rest of the day.

The sympathy cards had poured in, one after another, terrible Hallmark sentiments that missed the mark and sometimes made it worse. In one of them someone had written "You're halfway there," as if to console her. Her son had just died but she was halfway there, as if she were running a marathon. But that was five years ago and the finish line isn't anywhere in sight.

Julia rolls over to stare at Mark's side of the bed, the side he doesn't sleep on anymore. She's alone in this boat of a bed, a California king they splurged on after they bought the house. It had been almost as painstaking a decision as the house purchase itself—should we get it, should we not, should we wait, and so on—but in the end they decided to go for it even if it meant working extra hours to cover the additional expense. When they realized later they would need new sheets and blankets, too, they just laughed and agreed to buckle down and work a little harder. So they did.

Julia knows she has choices. Working again would help their income, though Mark's business is starting to pick up and they still have some savings left. Julia used to love work, but she can't see herself back at Bertram Berry, the small paint company in Freeport where she was an HR manager. She doesn't want to have to dodge the tentative smiles, have to answer the never-ending, probing question masked with three simple yet ever intrusive words: "How *are* you?"

How is she? Let's see. She has a child and yet she's childless. She is married to a man who was her first and only love, someone who has morphed into a stranger who passes her in the hallway of the home they share. Her parents have taken refuge and retirement in sunny Florida, where exuberant postcards arrive that have nothing to do with what they've left behind. *Canasta! Poetry readings! Visits to Butterfly World—Gracie would love it! Call! Visit! We miss you! How* are *you?*

How is she. No longer a question, but a statement. Because there really is no point in asking—how would anybody be if they lost their son?

Julia wasn't there when it happened. There's Livvy's account, and the coroner's, but in her mind, this is what Julia sees.

It is May 26. Five years ago. Livvy is picking up ten-year-old Josh after school. He was supposed to have an hour and a half of baseball practice but the parent-coach called in sick. Julia and Mark are due at the doctor's office for a five-month ultrasound so she calls on her younger sister to help as she has so many times before.

Livvy has a meeting so they agree she'll drop Josh at the house to finish his homework. A teenage babysitter will meet them there, taking over for Livvy so she can get back to work.

Aunt and nephew are chatting amicably in the car as they pull up to Julia's—no, Livvy's—house. Livvy has forgotten to return a black skirt she borrowed from Julia, and has stopped by her place to get it before taking Josh home.

Livvy parks the car in the driveway, cuts the engine, then sprints across the lawn to the front door of her unnecessarily large 4,500-square-foot house. She notices that the dog bowl has dirt floating in it, leaves maybe, and asks Josh to please give the dog some fresh water. They'll be back on the road in less than ten minutes, but Livvy automatically presses the button on her car remote before heading into the house. There's a beep and flash of headlights as the doors lock.

Julia can picture her son strolling over to the water bowl on the porch and dumping the old water in the bushes nearby. He heads for the garden hose on the side of the house. There's no warning when an angry yellow jacket wasp stings him on his fingertip.

Josh must have known something was wrong. He probably called to his aunt, but Livvy was rummaging through her bedroom closet on the second floor, searching for a skirt she should have returned months ago. She can't hear him. Josh stumbles a few feet, then collapses. A man driving by sees this odd behavior and pulls over to help, but it's too late.

Livvy emerges from the house triumphant, clutching the skirt like a trophy. It takes her a moment to digest the scene in front of her. Josh is lying there with a man standing over him, his car stopped in the middle of the street, the driver's side door still open. At first Livvy thinks Josh has been hit by the car.

A neighbor dials 911—it takes the EMTs five minutes to get there. They're performing CPR and questioning Livvy when it hits her.

"He's allergic to bees," she says, turning to look at the locked Honda Pilot in the driveway. Josh's knapsack is in the backseat, his EpiPen inside.

The EMTs immediately give him a shot of epinephrine, then take him to the emergency room where doctors administer thirty more minutes of treatment.

Meanwhile Mark and Julia are in the OB-GYN annex, staring dreamily at the milky image of their unborn baby, their cell phones off so as not to interfere with the equipment. The doctor asks if they want to know the sex, and they both demur. Should it be a surprise? Julia thinks it's a girl. They decide to wait, so Josh will be surprised, too.

Julia's doctor prints out several 3-D pictures of their baby, then strings them together to produce a 4-D ultrasound—the baby's first video. A video! It's amazing what technology can do, they all marvel. They spend a few more minutes chatting about walking epidurals and how it's a relief the long, hot summer has finally passed.

Back in the ER, doctors are able to get Josh's heart going again but the excessive swelling of his larynx has severely slowed the flow of blood to his brain and has caused a massive stroke. Josh is comatose.

Brain dead.

By now Julia and Mark have left the doctor's office and are in the car driving away when Julia checks her messages. "Turn the car around!" she screams.

This all happened on a Tuesday. On Saturday they disconnected Josh from life support and watched him slip away.

Circulatory collapse. Respiratory arrest. Cerebral hypoxia, fatal anaphylaxis. Julia knows his throat closed up in seconds, but that doesn't stop her from hearing him, calling to her for help.

This is what Julia sees. And hears. Over and over again.

Julia pushes herself out of bed, stares into the empty hallway. There are spots on the walls, bright rectangles that have been shielded from sunlight for many years. Julia meant to replace the pictures that once hung there but hasn't gotten around to it—she hadn't realized how many pictures there were of Livvy until she started taking them down. Livvy appears almost everywhere, at every turn. From the moment Julia got her wish for a baby sister, there was not a moment in her life where Livvy was absent, no such moment until the day after Julia buried her son.

And then it starts, the hurt and anger that washes over Julia like a wave. It's not like before when it would consume her so she couldn't see straight, but still Julia can hardly bear to think of it. When Mark and Julia were deciding where to live, Avalon was an easy choice because Livvy and her parents were here. Mark's family lives in St. Louis, but he's not close with them, not the way Julia is with her family.

Was. The way Julia *was* with her family.

Julia decides to forgo a shower and drifts down the stairs, grateful for the quiet house but feeling the dull melancholy of loneliness, too. It's like this for the next hour as she pulls herself together, going through short "to do" lists in her mind.

By the time the phone rings, Julia's changed into a pair of jeans and a short-sleeved knit top, her hair knotted into a ponytail.

Nobody really calls anymore, and Julia debates whether or not she can be bothered to answer it. Before Josh's death she and Livvy would talk several times a day, about everything and nothing. Julia hasn't let herself miss those calls, those long and sometimes pointless conversations, but today Julia finds herself thinking that if it is Livvy who's calling, maybe she won't hang up the phone this time, maybe she'll just listen to whatever it is Livvy has to say.

But what would Julia say to her?

"I don't think I'm doing this right." It's Hannah, the young Asian woman Julia met last week at the tea salon. She sounds discouraged. "I found your name in the phone book—I hope it's all right that I'm calling."

"No, no, it's fine." Her first words of the day. Julia coughs, clearing the sleep from her throat. "You're not doing what right?"

"The Amish Friendship Bread. It's so runny! Should I add more flour? My roommate had a breadmaker in college and I remember it being more doughy . . ."

Julia realizes she's been holding her breath as she listens to Hannah talk, her voice anxious through the telephone line. It's such a small thing—this simple telephone conversation—and yet Julia can't quite believe it's happening. A normal conversation that has nothing to do with her, or Gracie's school, or Mark coming home late from work. There's no hint of concern, no careful treading around Julia. In fact, Hannah is speaking in such a rush that Julia finds herself in the unusual position of stopping another person from getting worked up into a frenzy.

"Hey, it's fine," Julia says. She hears the amusement in her own voice and it makes her smile. "I should have told you. It's called Amish Friendship Bread but it's a sweet bread, more like a cake. Like banana bread."

"Oh!" Hannah breathes. "So this is okay, then?"

"It's okay. Did you put it in the oven yet?" Julia leans against the kitchen counter, the phone cradled between her ear and her shoulder.

"No. I thought I should call you first."

"Put it in and then call me in an hour when it's ready," Julia tells her.

Hannah hesitates. "Are you sure? I don't want to put you out."

"You won't." Julia can't remember what she was going to do this morning—as usual her plan was no plan. "Talk to you soon."

They hang up and Julia turns to look at her own bag of starter, which is ready to be divided. They'll bake when Gracie comes home. They've already copied the instructions and Gracie has preselected more friends at school she wants to give the extra bags to. They'll bake a loaf to keep and maybe one for Mark to take to work. If he wants to.

Julia is restless, checking the clock to see if the hour is up yet. She has a burst of energy and finishes organizing *and* wiping down the refrigerator with bleach in record time. When was the last time she'd done that? A year ago, maybe, and it had taken her forever. She did a shelf a day, then the door, then the freezer over another three days. A week. It took her a week. And now she's done in just under an hour.

Julia thinks back ten days ago, when she first met Hannah at Madeline's. She had no idea what Hannah was crying about that day, but Julia was grateful. For once she didn't feel like the only person in the room with a tragedy.

When the phone rings, Julia practically leaps at it. "Hello?"

"Hi, Julia. It's Hannah. I'm so sorry to have bothered you. You were right—the bread came out perfect! I'm waiting for it to cool and then I'm going to have a slice." Hannah sounds pleased, and Julia feels oddly proud.

"That's great to hear. I'm glad it turned out okay."

"Me, too. I've got two left thumbs in the kitchen so I was sure I'd done something wrong. Thank you for sharing it with me."

"Anytime." Julia doesn't want to hang up the phone but she can't think of anything else to say.

"There's just one more thing . . ."

"Yes?"

"It was fun, but I really don't bake or cook. What am I supposed to do with these bags of starter?"

Julia laughs, remembering what it felt like to be in Hannah's exact predicament ten days ago. "My daughter would be thrilled to take the extra bags to school," she tells Hannah. "I think there's a waiting list of kids who want to try the bread at home."

Hannah gasps. "I'm so glad! I was afraid it would go to waste."

"I know what you mean." Julia's been thinking about this and has come up with a theory. Her theory is that doing a little something every day to the starter somehow endears you to it. You become too attached to just throw it down the drain, to let it go to waste.

"I really appreciate you sharing this with me and helping me out. Can I treat you to lunch?"

"Oh, you don't have to do that, Hannah," Julia says. She immediately wishes she could take it back. It sounds like she doesn't want to go out, which couldn't be farther from the truth. She quickly adds, "I mean, I'm happy to pay for myself." She sees her reflection on the oven door. She'll need to fix her hair, put on a little makeup.

"How about you pick up next time?" Hannah proposes, and Julia feels happy at the suggestion that there is the possibility of more to come. "And is it okay if we go back to Madeline's?"

Julia can't think of any place better. "I'd love to go back to Madeline's."

"Is noon okay?"

"Noon." Julia says the word slowly, remembering what it feels like to set a date, to make a commitment. "Noon would be perfect."

Hannah rests her forearms on the counter and inhales deeply, taking in the sweet scent of the bread. The cinnamon crust is dotted with small sugar crystals, tiny edible diamonds. The bread is warm to the touch so Hannah gently taps it out of the pan and puts it on the wire rack to cool. She still can't believe that she baked something by herself. And from scratch! Ever since she started playing professionally at the age of sixteen, her meals have primarily been on the run—takeout, something quick and microwavable, dinner at other people's houses. The habit sort of stuck, even after she stopped playing for a living. Plus Philippe preferred eating out—he liked the attention that came with favoring a few restaurants that made it their business to know him by name.

Since living in Avalon Hannah has tried her hand at cooking, mostly because she hates eating alone in public, but she doesn't really know what to do in the kitchen. She doesn't have a well-stocked pantry and everything seems to take so long—the preparation as well as the cooking, not to mention the cleanup. She wonders if Philippe is right, that it's just easier to eat out. She's tired afterward, not even hungry anymore.

But the Amish Friendship Bread looks and smells so wonderful that Hannah can't resist. She breaks off a piece and pops it into her mouth. It's fabulous. She wishes Philippe could see her now, could see the woman she's becoming and that he's missing out on. He had been furious that she hadn't followed his instructions to the letter and let the movers do the packing. For a second she was scared, thinking that she was making a bad situation worse. And then she stopped herself.

Why is she the one feeling bad? She's been the agreeable one since the beginning of their relationship. When Philippe suggested they move in together, she agreed. When he wanted to get engaged a couple years sooner than Hannah would have liked, she agreed. When he wanted to move to Chicago, she agreed, even though it meant that she was the one flying back and forth for those couple of years to make their long-distance relationship work. After they got married, it was Philippe who called the shots, who picked the furniture, who chose their cars and where they would live, what vacations they would take. It had been his idea to move to Avalon, a decision that surprised Hannah, but delighted her, too. She had agreed to everything, and now she is filled with regret.

He assures her that he will take care of her, that everything won't be any more complicated than it needs to be. He has his earnings and she has hers, it's always been separate. He'll give her the house in Avalon to keep or sell if she'll agree to give him their apartment in Chicago which, he points out, is half the size. He'll send Hannah her things from the apartment once the season is over in June. They'll each keep their respective cars—Hannah has a Toyota, Philippe an Audi—and that should be the end of that.

Jerk, she thinks as she eats another piece, stopping only because she wants to save room for lunch with Julia. They're meeting in a few minutes, but it's a short walk to Madeline's and Hannah doesn't want to seem too eager. Then again, since she's the one inviting she shouldn't be late, either. She puts the three bags of starter into her purse then gathers the rest of her things and steps outside.

It's a beautiful day in Avalon, still cold but with all the early signs of spring on its way. Hannah buttons her jacket and ties a scarf around her neck as she walks along the sidewalk. She looks at the houses adjacent to hers, noticing that their homes look lived in, cared for. Their street in particular has a row of single-story bungalow-style houses built in the late 1800s with wood siding and shingled roofs, all with garages that were added after the fact. Hannah and Philippe's house is one of the few properties that had undergone additional renovations to expand the size of the house, the appliances upgraded, the original wood floors refinished and restored. The ornamental fireplace—typical for these old homes—was replaced with one that actually worked. The small front yards belie their spacious backyards, one of the features Hannah loves about their home. It's what she missed the most in New York and Chicago. Space. Grass. Your own tree. Now Hannah has five, the royal empress being her favorite. The fragrant purple blossoms are just starting to bloom.

There's a pride in the simple upkeep and landscaping of their street, which isn't far from Avalon Park and the elementary school. Hannah likes that Avalon is big enough that you need a car to get around and at the same time there's so much within walking distance. Less than fifteen minutes away there's a bona fide neighborhood ice cream parlor with black-and-white checkered floors and a row of red vinyl stools at the counter. Hannah sees the kids go there after school, backpacks lined outside the parlor, an Avalon tradition. Hannah likes that.

Her pace slows as she nears Madeline's. There are more cars and more people coming in and out of the tea salon, reassuring activity for a place that seemed so quiet the first few months Hannah has been here. She spots Julia emerging from her car and smiles brightly when Julia sees her and gives a wave.

"I'm so glad you could make it," Hannah says as they meet up and head toward the entrance of Madeline's. "I've been going stir crazy in the house."

"Me, too," Julia says. "I was cleaning my refrigerator when you called."

Hannah looks like she's about to apologize but Julia quickly waves it away. "It's a relief for me to get out, too."

They step inside and are immediately enveloped in warm, delicious smells. Many of the tables are taken and Hannah sees a bob of silvery white hair as Madeline emerges from the kitchen with two plates of food, looking frenzied.

She takes a moment to chat with a customer, picks up a sweaty pitcher of iced tea, and begins to offer refills as she floats from table to table. Both Julia and Hannah hesitate, unsure if they should wait or come back another time. At that moment, Madeline looks up and a wide smile spreads across her face.

"There you are!" she exclaims, as if she's been expecting them. She puts down the pitcher and hurries over, greeting them with a big hug before the women can say anything. "Most of my tables are almost finished. Are you in a rush?"

"I'm not." Hannah looks to Julia for confirmation.

Julia shakes her head and says, "Me, neither. I don't have to pick up my daughter for a while."

Madeline's eyes twinkle. "Perfect! Make yourself at home and I promise I'll take good care of you." She scurries away.

"Gosh, she's getting busy." Hannah looks around, a little intimidated by the small crowd. It's a funny thing—she can perform in front of fifty thousand people in Central Park but freezes up in a room of twenty-five. It's a bit of a relief when Julia spots a table and leads the way—Hannah just has to follow.

"Avalon isn't exactly a huge draw for new businesses so I'm glad to see that business has picked up for her," Julia says. Her eyes quickly scan the room before dropping down to her menu. "Looks like she has a few locals. Mostly tourists, though."

"Avalon doesn't seem like much of a tourist town," Hannah notes.

Julia nods. "We're not really, but people like to drive up and down along the river. Avalon's an easy stop along the way."

That makes sense, seeing that's exactly how Philippe and Hannah found it. She remembers the quaint wooden sign that welcomed them to Avalon when they first drove in, unsure of what to expect but curious just the same.

Julia points to something on the menu. "Look at this—'A Trio of Finger Sandwiches.' Salmon and cream cheese, turkey with a cranberry relish, fresh goat cheese with watercress. That's what I'm getting." She seems pleased by her selection. "What about you?"

Hannah glances at the menu, at the soups, salads, quiches, and sandwiches, and has no idea what to order. It's not an extensive menu but the choices seem overwhelming. Hannah is not a picky eater—she never has been. She usually goes along with whatever Philippe wants, not because she's a pushover but because it's just easier. Hannah has never had to give it much thought before.

Everyone around her is eating something that looks good. Julia already knows what she wants. What does Hannah want? It's just lunch, after all—not the rest of her life. She finally gives up. "I'll ask Madeline to recommend something." She puts down her menu, disgusted that she can't even make this one simple decision.

Madeline comes by with a carafe of iced tea and two tall glasses. She places it all on the table. "An iced ginger green tea," she announces. "My own special blend. There's some simple syrup on the table if you'd like to make it sweeter. And today's special is a lovely

Croque Madame with a Mornay sauce. A neighbor brought over a flat of organic eggs from his farm and I couldn't resist. Comes with a side of fresh greens. Nine ninety-five."

"That's the one for me," Hannah says immediately. She reaches for the iced tea pitcher and pours herself and Julia a glass. "Madame de Brisay will have the Croque Madame, *s'il vous plaît.*" She feigns a French accent but it comes off funny.

"I'll have the finger sandwiches," Julia says. She looks at Hannah. "Who's Madame de Brisay?"

"Me." Hannah stirs some syrup into her iced tea. "My husband is French." She doesn't look up.

Madeline's eyes widen in sudden recognition. "I know who you are!" she exclaims. She puts her hands on her hips and looks at Hannah as if she's been holding out on her. "Hannah de Brisay, née Wang. I've read about you in the *New York Times.* You're a concert cellist!"

"Was," Hannah corrects.

"I think I heard an interview on NPR. Didn't you start playing the cello when you were three?"

"Three?" Julia gapes at her and Hannah is embarrassed.

Madeline continues, unabashed. "I remember Joel Rose saying that you could hear a piece and play it back in its entirety by age seven."

It was age six, actually, but Hannah doesn't correct her. She's a little flattered someone knows something about her in this town. It feels good, like her identity hasn't been completely wiped out.

Madeline is excited, and it must be contagious because Julia is grinning, too. "You used to play with the New York Philharmonic. I can't believe it—there's a celebrity in our midst!" Madeline's voice reaches an exclamation and a few heads turn to look at them, curious.

"No, no," Hannah says hastily. "I'm retired from playing professionally. Besides, that was a long time ago."

"It couldn't be that long ago. You're still too young and beautiful." Madeline gives her a look that's both kind and stern, and Hannah wonders if Madeline knows more than she's letting on.

Madeline glances around the tea salon, which is still full of customers. "And wouldn't you know it, I have to get back to work just when it's getting interesting. I'll swing by when things settle down. Dessert is on the house—your pick." She hurries off before the women can protest.

Julia looks at Hannah, intrigued. "Is your husband a musician, too?"

Hannah manages a nod as she takes a sip of her iced tea. It warms her throat—the ginger is a little spicy. "Philippe plays the violin. He's assistant principal for the Chicago Symphony Orchestra." *And he left me,* she wants to add, but decides against it. It's not the kind of thing people want to know about.

"Why aren't you playing anymore?" Julia asks.

"Three years ago I had a back injury after touring hard one season. I couldn't sit upright for a long time—the muscles in my back were constantly in distress. I'd had chronic back problems before—a lot of cellists experience this, unfortunately—but this was much, much worse. I took a leave but it was clear I wouldn't be able to perform like before."

"I'm so sorry."

"It's okay," Hannah says, even though it's really not. She misses it more than anything, especially now, and it makes her wonder what all her hard work has been for. "Philippe and I were also tired of having a long-distance marriage, so it made sense to give up my apartment in New York and move to Chicago. Then this year we started looking in the suburbs for a place to live. We couldn't find anything we liked so we kept driving until we found Avalon." She doesn't say that she resisted the idea of moving to a small town that seemed a bit too far away from the city, too far away from civilization as they knew it, but Philippe had insisted, convincing Hannah that he was thinking about their future. Now she knows he was just thinking about a future without her. "It was Philippe's choice to move here."

"Is he enjoying it?"

"He said he was, but he was never here." Hannah realizes she's speaking in the past tense but Julia doesn't seem to notice.

"Did you say you have children?"

"No." Hannah can't imagine what she would do if they had children. She adds, "We've talked about starting a family but I don't think that's going to happen." She doesn't say any more and Julia doesn't ask.

Julia turns to gaze out the window. "I'm trying to remember if I saw something about your arrival in the *Avalon Gazette,* but I don't really look at the paper much. They make such a big deal about anything that happens in this town, I'm sure they were thrilled to hear that you and your husband are residents of Avalon now."

Hannah gives Julia a bemused smile. Avalon is such a far cry from New York or even Chicago that she doesn't know where to begin. She remembers a time when she and Philippe were constantly in the press, music fans and photographers in love with the young couple who seemed destined for stardom.

"With the exception of Madeline, I don't think a lot of people keep up with the classical music world anymore," Hannah says.

Julia looks sheepish. "I'm sorry to say I don't know as much as I'd like." In other words, she has no idea who Hannah is.

Which just makes Hannah beam. There was always that uncertainty if someone was enthralled by Hannah or just by her music. She has friends and acquaintances by extension, other musicians who travel in the same crowd, all with similar stories to Hannah's—they started playing young, went to music camp during the summer, attended Juilliard, and so on—but she's never known many people outside of their music circle. Constantly moving, plus four to seven hours of daily practice, made it impossible to get to know anyone.

When their food arrives, Hannah dives in, starving. Her grilled sandwich has an egg on top, sunny side up, and a creamy cheese sauce on the side. She and Julia trade small bites, cutting off corners of their sandwiches and commenting on how good everything is, how Madeline clearly has a gift. Both of their choices are delicious, and Hannah decides next time she's going to pick something off the menu, something new that she hasn't tried before, and will keep going until she's sampled everything.

Hannah quizzes Julia about Avalon. What to do, where to go,

what to see. It's embarrassing how little she knows of the town she's living in, but Hannah thought she'd be discovering it with Philippe.

She pushes Philippe from her thoughts and turns her attention to Julia, finds herself intrigued by Julia's love for a town that is clearly home for her.

Home. The concept of setting down roots or even having roots is foreign to Hannah. Seven moves over her lifetime, either for music or for when her mother was sick and they camped out near Cedars-Sinai in Los Angeles. Hannah feels like her life has been in perpetual storage—some things here, some things there, nothing ever all in one place, not even now. Her possessions are divvied up between Avalon and their apartment in Chicago, and her brother Albert recently told her that he still had three of her boxes from their parents' old house up in his attic in Maryland.

"I haven't lived anywhere for more than four years at a time," Hannah tells Julia. "I used to tell myself that it was wanderlust, that traveling was in my blood. But it was just my way of justifying why I was never anywhere for too long. I didn't want to admit that I didn't have a place to call home."

"Where would home be, if you had a choice?" Julia asks.

"I don't think it's the place so much as the feeling. Does that make any sense? I have this sort of Norman Rockwell ideal of what home would feel like, of everyone being together, of kids riding their bikes, of lemonade stands and lazy summers." Hannah gives a wry smile—she has never had a lazy summer, and there was no way her father would have let her set up a lemonade stand on their street. Neither she nor Albert has ever owned a bicycle, not even now. "We celebrated American holidays—sort of—but there was usually some kind of Chinese spin on it."

Julia looks confused so Hannah explains how her parents made a turkey one Thanksgiving, and after agreeing that there wasn't enough flavor, reverted back to roast duck with its crispy skin and moist, sweet meat. Hannah remembers sitting alongside the banister next to Albert, both of them up past their bedtime, watching the men smoke and talk in Chinese while the women played mah-jongg, their hands moving fast over the colorful resin tiles, mixing them up as they laughed and chided one another.

Julia smiles. "I think that sounds lovely, Hannah."

"I guess," Hannah says. "But I always thought it would be nice to have an old-fashioned holiday, you know? I wasn't born in Taiwan, I was born here. I just want to experience things like everyone else."

"Being a concert cellist is hardly like everyone else."

Hannah smiles. "Tell me about it. And then, of course, I had to marry someone who was French, so there were always French celebrations we participated in like Bastille Day and La Chandeleur. It's not that I mind any of that, it's just that I want . . ."

"A Norman Rockwell Christmas," Julia finishes for her.

"And Thanksgiving and Easter." Hannah gives a sigh.

Julia smiles. "You know, Hannah, you can have all of that here. In Avalon."

Hannah thinks about this. Even though Avalon was Philippe's choice, it does have that classic Americana feel to it. "Maybe you're right."

The lunch rush has passed and there are only a few lingering customers other than Hannah and Julia. When they finish eating, Madeline brings over a pot of tea and three cups and pulls up a chair.

"Finally!" she exclaims, her face flushed in happy exhaustion. "I've been anxious to try this tea. It's peppermint with a touch of cocoa beans. Helps the digestion."

Julia smiles. "You're spoiling us."

"Oh, pshaw." Madeline feigns indifference but the women can tell she's pleased. Madeline drops her hands into her lap and nods toward the buffet of desserts. "Go on and help yourself—plates are on the left." She checks the tea for readiness, but it's still steeping.

Julia is the first to fill her plate: dark sticky gingerbread, vanilla sponge cake with a passion fruit filling, a wild blueberry scone. Hannah chooses to satisfy her chocolate craving with a single, albeit decadent, fudge brownie.

"We're going to eat all of your profits," Julia warns Madeline, who dismisses the comment with a wave of her hand. Julia glances at Hannah's modest choice. "Or maybe just I am."

Madeline checks the tea and, satisfied, pours each of the women a cup. "I am just thrilled to have people eating my food," she tells them.

"It looks like everyone's eating your food now," Julia says. "You were packed today."

"I know, isn't it glorious? It's been like this since . . ." Madeline thinks, then brightens. "Since you girls came in a couple of weeks ago. Here I was thinking that maybe it was spring coaxing everyone out, but maybe it was the two of you. My own lucky charms."

"Or," Hannah adds, "your food is just amazing and one taste is all it takes. That's how it was with me."

"And me," Julia says. "Sometimes it takes our town awhile to try something new, but once they do, if it's good, they're hooked. And word travels fast in Avalon."

"Whatever the reason may be, I am grateful," Madeline says. She takes a sip of her tea, considers it. "Oh, that's nice." She pours some more for all of them then settles back in her chair. "Those first few months were concerning, let me tell you. The downstairs freezer is filled with baked goods I didn't want to spoil. The local food bank only wants nonperishable food and I like to bake fresh. I guess I'll be saving it all for a rainy day."

That reminds Hannah, and she reaches for her bag. She hands Julia four Ziplocs of starter.

"Are you sure you don't want to keep one?" Julia asks her.

Hannah wants to say yes but isn't confident she'll be as enthusiastic to bake again next week. "It'll take me forever to get through the two loaves I made. Plus I'm more of a chocolate person." She takes a bite of the brownie and is surprised by how moist it is, practically melting in her mouth. "This is heavenly. I should probably try to tackle brownies someday."

Madeline gives Hannah a sly smile. "Funny you should say that. I made those brownies using one of my bags of Amish Friendship Bread starter."

"Really?" Hannah takes another bite. It's delectable. So long as the recipe isn't complicated, she wants to try it. "If it's not too hard to make, I'd love the recipe."

"Me, too," Julia says.

"Of course," Madeline says. "And rest assured it's surprisingly easy. If you made friendship bread, you can make this."

Hannah gives Julia a sheepish look. "Do you mind if I ask for one bag back? Will your daughter mind?"

"Of course not." Julia hands a bag back to her. "Gracie will just be thrilled to have any extra bags to take to school."

"I would love to meet her sometime," Madeline says. "Promise me you'll bring her in, Julia. I'm toying with the idea of afternoon tea parties for little girls, or maybe offering my place as a birthday party venue on weekends. She could be my test market."

"Gracie will be in heaven," Julia says, beaming. "In fact, she might never leave."

"Do you have any other children?" Hannah asks, curious. Julia looks like the sort of woman who would have a handful of children. Hannah can picture Julia managing her familial chaos like a traffic cop, a smile on her face as she wrangles her children into a minivan.

But a shadow crosses Julia's face as she looks down at her teacup. There's an obvious shift in her mood, and Hannah wishes she could take it back, wishes she hadn't said anything, not wanting to have disrupted this otherwise perfect moment. Hannah sees Julia's shoulders tense and for a second Hannah wonders if Julia is going to leave. But she doesn't.

Instead she looks up at Hannah and says, "Yes, I do. I have a son."

CHAPTER 8

If you don't see anyone, you never have to talk about it. It's been a
long time since she's had to say anything about it, because everyone
in Avalon already knows some version of that day.

Julia feels it hanging in the air, lingering. Waiting. Her voice is un-
even, shaky, as she begins in a low voice, uncertain of how much she
will say, of how much she *can* say. Then suddenly the words swoop
down and she's telling them everything.

The three women are quiet. Julia can't quite believe that she's actually recounted the events surrounding Josh's death aloud. She's
never discussed it, not even with Mark, and if anyone were to ask her
what happened, she simply got up and walked away.

Madeline is the first to speak. "I'm so sorry for your loss, Julia."
She takes Julia's hands in hers, her wrinkled skin soft. A balm.

Hannah looks stunned, her eyes filling with tears. Julia is familiar
with this, the shock of hearing about Josh for the first time. That

Hannah is completely speechless and not rushing to fill the silence with words is a relief.

Madeline's eyes are wet but her gaze is steady on Julia, who pulls her hands back and uses her fingers to rub her eyes. She suddenly feels tired. She wants to sleep.

"I am so sorry," Hannah finally manages. Madeline hands her a tissue and Hannah blows her nose. "I just . . . I don't know what to say . . ."

Julia opens her eyes to look at the young woman weeping in front of her, trying to stop but unable to. "It's okay, Hannah." In the past, it angered Julia when people would break down in front of her, mourning the loss as if it had been their own, as if expecting her to comfort them. Now, however, she feels differently.

Madeline excuses herself to tend to the few remaining customers, promising to be right back. She gives Julia a hug and kisses the top of her head.

The tiredness passes. Julia is suddenly aware she's sitting at the table with a pretty blue chintz tablecloth, her hand wrapped around a cooling teacup. She notices the vintage salt and pepper shakers, the purple crocus buds tucked into a small glass vase. In the past, the tired feeling would have camped out in her body for days so that the only viable solution was to crawl back into bed. But today, the tired feeling has come and gone. Her chest still feels hollow and as fragile as an eggshell, but she is sitting at this table, drinking her tea, and talking about Josh.

She's stunned.

Madeline returns to the table, a fresh pot of hot tea in hand. They are the only ones remaining in the tea salon, and Julia notices Madeline has turned the sign on the door to CLOSED after bidding farewell to the last customer.

Julia doesn't argue with her, doesn't protest. These women don't know her, they don't know Josh, and yet she feels like they know her grief.

The three women sit there, in comfortable and uncomfortable silence, giving themselves a little time before eventually talking in low voices about matters of the heart that can never be forgotten.

Dr. Norma Meehan, 37
Therapist

"Just let it out," Norma Meehan coaxes. "How did it make you feel?" She leans back in her chair, her eyes glancing surreptitiously at the small clock behind her client's head. Forty minutes to go.

"Terrible, Dr. Meehan!" Phyllis Watts sniffs, clutching a tissue. "I told him I didn't want the extended warranty, but he didn't listen. He told me I needed it and wrote it up anyway. He was such a bully!"

Dr. Meehan makes a clicking sound with her tongue. The sound is supposed to reassure Phyllis that she's listening and being hugely sympathetic, yet at the same time not passing judgment on what has happened. "So then what?"

"I told him I wasn't going to pay for the extended warranty, because *Consumer Reports* says that extended warranties aren't necessary. And then he ... he ..." Phyllis starts to get agitated again, her breath coming in short, angry puffs.

"What did he do, Phyllis?"

"HE LAUGHED! I ended up walking out of the store, thinking

that I would show him, but the thing is, I *really* like that new Hoover and nobody else in town is selling it. Now I have to go back there if I want to get it, and he's just going to laugh at me again!"

Dr. Meehan suppresses a yawn. Early afternoon is a hard time for her, right after lunch. She's always a bit sleepy.

Phyllis is thunderous now. "I mean, he shouldn't be allowed to treat a customer like that! I AM A PERSON! He made me feel so little, like I didn't know anything. But I did my research, Dr. Meehan. That Hoover got the highest rating and was a Best Value pick! I'm so angry I just want to punch something!"

Upon hearing this, Dr. Meehan straightens up. "You want to punch something?"

"Yes! A pillow or maybe that foam bat you have . . ."

Dr. Meehan stands up and hurries to the little kitchenette that's attached to her office. She returns a few seconds later, handing Phyllis a baggie of the Amish Friendship Bread starter. "There you go. Give it a good squeeze! Let out your frustrations! Be careful not to pop it, though. It'll be an awful mess."

Phyllis looks at the bag in her hands, not comprehending. "You want me to squeeze the bag?"

"Yes. In fact, I'm writing you a prescription." Dr. Meehan scribbles something on the back of a piece of paper.

"I don't really want to go on any medication, Dr. Meehan." Phyllis looks worried.

"This is a different kind of prescription," Dr. Meehan assures her, handing Phyllis the instructions for Amish Friendship Bread with a few extra pointers on the back. "Squeeze it, pound it, or wring it, once a day for ten days. Oh, you'll have to add some things on Day Six, but it will only take you a minute."

Phyllis looks confused. "That's it?"

"That's it! Oh, and on the tenth day, if you want, you can bake two loaves of the bread. It's quite delicious."

"But how is this going to help me, Dr. Meehan?"

Dr. Meehan doesn't know, but at least she has one less bag of starter. One of her clients had given her several slices of the bread and she'd made the mistake of saying how good it was. An hour later, a bag of starter and the instructions were sitting in her mailbox. There was a hint of burned rubber in the air, evidence of her client's quick getaway.

Dr. Meehan doesn't know why she didn't think of this earlier. It's the perfect way to manage these extra bags of starter while still leaving some for her. Genius.

"I can't explain my process," she tells Phyllis briskly. She has two more appointments today, and this time she'll have the starters sitting on the couch, waiting for them. "Let's just go with it, shall we?"

CHAPTER 9

There's a small gift on his desk, a pale blue box tied with a generous white ribbon. Mark slips off his jacket and hangs it on the hook on the back of his office door, wondering who it's from even though he has a pretty good idea.

The office is quiet. Everyone is busy on projects and Victor is at an AIA conference in Istanbul. The annual meeting is in Miami in a couple of months, but Mark didn't think Victor would make it to June. Victor has given up vacations and even sick days to cover for Mark, to make sure it's business as usual for Gunther & Evarts. It's been like this for the past five years and now, by some miracle, Mark finally feels he's ready to come back. So he sent Victor and his wife to Europe for two weeks, and in the meantime, Mark is the one in charge again.

He didn't see Vivian this morning at the gym, not that he was looking for her. It's just that it's become something of a routine, this informal meeting up in the mornings. They'll see each other and chat briefly before moving on to their respective workouts. He's aware of her, of wherever she may be in the gym, but tries not to look her way. They'll run into each other again on the way out, and then bump into each other twenty minutes later at the coffee shop outside the office. It's not unusual for them to walk through the doors of Gunther & Evarts Architects at the same time, already caught up on whatever it is they need to discuss, laughing and at ease with one another.

He knows it's a fine line between friendship and something else, but he appreciates her energy and vivaciousness. She has a brilliant mind, and she's driven to succeed. He knows at some point they'll lose her to someone else or she might even go out on her own, but until then he's grateful to have her talent in the firm.

Mark feels a funny twinge inside and instantly turns his thoughts to Julia, his wife. Not that he needed any reminding. Why should he? He's lived and breathed her for almost twenty-two years. He loves Julia, has loved her ever since they met at the University of Illinois at Chicago, in the dining hall at Student Center West. He fell for her instantly—her laugh, her wild, untamable hair, her love for organizing and reorganizing things.

"Ta-da!" she'd proclaimed one day. He'd come back to his dorm room after class and found his entire closet rearranged. There were clothes he hadn't seen in months, cleaned and pressed, hanging side by side. Julia had replaced his ratty wire hangers with white plastic ones. There was some kind of order to the clothing—casual shirts to pants to jackets. A scented girly sachet dangled from the closet bar.

"You didn't have to do all this," Mark protested, secretly pleased.

Julia raised an eyebrow. "Actually, I did," she confessed. "It's been driving me crazy ever since we met. This place is a pigsty."

Oh. "It's not that bad," he had said defensively.

"You think?" Julia seemed to be waiting for that moment, because she pointed to something on his desk. Upon closer inspection, Mark saw that it was a half-eaten fast-food burrito, still crumpled in its wrapper, sprouting mold like a Chia Pet. "I found that in the pocket of your barn jacket. But I'm happy to put it back. This stuff, too." She nodded at his cheap garbage can, which was filled with all sorts of disgusting trash.

It was enough to make Mark grimace, and he had a pretty tough constitution. Julia had laughed, tossing the burrito into the trash. She collapsed onto the bed, which, he noticed, was perfectly made. He flopped down next to her and slipped his hand under her shirt, feeling her flat stomach warm beneath his palm. "I'd like to find a way to repay you, but it might require messing up these nice hospital corners that you did."

Julia had giggled, then stretched herself out on the bed, beckoning him. "Go for it," she said. So he did.

Mark loves Julia's body, the smattering of freckles across her nose, her fair skin that burns no matter how much sunblock she slathers on. He loves how she's up for almost anything, how can she do whatever she sets her mind to. He remembers the year she wanted to go camping, when Josh was eight. She bought all the gear—the tent, the sleeping bags, air mattresses, a camping stove, folding table and chairs, a portable toilet, rain gear, fishing gear, a hammock. She had a full-on medical kit for any potential camping-related mishap for Josh or anyone else at the campsite. They had new backpacks, fancy waterproof flashlights, a crank radio.

Then Julia sprained her ankle. They'd been at the Johnson-Sauk Trail State Park for all of five minutes when Julia tripped over a tree root in the parking lot and went down. They went to the ER, got her ankle X-rayed and wrapped, then drove home. Mark went to the pharmacy for some prescription Tylenol and when he got back, Julia and Josh had somehow managed to pitch the tent in the backyard along with the rest of the gear. Julia stood over the cookstove cracking eggs into the cast-iron skillet while Josh swung in the hammock, happily reading a comic book.

He loves Julia, he loves Julia, he loves Julia. Even with everything that's happened—the closing off, the withdrawal, the distance—he loves Julia. But he's coming to realize that he loves his life, too, and he's ready to move forward, even if Julia is not.

The box sits in the center of his desk, a silent beacon.

Mark busies himself checking his voice mail, taking more time than is necessary to jot down the details of each message, listening to a couple of them twice even though they're of no consequence. He powers on his computer, waits to see if there are any important emails. There aren't. When he finishes straightening his desk and shuffling plans around in his vertical filing cabinet, he finally turns his attention to the light blue box in front of him.

His name is written on the envelope in Vivian's precise script. The notepaper is thick and crisp, embossed with her initials. A light fragrance tickles his nose and he recognizes her perfume.

Mark,

Just a little something to congratulate you on getting the Lemelin deal—I knew you could do it. Thanks for letting me be a part of the G&E family.

Best,
Vivian

Victor, Mark, and Vivian met with Bruno Lemelin shortly after the dinner at Roux, and then worked around the clock to get a proposal to him for his new restaurant concept in the city. He awarded them the project two days ago, and Mark has been on a high ever since. A frenzied high, because Lemelin is every bit the demanding client that Mark has heard about, with no sense of boundaries or office hours, calling Mark at any time during the day or night to add a comment or change his mind. Mark knows the next few months will be all late nights and caffeine, but he doesn't mind—in fact, he welcomes it. It's worth it. It could change a lot of things. It could change everything.

Despite his elation, he hasn't said anything to Julia. She's been out of the loop with the business since Josh's death. Understandably so, of course—look how long it's taken Mark to get back into the swing of things. Julia hasn't lost her capability, but considers everything overwhelming or unnecessary. Julia will do the bare minimum if she can get away with it.

One of the grief counselors, a woman who wore Birkenstocks and flowing dresses, had gently suggested that maybe Julia wasn't doing more because she didn't have to—Mark was stepping up before Julia had the chance. "If someone loses an arm, they feel helpless until they realize they can use their other arm," the counselor had told him. Mark had just stared at her—he hated metaphors. "If left to her own devices, Julia might help herself," the woman clarified.

Maybe, but "might" is not a powerful enough word for Mark. Julia might—but she also might not. It seemed like a small thing at first, something any loving husband would do to help his wife. Pick up the slack wherever he can, to try and make it all better.

But now Mark is wondering if maybe that hippie counselor was right, that he's painted himself into a corner with no way out. It's become their routine, their dynamic, and he wants to change it. But how?

Strangely enough it isn't Julia's reaction that Mark fears, but her lack of it. He can't bear her possible apathy about the Lemelin news. He doesn't want to think of what he might feel—or do—in the face of this indifference.

The box sits there, patient. Mark decides to open it.

The white satin ribbon falls away easily. He lifts the lid off the box and sees a soft pouch inside. He reaches inside the pouch and his fingers touch something cool, hard. He pulls out a stately sterling silver compass.

His initials are engraved on the inner lid. The rim of the compass is stamped with 925 T&CO 1837. He doesn't know the cost but it has to be worth a few hundred dollars. Either way it's by far one of the most elegant and expensive gifts he's ever received in his life. He wonders how Vivian had time to do this for him with everything else they have going on.

There's a knock on his door and he gives a start. His secretary, fifty-four-year-old Dorothy Clements, sails in.

"Good morning," she says briskly, her eyes trained on her notebook, not bothering to give him any eye contact. Dorothy is fixed in that way, always with her checklists, always wanting to make sure she doesn't overlook a single thing. She makes it her business to know everyone else's business, which was invaluable when Mark was here in body but not spirit. She kept him in the loop, the real loop, of what was going on while he did little more than show up and sign paychecks.

It hasn't escaped Mark's attention that Dorothy has failed to comment on the gift on his desk, that she doesn't show the least bit of interest in wanting to know more. "Victor called early this morning to say that things are going well and he sends his best. He also wants to know if you've had a chance to talk to Ted Morrow who's heading up the development of that new housing project over in Edison. Says Ted gave a well-received presentation on green modular architecture that was posted on YouTube."

Modular architecture? Please. Mark isn't a snob, but at the same time he's always craved to be a bit more cutting edge and modular/prefabricated housing somehow doesn't fit the bill. But Bruno Lemelin's project does.

Mark notices a smudge on the sterling silver surface of the compass. He uses the felted pouch to buff it clean, careful not to press too hard. "Okay, I'll give him a call."

"Victor says he'd talk to him but Ted wants to get in touch with you, hear your ideas." Dorothy pretends to be writing something in her notebook as Mark admires the compass. "If you're not going to follow up with Ted, you should tell Victor."

"Uh-huh." He gives a slight nod.

She clears her throat. "Because if you're not going to, a courtesy heads-up would be nice."

Mark looks up, annoyed. "Dorothy, I *am* going to follow up with Ted."

She gives him a pointed look. "When? It's been two weeks."

"Well, it's been a busy two weeks, in case you haven't noticed." He gives her a pointed look back, enjoying the banter. It used to be like this, didn't it? He's missed it. "Anyway, I want to talk to Victor first but I can't get the whole time difference thing figured out."

"Turkey is seven hours ahead."

"Got it."

Dorothy goes on to tell him a few more things, and suggests a simple office party tomorrow to celebrate the Lemelin deal—champagne, cake, movie tickets, that sort of thing. Mark agrees. It's a great idea.

Dorothy lingers by the door. "Oh, and Vivian went home sick today. Stomach flu." The look on her face is inscrutable. Or is Mark just reading into things?

She leaves and Mark is immediately on the phone, dialing Vivian's number. She was a key team member in landing the Lemelin project, and it doesn't make sense to have a party if she can't be there to celebrate with them.

She answers her phone on the third ring, her voice drawn. "Hi," she says weakly.

"Hi." Mark clears his throat, his mind emptying of whatever it was he was supposed to say. "How are you feeling?"

"Honestly? Like hell. I must have caught a bug."

"I'm sorry." He's genuinely sympathetic. Vivian seems so tough, it's strange to hear her so down.

"It happens. I'll get over it."

She's tough, just like he said.

"Can I get you anything?" The offer comes out before he has a chance to think twice and he's relieved when she says no.

Then she asks, "Did you get my gift? I dropped it off late last night."

Mark's eyes fall on the compass. The red-tipped orienting needle is over the E so Mark turns the compass until the needle lines up with the N. He tries to ignore the niggling memory of Julia learning to read a compass before that camping attempt a few years back. He couldn't get her to stop saying "left" or "right," which of course always changed depending on your location. Cardinal points, however—north, south, east, and west—are constant no matter what direction you face. "I did, and you shouldn't have. It wasn't necessary."

"I know it wasn't necessary, but I saw it and I instantly thought of you. It suits you, I think."

He tries for a joke. "You mean in case I ever get lost in the wilderness?"

Vivian's voice is strained but serious. "In case you ever need any direction."

There's an awkward silence. Mark hurries to fill the empty space. "So Dorothy and I were thinking about finding a good time to have a little champagne and cake with the team, hand out some movie tickets or something. But I want to wait until you're feeling up to it and back at work."

"That's so sweet," she says.

"Well, it's true. I couldn't have done it without you." He needs to stop talking. Why did he say that?

"I'm hoping this is just a twenty-four-hour thing," Vivian says. "Maybe plan it for the day after tomorrow, just in case?"

"The day after tomorrow." He repeats the words slowly, writes them on a piece of paper. "Okay. Great. Take care and get some rest, Vivian."

"Mark . . ." Vivian is sighing now, sounding so tired, sounding almost exactly like Julia used to. "There actually is something you can get me, since you offered."

Damn. He wants to hang up, and at the same time, he wants to know what she needs.

"Some sparkling water with lemon, maybe? Or a loaf of French bread? I'd love something simple to settle my stomach. I'd get it myself but I don't trust myself to drive. If you can't do it, I completely understand . . ."

Mark is trying to think of alternatives but nothing comes to mind. Fine. "No, no, it's not a problem," he assures her. He can grab what she needs, drop them off, and be back on the road in ten minutes or less. He won't let himself be drawn into a conversation or get a tour of her place even though he's admittedly curious. Where does a woman like Vivian live?

She gives him directions and he tells her he'll stop by briefly after work. He emphasizes the word *briefly*.

"Of course," Vivian says. "And if I'm resting, I may not come to the door. Is that all right? Just knock and if there's no answer, you can leave it on my doorstep. I really appreciate this, Mark."

They hang up and Mark lets out a sigh of relief, and then a chuckle. He's acting like an idiot. Vivian isn't interested in him—he's too old for her, for starters, and he's married. Vivian's met Julia before, hasn't she? He frowns, trying to remember. Maybe not, but it doesn't matter. Vivian is a professional, a single woman with the time and energy to build relationships with her peers and superiors. It's why she's so good at what she does, why their clients love her.

The phone starts ringing and an associate is waiting to talk to him. Mark gratefully turns his attention to his work, eager to get back into the rhythm of things, the rhythm of his life.

The kitchen is a mess. Flour is everywhere, the sink filled with pans needing to be washed. The air is warm and sweet. Four loaves of Amish Friendship Bread are cooling on the racks, and two more loaves are in the oven.

It's chaotic, but wonderful.

Gracie is barefoot, and there are little footprints in the fine dusting of flour on the floor. She really wanted an apron like Julia's, but Julia only has one and it's far too big for Gracie. Instead, Julia fastens something together from a dishtowel and ribbon, with help from a stapler, a quick and easy solution that delights Gracie to no end. Julia even feels a little proud of herself.

The bags of starter are quickly starting to get ahead of them. Gracie brought another three bags to school last week, and this week planned on bringing more. But apparently some of the other children had the same idea. There are now over twenty bags of Amish Friendship Bread starter in the little Montessori schoolhouse. The other children were clearly instructed by their mothers *not* to bring home any more starter, so Gracie brought hers back, disappointed.

So now they're baking.

Feeding four bags over the next week is going to result in sixteen new bags. Julia's made the executive decision to use what she can now to cut back on what will become an unwieldy amount of starter in the days to come. She's reserved one bag because she's grown quite fond of having the starter and a regular schedule for baking.

She'll give a few loaves to Mark to share with the office, and she'll pass some around to the neighbors. Next week they'll be back down to their three bags of starter to gift to some lucky person, and things will be back to normal.

Julia is trading recipes with Madeline, and Hannah is scouring the Internet for more variations. She talks on the phone with them daily, conversations Julia enjoys and even looks forward to. Yesterday Madeline suggested that the three women get together at least once every ten days, their visits corresponding with the days they're due to split their starters and bake, which happens to be today. They'll meet after the tea salon is closed. Mark has agreed to come home early and watch Gracie. And Julia is actually looking forward to going out.

The sun is streaming into the kitchen. Oh, she really doesn't want to wash all these dishes! She'd rather do something else instead. She sees Gracie hopping from one foot to the other, and reaches over to turn on the radio.

An old Crosby, Stills and Nash song is playing and even though Gracie doesn't know it, she starts dancing and waving her little arms in the air.

Julia laughs, watching her daughter. Gracie is trying to sing, making up words one beat behind the song, and Julia feels her heart swell almost to the point of aching. Still, she can't stop laughing, can't stop smiling. She feels happy. *Happy.* If she doesn't think about anything else, just keeps her attention on this one flour-covered, "Too Much Love to Hide" moment, Julia is happy. She's laughed with Gracie before, and lately with Hannah and Madeline, but there was always something tight about it. Clenched. Now Julia feels as if something has just cracked open.

She puts her arms up, too, and starts to dance.

• • •

Mark walks up the steps to Vivian's apartment. It's a nice condo in a development right outside of town, more urban and hip than the older family homes in Avalon. He has the bread and the Perrier, even though the woman in the store didn't recommend carbonated drinks for someone with stomach flu. She suggested apple juice, so he got that. Then he remembered that Gracie had a bout of stomach flu last year. Bananas, applesauce, and saltine crackers were her best friend. He got those things as well.

He's decided that he's not going to knock on the door, but leave the bag on her doorstep and then give her a call to let her know it's there. It's stupid that he's even doing this, but then he tells himself that if Victor were sick, he'd do the same thing. Dorothy, too. It's really not that different.

The door opens just as he gets to the top of the stairs and there's Vivian, modestly dressed in a silk bathrobe with unexpectedly endearing fuzzy slippers on her feet. Her hair is twisted up and clipped to the top of her head, casual and a little messy—even sick she still looks good. She does look pale, though, and despite the smile on her face, Mark can tell she feels lousy.

"I thought it might be you. Didn't want you to escape without saying thanks."

"Oh." Mark isn't sure if he should hand her the bag. It's pretty heavy with all the drinks. "Should I put this somewhere?"

"Please." Vivian steps aside, and Mark walks into her home.

He's immediately struck by how clean and organized everything is. Just like Vivian. Her place is well decorated (no surprise there) and he can tell that every design decision has been well thought out. There's a green chenille blanket on the couch where she was obviously lying, and he can see the imprint of her body against the cushions. He quickly looks away.

This is a huge contrast to his own home, which is scattered with Gracie's toys and mismatched furniture in various stages of decline. The plan had always been to buy a new living room set and paint the walls, but for reasons that are now quite obvious, it never happened.

Mark knows his home is the antithesis of his career, which is all about marrying beauty and function to create shelter. He knows there are jokes out there about what architects do—and don't do—and while he doesn't wear black turtlenecks and trendy glasses (he's been gifted with 20/20 vision), he does consider himself the genuine article. He's just forgotten this for the past few years.

He puts the bag of groceries on the granite countertop. He's struck by her open-plan kitchen, which has classic shaker styling with a sleek minimalist twist. The walnut keeps it warm and homey but the stainless-steel appliances keep it state of the art. He lifts his head and finds himself staring at an elaborate branched pendant lamp hanging from the ceiling.

"It's got twenty-four lights," Vivian informs him, peeking into the bag and pulling out the bottle of Perrier. "I actually ordered it for the McAllister renovation, and Mrs. McAllister nixed it. I called the supplier, and he offered it to me at cost. Didn't want to deal with restocking it."

"Ah. So you got into the business so you could design your house on the sly?"

"I won't lie. Home accents and fixtures are to me what shoes are to other women." Vivian gets two glasses. "What about Julia? Is she a shoe person?" She pours some Perrier into the glasses and offers one to him.

Vivian was hired a couple of years after Josh's death, and he knows she's heard the story from someone in the office. He's never discussed it with anyone from work save Dorothy and Victor, and he doesn't want to start now. Somehow Vivian's seemingly innocent question about Julia puts him on the defensive. And then he remembers—he was supposed to be home early to watch Gracie so Julia can go out. He was shocked at the request and readily agreed, not even bothering to ask where she would be going. And now he's late.

Mark declines the drink. "Thanks, but I have to go. Feel better soon, okay? And thank you again for the gift. It was really generous and you didn't have to do that." The words spill out quickly as he makes his way to the front door.

"I know, you already said that," Vivian says in a teasing voice, following him. "I wanted to do it, okay?" She tilts her head and gives him a smile, resting a hand on his arm.

Mark feels a jolt of adrenaline shoot through his body. He turns quickly so that her hand slips off without it seeming like an intentional thing, and edges closer to the door. Why did he come in? He wishes he hadn't come in. "Okay. I'm just saying it wasn't necessary. It was really thoughtful and it means a lot that you were thinking of me and . . ."

"God!" Vivian gives a small laugh, shaking her head in charmed disbelief. "It's not an engagement ring, Mark—it's just a compass, okay? We don't have to talk about this anymore. But, for the record, *again,* you are welcome."

He gives her a sheepish look, embarrassed over his behavior. "Okay." He pulls open the front door.

Vivian hits the side of her head with the palm of her hand. "I almost forgot. I have season tickets for the Chicago Symphony Orchestra. Do you want to catch a performance sometime? I get access to all their post-concert receptions . . ."

"Vivian." Any fogginess he's had before suddenly clears up. He feels oddly grateful that she's done this, because now he can set the record straight. "I'm sorry, but I can't. I think you're terrific and an asset to G&E, but it's not appropriate for me to be doing things with you outside of the office. My wife . . ."

"Your wife doesn't care." Vivian says this evenly, her eyes trained on his.

He's shocked by her boldness. "My wife *does* care," Mark says vehemently. He leaves, not bothering to close the door on his way out.

"You're late." Julia is angry, her anxiety for the past hour giving way to fury. "I told you I had somewhere to be at five o'clock. It's almost six." She rummages in her bag, looking for something.

"I'm sorry, I'm sorry." Mark looks guilty as she checks the time again, frustrated.

"God! I was all ready to go and now . . . where are my keys? Have you seen my keys?" She just had them but now she can't find them.

Julia dumps the contents of her bag onto the hallway table. Her eyes search through miscellaneous pens, mints, scraps of paper, loose change, wet wipes, tampons, Band-Aids, rubber bands, sunglasses, a stray earring, ChapStick, wallet, stamps, safety pins, a couple of hair ties, a roll of Scotch tape, ibuprofen.

"You could have called to remind me," Mark says lamely. He pushes aside earplugs and a packet of garden seeds in a feeble attempt to help.

Julia's mouth opens and closes but she doesn't say anything, not trusting herself to speak. All the good feelings from her day have evaporated. Julia just wants to leave, to get out of this house that has held her prisoner for five years. She never felt that way before, but suddenly staying home is making her crazy.

"Here they are." She holds up a ring of keys and shoves everything back into her bag. She hefts it onto her shoulder and lets out a breath, willing herself to calm down. She still has a couple hours ahead of her with Madeline and Hannah—it will be okay. The anger drains from her body, leaving her empty and feeling rotten for yelling at Mark. "Sorry. I was just   well, I'm sorry. For overreacting." She shakes her head. Mark does a lot for her, she knows this and feels equal parts guilt and shame. It's this constant reminder that makes it so hard for her to stay in the house, to see him so apologetic.

Mark looks surprised, a strange look on his face. "It's okay. I shouldn't have been late."

This just makes her feel worse. She can tell that Mark wants to talk more, that somehow this is a segue into a conversation that may be long overdue, but Julia just wants to get going. "Gracie is already bathed."

Now her husband looks genuinely baffled. True, she probably wouldn't have done it if Gracie hadn't been covered with flour and melted chocolate chips, but it was just easier to put her in the tub and get her cleaned up. Gracie smelled so sweet afterward that Julia sat her in her lap and inhaled her.

Now Gracie is watching a video while Mark follows Julia to the door. "So where are you going?"

Julia ignores the question. She doesn't want to have to explain herself, explain these women. Not yet. "There are a couple of loaves of Amish Friendship Bread for you to take into the office. And there's one that's already sliced if you want to have some with Gracie before she goes to bed. Just make sure she brushes her teeth again."

"Oh. Okay. That was nice of you." Mark's politeness throws her off and there is a moment of extreme unease as they stare at each other, standing only inches away. Mark has a hopeful look in his eyes and Julia knows his body language, knows he just might kiss her. But why? They haven't had sex in a long time—maybe twice in the past five years. They don't even kiss on the lips anymore. Sure enough, Mark moves toward her but Julia steps back, her heart racing as she feels for the door.

She escapes just as he's reaching for her and feels nothing but relief as she hurries down the walk toward her car. When she pulls out of the driveway, she sees his shadow in the doorway, watching her.

CHAPTER 10

❀

Hannah is looking forward to seeing Madeline and Julia again. In fact, it's all she's been thinking about since the last time they got together ten days ago. It's the one thing that keeps her grounded, keeps her from obsessing about Philippe and her disintegrating marriage.

Last week Philippe had called and left a message on the machine, saying he wanted to talk about their bank accounts. When Hannah finally found the courage to call him back, a woman answered the phone.

"Who is this?" Hannah had blurted out. There was a muffled silence and then a dial tone.

Hannah had called back, incensed. This time Philippe picked up.

"Hannah!" he'd exclaimed, as if he were happy to hear from her. "How are you?"

She hung up, fuming, tears of disbelief stinging her eyes. When her computer dinged to let her know that she had a new email, Hannah unplugged it from the wall and went into the kitchen.

The kitchen has become her safe haven. It's not large, which may be why she likes it—there's no room to get lost and everything is practically within arm's reach. In Chicago their tiny apartment had an unusually large professional kitchen—the previous owner was a chef—but neither she nor Philippe spent much time there other than to use the microwave. Hannah always felt intimidated by the stainless-steel Sub-Zero, the oversized burners on the Wolf stovetop. In Avalon, the kitchen feels welcoming and unassuming, a place where Hannah can linger as she heats up a pot of tomato soup or makes herself a sandwich.

With the exception of when she was hurt, Hannah's ritual has always been to play her cello first thing in the morning. But when things started to fall apart with Philippe, Hannah found herself less and less interested in going into the music room to play. She stays in the kitchen, familiarizing herself with every appliance, every spice jar, every utensil. She knows where everything is and can now say, unequivocally, that this kitchen is *hers.*

The best thing was this morning, when she woke up and her thoughts went to Philippe for only a moment before she remembered that this was the day she'd be trying Madeline's recipe for Amish Friendship Bread brownies. She headed straight to the kitchen in her pajamas, washed her hands, and got to work.

Unlike ten days ago, Hannah now has an inkling of what she's doing. That's always the benefit of doing something repetitively—it's inevitable that you'll get better at it. Some of the best musicians are the ones with moderate talent who practice incessantly while others who are truly gifted squander their talent by being lazy and ultimately go nowhere. Hannah knows better than anybody that practice makes perfect, and she needs to remember that the same rule applies in the kitchen, too.

Hannah adds the flour, sugar, and milk with confidence, then divides the batter—one portion for her, the other three into Ziploc bags. She follows Madeline's recipe, loves how her kitchen is quickly filled with the aroma of rich chocolate.

As the brownies are baking, Hannah readies the extra bags. In all the months she's been here, she hasn't officially met the neighbors. Philippe is the sociable one between the two of them, but Hannah finds it next to impossible to meet new people, to strike up a conversation with someone she doesn't know. That's what makes this unexpected friendship with Madeline and Julia so precious to Hannah, and she is counting the minutes until it's time to meet them later this afternoon.

She doesn't bother trying to photocopy or type out the instructions, but pulls out a box of stationery and takes the time to write it out by hand. She adds little notes on the side, even copies down the recipe for the brownies on the back. When the brownies are out of the oven and cooling, she changes out of her pajamas and washes up. Then she wraps three generous brownie rectangles in wax paper and heads out the door.

The immediate neighbor to her right, Marion Krum, is a frazzled mother of toddler twin boys. She mistakes Hannah for a high school student selling candy bars. *A high school student selling candy bars?* Hannah is almost thirty! She knows her Asian genes make her look young, but still. It takes all of Hannah's willpower to keep a straight face as she explains about the bread.

Next is Joseph Sokolowski, the part-time car mechanic whose hallways are lined with old hubcaps and license plates polished to a shine. He kindly invites her in and fixes her a cup of espresso that tastes a bit like sludge.

The woman living next door to him flatly refuses the starter before Hannah even has a chance to explain what it is. Henry Tinklenberg, the last neighbor, is an elderly African-American baggage handler who recently retired from United Airlines. Hannah likes the way his eyes crinkle when he considers the bag of starter and then decides to give it a try for his grandkids who'll be coming to visit next week.

When Hannah returns home, she doesn't even blink when she sees she has another message on the machine. She hits DELETE and then takes her time cleaning the house from top to bottom. By the time she's finished, the house smells like lemons. The afternoon sun has filled the house with light and contrary to feeling tired, Hannah is ready to go.

The CLOSED sign is up when she arrives at Madeline's, but the door isn't locked. She knocks gently before letting herself inside and calling out her name. Madeline comes out of the kitchen wiping her hands on a dish towel.

"Hannah!" she exclaims. She hurries over to give her a hug. "I'm almost done straightening up. I just have a few more things to do in the kitchen—I'll only be a minute."

"I can help," Hannah insists, and it doesn't take much persuading. She follows Madeline into the kitchen where a large cooking pot is on the stove. She washes her hands as Madeline fishes around for an apron.

"Halve and quarter these," Madeline says, handing Hannah some yellow onions. "Then quarter them again. I want them about a half an inch thick. You can grab a knife from the knife block over there."

"Er . . ." Hannah stares at the onion. An inch thick in which direction? She peels off the papery onion skin then hesitates as she's about to make the first slice.

Madeline liberally drizzles the pot with olive oil then grabs an onion and knife for herself. "Like this." She demonstrates, slicing straight through the root to the other side. "Once you cut it in half, it's easier to peel off the outer skin. Then you can use the root to keep the onion together as you cut."

Hannah mimics her, following Madeline's directions as they lay the onion halves flat on the wooden cutting boards. They trim one end and then begin to make thin parallel cuts across the onion. Madeline shows Hannah how to curl her fingers over the onion, letting her knuckles hit the side of the knife so that she doesn't risk losing a finger.

Madeline glances at the clock as she tosses the onions into the pot, leaving Hannah to finish the rest. "I do hope Julia will still be able to come by," Madeline says. She takes a block of butter and cuts it into rough chunks, adding them into the pot.

Hannah hopes so, too. Even though Julia is older, she isn't condescending, doesn't treat Hannah as if she doesn't know any better. She's secretly added Julia to the speed dial on her phone—Madeline, too—but she won't admit this out loud because it seems premature and a bit needy. "What are we making?" Hannah asks.

"Tomorrow's special: French onion soup with Gruyère cheese croutons." Madeline gives the onions a quick stir in the pot, adds a generous pinch of salt. "We'll pop this into the oven and give the onions a chance to brown. Come, you've done enough. Let's take our tea in the back parlor."

The back parlor is in Madeline's private quarters overlooking the gardens. "Oh," Hannah breathes when she sees the yard through the large bay window. It's still bare from winter, like her yard, but there's just so much more of it.

"It's about an acre." Madeline gazes outside. "I've let it go, I'm afraid. It used to be beautiful but the upkeep is expensive when you have negative cashflow. When it was the Belleweather the owners managed the grounds themselves, but it's too much for one person. I don't really use it with the tea salon so it doesn't make sense to hire a gardener, though it would be lovely to have some tables outside during the summer." The expression on her face is wistful. "But I'm getting ahead of myself. I want to know about you, Hannah. What on earth are you doing in Avalon?"

"Oh." Hannah is suddenly shy. She finds a comfortable place to sit on the couch and curls up, tucking her feet under her. "My husband, Philippe, wanted us to get a place outside of the city. So we did."

"I see." Madeline doesn't press for details and Hannah doesn't offer any. What exactly would she say? Madeline walks over to close the window, but it's stuck and refusing to budge. Hannah's about to get up and help when Madeline puts her weight on it and it closes with a reluctant groan. "There," she says, satisfied as she flips the latch to lock it in place.

The sun begins its slow descent. The sky is filled with dark yellows and warm oranges, but there's a tinge of gray clouds multiplying and filling the sky. There's a slight chill in the air. Madeline passes a soft wool afghan to Hannah, who thankfully wraps herself in it. "What about the cello? Are you still playing?"

"Not lately." Not since the day Philippe told her he wasn't coming home. "I used to play for three hours in the morning."

"Really?" Madeline arches an eyebrow, impressed, but three hours is nothing compared to Hannah's once-rigorous schedule.

"I'd play more but then my back starts to hurt or the tendonitis in my shoulder flares up and I have to stop."

Madeline winces. "It must be difficult."

"It was. I'm used to it now."

"Do you miss performing?"

Hannah smiles. She misses the heady rush before a concert, the sound of the orchestra tuning up. The lit stage, the darkened auditorium. The applause. "I do."

"So what now?"

Good question. Hannah has never done anything other than play the cello. She knows it's an impressive accomplishment to many people, but to her it's just part of who she is. Her parents started her playing at five and she had relentless two-hour practices every day until middle school, when she doubled her practice time. By the end of her first year at Juilliard, Hannah had logged in more than ten thousand hours of practice and performing time. And while she doesn't regret a moment of it (well, not usually), she does wish she'd had a chance to try different things, to learn some different skills, to experiment, to dabble.

"I don't know," Hannah admits. It hadn't been a pressing issue before, because she had Philippe. Hannah had assumed they would figure out the future together. Now that the decision is hers alone to make, Hannah doesn't know where to begin. "I'm not sure where to go or what to do, Madeline." Her voice wavers, full of uncertainty.

"The world is your oyster, in other words." The smile on Madeline's face is expansive, contagious, and Hannah feels a small smile tugging at the corners of her own mouth despite her anxiety.

"I hadn't quite looked at it that way," Hannah concedes, "but I suppose that's true."

"It absolutely *is* true," Madeline says.

"I know," Hannah says even though it doesn't feel like the great adventure that Madeline is making it out to be. "It's just that I always thought my life would be about the cello."

"And it still might be," Madeline says. "Who knows how things will work out?"

"Who knows," Hannah echoes. But instead of feeling encouraged, she feels awash with despair. It would take a miracle for her to be able to play professionally again, and she's not even sure she wants that. She doesn't know what she wants.

Madeline seems to notice this and her face softens. "You know, Hannah, it's the unexpected turns that make life rich. You have already accomplished so much that I have to admit I'm curious to see what comes next. I just know good things are in store for you."

"I wish I knew for sure."

"Well, of course. And you will, Hannah, when it's time. But for now try to get comfortable with the unknowing. Plans are an illusion anyway. Goodness, if I had followed my plan to go back to Chicago, I wouldn't be here now. Blame it on my poor circulation!" She chuckles.

"Your circulation?"

"If I hadn't needed to stretch I wouldn't have pulled over when I did." Madeline gives her legs an affectionate pat. "So really, I should be thanking this old body."

This Hannah understands. "I feel that way about my body, too. It gave me many good years when I played professionally."

"Was it always your dream to play the cello?"

Hannah can't think of life without her cello being a major part of it. "I think I was too young when I started to really understand what it meant. But it was my parents' dream. My father's especially." She can still remember the stunned silence on the other end of the phone when she told him she couldn't play professionally anymore. "He moved back to Taiwan when my mother died a few years ago. We don't talk much."

"No?"

"There's the time difference, but really it's because we don't have anything to talk about. It used to be about my music, my schedule, certain performances. Now that's gone, so there's not much else. It's like that with my brother, too." Hannah thinks about the first time Philippe left, how she had called Albert under the guise of saying hello when really she wanted him to tell her that everything would be okay, or that Philippe was a creep and she could stay with them. He'd said neither. She'd been stunned when his reply was exactly something her father would have said, that she needed to figure it out and make it work. Was there anything else?

"What was it like when your mother was alive?" Madeline asks. "Was it any different then?"

Hannah gives a faint smile. "Oh yes. My father was still strict—she was, too, in her own way—but she tried to give us a normal childhood, an American childhood. Like once she let us take a break from practice to get a Popsicle from the neighborhood ice cream truck. My father was furious, of course, because he considered it both a waste of time and money. But my mother stood her ground and he eventually backed down. She was the only one who could do that with him—the rest of us were too scared. But not my mom." Hannah doesn't add that she misses her, even though it's been more than ten years since her mother died. She doesn't have to. Madeline seems to understand this.

Hannah burrows deeper into the afghan and shivers, tucking her legs under her. She admires the perfectly crocheted rows, her slender fingers running along the pattern. "Did you make this?"

Madeline shakes her head. "I have a gift in the kitchen, but that's pretty much it. I bought it at a small gift shop in town that sells lovely items made by fellow Avalonians." She pulls a worn fleece throw over her own legs.

Hannah admires Madeline, admires what she's done. She's all alone from what Hannah can see and it doesn't seem to bother her. Hannah hopes that she'll someday be as comfortable with her independence as Madeline is, but right now she can't imagine it.

"How do you do it?" She gestures around her. "The tea salon, all the cooking and baking. How do you manage?"

Madeline ponders the question. "I guess I don't really think about it like that. Like I said, when I came through this town, I just knew this was going to be my home. I hadn't thought beyond that. After a couple of days, it seemed like a waste to be rattling around in such a big house by myself. I didn't want to do a bed-and-breakfast—I like my nights quiet and I need my privacy—but I did like the idea of serving people food. There was already a food and beverage permit for the property, so that helped me make up my mind. I guess I thought it would be a fun thing to do, so that's what I did." Madeline shakes her head and Hannah can see that Madeline's amused by her own folly. "Little did I know it would be so much work. I'm getting the hang of it now, which is good. For a while there I was afraid I'd have to sell everything and move on."

"Oh, you can't!" Hannah's own vehemence surprises her. Madeline and Julia are the only things that anchor Hannah to Avalon.

"Oh, I'm not going anywhere," Madeline assures her. "At least not anytime soon. I like the people too much." She leans over to give Hannah's hand an encouraging squeeze, and Hannah smiles.

They spend the next hour talking about music, art, books. Madeline and her husband, Steven, were widely traveled, true patrons of the arts. Fat copies of the Sunday *New York Times* are piled up in a corner of the parlor, along with literary magazines and sophisticated academic journals. Madeline is a true learner, and Hannah envies this.

"*Pah,* I'm just bored," Madeline says when Hannah points this out. She sips her tea. "When business was slow, I had nothing but time. I'm not much of a TV person, so I read. And bake."

"Philippe never cared much for my cooking," Hannah says. Not that she blamed him—she burned *pudding* once, for God's sake. "I've never been very good at anything other than playing the cello. We just ate out a lot and whenever I did cook, it was either alarmingly simple or a complete disaster."

"There's nothing wrong with simple," Madeline says. "I enjoy simple cooking tremendously. So much is overprepared or over-thought these days." Madeline gets up to peruse a stack of books. "The previous owners had a lot of cookbooks—these came with the house when I bought it. There are some real classics here." She selects a book and brings it to Hannah, wiping off a thin layer of dust.

Hannah accepts the book. It's a heavy, intimidating tome with a simple cover and three words.

"Joy of Cooking," Hannah reads. She recognizes the cover and of course has heard of it, but this is her first time actually looking through it.

"It's the backbone of many a kitchen," Madeline says. "Restaurants, too. The author, Irma Rombauer, wrote it back in the 1930s right after the stock market crash."

Hannah flips through the book and comes across a recipe for turtle soup. She's way out of her league here, plus there's no way she's going to cook a turtle. She's about to close the book and hand it back to Madeline when she comes across instructions for how to boil an egg.

Boiling an egg has always been a point of contention between Hannah and Philippe. He likes his eggs soft-boiled, runny on the inside, whereas Hannah likes hers hard-boiled. And in all the years they were together, Hannah has never been able to get it right.

She'd overcook his egg even if she left it in for the prescribed three minutes. And now, as she reads the instructions for how to do it, she realizes that she should have reduced the heat the minute the water hit a boil, and then let it simmer for three minutes. She didn't know that. And Philippe, for all his complaining about how she couldn't do it right, never bothered to figure it out himself.

Hannah's eyes skim the rest of the page, and she suddenly understands why her eggs are sometimes hard to peel. Fresher eggs don't peel as easily.

It's not until Madeline lets out a dainty cough that Hannah realizes she's been engrossed in the book for almost ten minutes. The sun has slipped past the trees on the horizon, the sky dark and moody now.

Hannah blushes, embarrassed. "I'm sorry, Madeline. It's just all so interesting. Would it be all right if I borrowed this?"

"Hannah, you can have it," Madeline says graciously. "And you know, *Joy of Cooking* was initially self-published. Irma was just a simple homemaker struggling to make ends meet after her husband committed suicide the year before. She was fifty-four, I believe."

Hannah definitely wants the book now. If Irma Rombauer can

write a book at fifty-four, Hannah can certainly find a way to pull her life together. She clutches it to her chest. "Thank you, Madeline."

There's a low rumble of thunder. Both women look out the window as fat drops of rain begin to pelt the side of the house.

Well, that came out of nowhere. Madeline is starting to see how she's been spoiled living on the sunny west coast, plentiful with its bright sun and blue skies. She's forgotten how the weather here is much less forgiving, how it can be dry and sunny one moment then pouring down rain the next.

She leaves Hannah with *Joy of Cooking* and goes to check on the onions. She cracks the oven door open and the most divine aroma fills the kitchen. Perfect. She carefully eases the pot out of the oven and places it on the stove over medium heat. The onions are a beautiful golden brown. She stirs them, watching the liquid reduce until a light crust has formed on the bottom of the pot.

She adds water and then gives it another good stir, mixing the crusty pieces back into the onions. She'll need to do this a few more times until the onions are dark brown. As she waits for the liquid to evaporate, she takes a thin baguette from the bread basket and slices it, lining up the pieces on a baking sheet. She'll bake them for ten minutes until they're crisp and golden. Tomorrow when they serve the soup she'll put a slice on top, sprinkle it with Gruyère cheese, and set it under the broiler before serving. It's one of her favorite recipes from *Cooks Illustrated* and she can't wait to eat it again herself.

A clap of thunder shakes the walls of the house, causing her to start.

"Did you hear that?" Hannah asks as she comes into the kitchen. She has the afghan wrapped around her body, the book cradled in her arms.

Madeline nods her head. "I did. Cats and dogs. I suppose we have two more months of this."

"No, I mean I think someone is at the door."

The two women look at each other for a moment. Madeline listens intently, her ears alert. At first she thinks it's a branch hitting the house but then she hears it again. A definite knock.

"Perhaps it's Julia," she says, and Hannah nods though she doesn't look convinced. There's hardly any crime in Avalon so Madeline isn't worried about that.

Well, maybe just a little. You can't be too sure these days and she knows better than to be too complacent about anything. It's completely dark outside and Madeline notes how everything seems so much more foreboding at night. "Come," she instructs Hannah. On the way out, she decides to grab a rolling pin for good measure.

Madeline hasn't had a chance to turn on the exterior lights but she can see a figure looming on the porch. She senses Hannah's apprehension next to her and realizes how ridiculous they're being. If Steven could see her now, he would never let her hear the end of it. She can hear him chuckling in her ear, and it's enough to make her straighten up and toss the rolling pin aside. She flips a switch and suddenly the hallway and porch are flooded with light.

"Mystery solved." She opens the door and ushers in a soaking wet Julia.

"I'm sorry I'm late," Julia stammers. She's shivering despite wearing a coat, her curly hair pasted to the sides of her face. At Madeline's nod, Hannah quickly tosses her blanket over Julia's shoulders. "My husband was late and when I got here I didn't know if I should come in so I was just walking around and thinking . . ."

Walking around and thinking? In this weather? Without an umbrella? Madeline knows better, and she suspects Julia does, too. "Come," she orders. She wants to get them back into the warmth of the kitchen and she'll start a fire. She takes Julia's hand, which is ice cold. "I'm glad you came in."

"I had to," Julia says. Madeline can see that she's been crying. "Because I can't bear to go back home."

Julia is wrapped in a blanket as Madeline adds kindling to the cast-iron stove. Julia has peeled off her wet clothes and is wearing a soft flannel nightgown that is short and a little tight around the shoulders, the only thing Madeline could find that would fit Julia's tall frame. Julia is shivering even though her body has warmed up, unable to stop her teeth from chattering, unable to stop the violent shaking that overtakes her every now and then.

"I can't go home," she says again, and both Madeline and Hannah nod. They seem to understand, and yet she hasn't explained anything. How can this be when for so long nobody could understand what Julia needed no matter what she said?

Except for Mark, who saw her retreat and let her go, knowing that no one could go there with her. It's been like this for so long that tonight, when he came home and looked into her eyes, Julia was struck with fear. She saw the gentle suggestion of life returning to them as they once knew it, and yet this is impossible. How can things ever be the same?

What is it like to lose a child? Julia has never been able to put words to the grief. The shock. The devastation. What can you say when your life is suddenly destroyed?

In the days and then months that followed Josh's death, Julia was in a daze. It was like a nightmare she wanted to wake from, but couldn't. When Gracie was born four months later, Julia had cried so hard the doctor had to sedate her. Nobody understood why. She heard groggy murmurs about grieving for Josh *still,* as if it were something she'd eventually stop doing. What nobody could understand was that she was grieving for her daughter. For Gracie. Gracie was now out in the world where anything could happen to her.

Their friends offered awkward comfort in the beginning and then evaporated into thin air. Julia never felt like going out but when she did, people smiled uneasily and looked away. This was the town she grew up in, these were people who knew her, but suddenly no one wanted to be around them. They say that tragedy is supposed to bring people together, but that hasn't been Julia's experience. Instead, everything became more separate.

Everyone fell away eventually, even her parents. Her mother and father had cried alongside her in those early weeks but then they seemed to quickly find their footing, seemed ready to come back to a world that was filled with nonsensical tasks like grocery shopping and mowing the lawn. They tried to coax Julia to eat a little more, to take a shower, to come outside and take a walk. She refused.

On the first anniversary of Josh's death, they were hurt when Julia refused to watch a slide show they had painstakingly put together. On his first birthday following his death, they had been appalled when Julia plucked everything from the tombstone that had been left for him—balloons, small gifts, a T-shirt from his favorite baseball team—stripping it bare except for the flowers she had brought. What nobody seemed to understand—nobody except for Mark, who had silently helped her and then took everything to the Salvation Army—was that none of these things were for Josh. They were for everybody else, so they could feel some sort of misplaced peace about his absence, as if he were still a guest at his own party. It seemed to escape everybody's attention that Josh could do nothing with those things, because he wasn't there.

Managing Julia became overwhelming for her parents, she knows. Not that she asked to be managed, but they would do it just the same, talking about her in the third person as they planned the week, coordinating Gracie's care with Mark. Her parents would look at each other, their eyes in silent conversation as they nodded toward Julia as if she weren't there. She knew they wanted her to move on, and when it was clear that she couldn't, they did.

On the day they were scheduled to fly to Florida, her mother came to the house for one last goodbye. It was three years after Josh's death. Rebecca Townsend was all dressed up, her hair done, her nails done, made up as if she were going to a party. Julia couldn't even look at her.

"Julia." Her mother took her hands. "Julia, we all miss Josh, but you need to get past this. You need to give some love to your husband, to Gracie. You still have a long life in front of you. There is still much happiness waiting for you, Julia." When Julia didn't respond, Rebecca just sighed and kissed her older daughter goodbye.

At the door, Rebecca hesitated. She surprised Julia by turning to gather her in her arms, holding her tight. "Call Livvy," she had whispered in her ear, and Julia felt the dampness of her mother's cheek, unsure of who was crying. *"Talk to her, Julia."* And then her parents were gone.

For days Julia considered this, thought of making a phone call to Livvy, a visit even. But in the end she couldn't do it, couldn't bear to hear any explanation or excuse. She saw her sister's hesitation at the hospital, recounting for the police what had happened, her nervousness, the way her eyes darted back and forth, worried she would somehow be blamed.

Well, she's right. Julia does blame her. Livvy should have driven Josh straight home as they had planned. She shouldn't have left him alone in the yard, asked him to do a task, and then not supervised. She shouldn't have locked the car door. She shouldn't have left him for a moment.

What *should* Livvy have done? She should have gotten her lazy husband to properly tend to their yard like all other Avalon homeowners so that there wouldn't be any yellow-jacket nests so close to the house. She should have returned Julia's skirt on her own time or, better yet, never have borrowed it at all. She should have kept a cool head while Josh was lying there, remembering that a single shot of epinephrine would have saved Josh's life. By the time Livvy remembered, it was too late.

What Julia doesn't understand is how Livvy could forget. Livvy has known this boy all his life. She was there when he was born. She was the godparent. Josh adored her. And at the beginning of every school year, every summer camp, it is the first thing that goes down on the paper.

ALLERGIES. BEES. RISK OF ANAPHYLACTIC SHOCK. CARRIES EPIPEN ON PERSON AT ALL TIMES.

Julia knows Livvy knows this. She's filled out forms on Julia's behalf. Of all the times for Livvy to freeze up, to not think clearly, why did it have to be then?

At the hospital they all stood there in shock, and eventually Julia's father had ushered them back to the waiting room where they had paperwork to fill out, organ donation to consider, everything that shouldn't be happening in that moment, on that day. Julia sat on the unforgiving plastic chairs, flanked on either side by Mark and Livvy, her parents and Tom opposite them. They were all crying and Julia couldn't think straight, couldn't hear a word that was said to her. All she could think about was seeing Josh head to school that morning, that last goodbye she had barely paid attention to. She had told him to tuck in his shirt and he had, rolling his eyes. That was it.

That was it.

She felt the wall go up almost immediately, everybody fading into the background—her husband, her sister, her parents. She couldn't believe that Livvy had let this happen, and even when she started to accept that it may not have been Livvy's fault *exactly,* she couldn't believe that Livvy had been the last person Josh had seen before he died. It should have been Julia, not Livvy.

Her parents visit once a year. They call and sometimes write, mostly birthday cards for Gracie with a ten-dollar bill carefully taped inside. They've begged Mark and Julia to come for a visit, promising to watch Gracie and show her the time of her life, but Julia doesn't want to go anywhere. She wants to stay right where she is, near Josh. She's not leaving him.

At first, Mark would join her when she went to the cemetery, sometimes with Gracie, sometimes not. But the daily vigil wore him down and eventually she found herself making trips to Josh's grave alone. She knows Mark comes on his own time, because sometimes there will be fresh flowers or a new baseball. Once there was a strawberry Charleston Chew resting on the top of the memorial marker, no note. Josh loved Charleston Chews but he always had so many cavities that Julia banned it from the house. The only person she can think of who would ignore the rules laid down by Julia would be Livvy. Julia had clutched the candy bar, wanting to throw it away, but she couldn't. She put it back and left, drove home and crawled back into bed.

She suffered from insomnia, from migraines, from too much of everything. Life—the world—it was all too much. The doctors gave

Julia pills but she didn't take them. She didn't want relief—that's what nobody could understand. The pain was real. Her son had died. Why should she get relief when he didn't?

She sees the concern in Madeline's and Hannah's eyes, their genuine desire to help her however they can, but there is a touch of alarm, too. Julia is like a woman insane—she can feel herself losing it, reality slipping away. They'll lock her up. They'll have no choice but to lock her up and throw away the key, punishing her for something she should have been punished for long ago.

She should have been there. She should have been there.

Julia closes her eyes, unable to stop shaking while her whole body feels like it is on fire. She feels it in her belly. The heat is visceral, and it's consuming her.

And then—blackness.

Madeline is no stranger to grief. She remembers the pain from Steven's death as if it were yesterday. Sudden death gives you no warning, no preparation, no time to say goodbye or I love you.

Madeline cannot comprehend the depth of pain that must come from losing a child. It's not the natural order of life. Your children are supposed to outlive you. They're supposed to have a full life. They're supposed to grow up, get married, have children of their own. No one prepares you for this kind of despair—there is no despair that can rival this.

When she lost Steven, she also lost Ben. In a different way, of course, but it was difficult nonetheless. To think that for so many years she had been relieved when Ben wasn't around to cause them more heartache, and yet when Steven died, Ben was the only person capable of understanding what this loss really meant. She wishes now they hadn't grieved alone, Ben especially, because there is no question that loneliness is sometimes the worst of it.

It took some time but Madeline was able to eventually move forward with her life, and when she did, she simply took the sadness with her. You can never recover from losing a person you love, but you can find a way to let it be a part of your life rather than letting it take over every part of you. Still, there is no set timetable, no magic bullet. Julia, like Madeline, will have to find her own way out.

"What should we do?" Hannah's voice is a whisper.

Madeline thinks about whether or not they can get Julia upstairs but decides that the couch in the back parlor is closer. They get her arranged and then return to the kitchen so Madeline can finish the French onion soup.

"Will she be okay?"

Madeline gives a firm nod to allay Hannah's concerns, but she's not sure. She doesn't want to wake Julia because she doubts Julia has really slept since Josh's death. If the heart can't heal, the mind doesn't rest—Madeline knows this all too well. That's not what worries her. Madeline learned a long time ago that death's most painful companion is guilt, and Julia has that in spades. "She just needs some rest— we'll leave her be."

The storm subsides to a steady downpour of rain. Hannah helps Madeline scrape down the sides of the pot. "Add some water now," she tells Hannah, "then scrape the bottom and the sides again, stirring it all back into the soup. It's called deglazing."

"Deglazing," Hannah repeats obediently, holding the wooden spoon like an expert.

"Do it one more time with the cooking sherry instead of water— that will really pull the flavor out."

Madeline slides the baking sheet with the baguette slices into the oven, then checks on Julia, who is sleeping peacefully. She tucks the blanket around Julia, feeling a bittersweet pang of sorrow and hope, and returns to the kitchen. She considers what to do as she sets out three bowls on the table, resting the spoons on folded cloth napkins. She goes to her junk drawer and pulls out the telephone book, squinting as she tries to read the small print. Her finger trails down the names until she finds the one she's looking for. She gives Hannah a pat on the shoulder as she leans over to check the onions. "Almost there," she tells Hannah with a smile.

Then she reaches for the telephone to call Mark Evarts.

Sergeant Robert Overby, 55
Avalon Police Department

Sergeant Robert Overby reviews the incident reports for the day.

One disturbance of the peace. Teenager was playing on a new set of drums in his garage. An officer was sent out and witnessed heated argument between teenager, parent, and neighbor. Officer helped move the drums to the basement and suggested soundproofing options. Issue resolved.

One suspicious vehicle on Elwood Drive. A naked man and woman found in the backseat. They claimed they were not engaged in any illicit activity, but merely talking. They were asked to move along. Issue resolved.

Sergeant Overby chuckles. All in all, a pretty good day. He has four patrol officers on duty and in an hour he gets to go home and get some blessed sleep.

He lets out a yawn just as an elderly woman in a trench coat is escorted into the department by Officer Joey Daniels. "I got a live one here, Sergeant," he says importantly. Officer Daniels is new to Avalon and is still getting to know the residents, which is why he doesn't recognize the woman as Avalon's former Miss Sunshine.

Cora "Miss Sunshine" Ferguson had a brief television career as the pretty homemaker in the ever-popular Sunshine Detergent commercials that ran in the 1970s. She had been spotted in the downtown Chicago Marshall Field's on State Street one Thanksgiving weekend, shopping early for Christmas bargains. The talent scout handpicked her out of the crowd and had her audition on the spot, which Cora did with a flourish. The scout found her charming, oblivious to the scent of hot buttered rum on her breath, and took her to the headquarters of Sunshine Detergent down on Lake Street. She did a screen test and the rest, as they say, was television history.

Sunshine Detergent eventually went bankrupt, and Cora returned to Avalon with a small savings account, which she drank through in less than a year. After that, despite attempts by friends and well-meaning neighbors to get her into a good alcoholic treatment program, Cora Ferguson became known, affectionately, as the town's resident drunk.

"I have a Miss Ferguson here . . ." Officer Daniels begins, reading from his notebook.

Cora yanks her arm free of his grip. "That's Miss Sunshine to you." She sways a bit as she glares at him.

"Now, Miss Sunshine, what are you doing here?" Sergeant Overby gets up from his desk and comes over to her. "Can I offer you a cup of coffee?"

"Do you have any whiskey?"

"No, ma'am, I do not," he replies politely.

She pulls the trench coat tight around her body. "Then coffee will do just fine. Thank you." She gives Officer Daniels the stink-eye, then sits in the chair Sergeant Overby has pulled out for her.

He fills a Styrofoam cup with coffee, picks up a couple packets of sugar and cream and places it all on the table in front of her. "Now why did Officer Daniels have to bring you in today?"

"Theft." Officer Daniels says the word loud and clear, then gives Miss Sunshine a stink-eye of his own. "Perpetrator was seen lurking around a private property on North Davis Street. She fits the same description as the call we received last week about someone in a trench coat stealing newspapers from people's walkways."

"I was REDISTRIBUTING them," Cora says loudly.

This is not the first time Cora has been brought in, and Sergeant Overby knows it won't be the last. "What did you take this time, Cora?"

Cora is sulky. "Nothing."

Officer Daniels attempts to open Cora's trench coat but she fends him off. Frustrated he steps back. "It's in her coat, Sergeant. I saw her put something in it right before I apprehended her."

Sergeant Overby sighs. He hopes to God it's nothing serious, because he really doesn't want to have to arrest Cora. Most of the town knows her and understands she's harmless, but the recent influx of new residents means that Cora's colorful history in Avalon may be coming to an end. "Can you please remove your coat, Miss Sunshine?"

She wraps the coat tighter around her body. "I'm afraid I can't do that."

"Why not?"

"Because today is laundry day and I only have my unmentionables on while I wait for my clothes to dry." She gives him a smug look and then proceeds to add cream to her coffee.

He sighs. "Officer Daniels, can you please call Roxy Hicks? She just left and can probably get back here pretty quickly." He explains to Cora, "Roxy Hicks is one of our new Police Services Aides. She's not a police officer, but she helps us with a lot of official tasks around the department."

"Is she a hooker? Her name makes her sound like a hooker."

"Roxy is not a hooker, she's a very nice lady. You don't want me to call Officer Tripp in here, do you?"

Cora presses her lips together, then shakes her head. Juanita Tripp is a female officer, but one of the toughest cops in the department. She's brought Cora in enough times to have lost patience with her.

When Roxy arrives, Cora is taken to the debriefing room. A few minutes later, Roxy emerges holding a cardboard box, an unpleasant look on her face.

Lord, what has Cora Ferguson gotten herself into now? Sergeant Overby straightens up. "What is it, Roxy?"

Roxy begins pulling items out of the box: two issues of the *Avalon Gazette,* a couple of golf balls, a chewed up dog toy, and a puffy Ziploc bag filled with a suspicious substance. On the bag written in bold permanent marker, "AFB. Day Ten." Today's date is printed next to it.

"What *is* that?" Officer Daniels strains for a closer look then jumps back when Roxy gives it a poke.

"I have no idea." Sergeant Overby wonders if maybe he should send it to the lab. The bag is just about bursting, and he has no idea if what's inside is toxic, or worse.

"I asked her, but she wouldn't say anything," Roxy says. "Though she did call me a hooker. That was nice."

"Get her back in here," Sergeant Overby orders. He's willing to give Cora the benefit of the doubt, that she picked up something she shouldn't have, but he doesn't like the look of this. Something doesn't feel right.

Roxy returns with Cora, who eyes her things hungrily. Sergeant Overby pushes them out of her reach and holds up the bag. "What is this, Cora?"

Cora refuses to say anything.

"Cora." His voice is stern. "I'm serious now. I don't want to have to book you on trespassing or petty theft, but if this is a potentially dangerous substance, I need to know. *Now.*"

"Should I call the fire department and have them send a hazmat team, sir?" Officer Daniels has the phone in his hand.

Sergeant Overby holds up a hand. "Cora, if I were to open this bag, what would happen? Do you know?"

"I have a vague idea," she smirks. "Just don't let it interact with any metal or you'll be sorry."

One minute later, the Avalon Police Department is evacuated.

CHAPTER 11

❧

A hazardous materials incident in Avalon! Edie still can't believe it. The call came into the *Gazette* a few minutes ago, a concerned citizen wondering if they knew why the police department had been evacuated and the fire department summoned. Edie was quick to make a few calls before grabbing her backpack and running down the street.

She hears the sirens and feels adrenaline coursing through her body. It could be nothing but it could also be something. Something that could put a small town on the map, put Edie on the map. It's a long shot, true, but look at Benson, Minnesota, which has a population even smaller than Avalon. A small story about turkey manure fuel generation made it into the *New York Times*. A story in the *Chicago Tribune* about a ten-second tornado in Utica, Illinois, garnered the reporter a Pulitzer Prize. So why can't there be a story about Avalon? And why can't Edie be the one to write it?

Several possible headlines run through her mind. She sees it being picked up by the major newswires: AP, UPI, Reuters. And, of course, her byline.

By Edith Gallagher.

Maybe she's making this into a bigger deal than it is, but she's a good writer, a good reporter. She knows she can write a story that will make a difference if only she can find the right one. Disappearing garden gnomes and steak frys aren't going to do much for her career—she knows this. But there are many prominent journalists who got their start with that one great story, and that's what Edie is after.

As she approaches Main Street, she sees a Ford F650 Utility Truck. She's never seen one in Avalon, which means it must have come from a neighboring town. A deck gun is mounted on board and Edie knows there are probably several hundred gallons of foam concentrate at the ready. A small crowd has gathered across the street, with officers managing the crowd and traffic. She sees two men, presumably the hazmat team, already dressed in fully encapsulated suits and getting ready to make their way into the police department.

This is the most thrilling thing to happen since she's moved here. While Edie sincerely hopes that everything is fine and that no one is hurt, she knows this incident will be on the front page for at least a week.

Without even knowing any details Edie has an idea of how she can craft the story, something about the fragility of life and how, in this world, we need to help each other out. She may not be great with one-on-one relationships, but she's all for the greater good. It's why Edie signed up for the Peace Corps, why she spent twenty-seven months in Benin, Africa. She wanted to make a real difference in real people's lives. Those two and a half years opened her eyes.

She loves being an American, but being an American overseas is quite a different thing. Edie was able to see herself, and her country, through other people's eyes—through the eyes of aid workers from Europe and Asia, through the eyes of the people they were trying to help. She knows that Americans are often viewed as arrogant and frivolous, clueless about their own country, and she hates that this is true.

Edie remembers one night when she and two other Americans lost an impromptu game of pseudo-Jeopardy to a group of Swedes. The category: American history. The Swedes—Vilde, Max, and Frej— knew more about American government than they did: They could name the presidents, their term of service, why their presidency ended. Edie and her colleagues, one of them a history major from Vassar, held their own but in the end were still blown away. But the real clincher was when the Swedes offered them a bonus question, an all-or-nothing shot at winning the single bar of Hershey chocolate and tin of Pringles that was at stake.

Name the current president of Sweden.

They lost.

Later, when Edie recounted the details for Richard, he had laughed so hard that tears were running down his face. "Edie," he said. "Sweden is a constitutional monarchy. They don't have a president; they have a *king*."

Edie was embarrassed, but it just drove home the point she was trying to make. It's a big world out there, and everyone has a responsibility to make it a better place, everyone including Edie. The thing that really gets her is that it doesn't take much. Does she really need a four-dollar cappuccino? Or a pair of shoes that cost a hundred twenty-five dollars, made in a sweatshop by child laborers in Indonesia? How does a country with so much consumer debt manage to have women running around getting boob jobs and highlights? Does she really need to be asking these questions?

"Chief Neimeyer, what's happening?" Edie calls out over the din of the sirens. Several other people are asking the same question, and while they're not reporters, their voices carry over hers. Edie pushes her way to the front of the line, her digital tape recorder already on. She repeats her question, louder this time, and catches the chief's eye.

"Folks, just give the teams a chance to do their jobs, and we'll let you know what's going on as soon as we know something." Chief Neimeyer signals for Sergeant Overby to take over so he can check with the fire chief and get the latest update.

Edie tries again with Sergeant Overby. "Sergeant, can you tell us what's happening?"

"Sorry, Edie. Can't do that."

"Sergeant Overby, our phones are ringing off the hook. The people of Avalon are concerned." Okay, that's a slight exaggeration, but it's possible. Her boss, Patrick, told everyone to come down and find out what they could, save Livvy and the receptionist. They're holding down the fort.

Edie sees the rest of the *Avalon Gazette* team coming up on her rear. She wants this story—she *needs* this story. "Sergeant, please. Is there anything you can tell us?" The desperation in her voice is real.

He throws her a bone. "All I can say is that a woman was brought in carrying several items on her person, including a bag containing a suspicious substance. Under the circumstances, we though it prudent to call the fire department and let the hazmat teams investigate the substance and make a determination."

"Can you assess the level of risk?"

"We were told that the substance would react to metal but we were unable to verify the validity of this statement before . . ."

Patrick runs to them, out of breath. Sergeant Overby straightens up, aware that he's said more than he originally intended. He gives them both a polite nod and turns away.

Damn. He probably would have told her more if Patrick hadn't shown up. Now she's going to have to wait like everyone else.

Edie chews on a nail, thinking quickly. In an hour this will be old news. Television crews will be here soon. A write-up in a small town paper may as well be used to line the bottom of a bird cage if Edie doesn't figure out a way to spread the word first.

"What's the scoop?" Patrick pants. There's mustard on the corner of his mouth.

She gives him a quick rundown, and in that instant knows what to do. She steps away, leaving Patrick to crane his neck in an attempt to peer into the police station.

She calls Livvy. "Livvy, it's Edie. I need you to do me a huge favor. Are you up for it?"

"Are you kidding? Please put me out of my misery. What do you need?"

Edie rattles off several Web addresses for news stations, then tells Livvy what to type. It's possible that being the first to share the news will give her a way in, too. Just as she's finishing with Livvy, she sees the hazmat team coming out, hoods off.

"Hold on," she says. She runs back just as Chief Neimeyer nods his head and turns back to the crowd.

"It's all right," he says in a loud voice. "The hazmat team has determined that the substance in question is not harmful or dangerous."

An audible sigh of relief tinged with disappointment sweeps through the crowd.

"Chief Neimeyer," Edie calls out. "Any idea what the substance is?"

He hesitates. "It's batter."

There is a murmur of confusion.

"Badder than what?" Edie probes.

"BATTER. Dough batter. Cake batter. Hell, I don't know. It's for something called Amish Friendship Bread. Apparently it's been circulating around town." He turns around and storms back into the station.

Edie tries to make sense of this in her head, but she can't. What is Amish Friendship Bread and why is it circulating around town? More important, *how* is it circulating around town?

"What should I write next?" Livvy wants to know.

Edie notices a burst of conversation in the crowd upon hearing Chief Neimeyer's news. "Hold on, Livvy."

"Hate the stuff myself," someone says. "Someone in my office always tries to pawn it off on me."

"Really? I love friendship bread!" someone else declares. "Twice a month I bake a couple of loaves. My kids can't get enough."

"My kitchen smells amazing when I bake it."

"Don't the instructions say you're supposed to leave it out at room temperature? That doesn't sound like safe food handling to me. There's milk in there!"

"It's like a sourdough starter," comes an exasperated reply. "It's *supposed* to ferment."

"What's Amish Friendship Bread?" someone wants to know. "Where can I get some?"

As the people around her begin to talk and quibble, Edie tells Livvy to forget about it. A hazmat false alarm isn't much of a story, and the TV reporters have it covered anyway. Besides, she has an idea for a better one.

A much better one.

The answering machine is blinking when Hannah gets home from the store. She takes her time putting away the groceries, humming Jean Sibelius's Impromptu, Opus 78. Maybe that's what she'll do, play her cello and then check her messages. She misses playing and yet she doesn't. She feels drawn to the music room but then veers away, heading toward the living room or kitchen instead, finding something else to do.

The machine blinks a digital 2. Two messages. From Philippe, no doubt. She's curious, but she doesn't trust herself to listen to the messages in case he says something that could ruin her day or, worse yet, make her call him back. Hannah has never been good at expressing her feelings and she isn't going to try to do this over the phone. If Philippe has something to say, let him come to Avalon and say it.

She gets a glass of water and a slice of Amish Friendship Bread. It's made with zucchini and Hannah found the recipe by herself online. The first batch had been too wet and took twice as long to bake. Hannah was about to call Madeline when she decided to consult *Joy of Cooking* and discovered that she should have squeezed some of the moisture out of the zucchini after grating it. Hannah plucked a second bag of starter and tried again, this time with more success.

So now she has four loaves of zucchini bread, two bags of starter, and she couldn't be happier.

Well, that's not true. Hannah wishes she weren't alone, wishes her husband was with her and still in love with her. She's struck by the sad truth of her situation. Despite what he's done, despite what he's doing, she'd take him back in a second if he asked her to.

Knowing this only makes her feel worse. Hannah knows it's the sort of thing spineless women do, the ones who are afraid to be on their own, but let's be honest—that sums up Hannah pretty well. She doesn't like being alone, doesn't want to be alone. She isn't built like these superwomen she reads about—women who start their own businesses, who make bold decisions, who take risks. She knows she's smart, but she doesn't have that fearlessness that seems to be a staple requirement for these sorts of women. She's just Hannah, a woman with a musical gift, a woman with a marriage that might be over. And she has no idea what to do.

Hannah wishes her mother were alive. She'd know how to counsel Hannah, how to keep her calm and focused. Her mother wasn't the warm and fuzzy type—she was practical and highly efficient—but Hannah knows her mother loved her and that knowledge would be enough to give Hannah the courage to figure out the next step.

Her parents were like every other set of Chinese parents—they set the bar high, pushed their children to reach it, and didn't accept anything less. There wasn't any discussion or choice about the matter—you just did it. Her father, in particular, demanded a high level of excellence. Hannah's mother was the soft one, adding little bits of laughter to their otherwise solemn household. If Hannah was taking a break from practicing or Albert wanted to play outside with the neighborhood kids instead of studying, it was her mother who would relent. Her father? Never. He would complain that Hannah's mother was too yielding with the children, which she wasn't. She would just give them a break every now and then, give them a small bit of childhood they would have otherwise missed.

Hannah saw the way her father would defer to her mother whenever there was something she felt adamant about. Sometimes it was a big thing, like helping relatives who were struggling financially, or a seemingly inconsequential thing, like celebrating Christmas.

For many years all they did was hang a simple plastic wreath on the door, more for the benefit of the neighborhood than their family. No lights, no decorations, no tree. She and Albert received one or two gifts each, and that was it until Hannah turned nine. Suddenly her mother began to rally for a full-blown Christmas. They were living in North Carolina at the time, their first white Christmas.

"*We are going out to buy a tree,*" her mother called out to her father in Chinese as she ushered an overwrapped Albert and Hannah toward the garage.

"*Shenme?*" Hannah's father came barreling out of the study where he had been preparing his lecture notes. "*No! No tree! They're too expensive! We do not need a tree!*"

"*We do need a tree,*" Hannah's mother informed him coolly as she put on her gloves. "*And I am getting Christmas lights, too. You can put them up when we get home.*" She wasn't going to budge and Hannah's father could see this.

"*Next year,*" he suggested in an attempt to compromise. Albert rolled his eyes behind their father's back. "*We'll buy everything the day after Christmas, when it's marked down. Buy a fake tree and plenty of ornaments then.*"

"*We are getting a live tree,*" her mother said. "*And we are getting it this year. I want the children to have Christmas. Albert is almost a teenager and Hannah will be ten. We are celebrating Christmas this year.*" And with that she marched out the door with the children in tow.

They returned home four hours later, the car filled with Christmas paraphernalia Hannah never dreamed she'd see in her own home. For the first time she and Albert had Christmas stockings. Albert didn't seem to care for his, but Hannah loved hers. She loved when they got home their father had the ladder out, the hammer and nails. Hannah didn't know if this had been part of a larger argument than she had witnessed, but her mother looked smugly satisfied as she handed him the six boxes of lights. When he finished putting them up, he went out and bought five more boxes, using the excuse that the stores were already starting to mark down the prices and they may as well buy them now. Hannah's mother didn't say anything, just prepared the *huoguo*—Chinese hotpot—for dinner, her father's favorite and something that was ordinarily reserved for guests.

Hannah knows her parents' marriage might not have been perfect, and yet at the same time it was. She can't imagine them without each other, and even when her mother passed it never occurred to her that her father might remarry, which he hasn't. Maybe Hannah is more like him than she wants to admit—she wants to stay loyal to the person she first said yes to.

Philippe is her husband. She had pictured a whole life together, touring together, playing together, growing old together. Hannah tries to see them both in their seventies. Sixties. Fifties, even, but she can't. She can't see beyond where they are now. And now that they are not equal playing partners, what is left? What else is there for her to share with him?

She hurries to the answering machine and presses the PLAY button, holding her breath. The first message is an automated message from her credit card company. Annoyed, Hannah deletes this. The second message is from her neighbor Henry Tinklenberg, thanking her for the Amish Friendship Bread and inviting Hannah to join him and his family for dinner. He has a daughter her age, Pauline, whom he'd like her to meet. Hannah saves this message and falls back against the cushions of her sofa, defeated.

The doorbell rings just as the tears threaten to come. Instantly she thinks, *Philippe*. He doesn't have a new key so of course he can't walk right in. If it's him, and if he's here to apologize, she will accept it. There's a spare key in the kitchen drawer—she'll hand it to him, say she's been waiting to give this to him. They'll learn from this experience, and their bond will be stronger than ever.

The doorbell rings again, followed by a knock. Hannah licks her lips, wishing she had time to put on a little makeup. She hurries to the front door and takes a quick look through the peephole. But it's not Philippe.

It's Julia.

• • •

What if.

Ever since she woke up in Madeline's house the other night, Julia hasn't been able to stop thinking, *what if.*

What if Josh hadn't died? What if he'd never been stung, was still waiting on the lawn when Livvy came downstairs? What if for the past five years they were a family of four—her, Mark, Josh, and Gracie?

What if.

Would they be going on family vacations, having date nights, redecorating the rooms as the kids got older? Would they have had another baby? What would have happened if Josh had not died? What?

Julia has no idea. It pains her to think about it and yet she can't stop. It's the last thing on her mind when she goes to bed and the first thing when she wakes. She can't sleep in anymore—her eyes open as soon as she hears Mark and Gracie moving through the hallway, chattering and laughing. At first she had lingered, seeing if her body wanted to go back to sleep, but it was pointless—she was awake. Even if she wanted to stay in bed, she couldn't. She had to get up, unable to lie there any longer, so she now joins her family for breakfast.

Julia stirs granola into her yogurt, staring at the one empty chair around the table. They had bought it years ago as a set—a square maple wood table with four matching chairs—and wonders what it would be like if Josh were there with them, sitting in that fourth chair. She glances at her husband and daughter for signs that they may be thinking about this, too. But Gracie is listening to the crackle of her Rice Krispies and Mark is occupied with small talk, with language that tiptoes around Julia, as if he's uncertain of what she will say or how she will react. He's somewhat wary about her presence at the table, unsure if she'll change her mind again. The result is a conversation of little consequence to her and, she suspects, to Mark.

What if she and Mark were no longer together?

Julia doesn't know what to make of this and at the same time feels a subtle shift in her spirit, of something falling into alignment. What if she could start over, like Madeline or Hannah?

What if.

The rest of the day Julia keeps herself busy but her thoughts drift back to her two new friends. The other night she woke up feeling more rested than she had in years. She saw herself surrounded in the warmth of friendship, her hands wrapped around a bowl of French onion soup that tasted like heaven. Her body gave a sigh, felt something dissipate into nothingness. She knew in that moment that something had changed.

Madeline—who only had Julia's cell number—had called Mark at home and told him that Julia was staying late. He didn't seem alarmed when Julia returned home after midnight. Didn't ask any questions, just bade her good night. Perhaps this is the way things are going to be. She and Mark will have their own lives, independent of each other. Lives that don't require explanation or even checking in, just a coordination around Gracie, figuring out drop-off and pickup times. Julia knows this doesn't look like much of a marriage, so the next question that comes into her mind is, Should they even bother?

By mid-afternoon Julia can't stand it anymore. She gets in her car and drives to Madeline's. She's a bit early for their get-together, but she doubts Madeline will mind.

When she arrives she sees that the tea salon is crammed with local Avalonians, a meeting of some kind given the way all the women's heads are turned to see Margot West, an independent Avon representative, holding up a gift basket stuffed with beauty products as she points to each item in turn. Julia recognizes several people through the window and doesn't want to see any of them. She puts the car in reverse and drives away, heading down the street. Then she sees a house that she knows must be Hannah's. A second later Hannah walks past the window, engrossed in a book.

Julia makes up her mind. She cuts the engine, grabs her bag, and heads up the walk.

"I was driving by and thought I'd say hi," Julia says now. "I didn't realize you were this close to Madeline's. I hope this isn't a bad time."

"Of course not." Hannah gives her a hug and invites her in, offering her tea and a slice of zucchini bread. "You cut your hair!" she exclaims.

Julia's hand flutters self-consciously to her short locks. She hooks her finger around a loose strand by her ear, giving it a tug. "It isn't too short, is it?" she asks. She cut it the day after she'd spent the night at Madeline's. She had stepped out of the shower, her body soft and pliable from the heat. The mirror above the sink was covered in steam, obscuring her reflection, and she thought she saw a movement behind her, something familiar. She quickly brought her palm to the mirror to wipe it clear but when she did she only saw herself looking back at her, her wet hair streaming down past her shoulders. She dug through the drawers until she found the hair shears and thought, *Enough.*

"It's *perfect,*" Hannah says enthusiastically, and Julia smiles, encouraged. They walk into Hannah's sunny living room. "You caught me in the middle of daydreaming."

Daydreaming. Maybe that's what Julia was doing all morning. Down the hallway she sees a room with framed articles on the wall. "I was doing the same thing," she says. "Of roads not taken."

"That's funny," Hannah says as they settle on the sofa. "Because I was dreaming of the opposite. I was thinking about the road I did take, though I don't know what else I could have done. Playing cello seemed like the only choice available to me. And marrying a man who was also a musician. It made sense to be with someone who understood music, who knew the demands of playing professionally, you know?"

"Maybe," Julia says. "But I'm not an architect and Mark used to say that it was a huge relief, because all other architects want to do is talk about architecture. He used to say I kept him normal."

"Normal." Hannah looks at her, genuinely perplexed. "What is normal, anyway?"

Julia laughs. Hannah is asking the wrong person. "I have no idea," she says honestly. She spots a familiar book in front of her and picks it up.

"Joy of Cooking?" Julia is impressed.

"Have you read it? Madeline gave it to me. So far I've learned how to core an apple, that pancakes shouldn't be turned more than once, that cooking a pizza on a grill results in a crispy yet chewy crust." Hannah holds up a simple lined notebook. "I'm writing down recipes I like. I think I might actually try to bake an apple pie." She opens the notebook and flips through the pages. "Or maybe a risotto with mushrooms. Philippe loves risotto, but I never had enough guts to try it." She bends the corner of that page, a reminder.

Julia is confused. "Is Philippe coming home?" From what Hannah had told her, it sounded like their marriage was heading straight for divorce court. His choice, not hers.

Hannah reddens. "No. I mean, I don't think so. Everything is so distorted on the phone, you know? We need to talk in person. I found the names of some marriage counselors and thought seeing someone would help us communicate better. Not that we're going to get back together or anything . . ."

Julia hears the guarded hope in Hannah's voice. She respects Hannah's willingness to try, but doesn't want to see this young, beautiful woman waste her life on someone who isn't going to love her back or give her the respect she deserves. How well do you have to know someone before you can share what you really think?

Julia has never met Philippe and she doesn't know the details of their marriage. It's really none of her business. Julia remembers how she bristled when her own mother gave her unsolicited advice about her marriage, but Julia isn't Hannah's mother. She's a friend, a new friend who brings a certain level of objectivity to the situation, who can see what is happening to the young woman in front of her. Julia wants Hannah's happiness and, for the first time in a long time, her own.

She decides against saying anything and instead comments on Hannah's home, on how everything is perfectly put together.

"Oh, that's Philippe," Hannah says, blushing, gesturing to a few expensive art pieces that are arranged just so. "He's particular about where things should go and how they should look."

"No, it's not just that. You've made this into a home, Hannah."

Julia can see Hannah's femininity in the house, the small touches that soften the otherwise sharp edges.

On the mantel Julia sees a series of square photos, each in their own individual porcelain frame, slightly different but complementary. They're of Hannah, taken when she was a little girl and then all through adulthood, all with her cello.

Julia gazes at a picture. "You look so little here. When did you start playing?"

"When I was five."

Five. That's how old Gracie is. "Could you teach my daughter to play?" Julia asks suddenly. She doesn't know if Gracie has the attention span to learn an instrument—Julia hasn't given the topic much thought until now.

Hannah brightens and sits up tall. "Is she interested?"

"I don't know. She loves to sing and dance. I never had music lessons growing up, although Mark played trumpet in his school band for a few years. Hopefully she hasn't inherited our musical genes." Julia carefully touches the frame. A pint-size Hannah with her hair in two braided plaits dressed in a simple jumper is holding her bow and cello, a huge smile stretched across her little face. Her parents stand behind her, proud. "You all just look so happy. I want Gracie to be happy." There's a determined look on Julia's face. "How much do you charge for a lesson?"

Hannah knits her brows, thinking. "Um, I don't know. Maybe we could do one lesson to see if she likes it first. It's really important for the child to have some interest. Would that work?"

Julia finds herself warming to the idea. Gracie will love it or hate it, but she wants to find out. "Of course."

Hannah excuses herself to put a kettle of hot water on. In the kitchen, she calls to Julia, "I don't have a huge selection of tea like Madeline's. Is black tea all right? I have a nice one with citrus, vanilla, and lavender."

Julia sees a UPS truck pull up to the curb and a young man get out. "That sounds great."

Julia puts down the *Joy of Cooking*. She watches the delivery man stride up Hannah's walkway, a package tucked under his arm. Could it be possible? Julia quickly crosses the living room, opening the door just as he's about to press the doorbell.

His eyes widen. "Mrs. Evarts?" he says.

"Jamie," she breathes. It *is* Jamie, one of Peter Linde's older brothers. Peter is—was—Josh's best friend. The last thing Julia remembers is that Jamie was graduating from college but that was more than five years ago. She lost track of the Linde family after Josh died, never bothering to return any of Sandra Linde's phone calls. "Hi. You . . . you're working for UPS?"

He gives her a sheepish grin. "Part-time while I finish up graduate school. UPS has great benefits. And it keeps me active."

She gapes at him. "Graduate school?" Just yesterday it seemed like Jamie was bringing home trash bags filled with dirty laundry for his mother to wash. Does Sandra know how much her son has grown up?

"Yeah, I decided to go back for a master's degree. Education. Part-time also, but I'm almost done. I'm thinking about teaching."

"Wow, that's great. I'm really happy for you, Jamie." How did he get so big? She can't even imagine what Peter must look like now. She licks her lips and decides to ask. "So how is Peter?"

"Oh, he's great. Playing freshman football for Avalon High. He's running back." He says this proudly. Julia recalls that all the Linde boys were football players. "Other than that, cutting up in class every now and then, starting to like girls, you know, the regular stuff . . ." His voice trails off, suddenly aware of his mistake. Julia obviously doesn't know.

"That's wonderful," Julia says, forcing a smile. "Will you tell your mother I say hi? And Peter, too."

"Of course."

Julia turns to get Hannah, and sees the young woman standing in the living room with a tray of empty teacups, a startled look on her face.

"Hi," Jamie says, spotting her. Julia notices he's standing taller. He holds up the package in his hands. "Got another delivery. Crate and Barrel. Fortunately I know how to say that." He puts the large, rectangular box on the inside of the doorway.

Hannah manages an awkward smile, but still hasn't said anything.

"This is Jamie," Julia says, clearing her throat. "We're old family friends. His youngest brother used to be best friends with Josh. My son." She blinks rapidly, hoping to keep the smile on her face.

Hannah finally puts down the tray and crosses the living room. "Do I need to sign or . . ."

Jamie shakes his head. "Nope, you're good."

"Oh. Okay. Well, thank you," she says. Julia notices the tips of Hannah's ears have turned pink.

"My pleasure."

"It's a KitchenAid stand mixer," Hannah says to no one in particular, pretending to inspect the shipping label on the box. "I just thought, since I've been baking so much . . ."

"Oh, you bake?" Jamie looks interested.

Julia doesn't know how this fact is particularly riveting, but she can feel something stirring between these two young people. The kettle in the kitchen starts to whistle. Relieved to have something to do, Julia volunteers to take care of the tea and hurries off before Hannah can respond.

In the kitchen, Julia turns off the stove and takes the kettle off the heat, then leans heavily against the counter.

Fifteen years old. That's how old Peter is, the age Josh would be if he were alive. She stares out the kitchen window. There are rumors of more bad weather, but today the sky is a clear blue, the sun shining. It's an easy seduction, one that lures you into thinking that everything is all right.

Is it or isn't it? Julia isn't sure anymore. She's readied herself for a lifetime of hopelessness despite the little bursts of good moments here and there, but maybe it's really the other way around.

Hannah enters the kitchen, her face flushed. She reaches for a loaf of Amish Friendship Bread cooling on a wire rack and fumbles, almost dropping it. She manages to wrap it in plastic, then grabs a bag of starter, and dashes back out of the kitchen.

Julia edges to the doorway to take a peek. She sees Hannah give the loaf and bag to Jamie, trying to explain what it is and how to prepare it.

Jamie wears an amused look on his face, but he's also gracious as he thanks her and waves goodbye.

Hannah returns to the kitchen. Her eyes are bright. "I just thought he might like it . . . for his mother maybe . . ." She's stuttering a bit and Julia sees the tips of Hannah's ears grow pink again.

"Hannah," Julia says gently, because she knows where this is going. Jamie is a nice boy—a nice young man—and Hannah an even nicer young woman, but Hannah is still married. Julia wants to say something, wants to offer advice before things get too complicated. She pauses. "I think you're right—you need to see Philippe."

"Oh." Hannah flushes as she fiddles with a drawer pull. "Well, yes. It's just that . . ." She takes a deep breath. "It's just that I don't think he's coming back to Avalon."

"Then you need to go see him in Chicago. Find out where things really stand." Julia can't believe she's handing out marital advice, but she doesn't want Hannah to do anything she might regret. "Just go see Philippe," she urges again. "Chicago isn't that far away."

"I know." Hannah looks up, her eyes filling with tears. "But what if Philippe doesn't want to see me?"

Clyde Thomas, 64
Pharmacist

"What the fresh heck is this?" Clyde Thomas, Avalon's lone pharmacist, spits into a napkin. He looks inside a large ceramic bowl sitting on the kitchen table and grimaces. "I thought this was my oatmeal, for crissake!"

His wife, Hazel, swats his hand. "Don't touch. And don't swear. I'm going to be baking today." She hums as she hands him a clean bowl and spoon from the dishwasher. She picks up the bowl of starter and tucks it under her arm.

Clyde pours the oatmeal into the bowl and adds hot water. He dutifully eats it every morning and recommends it to anyone who comes to pick up their cholesterol medication, but he can't stand the stuff, truth be known. He picks up the *Avalon Gazette* and starts reading. "What are you baking?"

Hazel is pulling out flour, a carton of eggs, a tin of sugar, and some other ingredients. She lines them up on the counter, frowning as she inspects them. "Amish Friendship Bread. *Delicious*. I had some last week at our Bunco club. Mary Winder was hosting and she made three kinds. Only difference was the pudding, so I'm going to try the same thing." She holds up a handful of pudding boxes. "I've got vanilla, devil's food, and a banana cream."

Clyde looks up, suddenly interested. He does love banana cream pie.

Hazel preheats the oven, then starts combining ingredients. The pharmacy doesn't open until nine, but Clyde likes to get there early even though he has an assistant who checks the packages and makes sure everything's in order before they open.

"When's it gonna be ready?"

Hazel shrugs nonchalantly as she greases two medium-size bundt pans and then dusts them with sugar. "In about an hour."

An hour! He could easily wait an hour. Clyde folds the paper and brings his empty bowl to the sink. "I'll just go check the weather channel," he says.

"That'll be fine." Hazel watches him leave out of the corner of her eye. She isn't surprised when a yelp comes from the living room.

"What's this?!"

"That would be the church's volunteer form for the Easter potluck."

"I can read, Hazel. What I want to know is what is it doing in my chair?"

"They need big strong men to help set up tables and chairs, then go out and hide the Easter eggs for the kids. Pen's clipped right there on the top and your spare reading glasses are on the side table."

Clyde groans. "Hazel!"

She pours the first batch of batter into the pans and slides them into the oven. "Should be ready in about forty-five minutes," she calls out to him. "And I'm putting on a fresh pot of coffee for you. I got that vanilla-flavored kind that you like. On sale."

Clyde grumbles as he slips on his reading glasses. He works six days a week as it is, and he likes to keep his Sundays free for sleeping in. He'll go with Hazel to church so long as it's the 10:30 service and not the 8:30 service, but this is really pushing it.

He holds the form out in front of him and reads the long list of volunteer duties. This is an all-day gig! Well, forget it. Hazel can keep her banana-Amish-whatever bread. He doesn't appreciate being coerced into anything.

He stands up, ready to march into the kitchen and give her a piece of his mind when the smell of cinnamon and bananas hits him. There's a hint of walnuts, too. Hazel is humming, and there's the sound of coffee percolating. Suddenly his entire house smells too damn wonderful for words. He sits back down with a sigh and begins filling out the form.

Dang that woman.

❧

CHAPTER 12

"Tell me again," Livvy says eagerly. Her eyes are lit up with interest.

Edie tears off a piece of pizza. "Okay. Supposedly there's all this cake batter floating around Avalon. Amish Friendship Bread, though it has nothing to do with the Amish." She picks off the pepperoni slices then takes a bite of her pizza, chewing thoughtfully. "I did some research online and apparently it's pretty popular. It's like a chain letter, except it doesn't say anything bad is going to happen to you. Just that you're supposed to take care of this batter and then, ten days later, split it up into four cups. You bake with one and give the remaining three cups to three friends."

Edie holds up a plastic bag filled with the starter. She got it from Bettie Shelton at last night's scrapbooking meeting. Turns out the women of the Avalon Scrapbooking Society know more about this town than she'll ever find out on her own so she plans on attending their meetings for just a little while longer. For research.

"Got another meeting," she told Richard last night as she headed out the door, letting out an exaggerated what-can-you-do sigh. "It's for work." Under her jacket she hid the small plastic box that contained an X-Acto knife, plastic erasers, glue erasers, scissors, an assortment of colorful eyelets and mini brads. The group is always happy to share supplies and paper, but Edie already favors certain scrapbooking tools over others and just figured it would be better for her to get her own. It's a legitimate business expense because, of course, she wouldn't be doing this otherwise.

"Whatever you say," Richard had responded good-naturedly.

Now, Livvy takes the plastic baggie from Edie and stares at it in wonderment. "This is the same thing that Miss Sunshine—I mean, Cora Ferguson—had at the police station?"

Edie nods. "And, given the way this stuff proliferates, it probably came from the same original starter somewhere down the line."

"Where?"

"Or, more precisely, who? That's what I want to find out. Nobody was doing Amish Friendship Bread in this town when I arrived, and now everyone's got a bag."

"I don't." Livvy looks disappointed.

Edie grins as she helps herself to another slice of pizza. "Well, you're in luck. In nine days I'll have to split this, so you can have one of my bags. How does that sound?" She begins to pick the rounds of pepperoni off this slice, too, adding it to the pile, then looks up to see Livvy beaming at her.

Judging by the pleased look on Livvy's face, Edie can tell that it sounds pretty good.

Livvy is grinning. "That sounds great, Edie." Livvy likes that their friendship has evolved beyond the office, that Edie has taken her into her confidence. She doesn't quite understand what the big deal is with this Amish Friendship Bread thing, but she likes that Edie wants to include her. She wonders what she can do for Edie in return. "Thanks!"

Edie barks out a laugh. "Don't thank me yet," she says. "From what I've read, plenty of people will disown blood relatives if they show up with a bag of this stuff. You'll hate me in a month when your house is overflowing with starter."

Livvy knows that Edie is joking, because Livvy could never hate Edie, never hate anyone. Not even Julia who has been freezing her out for so long that Livvy is starting to think that there's no real hope of reconciliation. It's sad and unfair, but Livvy still doesn't hate Julia. She feels her eyes getting wet so she blinks quickly as she clears her throat. She wants this friendship with Edie to work. "What is it that you want me to do?"

"Help me ask some questions—you know this town better than I do. We'll start tracking when people started getting bags, who they got it from, when they got it, and so on. Eventually we'll find the source. I know we will." Edie takes a swig of soda.

"Okay." Livvy tries to remember what Edie just said. Maybe she should have taken notes. "And, um, why again?"

"Why what?"

"Why are you writing this? Is it like a cooking piece?"

Edie shakes her head. "No, no. It's like . . . a reminder of how we waste our time doing things that don't matter, when there are things we could be doing that *do* matter. I mean, if you're going to have a chain letter thing going on, why not ask people to give a dollar a day and ask three other people to give a dollar a day and so on? Or plant a tree? Or give up some useless piece of crap that just clogs up our landfills and depletes our ozone? I think we could all do well to have one less lipstick in our purse, you know?"

Livvy makes a note never to let Edie look inside her purse.

Edie continues on, talking about social mores and how, if they do this article right, they'll be able to set an example for how people can better use their time and resources to help the greater good. "I mean, you should have heard the women last night. It's all they talked about! And then you factor in the time to shop, bake, care for the thing, pass it on to others. There are so many other ways people can make a bigger impact on the world in much less time. It's like, get real. This is *cake* we're talking about here."

"Okay." Livvy nods. This could be fun, an adventure almost. She wants to help, wants to make this into the great story Edie is talking about. "Patrick must be pretty excited. He loves human interest stories."

Edie lowers her voice, suddenly serious. "Livvy, I'm not doing this for the *Gazette*. I mean, I might if it turns out to be nothing, but I think I can really angle it and get some of the larger metropolitan papers interested. That's why he cannot know, okay?"

"But why?"

"Because even though Patrick knows I want to write for other publications, he may want this for the *Gazette*. I think it's a much bigger story. A piece that goes beyond this small town."

Livvy winces. Is being in a small town a bad thing? "But it's about Avalon . . ."

"Look, Livvy, you don't have to help if you don't want to." Edie gives her a look, then shrugs.

Livvy feels a rise of panic, not wanting Edie to find someone else. "No," she says quickly. "I do want to help. I was just asking."

Edie raises an eyebrow as she chews on some crust. "Are you sure? What about Patrick?"

"What about him?" Livvy forces herself to give an indifferent shrug. Livvy still doesn't get what the fuss is about, but she doesn't have a problem doing something behind Patrick's back, especially after he praised Tracy for the Web-based advertising proposal that Livvy wrote. "I'm in sales. He doesn't care what I do so long as I show up at the meetings and make coffee."

Edie nods, at ease again. "Great. So I'll take care of this bag and see what happens. If you want, you can come over when I'm baking and tell me what you've found. Each starter bag makes two loaves, so you can take one home."

Livvy brightens. "When? Today?"

"What? No, Livvy, I told you. In nine days." Edie gives her head an impatient shake.

Livvy picks at her pizza, wishing she hadn't said anything. She's going to blow it if she's not careful, asking questions Edie's already answered. "Oh, right. Nine days. Okay."

This friendship is important to Livvy, not only because no one has really talked to her since Josh's death, but because Edie is the friend that Livvy's never had—smart, conscientious, worldly. She's seen so much and done so much that Livvy could listen to her all day. Edie is so sincere in her desire to make the world a better place that Livvy wants to help, even if she doesn't quite understand exactly what they're doing.

The other thing Livvy likes about Edie is that she never says anything negative about Richard, never complains about him or says anything that's less than complimentary of him, unlike Carol and Jo Kay who are constantly lamenting about their demanding children and hapless husbands. Next to Mark and Julia, Richard and Edie are the kind of couple Livvy hopes she and Tom might be someday.

She feels Edie's eyes on her, but doesn't look up, afraid she'll give herself away or say something dumb again.

"Hey, I have an idea," Edie says. She wipes her hands on a napkin and stands up. "Want to go do a pregnancy test?"

It's humiliating, peeing on a stick. Edie's done stranger things living in a third-world country, but Avalon is not a third-world country. Richard would crack up if he knew what she was doing.

Edie sighs as she shifts uncomfortably in the tiny stall. She's only here because she could tell that somehow she'd let Livvy down, could sense her pulling back. Livvy has become a part of Edie's day in an unexpected sort of way and Edie has gotten used to it, even looking forward to their coffee breaks and pizza runs. So when Livvy looked uncomfortable, she decided to propose the one thing she knew would cheer Livvy up.

"Is it doing anything?" comes Livvy's voice from outside the stall. "A minus means you're not pregnant. Plus means you are."

"There's nothing, Livvy. I just went to the bathroom." But there's a tinge of pink already starting to form. A faint minus, thank God. Not that she was worried, but . . .

"The instructions say it may take longer if it's early in your pregnancy." Livvy had selected a brand that boasted the highest accuracy five days before your period was even due. It had cost almost eighteen dollars for the two-pack box with one "bonus" test. How accurate can it be, Edie had asked, if they have to give you three?

It was difficult handing over the cash, especially when she knew that the same amount easily could buy three mosquito nets in Africa, where a child died from malaria every thirty seconds. *Grrr.* But Edie forced herself to keep the big picture in mind. The sooner she could start freelancing for the larger papers, the higher her income, which would then let her do a lot more good.

"Anything?" Livvy's voice is both excited and anxious.

Edie unlocks the door and shows the stick to Livvy. "Minus." She tosses it in the trash then goes to wash her hands.

"What are you talking about, Edie? That was a plus." Livvy goes to the trash can and uses a paper towel to fish it out. "See?"

Sure enough, in pink and white, there is a plus.

Edie grabs the instructions. Livvy must have read it wrong.

Livvy looks a little surprised, too, as if she really hadn't expected Edie to be pregnant. But a second later she's giddy and giving Edie a big hug. "Congratulations! You should wrap this up and take it to Richard. What do you think he's going to say?"

Edie honestly has no idea. He'll probably be overjoyed, having dropped the hint repeatedly about babies and marriage, not necessarily in that order. But he's not the one who has to carry the baby or give birth.

"This can't be right," she says instead. She skims the directions once, then twice, then checks the stick again. "Look, it says there's a chance of a false positive . . ." She shakes the remaining two sticks out of the box. They're individually sealed. "I'm taking it again. You take the other one."

"Me?" Livvy looks alarmed.

"I need a control group." Edie storms back toward the stall. *This can't be happening.*

Livvy opens her mouth to protest, then shuts it. "Honestly, Edie,

I'll just waste it. I've done these tests before and I've never seen a plus. I'm not even late. It's pointless for me to take a test."

Edie rips off the paper and slides a new test out of the wrapper. Her mouth is dry and she feels nauseous. It's all in her head, she tells herself. "Livvy, this was your idea to begin with. Come on." The stall door closes with a slam.

"Okay, fine." She hears Livvy walk into the stall next to hers.

Edie stares at the stick, willing a single horizontal line. A minus. A minus, that's what she wants. One line. She hears the toilet flush next to her as a pink plus forms in the window.

Shit.

Edie is in a daze as she exits the stall and goes to wash her hands. Her only hope is that somehow they got a batch of irregular tests. She dries her hands with the coarse paper towel as she waits impatiently outside of Livvy's stall. "Well? Tell me yours is a plus, too. Then we can throw this whole test into the trash."

Livvy unlocks the door and steps out of her stall. "Here," she says, and holds up the stick.

Plus.

Four boxes and nine tests later, Edie and Livvy have confirmed the unexpected.

They're pregnant.

Edie had practically frog-marched Livvy back to the drugstore, then proceeded to buy four more tests from different brands, some with two tests, some with three. Then they went back in the bathroom, Edie gloomy, Livvy ecstatic, as each test came back positive.

They're standing in the bathroom, unsure of what to do next, when Livvy's cell phone rings. It's Patrick, and he wants to know where she is. It's an hour past their lunch break, and she missed the meeting with him and Tracy. What the hell?

"I'm sorry, Patrick," Livvy starts to apologize, and then stops. She hasn't missed a day of work since she started at the *Gazette,* nor has she taken a single vacation day since she came on board three years ago. She thought her dazzling work ethic would impress him, but clearly the only thing she's good for is another warm body around the conference table. "I'm taking the rest of the afternoon off," she informs him.

"What?"

"Sick day," she says. She hasn't taken any sick days, either, not even when she had what she was sure was bronchitis. "Maybe two." Maybe the rest of the week. And then to stop him from asking more questions, she adds, "It's a female thing," and shuts her phone.

Edie is staring at her pile of pregnancy tests. Livvy feels bad, can tell that this isn't good news. Will Edie keep the baby? Take maternity leave? Livvy's mind swirls with the possibilities. She knows Edie is focused on her career, but lots of women do both. And if Edie keeps the baby, Livvy can help. She'd love to help. She missed that part of Gracie's life, those early months, those early years. She'd been just as excited if not more that Julia was having a little girl. Seeing Gracie grow up without really knowing Livvy is almost as painful as Livvy's estrangement from Julia.

But this is a sign, a sign that everything will be okay.

She's pregnant.

"Edie, are you okay?" Livvy can't wait to get home to tell Tom. She used to dream about this day so she knows exactly what she's going to do. She'll buy a card, make a nice dinner, a nice dessert. She'll put the pregnancy test in a box with a note that says, "Your real present will be here in nine months!" and give it to him once they've finished eating.

Or maybe she'll just show him as soon as he gets home.

"I need to see Richard," Edie says abruptly and then turns to Livvy. "Are you okay?"

Livvy is touched that Edie is asking after her since she knows Edie's been dealt a blow. She nods even though she's shaking, and applies a fresh coat of lipstick to her lips. *At this moment, there is a baby growing inside of me.* While Livvy never said it out loud, there was always the fear that she wouldn't get pregnant because of what happened to Josh. After all, what kind of mother would she make? Mothers don't make the kind of mistake that Livvy did, do they?

Olivia Scott is going to be a mother.

Madeline squints at the computer. She finds it both fascinating and a little disconcerting that so much personal information can be easily obtained on the Internet. Or is it the Web? She doesn't even know what to call it.

The website has been dramatically updated from when she saw it last, almost ten years ago. There's music and a collage of images that parade across the screen, then disappear only to be replaced by new images. The shoes are basically the same, with some modern twists, and she's pleased to see that they haven't changed the classic buckle shoe, which is the style she always wears, even though the price has gone up. There are more color choices, too, with names like Buttercup and Raspberry. She hadn't planned on buying anything— that's not why she went to the website, anyway—and the shoes come with a lifetime warranty so all Madeline really needs to do is mail hers back in to get resoled. But she wants to try a different color, like Orchid, and maybe a different sole, so she clicks on the appropriate buttons and orders a new pair of shoes.

After she's given her credit card information and received a confirmation, her eyes skim over the tabs on the top menu bar. ABOUT US. She remembers what it used to say, and that one time even her picture was on it (they loved having family members model the shoes, and had hired a professional photographer who made everybody look good). She wonders what it will say now. She clicks on it, and holds her breath.

The Caitlyn Shoe Company. Madeline still loves the name. Named after Steven's great-great-grandmother, Caitlyn Dunn, who sold handmade custom moccasins to her neighbors. The company grew slowly, taking its time when introducing new lines: buckle shoes, women's pumps, gorgeous leather boots. Each pair handmade in a workshop in Devon, England.

The information contained on the page is generic, talking about the history of the company, their commitment to quality. The pictures of people have been replaced by pictures of storefronts and close-ups of these lovely, well-crafted bespoke shoes. In other words, there's no information that's of any real help to Madeline.

So while Steven was a shoe salesman, he was a shoe salesman with a capital *S*. A dollar sign *S*.

Madeline turns off her computer. She holds the printout of her shoe order in her lap and notices, as she has every day since she's moved to Avalon, how quiet and still her house is when nobody else is in it.

In California, even though she lived alone (with one brief but disastrous attempt at a roommate), there was always somebody around, somebody stopping by, noise from the street, car alarms, an airplane flying overhead. She'd wake up twice a week to the sound of the garbagemen throwing—throwing!—the metal cans back onto the sidewalk. Chicago was the same way. But here in Avalon, there's more silence and long stretches of quiet than Madeline is used to.

Which has been leaving her with lots of time to think.

Madeline feels her age, her exuberance from earlier in the day waning. Today it was a full house again from breakfast until after-noon tea time. She loves it, she does, but once everyone is gone, Madeline is exhausted. She needs help in the kitchen, or with the bookkeeping. Either or both, all of the above.

She looks at the printout of her order confirmation. THANK YOU FOR YOUR ORDER, MADELINE DAVIS DUNN! So cheerful, as if they know her or have some relationship with her, but Madeline knows that this response is automatically generated. She's just another name, another customer, and nothing more.

CHAPTER 13

"I'm leaving!" Julia calls outs.

Mark made a special point of being home early today, not wanting to screw up again. He'll never forget what happened that night he was late because of Vivian. Avalon was being pounded by rain and he became anxious when Julia hadn't returned home by nine. He finally moved a sleeping Gracie into the car and went out looking for his wife. They drove all the way out to the cemetery, which was closed, and then randomly through the streets of their small town.

They had returned home, Mark worried out of his mind. For a second he thought Julia had left them. Then a woman called him out of the blue. She introduced herself as Madeline Davis and told him that his wife was fine, but resting in her home. The old Belleweather B&B turned tea salon, just a few minutes away. A few minutes away! How could Julia be so close and Mark not know?

He wanted to go get her, but the woman was quick to suggest that they just let Julia sleep, if Mark was okay with Gracie at home. Of course he was okay, but he was a little put out by this stranger who seemed to know something about him whereas he had no idea who she was. No idea at all.

Mark has come to the realization that Julia has secrets. Secrets she is not willing to share with Mark. He finally sees his wife emerging from her shell, but instead of returning to him, this Julia wants nothing to do with him.

When Julia finally came home late that night, she didn't say what had happened and Mark didn't ask. The next day Mark heard the shower running when he woke up. When Julia emerged, he saw she had cut her own hair. Julia used to cut her own hair—Josh's, too—but for the past five years it had grown longer and thicker, a mass of beautiful curls that Mark loves. Now those curls are gone.

But she looked beautiful, so much so that it took his breath away. He didn't know what to say to her. Waves of strawberry-blond hair that brushed her chin, softly framing her face. He could see how the weight of her hair, of Julia herself, had changed. She looked younger, lighter. He caught a glimpse of the back of her neck and was overwhelmed by a desire to press his lips against her skin, to inhale her once again, to simply *smell* his wife, but he didn't.

Gracie clamored for a haircut, too, saying she wanted to look just like Julia, which is unfortunately impossible. Gracie takes after him with straight brown hair that tucks obediently behind her ears, hair that smoothes itself easily into a ponytail or braids. But still Gracie begged for Julia to do something—*anything*—so Julia had laughed and agreed.

Mark watched from a safe distance in the living room as Julia brought down the cutting shears, draped a towel around Gracie's neck. It occurred to him that Julia had never cut her daughter's hair before, sending Mark and Gracie to the Avalon Beauty Salon instead.

Julia did a quick trim, but gave Gracie bangs, which Gracie loved.

"Now it's Daddy's turn," Gracie had announced when Julia was done.

"Sure." Mark was game.

Julia shook out the towel in the sink. "Maybe some other time," she said. Then she shooed Gracie into the tub.

Now, Mark steps around the corner, Gracie riding piggyback, her thin arms wrapped around his neck. They watch as Julia checks herself in the mirror, seemingly oblivious to either one of them.

"When will you be back?" he asks.

She gives a shrug. "I won't be too late. A couple of hours. Four, max."

He clears his throat. "Maybe we should invite your friends over for dinner sometime." There's supposedly another woman, too, another newcomer to Avalon. He wants to meet these women, see what they're like and why Julia prefers spending time with them instead of him. How well do they know her? How well does she know them? Do they know about Josh?

Julia doesn't respond, but gives Gracie a peck on the head. She's about to turn away when Mark takes a chance and gives his wife a quick kiss. On the lips.

Julia is obviously stunned. She manages a weak smile, then backs away, grabs her things, and leaves.

If she had wiped the back of her hand across her mouth, it would have had the same effect on Mark. He hears the car start, then the sound of Julia backing down the driveway and speeding off.

Running away.

On the drive to Madeline's, Julia pounds the steering wheel in frustration. Why did he do that? And in front of Gracie? *Why?*

Julia doesn't know why there is so much anguish around a single kiss from her husband. They used to kiss all the time—deep, soulful, sexy kisses before Josh was born, and then snuck in here and there as they managed their busy lives as parents and launching Mark's business.

After Josh's death and Gracie's birth, Julia would feign sleep in the morning, not wanting to open her eyes until she knew Mark was gone. The kisses were feather-light and timid. They soon became perfunctory, but they never stopped, even though Julia rarely kissed him back. It became easier to avoid it altogether, which Julia had managed with some success until, that is, today.

Julia knows that their marriage is scarred, maybe irreparably. For a long time she was indifferent, but now she's just sad. Is this her fault? Is it Mark's? She knows the statistics about children being raised in a broken home. How about one that's been ripped apart, turned upside down, missing a vital piece?

Some well-meaning person gave her an article about bereaved parents and she made the mistake of reading it. It talked about how, when a child dies, a branch on the family tree is broken. New branches can grow, but they'll never replace the branch that has broken. For Julia, it's not just the branch that has broken.

She feels as if the whole tree has been uprooted.

"I've made a decision." Hannah twists her diamond ring and wedding band. They're snug on her slender fingers but she doesn't want to risk taking them off to get resized in case Philippe sees her without them.

Madeline lines a plate with cookies and finger sandwiches—Julia is helping with the tea. "You've made a decision about what?" Julia asks.

"I'm going to see Philippe. I tried to call him the past couple of days, but he won't take my calls." It's coming up on three months since she last saw him. They've toured independently before, but always there was some sort of contact, phone calls or faxes, emails. But now there is nothing. She takes a deep breath. "I'm going to go to Chicago."

She outlines her plan to them. Since she can't get him on the phone and she's not sure what the situation is with a female in their apartment, she's aiming for neutral territory. Philippe is playing this weekend, so she'll catch him after the performance. She doesn't want to give him a chance to escape or come up with an excuse. Hannah isn't quite sure what to expect, but she wants to see him. She wants to see what he looks like. Is he happy? Miserable? Does he miss her? Maybe seeing her will remind him that he still loves her, that he still wants to be with her. It's possible, isn't it?

"I'm not going to tell him I'm coming," Hannah continues, then hesitates when her friends exchange a look. She hurries to add, "I mean, I'm not going to sabotage him or anything. I'm not the kind of person who would do that." She stops herself. A sane person wouldn't even be thinking that, would they? She feels her confidence waning and in its place, a swell of humiliation. She can't imagine what they must think of her, these wonderful women who've become her friends unless, of course, they're having second thoughts. "I'm so embarrassed you've had to meet me with my life being such a mess."

"Life *is* messy, Hannah," Madeline declares. Julia nods her assent.

Hannah bites her lip, grateful for their kindness but not convinced. "I know Philippe and I must look like two spoiled children to you . . ."

"Oh, let's face it," Madeline says. "First of all, both you and Philippe are musicians. And not just any musicians—you're magnificent performers in the public eye. You have a rare gift that you've chosen to share with us. You put years into your training. And your passion is also your livelihood. It takes a certain kind of person to pull that off, Hannah, much less succeed. Quite frankly, I'm surprised you're not completely unbearable!" She makes a face.

Hannah laughs and wipes her eyes, leaning over her cup of tea.

Madeline goes to her stereo and holds up a CD, her eyes mischievous. "Look what I found."

Hannah recognizes the cover and puts a hand to her forehead, embarrassed. "Oh no."

"Oh yes." Madeline pops the CD out of the case. "I can't imagine what it must be like to play under Lorin Maazel *and* Kurt Masur." She comes back to the table and hands the CD cover to Julia.

As the melodious strains of Strauss begin to fill the room, Hannah feels her body relax. Even Julia has her eyes closed, her mind somewhere else.

Madeline lowers herself into her chair. "You and Philippe are just as human as the next person, Hannah. There's no need to berate yourself for being human."

Hannah appreciates the kind words, but she can't imagine Madeline being as foolish as her. "I just wish I could be more like you," she says. "You're independent. You embrace opportunities. No regrets."

Madeline raises her eyebrows as she reaches for a basket of freshly laundered cloth napkins. "Oh, I wouldn't say that." She starts folding. "Like I said—we're all human. Everyone has regrets."

Julia reaches over to take a handful of napkins. "Well, of course, but look at your life, Madeline. You carry yourself with such confidence and dignity, and you're so kind and generous to everyone . . ."

Madeline interrupts her brusquely. "No, not everyone. You're giving me way too much credit, Julia. Both of you." There's an unexpected edge in her voice. She continues folding the napkins a few seconds longer, engrossed in the task until she suddenly pushes her chair away from the table and stands up. "Excuse me."

The two younger women watch her leave in bewilderment.

"Was it something we said?" Hannah asks, worried.

Julia seems just as surprised by Madeline's abrupt departure but shakes her head. "I think she just needs a minute."

The two women sit there, feeling Madeline's absence, and continue to fold napkins.

There's a turn in the music—a blaze of brass, reeds, and horns, the unmistakable fervor of violins. Hannah sighs. "I love this part."

Julia tilts her head, listening intently. "Are there cellos playing in this piece?"

Hannah nods. "Yes. Cellos are wonderful solo instruments, but in an orchestra, we play more of a foundation role. We provide stability and structure to a piece. So while you may not be able to hear us, we're there. You'd miss us if you took us away."

"I wish I could have seen you perform," Julia says. "I'm sure you were quite remarkable."

Hannah blushes. She's about to deny it but that would be a lie.

Julia folds a few more napkins, listening carefully to the music.

"I've only been to a concert once or twice in my entire life but I've never had the opportunity to really appreciate it. Now that I know you, I want to learn more." She gives a laugh. "Maybe I'm the one who should be taking lessons from you, not Gracie."

"Why not?" Hannah asks. She hadn't really thought about it before, but the idea of a mother-daughter lesson seems perfect for Julia and might give Gracie the extra incentive to practice. "It might be a fun thing for you to do together."

Julia stares at her. "I never thought about that. It *would* be fun, wouldn't it?" There's a thoughtful look on her face.

"I think it would be a lot of fun. For all of us." The two women grin at each other and Hannah summons the courage to ask Julia a question that's been on her mind for the past few days. "I wanted to ask you something, Julia."

"Sure."

"Would you be interested in coming with me to Chicago? For one night? I know it's awkward with this whole situation surrounding my marriage, but I could use a friend in case things go bad. I can get the tickets for free—they'll be great seats."

"Chicago," Julia murmurs.

"I mean, don't feel like you have to say yes," Hannah says hurriedly. She doesn't know if it's too soon to propose something like this, which seems like the sort of thing you would do with an old friend or someone you've known for a long time. But Hannah doesn't have anybody else and she'd love for Julia to be there with her. "I'll take care of the hotel and everything—I have to spend the money even if it's just me."

Julia folds the last napkin and puts it into the basket. "You know, I think I will. I just have to talk to my husband, but since it'll be on the weekend . . ." She nods, determined, a smile spreading across her face. "Yes, I'd love to come."

"Really?" Hannah clasps her hands in happy relief. "I'm so grateful!" Knowing that Julia will be there already makes her feel braver, more able to handle whatever might come. "I won't see Philippe until after the performance, and there's usually a backstage reception for season ticket holders and VIPs. It'll give you a chance to mingle with other music lovers and musicians."

Julia gives a shy shrug of the shoulders. "I don't know if I'm up for mingling just yet," she says. "I may just stick to you, or go back to the hotel."

"Whatever you want," Hannah says, wanting Julia to have a good time, too. It's funny how things can change in an instant. Hannah was anxious about Chicago but now she's looking forward to it.

A *night off*. The words take flight in her mind. A night where Julia can be an adult, a normal person without the pitying looks or the judgment. No Mark, no Gracie. She loves them and needs them, but right now maybe she needs this more.

Julia wants a break from her life.

Madeline returns to the parlor clutching a fat envelope. She wrote the letter when she first came to Avalon, when she seemed to have nothing but time. She places it in the center of the table and sits down heavily. "My regrets, girls." She presses her lips together, tight.

The women stare at the envelope but no one picks it up. It's addressed to Mr. Benjamin Dunn with a Pennsylvania address.

"It's his last known address," Madeline says. "Who knows if he's even there? I have no idea if he's even alive." That, more than anything else, is her worst fear.

"Who's Benjamin?" Hannah asks.

"My husband's only child from his first marriage." Madeline looks up at the vintage sign that hangs above the entrance to the kitchen. FRIENDS AND FAMILY GATHER HERE. She hadn't thought about it much, just liked the sign's charming and rustic feel, but now she sees the hypocrisy in that single, simple statement.

"Steven's first wife, Erica, died when her car hit a patch of black ice one winter. Ben was seven when I became his stepmother three years later and he was an angry, hurt child. He was one of those kids that I suppose you'd describe as ADD or whatever they call it now. He and Steven were always at odds, in part because I think they needed a woman in that house to help make things right."

Julia and Hannah listen quietly, nodding for Madeline to go on. Madeline sighs—this isn't a story she's told many people, and it's not one she likes to bring up, because it doesn't have a happy ending.

"Erica had become pregnant on their wedding night and Steven wasn't ready to be a father," she says. "He just didn't know how to handle a boy like Ben. Don't get me wrong—Steven was a very sweet man and he tried very, very hard. But he was still a man and it was hard for him to parent Ben in the way Ben needed to be parented. By the time I came along it was like adding fuel to the fire.

"It was a struggle. I tried hard in the beginning—offering to help him with homework, offering to chaperone class field trips, taking his side in arguments with Steven. The more I did, the worse it got. Or so it seemed. Thinking back now, there are small things I didn't pay attention to, like how he would stay home on the weekend instead of going out with friends. How he always seemed to be underfoot, his things everywhere. He seemed to be deliberately trying to get in my way. I would be so fed up that I'd have to go to my room to cool off, not realizing that Ben *wanted* my attention. I was too dense to see it at the time, to understand what his behavior really meant. He was a child who simply wanted love, like all children do, but didn't know how to ask for it." She sees Julia dab at her eyes, and feels her own eyes get wet. But it's been a long time since Madeline has cried about this. "I didn't get then that it was my job to figure that out, not his.

"When Ben went off to college, I have to admit that I was relieved. Out of sight, out of mind. Things were seemingly peaceful for a while, though there was the occasional Ben hiccup—academic probation, a DUI, that sort of thing. And then Steven died."

Madeline casts her eyes to the ceiling. "Steven's shoe company had been in his family for five generations. It was always his hope that Ben would somehow clean up his act and take over the business, so it wasn't a surprise that Steven left the company to his son. We had talked about it, and it was what Steven wanted to do. I wanted him to do it even though we hadn't seen Ben in years. It just seemed like the right thing to do, to keep this business in the family.

"Ben sold the company the minute he assumed possession of it. I couldn't believe it. He may as well have taken a stake and driven it right through my heart. I suspected he was an alcoholic even though he was still a young man at the time. Later I heard there were drugs, too. He was a drifter, unmarried and unmoored. I was actually relieved that Steven was dead so he wouldn't have to see what Ben had done." Her voice shakes. Madeline's talked about this before—many times, in fact—but it never fails to upset her as if it were yesterday.

"It's not your fault," Julia says quietly. "How could you control what he was going to do? You can't blame yourself for that." There's a startled look on her face and Madeline sees that the words echo in Julia's own heart.

"For that, no," Madeline says. She takes a deep breath and exhales, suddenly deflated. "But I was so angry, not just for what he'd done, but for *everything* he'd done—to Steven, to me, even to himself. Our little family saga had attracted a flurry of interest from the business media, and I was asked to do an interview. I accepted and then proceeded to blast Ben. Publicly. I don't even remember what I said exactly, but I was horrified when I read it in the paper—it just looked so ugly in black-and-white. I struggled with how best to apologize, but Ben hired an expensive lawyer and they were trying to get back the house that Steven had left me, the house that I was living in. It was a modest thing, nothing fancy, and with all the money Ben had, he could easily have bought himself several homes in high-end neighborhoods. I took it very personally that he was coming after me.

"The press was eating this up, and I was asked to do another interview—I declined. I decided that I wouldn't do anything anymore, just lay low and mind my own business, and let things die down so that life could return to normal."

Madeline looks miserable as she tells the rest of the story. They had the attention of the big papers now, and Ben was quoted in the *Wall Street Journal* as saying that Madeline had been a gold digger, a home wrecker, an alcoholic herself. It was all so ludicrous it was almost comical.

She remembers how quickly she found herself shunned by people she had considered friends. She received tight-lipped smiles from tellers at the bank, her neighbors offering no more than a short, curt nod when she went out to get her morning paper. After all these years, didn't these people know her well enough to see through Ben's lies? Apparently not.

"So I did the only thing I could think of. I donated the house to a foundation so that Ben could never buy it. I sold everything, not wanting to be burdened with more than was absolutely necessary. I took the proceeds, donated them to charity, and left town. California beckoned, so I went."

"Why did Ben want your house?" Hannah wonders.

Madeline dabs at her eyes. "Because, Hannah, while I was a grieving widow, he was a grieving son. He lost both his parents too soon, and the only thing he had was the house he grew up in. It really had nothing to do with me. I see that now. But I think, too, that he was doing the one thing that he knew would turn me against him, because he wanted to see what I would do."

"What do you mean?" Julia asks.

"He wanted to see if I would choose him over the house, over the shoe company. I obviously didn't, though I wish I had, more than anything. Now I have none of those things—the house, the shoe company, Ben. If I could do it again, I would have chosen differently. Would have acted differently." These last words linger in the air around them.

"So that's why you're back?" Hannah asks. "To make amends?

Madeline gives a smile, a small nod. "I needed to be closer—the west coast seemed so far away, another world almost. Chicago was my home for a long time—Ben's, too—and I foolishly thought that somehow we might both find our way back here.

"He could be anywhere, of course. The last address I have for him is in Pennsylvania, this one here." Madeline taps the envelope. She had used that Google function on the computer to see if she could find him but had been overwhelmed by the number of results—more than two million hits for Benjamin Malcolm Dunn, with every possible combination of his name. Madeline had clicked on link after link then eventually gave up. In the end, she decided to rely on the last known address given to her by her lawyer. Even if Ben's no longer there, the letter still might find him. "But I'm not so sure anymore that I should send it. It might just reopen old wounds." She sighs heavily. "It took me three months to write that letter. It'll probably take me just as long to mail it."

"I can mail it for you if you'd like," Hannah offers gently.

Madeline shakes her head and quickly reaches for the envelope as if she's afraid that Hannah might mail it right away. "No, no. I'll do it." She slides the envelope into her lap and covers it with a napkin. She takes a deep breath. "I'll do it when I'm ready."

Bernice Privott, 58
Town Librarian

"No, I'm sorry. I can't do it."

Bernice Privott stands safely behind the locked screen door, arms crossed, an apologetic but firm look on her face. She was rinsing her breakfast dishes when she spotted Helen Welch exit her house with several bags of the now-familiar creamy starter. Bernice had managed to dry her hands and hurry to the screen door, slipping the lock into place just as Helen came up the sidewalk.

Helen is smiling sweetly now. "Bernice, I wouldn't be asking if it wasn't an emergency." She cradles the bags in her arms.

Bernice shakes her head, refusing to be swayed. "Helen, I've gone through three cycles already. I have a bag of my own and as it is I haven't a clue as to what I'm going to do with it."

Helen clucks sympathetically, edging closer. "But I'm not *giving* them to you, Bernice—I just need you to babysit. Henry wants to visit his mother in Grand Detour and we won't be back until Friday at the earliest. Just give them a feed tomorrow on Day Six, and then I'll be back to take over again."

"No." The word comes easily to Bernice, who has been the head librarian at the Avalon Public Library for over thirty years.

Helen reaches into the front pocket of her dress and pulls out an index card. "Did I tell you that I found the most amazing recipe for a pumpkin cranberry bread using the starter? It's the best one by far. And doesn't Mr. Takahashi have a thing for pumpkin?" Helen's eyes narrow knowingly.

Koji Takahashi is the new library technician. He's a few years older than Bernice, a recent transplant from Ann Arbor, Michigan. He'd been instrumental in turning around the Ann Arbor District Library system, which has more than 500,000 books, magazines, audio books, DVDs, and the like. They have nothing like that in their cozy 2,000-square-foot town library, but Koji said it didn't matter. When Helen continued to insist that their needs were much smaller, he simply said that his were, too, and so she gave him the job.

Helen taps the card enticingly against the mesh of the screen door.

Bernice hesitates, but only for a second. She flips open the lock and pushes the screen door open. Helen jumps back just in time.

"Fine," Bernice says. "You're back on Friday?"

Helen nods and smiles broadly as she fills Bernice's arms, then hands her the index card. She heads back to her house, calling over her shoulder, "Oh, and in the event that I get caught up and don't make it back—you know how heavy the rains have been lately—do be a dear and make sure they don't go to waste. Thank you!"

Bernice knows now she's been duped. "Helen!"

But Helen is already hurrying home without a backward glance, her arms free, her kitchen free, with Bernice muttering under her breath as she wonders how many loaves of pumpkin cranberry bread it will take to win Koji Takahashi's heart.

CHAPTER 14

Livvy is buzzing with nervous energy. She's cleaned the house, washed the sheets, and cooked an amazing meal with the help of some heat-and-serve dishes from Kroger's. She found the perfect box for the pregnancy test and wrapped the whole thing in tissue paper the color of daffodils.

The second guest room is Livvy's choice for the nursery. It's the furthest away from the stairs (she's thinking ahead to when the baby will start crawling), gets plenty of sun, and has more than enough room for a crib, changing station, dresser, rocking chair, bookshelves. The closets are spacious and they can add a second rack since the baby's clothes will be so small. That's one of the things Livvy can't wait to do—shop for a layette. Maybe she and Edie can do this together. Maybe they can get a discount on furniture and things if they buy them at the same time.

The door slams and Livvy realizes that Tom is home. She hurries to greet him, a cold beer in hand.

"Hi, Liv." Tom gives his wife a kiss as he loosens his tie. He accepts the beer with a smile. "Wow. Nice. Thanks, honey."

He's had a good day. This couldn't be more perfect.

"Are you hungry? Dinner's ready." Livvy's anxious to get him into the dining room.

"I'm starving. Let me just change and I'll be right down." He tosses his briefcase to the side and climbs up the stairs.

Livvy hurries back to the kitchen to make sure everything's warm. She has his favorites: strip steak with mashed potatoes and carrots, soft dinner rolls, green beans. More beer for him, sparkling apple cider for her. A cheesecake for dessert.

She brings everything to the table except the cheesecake and sits down. She puts the napkin in her lap and waits, her heart pounding.

Ten minutes later, she's still waiting.

When a total of fifteen minutes has passed, Livvy throws her napkin onto the plate and marches upstairs. There, in their bedroom, she finds Tom lying on the bed watching golf, wearing boxer shorts, socks, and the shirt he wore to work. The empty bottle of beer is on the nightstand.

"Tom!"

He shushes her, his eyes on the television. "Liv, one more minute. They're doing a recap of the Players Championship . . ."

"Tom, I made dinner and it's downstairs getting cold!"

"Can we eat it up here?"

Livvy marches to the TV and snaps it off. "No!"

Tom swears. "Goddamn it, Livvy." He tosses the remote to the side and gets up. "Fine. Let's go eat."

She stares at him. "Aren't you going to finish changing?"

"I don't care. Let's just eat." He's the first to walk out of the room.

She follows him down the stairs, calming herself. With each step, her anger dissipates and she grows excited again, knowing how good this will be, knowing how this will change things.

At the table, Tom stops short of his seat. "What's this?" He picks up the box wrapped in yellow paper.

"It's a present," she says. Instead of sitting back down in her chair, she hovers by his.

He definitely looks surprised, and a little ashamed. He leans over to give her a kiss. "So that's what all the fuss is about. Thanks, Liv." He sits down and tears off the paper. "Is it a watch?"

She shakes her head, but doesn't say anything. She doesn't want to say another word until he sees what it is.

"What the . . ." Tom's face clearly registers shock as he reads the note and then holds up the pregnancy stick. "The plus means you're pregnant? You're pregnant?"

Livvy can't hold back. "I'm pregnant!" she gushes. "Can you believe it? I didn't have any idea, I was just being a friend to Edie and took the test to support her and . . ." She points to the window with the pink plus. "It's positive. We're going to have a baby, honey." She throws her arms around his neck and kisses him. "We're going to be parents!"

Tom runs a hand through his hair. "Wow. I mean . . . wow."

"I know. It's like they say, that when you're all uptight and anxious about getting pregnant, it's harder to get pregnant, but when you finally just let it go, it happens . . ."

"Are you absolutely sure? I mean, could this test be wrong?"

Livvy feels the smile fall from her face.

"What did the doctor say?" Tom asks.

"I didn't see the doctor yet. I have an appointment to go in tomorrow."

"So it's possible that the test is wrong? I mean, he has to check it first, right?"

Livvy doesn't know what he's saying. Or maybe she does. She grabs the stick from his hands. "It's possible, but it's not likely. I'm pregnant, Tom. It's what we said we wanted! Why aren't you happy?"

"I am happy, Livvy. It's just that . . ." Tom looks at her, distraught. "We're up to our eyeballs in debt, in case you haven't noticed. We have one car and we've borrowed against our mortgage. I don't think this is the ideal environment to be bringing up a child."

What *is* the ideal environment for bringing up a child? Financial security is only one part of the equation. What about love? Family? Money isn't the only thing that makes the world go round.

Tom adds reluctantly, "Also, I might be out of a job."

"You might be out of a job?" Livvy stares at him. She eases herself into the chair next to him. "What do you mean?"

He sighs heavily. "My numbers suck. It's been a crappy year for everybody. Even if they don't fire me, I should probably quit and look for a better job. You, too."

"Me? But I like my job at the *Gazette*."

"I know, Liv, but it doesn't pay. We're never going to get out of debt at this rate." He eyes the bottle of sparkling apple cider chilling in a bucket of ice and softens. "This is for real? You're really pregnant?"

Livvy nods, though she doesn't feel as happy anymore. "It's real."

"Have you told anyone else yet?"

She shakes her head. "Edie knows, because she was there, but I thought I'd go to the doctor first to see how far along I am. We should probably wait until the first trimester passes before telling anyone . . ." Livvy knows she's not fooling anyone. She plans to call her parents before she even leaves the doctor's office. She almost called Julia this afternoon, her finger hovering over the keypad of her cell phone. But she didn't.

Tom still looks overwhelmed. He pulls Livvy into his lap. "Pregnant." He swallows, digesting this. "Maybe I'll skip work tomorrow, go to the doctor with you. Would that be all right?"

It would be more than all right. Livvy is suddenly laughing and crying. "But what about work? The money?"

He shrugs, pretending not to care. "They're going to fire me anyway. We'll figure it out." He gives her a kiss and then holds her. Tight.

They sit this way for a long time. Tom, Livvy, and their little poppy seed of a baby, so full of possibility and hope for their future.

"Come here, *mamacita*." Richard pulls the covers back invitingly as Edie retreats back to bed from the bathroom.

"I know you think you're being charming, but it's not funny." She's been nauseous ever since she made Richard run the blood test to confirm the pregnancy, and she is definitely pregnant. They have an ultrasound scheduled in a couple of days to determine the due date and size of the baby since Edie's erratic periods (and her lack of interest in maintaining any record-keeping) are keeping them in the dark as to when she actually conceived. Correction: when "they" conceived. Edie is still getting used to the coupling terminology, and while she's happy to include Richard in every part of this, let there be no mistake that "they" will not both be giving birth.

Richard gives her belly an affectionate pat. "I'm not trying to be funny, sweetheart. You are going to be somebody's mommy." He bends down to give her tummy a gentle kiss then lays his head in her lap. "You know, it is kind of interesting that you only started having morning sickness after we confirmed the pregnancy."

Edie pops a ginger candy into her mouth and then decides on a second one to be safe. "Richard, first of all, it's not *that* interesting. I highly doubt anyone would be as remotely riveted as you. Second of all, it's not morning sickness because I feel nauseous *all of the time*." Case in point—it's 10:00 P.M. "Third, if you insinuate one more time that this is all in my head, I will personally put you out of *my* misery and then tell the police it was hormones."

Richard gives a chuckle. He weaves his fingers through Edie's. "So . . ." he begins quietly.

She groans, knowing what's coming. "Richard, if this is going to be one of those 'we should get married because of the baby' conversations, I don't want to have it." Edie shakes her hand free and burrows under the covers, her back to him. She just wants to sleep. All of the time, unfortunately.

Richard leans over her. "Edie, we've never had that conversation. I know your feelings on this. And I respect them."

Her voice wafts out from under the down comforter. "So why do I feel like we're going to have this conversation now?"

He gently tugs at the edge of the comforter until it falls away from Edie's fingers. "Because I need you to respect my feelings on this. Do you even know what my feelings are? We've known for three days that you're pregnant, and we haven't once talked about the future."

"The future." Edie says the words with a frown.

"Yes, the future. Our future."

"You want the future? Fine." Edie tosses off the blankets and props herself up on her elbows. "Here's the future. In nine months we're going to have a baby. Which means I have nine months to try and launch my pathetic career as a journalist before I become one of those breastfeeding mothers in Birkenstocks who hangs out by the bulk bins at the health food store. Is that future enough for you?"

Richard looks put out. "It's enough of *your* future. I'm not exactly clear as to how I fit into the equation."

"You're the guy who'll be changing diapers and getting up in the middle of the night with a bottle."

"Edie." Richard looks pissed now. "It goes without saying that I will be the guy changing diapers and getting up in the middle of the night. I don't have a problem with that, and you know it. But I do have a problem with you thinking that's all there is. What about marriage, Edie? *I want to marry you.* I know you want to marry me. So what the hell are we waiting for?"

Edie stares up at the ceiling. She doesn't know how she can make him understand. She's not discontent with her life or with Avalon exactly, but all of her alumni magazines show former classmates bragging about their successes, their publications, their good works, and it's starting to get to her. The only thing that doesn't bother her is hearing about people's growing families. To that she just rolls her eyes and thinks, *Better you than me.* She finds it ironic that the gods messed this one up and gave her the one thing she cares least about.

"Richard, I just want to focus on work for a little while longer. It's easy for you—you took over an existing medical practice and boom—office, patients, a secretary, a nurse, even an aquarium. You're Dr. Richard. Everybody loves you." She doesn't begrudge Richard's popularity but it's Richard's, not hers. "I just want to do my thing, make *my* mark. And reporting on a whack job who's been secretly stealing people's newspapers and switching their garden hoses isn't going to wow the major papers."

Richard falls back against the pillows, frustrated. He throws an arm over his face and grits his teeth. "Edie . . . Edie . . . Edie . . ." He says her name like a mantra.

"Richard, I just want one big story," she begs. "And I think I have it, with this Amish Friendship Bread stuff. And I found something else, too. There's a sweet bread, Hemin, circulating among believers of Saint Pio of Pietrelcina, also known as Padre Pio. You make this holy bread, read the prayer that comes with it, and, of course, split up the starter and share it with other people. Naturally the Vatican and official Padre Pio prayer groups deny this, but it doesn't stop people from giving it a try, just in case. The instructions differ a bit from Amish Friendship Bread, but it's basically the exact same thing. You should hear the stories of all the 'supposed' miracles that people . . ."

"Enough. Stop." Richard gently grasps her chin and turns her to face him. "I don't care about Hemin bread or Padre Pio, Edie."

Edie squirms. "Okay, but . . ."

"Hush." There's a determined look on his face, one that Edie hasn't seen before. "I know you hate surprises, so consider this fair warning: I will be planning a special dinner soon in which I intend to ask a particular question."

"Oh, Richard." Edie can't hide the crestfallen expression on her face. She loves in principle that her boyfriend of eight years is a romantic, but she has made it clear that she hates surprises, especially surprises that might result in any kind of photo opportunity. "Can't you just wait a little longer?"

"No, I most certainly cannot." He says this firmly. "Consider yourself lucky that I'm even giving you a heads-up. This is not exactly how I wanted to do it, but I want you to have time to think about this and who knows, maybe even get excited about it."

Edie never played dress-up where she pictured herself as a bride or getting married. She's not against it, she just doesn't think it's something every couple has to do. And for eight years things have been going so well. Why wreck it?

She's almost forgotten that she's pregnant (could there be a bigger wrecking ball?) until a wave of nausea makes her clap her hand to her mouth. It passes.

"So essentially this is the proposal before the proposal," she recaps, swallowing hard.

"No. I'm not proposing that I propose to you. I *am* going to propose to you, Edith Whitting Gallagher." Richard pushes himself out of bed and pads into the hallway, probably to get a late-night snack, or to make more toast for Edie. "So be ready."

Connie Colls, 21
Laundromat Attendant

The Avalon Wash and Dry is the town's only self-service laundry facility. Located on the corner of Main and Grove, the Avalon Wash and Dry boasts eight top loaders, thirty-eight front loaders, and thirty-six dryers. Hours are from 5:00 A.M. to 11:00 P.M. every day, including holidays.

Connie Colls started working at the Wash and Dry in high school. It was the perfect part-time job—sweeping and cleaning, stocking vending machines with change and small packets of detergent and dryer sheets, calling in broken machines. When she graduated high school with no real job prospects, Connie accepted a full-time position as the daytime Laundromat attendant.

She knows it's not as glamorous as some of the things her classmates have gone on to do, but Connie is happy. It's an easy job, and one that she does well. The pay isn't great and the benefits are lousy, but there are perks that keep things interesting.

She makes money on the side by helping her customers fold their laundry or taking their laundry out when the cycle is done. She's technically not supposed to do this, but seeing how she knows pretty much everyone who comes in here, she's not too worried about getting into trouble.

Other than that, there's not very much going on. Prompted by her own boredom, Connie suggested the addition of a few soda and water vending machines. She set up an informal kid's area for toddlers and little kids so that tired moms could have a moment of peace to fold their laundry. There's a lend-and-leave bookshelf and two neat stacks of magazines and newspapers. Connie painted the walls a light and airy sea foam green, replacing all of the hand-printed signs with ones printed from her computer. She added a couple more with clever puns, including one that said, "It's a dirty world out there—let us help you clean up!" It was her idea to offer free Wi-Fi (which lets her surf the Web at her leisure) and install a television in one corner that plays funny movies. Both have been big hits with the customers.

Connie is good at being inconspicuous. Her customers know she's there, but in a way she's considered part of the scenery—she doesn't really count. Which means that they'll say whatever it is they want to say in front of her. Connie jots down interesting anecdotes in a little notebook that she keeps in the back room, thinking that someday she might write a book. *My Life in a Laundromat* or maybe something catchier like *It All Comes Out in the Wash*. Something like that.

She knows business is good, because each week there are a few more new customers and the old ones keep coming back. Sometimes there's a wait for the machines. The owner seems happy each time he visits, and the last time he brought someone with him. They both praised her, said she was doing an amazing job, and when the owner was leaving he gave Connie a thumbs-up.

Her latest idea was the community bulletin board. She bought a framed corkboard and hung it under the clock, and in less than twelve hours it was filled with business cards. In twenty-four hours she had flyers, too.

Connie is careful to look through the board and remove any items that have expired or no longer seem useful. She hates the cheesy business opportunities (WORK FROM HOME! EARN $100,000 IN ONE MONTH!) and yanks those off the board right away. She likes the ones giving away cute puppies, the colorful flyers for yoga classes, the moving sales with lists of items going cheap or "OBO." The bottom line for Connie is that whatever is on the board has to be of service to the community. She's adamant about that.

A couple of months ago someone posted a question on a small card.

MY AMISH FRIENDSHIP BREAD STARTER GREW MOLD! WHY??

Another card quickly followed, written by another person.

WHY CAN'T I USE METAL FOR MY AFB STARTER?

And then,

I HAVE AFB STARTER COMING OUT OF MY EARS! CAN I FREEZE IT?

The responses filled the cards—some in pencil, some in pen, all in different handwriting. Then there were more cards, and more responses, until half of the community board was taken up with questions about Amish Friendship Bread.

The cards kept coming. Recipes, too. Yeast-free. Chocolate chip applesauce. Carrot coconut. Rhubarb muffins. Lemon poppy seed. All using the Amish Friendship Bread starter.

Connie finally came up with a solution. She went to the drugstore and bought two large index boxes, one for questions and techniques, another for recipes. She left a stack of blank cards and pens nearby for people to copy their favorite recipes or leave a new one.

Within a week, both boxes were filled. So Connie bought two more boxes.

She was starting to notice that women were coming in not just to do laundry, but to consult one or both of the boxes. Connie quickly added free coffee to the list of amenities for Laundromat patrons. Oftentimes two or three women would meet while waiting for their laundry to dry. They'd bring in different variations of the bread and share them, exchanging questions or commenting on whether one box of pudding was really enough or if whole wheat flour contained enough gluten to make the recipe work properly. Connie didn't really understand these discussions, but was more than happy to participate in any necessary taste tests. Soon she could count on a mid-morning and mid-afternoon snack, and sometimes a loaf to take home. She declined the many opportunities to take a bag of starter—it wasn't really her thing.

But helping coordinate the many women who did want a bag of starter, or who needed to get rid of their starter, *was* her thing. She quickly and easily hooked people up, letting them know what day the starter was on and how to care for it. She knew what to do and what not to do, and while she never spoke from experience (she let people know this up front), she also overheard enough to give good advice. She was like a lawyer who had never been in a car accident or subject to a lawsuit themselves. Just because she never actually made Amish Friendship Bread didn't mean that she couldn't tell people how to do it right.

Then the owner had come in a couple of days ago, his mouth agape at the bevy of chatting ladies poring over recipes and sipping the free coffee as they folded their laundry. He seemed genuinely sorry to tell Connie that he was giving her two weeks' notice. He had sold the business to a man from the city who already had ten successful Laundromats throughout the state. He was going to convert the Avalon Wash and Dry into a 1930s-themed Laundromat with laundry debit cards instead of coins. Dry cleaning pick-up and drop-off. Open twenty-four hours. It would be a complete overhaul using a proven formula. He was going to bring in a manager from one of his other operations to oversee the change, and they wouldn't be needing Connie anymore.

"I'm really sorry," the owner said to Connie. He handed her a card that said THANKS FOR A GREAT JOB and inside there was a hundred-dollar bill. Connie said thank you, but she could tell his mind was already on other things, like a vacation to someplace exotic or the new car he would be buying. He'd made his money, with Connie's help and brilliant ideas, and he was now hanging her out to dry. Pun intended.

The new manager comes in this week with the Laundromat's new signage and has already told Connie that the bulletin board must go.

They don't want clutter. So today, the bulletin board and the Amish Friendship Bread boxes, which are stuffed to overflowing, must find a new home. She wants to put them some place where people can freely gather and consult the cards at their leisure. She tried to put the boxes into the safekeeping of one of the regulars, but no one wanted the responsibility.

She'll try the library first, and while she's there she might pick up catalogs for the community colleges in Freeport and Rockford. Connie doesn't want to be at the mercy of a fickle employer anymore—she wants to have some options. Some real responsibility, with opportunities to grow. A career maybe.

She tries not to be angry at the owner for selling. After all, it was a good job while it lasted, and she learned a thing or two. More important, she had fun. She saved a little money, got to watch all the latest releases from Netflix, met a lot of good people. The customers are livid on her behalf but she tells them not to be. She knows they need a place to do their laundry, and she doesn't want them to feel guilty about coming to the new place.

In the three and a half years that Connie has worked at the Wash and Dry, she's come to realize that life is a bit like doing laundry—you have to separate the darks from the lights. One's not necessarily better than the other—they're just different. They have different needs, require different levels of care. She knows plenty of customers who don't give it much thought and throw all their laundry in together, and maybe that's the chaotic part of life that just happens, that no matter how hard you try, you can't always keep things separate. A red sock gets mixed in with a load of whites, or a delicate black top gets washed in hot water by accident. These things happen. All you can do is learn from it and move on. Tell your husband to enjoy his pink underwear, give your shrunken top to your little sister or niece. But it doesn't mean that you stop sorting your laundry. You keep sorting—lights from darks, darks from lights—and hope for the best.

CHAPTER 15

Mark pushes the grocery cart through the store, Gracie trailing beside him with her own mini version. She can only put lightweight items in her plastic cart, like tea boxes or bags of marshmallows, but that suits her just fine. It takes longer to do the shopping this way, but Gracie is happy, and it gets them out of the house so Julia can have more time to herself.

Today, however, Mark is steaming. He's been on a low simmer ever since that afternoon he kissed Julia, when she had recoiled as if he had been a stranger. No, correct that—a stranger probably wouldn't have evoked that response. That was clearly reserved for Mark.

Mark loads up on the bad starches, cheap carbs he knows he'll regret later. Well, more time in the gym then, which is quickly becoming his home away from home. White bread, pasta, crackers, chips. He throws in a sour cream dip just for the hell of it, and suddenly has a craving for nachos smothered with cheese and jalapeños.

Gracie is chatting animatedly to her stuffed elephant, Troy, who's sitting in the doll-size seat of her grocery cart. Troy is an elephant who thinks he's a bird. Right now she thinks it's important to humor Troy and then, when the time is right, she'll break the news to him gently.

Mark glances at her, worried that this imaginary play might be a mask for a more serious problem. He pictures the family therapist shaking his head and telling him that Gracie's lost touch with reality. She is now permanently damaged, unable to function in the real world, which is full of bad things and parents who fight and who don't know how to kiss. Even the admiring looks from other shoppers and the occasional coos don't soothe him.

He turns the corner. Rows of Hostess snacks come into view, junk he hasn't eaten since he was a kid. Boxes of Ho Hos, Twinkies, Ding Dongs, and Sno Balls end up in his cart. Even Gracie is frowning. But Mark doesn't care.

Julia is gone for the next two days, having some "down time" with one of her tea shop friends. Mark doesn't know where she is or what she's doing. As usual. Why should she tell Mark anything? He's just the husband.

A box of powdered Donettes sails into the cart. Mark pushes on.

After the grocery store, they're going to go to Avalon Video and rent the latest Disney movie. Some feel-good piece of la-la-land goodness that can only happen in the Disney studios. You want special effects? Try getting your wife to kiss you. You'll have to pull the whole tech team together for that one.

Julia used to get on her soapbox about the Disney epic cartoons. Did Mark ever notice how almost every movie had only one parent? And that it's the mother who's usually missing or killed off? *Cinderella, Snow White, Beauty and the Beast, Pocahontas, The Little Mermaid, Bambi,* even *The Fox and the Hound.* Mark had offered to write a letter but Julia wasn't humored.

The next aisle is frozen foods. He'll pick up one of those supposedly healthy organic TV dinners for Gracie and some Hot Pockets for himself. They've been advertising those new panini-style sandwiches— maybe he'll try one of those.

"Mark?"

He looks up. It's Livvy. She looks nervous at having run into him at the store, her own cart filled with groceries, too. Real food—vegetables and fruit, fish, yogurt. Surprisingly healthy food. Mark suddenly craves a salad and wishes he could just leave his cart somewhere and walk away.

"Livvy, hi." He's known Livvy almost as long as he's known Julia. Julia introduced them not long after she and Mark started dating. They all used to have fun together, Livvy driving Julia crazy, of course, and always spoiling Josh, but that's what sisters and aunts are for. Mark even misses her slacker husband, Tom, who is so predictably predictable that you can almost count on him. Mark misses all of this. He's tired of the awkward formality every time they meet, the careful greetings. He's so tired of all this bullshit that he steps forward without a thought.

He gives Livvy a hug.

He's surprised at the sudden rush of emotion that comes with holding her. It doesn't even bother him that he's standing in the middle of the grocery store, his eyes filling up with tears and blurring his vision. *Attention shoppers! Come see the weeping husband in Aisle Six!* God, why did they let things get so bad?

He steps back, wipes his eyes with a laugh. "Sorry, I wasn't expecting that. It's good to see you, Livvy."

Livvy's eyes are filled with tears, too, and soon they're spilling down her cheeks. She wipes them away quickly with the back of her hand. "You, too. Gracie, how are you?" She tries for a bright smile.

"Good." Gracie is polite, but cautious. Troy has a candy bar in his lap and she turns her attention back to him, telling him that he can have it later if he's extra good.

"I can't believe how much you've grown. You look just like your mother, Gracie."

At this Gracie's head snaps back up. "I have brown hair like my dad."

"Yes, you do, but your eyes and nose are all Julia. Your mom."

Livvy's voice is kind. "You even have freckles in the exact same spots she does." Livvy touches the bridge of her own nose.

Gracie looks between Livvy and Mark and then the widest smile breaks across her face. She's suddenly embarrassed. "Thank you."

Mark studies his daughter with affection and realizes that Livvy is right. Gracie has all of Julia's fine features. He gulps, wondering why they never saw it before.

"This is Troy," Gracie says, introducing her elephant to Livvy.

Livvy bends down. "He's a very nice elephant."

"He's a bird," Gracie says with that look that adults often give other adults when they're talking about children in their presence.

"Oh, right. Nice wings." Livvy has an admiring look on her face.

Gracie loves this, and beams. "How come we never see you?" she asks out of nowhere. She's warming up to Livvy now. "You can come to our house if you want. I can show you my room. It's pink."

Mark has never heard Gracie ask about Livvy. Usually by now they'd already be on their way, with no more than a handful of words having passed between them. He's composing the right response, one that doesn't hurt Livvy's feelings, when his cell phone rings.

It's Vivian. She's been decidedly cool toward him since that debacle in her apartment last month. If he walks by she conveniently turns away, speaks to him from across the safety of the large conference room table. She avoids him at the gym, pretending that she doesn't notice him or that she's too focused on her workout to say more than a brief hello. He feels a twinge of discomfort at this, but he's not sure what else he can do. He wishes they could rewind, preapartment, pregift.

"Bruno wants to pull the project," Vivian informs Mark now. Her voice is grim and there's background static.

"What? Why?" They've already invested over one thousand man hours and Mark even hired another associate to help them manage their workflow. They're on retainer and getting paid as they go, but the big payoff is at the end. Not just financially, but the potential press and media attention, something Mark has been counting on, even expecting.

"I don't know why, Mark." Vivian is irritated. "He called with the news so I convinced him to let us talk to him in person first. I'm on my way to Chicago right now."

Why did Lemelin call Vivian? Mark's the architect on this project. He glances at his watch. It's just past four. He looks desperately at Gracie who's chatting happily with her aunt. He can bring her, or maybe see if a neighbor can watch her. "I'll have to call you back, Vivian. I have my daughter with me and I need to make some calls. What time did you tell him we'd meet him?"

"Now, Mark! I basically hung up the phone and got in my car. He doesn't really want to see us. He's playing the 'I'm so busy card,' so this isn't something that can wait." Her voice is slightly accusatory.

Mark lets out a breath. Showing up with Gracie is definitely out of the question. "Okay, okay. Let me call you back. I'll be there." He snaps his phone shut.

"Is everything okay?" Livvy looks worried.

"Yeah. Just work stuff. Livvy, can you just wait here with Gracie for a moment? I need to call some people."

"Of course. We'll just keep shopping. Is that okay with you, Gracie?"

"Yes!"

Livvy looks pleased by Gracie's exuberance. "Let's go then. Come find us when you're finished, okay?"

He nods, already dialing.

It takes him almost ten minutes before he finds a parent of one of Gracie's classmates who is happy to watch her. He's feeling stressed now, and he abandons his shopping cart and goes in search of Livvy and Gracie.

He finds them in the baby food aisle, talking in low voices as they consider soft little hairbrushes and diaper ointment.

"Livvy, thank you," he says gratefully. "Come on, Gracie, we have to go. You're going over to Nicky Fischer's house for the rest of the day."

Gracie looks alarmed. "But Nicky Fischer still wets his pants!"

Mark isn't in the mood to discuss this. "Say goodbye to Aunt

Livvy," he orders. In his mind he calculates how long it will take to run home, pack up Gracie's things, change, and get on the road. Too long, but there's no way around it.

"And he hit Lisa Starkey on the head with a hula hoop," Gracie continues desperately, her eyes flicking between Mark and Livvy. "And then he didn't tell the truth when Miss Danielle asked him!"

Mark closes his eyes. Can he live with the possibility that Gracie might get hit on the head with a hula hoop by a five-year-old bully?

Yes. "Let's go, Gracie." He's losing patience now.

"I'm home all day, Mark. I'm not doing anything. I'd be happy to watch Gracie." Livvy swallows, nervous.

"Oh yes!" Gracie starts jumping up and down. "Please please please please please . . ."

Mark hesitates. This is either a good idea, or a terrible idea. He feels everything boiling down to this one minute, the future of his business, the future of his marriage.

Livvy continues, "Your home or mine, whatever works for you and Julia."

At the mention of Julia's name, Mark stiffens. Funny he didn't think to call Julia, to see if she would be willing to take a break from her girls' weekend to help him out with their business. He knows she'll probably agree to come home, but she'll be pissed. There's not enough time and it's just not worth it.

Of course, she'll be more pissed if she finds out that Mark has left Gracie with Livvy. Either way he loses. But who knows how long it will take to get in touch with Julia and then for her to show up? Mark knows what's on the line. He looks at Livvy whose full attention is on Gracie as she recounts in vivid detail other Nicky Fischer transgressions.

He never thought what happened to Josh was Livvy's fault, though it doesn't mean he wasn't angry. He was. But not at her, just at the injustice of all of it, and his place was by his wife, who couldn't even look at Livvy. There was never a good time to play peacemaker, and then he was busy trying to save his own marriage, so getting two sisters to reconcile has not exactly been on the top of his list.

Seeing Livvy now, too, Mark senses that something has changed. She's not as flighty, not as silly, a little bit more grounded. Age, he supposes, and time. It takes him thirty seconds to make up his mind.

"That would be great, Livvy."

Mark calls Mrs. Fischer to cancel as Livvy moves Gracie's car seat into her car. It's freeing not to have to run through any details because Livvy knows them, knows enough. Despite their years of being so distant, it's amazing how quickly things have fallen back into place.

He drives way above the speed limit in an effort to make up for lost time. On his cell phone, Mark finds himself arguing with Victor.

"Mark," Victor sighs. He's never liked Bruno Lemelin, never cared much for the project despite all the promise it holds. Victor is almost twenty years Mark's senior and he's been in the business a long time. Mark appreciates how steady Victor is, how levelheaded, but he also knows that Victor is planning his retirement. He doesn't care about going out in style or being profiled in magazines. But Mark does.

"Victor, big projects have big personalities—you know that. Lemelin just wants the attention."

"It's a black hole, Mark. A money pit. It's going to end up costing *us* to build this restaurant. I don't want to be stretched too thin and have everything on the line. We have other clients, other projects. What about Ted Morrow at Bluestem? Have you had a chance to get together with him yet?"

Mark hasn't. They've been playing telephone tag but Mark's energy is on Lemelin. "Let me just figure out what's going on with Lemelin first," he says. "Vivian's already on her way."

"Vivian?" Victor clearly doesn't approve. He's a bit of a purist in his own way, seeing interior decorators as peripheral to the architectural and engineering team.

"She helped us get this deal," Mark reminds him. He knows he sounds defensive but he doesn't want Victor knocking her. "Plus Lemelin likes her."

"I bet."

"Come on, Victor. I'll call you when we're done. Unless you want to jump in your car and come join us?"

Victor doesn't take the bait. "This is your project, Mark. If you want me there, I'll be there, but otherwise I'm fine to stay in the office and draw pictures of buildings that actually have a chance of going up."

Yeah, having Victor there will *really* improve their chances. "I'll call you later."

Julia is relaxing on the chaise lounge in the hotel suite when Hannah emerges tentatively from the bathroom wearing a simple black evening gown, a diamond pendant around her neck. Diamond studs twinkle in her ears. Her long hair is straight and sleek.

Julia puts down the hotel magazine and smiles at her friend. "You look beautiful, Hannah."

Julia's own outfit is a simple glittery stretch top and a long skirt, also in black. She hasn't worn it in years but when she took it out of the closet and tried it on, she was startled at the woman who looked back at her in the mirror, a Julia she didn't quite recognize even though she'd worn the outfit hundreds of times. She gazed at herself for what seemed like forever, touching her hair and running her hands along her hips, turning until the sunlight caught the silver sparkles on her top and made them dance. She had expected her face to look drawn and haunted but instead she saw a quiet elegance, a gentle maturing revealed only by a few fine lines around her eyes. And then she was smiling despite herself, filled with anticipation for this weekend, for this gift of a getaway, for the chance to be a new Julia of old.

Hannah turns to study herself in the mirror, somewhat forlorn, and picks at some invisible lint on her dress. "Maybe I should try to find another time to talk to him. He'll be so busy afterward, and he's not expecting me . . ."

"Hannah, he's still your husband." Julia gets up to get her evening bag. "And you tried several more times to call him this week."

"I know." Hannah looks miserable.

For a second Julia is tempted to give in, to let Hannah pass this opportunity by in exchange for some temporary relief. But that's all it is. Temporary. And Julia knows it will only be a matter of days before it comes back. She wants Hannah to do this, for herself and for her future. She wants Hannah to step fully into her own life, to be armed with everything she needs to make the right decisions for herself. So she says nothing, just gathers her wrap and waits patiently by the door.

Hannah follows reluctantly. "Do you mind if we walk to Symphony Center instead of taking a cab? It'll take us about twenty minutes. I think the fresh air will do me good." She's stalling, but Julia doesn't mind. They'll eventually get there, and that's what's important.

"Of course." Julia slips her arm through Hannah's and gives it a squeeze of support. For a second her thoughts flash to Livvy, to the many times Julia has done this same thing for her. Standing by her side when Livvy admitted to her parents that she tore up her report card, stole a few dollars from their father's wallet, played hooky from school. "Borrowed" the car without permission (five times), got drunk at prom. When Livvy wanted to go on the pill, drop out of community college, marry Tom. Whenever Livvy needed someone to lean on, Julia was there. Even when she didn't approve, Julia was there. Now Julia finds herself wondering about her sister, wondering if she's okay, all the way back in Avalon.

"Julia? Is everything all right?" Hannah studies her, a hopeful look on her face. Julia knows this look well, and smiles. Just like she's done for Livvy, she's going to do the same for Hannah—as hard as she knows it is, she's not going to let her off the hook.

"Yes," she says, and opens the door. "Come on—let's go."

"I'm just not sure about the direction anymore," Lemelin says. He's adopted a laissez-faire attitude toward them now, his original chumminess gone. "I want it to be strikingly original. Something like a Bentel & Bentel property."

Inwardly Mark groans. This has been going on awhile, this back and forth that threatens to continue indefinitely. Victor is probably home by now, having dinner with his wife or watching a little TV.

Flipping through a magazine at his leisure. Victor is relaxing in his comfortable home while Mark is sitting on plastic chairs in this shell of a building, a vicious Chicago wind whipping through the I beams and concrete.

Maybe he shouldn't have been so easily seduced. He gets now that Victor wasn't just talking about losing money on this project, but that if things really go south, it could tank Mark's career or at least be one of the things he'll be known for. He'll be the architect that Lemelin tossed aside, deemed unworthy.

"Beware," Victor had once warned him. "Architects have sold their souls for the sexy projects and never lived long enough to get over it. Stick with the bread-and-butter. There are good ones there, Mark. Ones that you can feel good about."

But Mark doesn't want to just feel good—he's no longer interested in playing it safe. If anything he is sick of maintaining the status quo. He wants things to change. No, he's desperate for a change—at work, at home, and everywhere in between. How does the old saying go? *Anything worth having doesn't come easy.* Mark just has to suck it up, do what has to be done. Lemelin's new restaurant is a high-profile project and Bruno Lemelin a high-profile client. There's not a lot of room for error.

Meanwhile Vivian is coolly talking about Lemelin's existing properties, careful to specifically point out the design elements and practical usable space that received so much attention and praise. This seems to mollify Lemelin—he likes Vivian's attention to his past successes. Mark notices Lemelin sizing her up again and feels a flare of indignation. This guy is scummy, no question. But Vivian is also too perceptive a woman not to notice, so she just cocks an eyebrow right back at him in return, giving Lemelin the once-over as well. Then they both chuckle over this, Lemelin's standoffishness fading, buddies once again.

Lemelin calls to his assistant.

"Go get a bottle of champagne for Miss Vivian," he orders. "A 1983 Millésimé."

Vivian gives Lemelin a demure smile. "Only if we're celebrating."

She taps her pen rhythmically on the makeshift table. Business first, her energy seems to radiate.

Lemelin won't commit. "I'll need a new design."

"We can do that." Vivian shoots Mark a decidedly pointed look, telling him that if he was planning on opening his mouth to say something—*anything*—now would be a good time. "But we would still like to include some of the original design. It's clean and innovative, incorporating noble materials against plain. The use of natural lighting during the day emphasizes all the textures and colors of the interior, and then the captured light from the solar panels will be redirected into the LED light strings draped throughout the restaurant . . ."

"Making this one of the most distinguishable, eco-friendly restaurants using renewable materials today." Mark sits up tall and feels an absurd pleasure in noting that he has a couple inches over Lemelin. "But what will make this restaurant stand out above all others is how we're integrating the surroundings of the city and bringing it into the space."

They are sitting in prime real estate in the heart of Chicago's cultural district, literally a stone's throw away from world-class museums and the Chicago Symphony Orchestra. The restaurant, which Lemelin is calling "227" after the number of square miles of land that make up Chicago, would reflect the tastes and neighborhoods of Chicago with a 2-2-7 degustation menu (2 appetizers, 2 entrees, 7 side dishes) served family-style. Mark has no doubt that the food will live up to Lemelin's reputation.

Mark pulls out the sketches and a rough mock-up of the plans they'd done in AutoCAD. He has definitely pushed himself with the design for 227, and it's good. No, great. He knows he can transform this space into something amazing. Lemelin listens to him with a look of bored skepticism, having heard the spiel before. When Mark finally says everything that needs to be said, Lemelin just shrugs.

"I don't really have a problem with the design itself," he tells them. "Though I have to tell you that I don't really give a shit about all that eco crap. I just feel that the artistry is missing. Where is the passion? I don't see it." He waves his hand toward the plans. "I want a firm that's going to give me passion. You understand?"

For once Vivian is caught off guard. "I can assure you, Bruno . . ."

"I don't want assurances. I have lawyers—they give me assurances. The firm that works with me has to have passion. Chicago isn't New York, but it holds its own promise of the American Dream. This town has had its fair share of fires—I want to bring that into 227. Something hot. Alive. Dangerous. And yet full of promise."

What the hell? A few weeks ago Lemelin was talking about an eclectic mix of colors, a bright mosaic. He wanted to use every color of the rainbow in a way that was fun and uplifting, natural, not tacky. Every element they chose to use, inside and out, was selected on that premise. While tasteful, they most certainly are not hot. That's not just a new design, that's a completely different take, a completely different project.

"I can look at the color palette . . ." Vivian glances at Mark, who doesn't know what to say.

"Do whatever you need to do. If you want this project, you're going to have to fight for it. Three weeks." Lemelin stands up and shakes their hands, then strides off toward his car without a backward glance.

"Damn." Vivian starts jamming things into her briefcase. "I should have taken that champagne while I had the chance."

Mark watches Vivian gather their things. She looks tired, her playful demeanor replaced by one of surrender, defeat.

Mark feels guilty. Vivian has done everything she can to help get this deal and hold it together. He doesn't want to give her too much credit and yet at the same time, she deserves it. "Sorry about all this, Vivian."

"What are you apologizing for?" Vivian rolls up the plans. "He's playing us. Always has. He just wants to see what we can come up with, and then he'll take our ideas to a bigger player with a bigger name."

With a sinking feeling, Mark knows she's probably right. "Well, I'm not giving up yet," he says. "We've gotten this far, we may as well go all the way." Three more weeks of hell. He can do it.

Vivian looks at him, suspicious.

"Come on," he says, nodding toward the street. It's still early. Julia is off with her friends and Gracie is in good hands with Livvy. "I'll buy you a drink." He owes her that at least.

They walk out of the building and are immediately greeted by a strong wind. The papers threaten to fly off but Mark grabs a firm hold of everything, including Vivian, and they battle their way to the parking garage.

Is that Mark? Julia can't be sure, but it looks like him, right across the street. He's with a woman and they're huddled together, braving a Chicago wind that has come up out of nowhere. Julia watches the man who looks like her husband turn the corner and disappear from view.

Should she run after him? What would she say? She's seeing things. It couldn't be Mark. Mark is in Avalon, at home with Gracie. He doesn't even know she's here. And why would he be here with another woman? It's dusk, too dark to really say for sure, but Julia knows his walk, knows his shadow. Doesn't she?

Hannah is next to her, her pashmina wrapped tightly around her. "I think I'm going to go back to the hotel," she says at that moment, turning on her heel.

"What? No, we're already here, Hannah." Julia gets a firm grip on Hannah's arm. "We'll sit through the performance and then if you don't want to see him, we'll go. Okay?"

Hannah nods. "I need chocolate," she says weakly.

"We'll order chocolate back at the hotel," Julia promises. She glances back to the empty corner where she thought she saw her husband. She shakes her head—it must have been an illusion. "We'll order up one of those chocolate fountains, just for you." She turns back to Hannah and gives her a distracted pat on the arm. "Now let's go inside."

Inside the lobby of Symphony Center, Julia is caught off guard by the throng of people. It's overwhelming at first, the bodies bumping into one another, a stray hand on her shoulder or waist, gently moving her in or out of place as people navigate their way around.

Julia finds herself relaxing, enjoying the anonymity, the busy cacophony that feels so appropriate, so carefree. Here, everyone is a stranger but oddly familiar. She glides along, content to follow Hannah through the wave of people.

A few men and women greet Hannah, give her hugs and kisses on the cheek, exchange pleasantries. Julia does catch a few concerned glances but Hannah doesn't seem to notice. It's a look of sympathy or, possibly, pity. It suddenly occurs to Julia that this is how people must have looked at her, too, not because of a wayward husband, but because of a lost son.

They find their seats. As their bodies sink luxuriously into the plush crimson cushions, Julia turns to focus on the stage in front of her. As the auditorium darkens, she feels a tremor of excitement, a thrill rushing through her body as the orchestra warms up. She knows they are here so that Hannah can see Philippe, but somehow that seems more of a means to an end. Perhaps the real reason they are here is so that Julia can have this moment, this perfect moment where she can witness 109 people of different ages, backgrounds, and ethnicities, each with their own stories and tragedies and moments of joy, play together in perfect harmony.

She sees him before he even steps foot on the stage. She pictures him slipping on his jacket, the black coat of his tuxedo. He nods and laughs, sharing a joke or two with the other musicians, but his mind will be on the music. People will be warming up everywhere, in the dressing rooms, in the hallways, but Philippe will play and walk, like a fiddler at a restaurant, moving between tables. He'll climb the stairs to the stage this way, playing as he goes, warming up his fingers, his neck. Then he'll stop, roll his shoulders, wait for his cue, then tuck his violin under his arm and walk out on stage, head held high.

Hannah's eyes skim over the musicians she knows. It's a comfort that with the exception of a handful of faces, she recognizes everyone. Perhaps things haven't changed as much as she had feared. She's been away from this life a long time but she hasn't forgotten the highs and lows of being a performing artist with a major symphony or orchestra. Madeline was right—she and Philippe are not like other couples. This is their home, this is their family.

When she sees the familiar mop of dark hair—*he cut it! When did he cut it?*—Hannah holds her breath. Can he see her, sense her in this crowd of two thousand people? It's a full house. Does he know she's there?

The box seats in section F give them a clear view of the violin section. He's so close that she can see his cowlick, the way his dark hair flips up at the peak of his forehead. Philippe has his eyes lowered, the corners of his mouth turned down in a slight frown. Hannah feels a flood of love for her husband. When the conductor raises his baton, Hannah is immediately swept away by the music and filled with hope.

CHAPTER 16

❀

The bar is right around the corner from Symphony Center. It's a restaurant, actually, and they have to fight their way upstream against last-minute stragglers on their way to catch a performance.

"You have season tickets, don't you?" Mark remembers.

Vivian nods. "I'm a bit of a buff but I hate going alone." She doesn't bring up what happened at her apartment. "I donated the tickets back for the rest of the season. I need to keep my focus on the Lemelin project anyway."

"Whoa. Philanthropic *and* a strong work ethic. I'm impressed."

"You should be," she says. "There's a lot about me you don't know."

They sit in the lounge and order drinks—passion fruit margarita for Vivian, vodka martini for Mark.

"That's some drink," he says when they bring out her margarita. It's like an art deco margarita, colorful and elaborate.

"Here, have a sip," she offers. She holds it out, the rim of salt perfect and untouched.

"No, no." Mark holds up his martini. "I'm set."

"Suit yourself." Vivian takes a sip then settles back in her chair. She takes a look around with a sigh of disgust. "God, what a scene. That's one thing I don't miss."

What scene? Mark looks around but doesn't see anybody making a scene. "What do you mean?"

"The whole dating scene. The first date, the blind date. The bad date. Ugh." She shudders and holds up her drink. "This is why I throw myself into my work." She seems to be gesturing to the crowd lined up at the bar but she's pointing her drink directly at Mark.

"So dating's not your scene," Mark recaps. "Is that what you're saying?" They both laugh.

"You got it," she says. She pulls out a thin wedge of pineapple from her drink.

"So what, then? You're just going to work forever, forget about romance, marriage?"

"Marriage." The top of her nose wrinkles. "I'm a realist, Mark. I know that romance and marriage don't last. I mean, I'm sure there are some exceptions, but I wasn't one of them." She looks away, takes a long draw on her margarita.

"You were married?" Mark asks. He's surprised. Vivian comes across as so fiercely independent, it's hard to see her as part of a couple. He had checked her personnel file one night and saw that she's thirty-one, thirteen years younger than he is.

"Twice. First time I was in college—I left with only one year to go. My boyfriend was going to medical school in Texas and gave me an ultimatum. We got married, moved to Houston. I worked two jobs to pay off his school loans. He left me four years later when he graduated.

"The second time I thought I did better. I went for the ambitious guy, the guy who didn't need me to wait tables so he could get a degree. He paid for me to finish school, bought me nice things, let me decorate the house. Money was no object." She gives a biting laugh.

"I made the most of that one. But I was good, you know? I oversaw the renovation for our house, for the properties belonging to some of his friends, some of his clients. He was in real estate, subprime mortgages, that sort of thing. We had a shitload of money."

"We don't have to talk about it," he tells her. He's uncomfortable seeing Vivian in this light, doesn't want too many details in case it makes a mess of things.

She looks up at him, shrugs. "I'm over it," she says indifferently, but Mark notices that she has a white knuckle grip on the stem of her margarita glass. "The economy went bust, his company went bust, my marriage went bust. Fortunately I had a feeling something was going to happen, so I'd been putting money aside for a rainy day. Then I ran out. Who knew it would be such a fucking downpour?" She finishes her drink.

"Come on, Vivian," he says, trying to cheer her up. "You've got so much going for you. You could have any guy."

She stares at him in disbelief. "Oh my God. You're giving me the break-up speech."

Mark is startled. "What? No, I'm not."

Vivian bursts out laughing. "The hell you're not! You're giving me the break-up speech *and there's nothing to break up*. We're not even dating!" She's laughing hysterically now, bona fide tears rolling out of her eyes. She motions to the waitress for another drink. "I know I'm in trouble when guys are giving me the break-up speech and we haven't even slept together. Jesus!" She erupts in laughter again.

"Vivian, I was not giving you the break-up speech, I was being serious . . ."

"Serious? Uh-oh. Are you going to give me the it's-not-you-it's-me speech next?" She cocks an eyebrow. "Because I'm a really great girl!" She says this sarcastically.

"You are a really great girl, Vivian," Mark says. "I'm sorry, I didn't mean to upset you . . ."

"For once, please stop being the nice guy, Mark!" Vivian grabs a cocktail napkin. She dabs her eyes, quickly composing herself. Her second margarita arrives and she doesn't look at the waitress, just accepts the drink and takes a sip, glaring at Mark. "You're the world's most perfect martyr," she snaps. "It's never your fault, no one can ever blame you for anything because you've had a personal tragedy. We've all had personal tragedies, Mark. You're not the only one."

Mark feels himself tighten inside. "I have never used my personal life as an excuse for my professional one," he says, clenching his teeth.

"You don't have to! Everyone else does it for you. Poor Mark, he just needs some time. Poor Mark, his wife won't talk to him."

"You don't know anything about Julia. You don't even know her." He debates getting up and walking out. Or firing her.

Vivian looks disgusted. "Oh please. It's a small office, Mark. You think people don't talk? And look, here you go, defending her again. There goes Mark, defending his wife! Isn't he great? He can't hold on to a client, he's blown his one chance at success, but what a guy!" She finishes her drink and picks up her purse. "What's it going to take for you to make a stand, take a chance? Bruno thinks you're weak, that's why he doesn't want to give you the project." She stands up, eyes flashing, taunting him. Challenging him. *"Be a man, Mark."*

The top button of her blouse has come undone. Mark can see the lace from her bra, the creamy curve of her breast. Vivian is right. He's been acting like a guy without balls, scared to make the wrong move, always wanting to keep the peace, keep everybody happy.

He watches Vivian sway, trying to keep her balance, all 5'9" of her plus a couple of extra inches for those sexy heels. She's beautiful even if she is a little tipsy.

Mark throws a few bills down on the table and stands up, getting a firm grip on Vivian's elbow. "I know what you need," he says. His voice is low.

She looks up at him, her lids heavy, and she leans into the curve of his body. She's the right height for a guy like Mark—physically he can tell they're a good fit. Even Julia is a bit too tall, almost the same height as him, a good match but not like this.

"What do I need?" Vivian whispers. Her words are almost slurring as her lips part expectantly. "Tell me."

Mark guides them out of the bar, aware that Vivian's hand is trailing suggestively down his arm. They approach the hostess stand at the entrance. "You need some dinner. Table for two, please."

"Philippe?" Hannah is backstage now, the concert having been over for half an hour. It had been absolutely brilliant, a selection of Beethoven's masterpieces including his Fidelio Overture, Opus 72, one of her favorite pieces of all time. The music left her on a high, and even Julia was glowing, ecstatic.

Julia surprised them both by deciding to brave the post-performance reception before returning to the hotel. Hannah is chatty and animated as she fights her way through the wave of familiar faces, all anxious to greet her, to find out how she's been. She knows people are happy to see her and while she does want to catch up, they're only serving to delay her reunion with her husband. As she approaches him, she sees why.

It's the violist, Janet Vandesteeg. She was a year behind Hannah at Juilliard. She teaches orchestral repertoire for viola at Northwestern, and it was Hannah who actually introduced her to Philippe when he first joined CSO. Given the way Janet's arms are wrapped around her husband, that was clearly a mistake.

Janet and Philippe are kissing. It's not a polite kiss or a social kiss, nor is it the airy double-cheek kiss that Philippe is so fond of. It's a romantic, passionate, intimate kiss. A whole-body kiss that is so entirely inappropriate and off-putting and yet Hannah can't turn away. It takes her a moment before she finds her voice, first a whisper and then louder. "Philippe!"

It's Janet who actually hears her. Their kiss interrupted, Janet is quick to disentangle herself and step away. The other musicians are embarrassed and mumble excuses or just leave. In a matter of seconds, it seems, the room has cleared. Philippe scowls as he crosses the room to where Hannah stands.

Hannah is amazed that Janet has the gall to stay, and at the same time finds herself unable to stop staring at her. Janet used to be as flat chested as Hannah, who struggles to fill a B-cup. But now Janet is all curvy and voluptuous with breasts that threaten to spill out of her dress. She's also done something to her hair—it's now glossy with a slight curl, like something out of a Pantene commercial. Or maybe it's more of a Lauren Bacall thing with that smoky look, full of allure and mystery. Hannah decides that she officially hates her.

"Hannah!" Philippe's voice is low but seems to fill the room. "What are you doing here?" Philippe blocks her view of Janet and Hannah actually has to crane her neck in order to see her again. Janet is pretending to look at something on the ceiling.

"I wanted to talk," Hannah says. She looks at her husband, tries to summon anger. He's cheating on her! With Janet! She knew he wasn't being faithful (it wasn't like she thought it was the maid who had answered the phone that day) and yet here she is, she's standing here in front of him—in front of them—and trying to have a conversation.

Wake up, Hannah!

Ironically it's Philippe who looks put out. "Hannah, now is not the time. I just finished a performance, for God's sake." His voice is curt. "Go home. I'll call you tomorrow." His hand is on her elbow as he steers Hannah toward the door.

"Go home where?" she asks. "The apartment, you mean?"

By the way Janet whips her head in their direction and Philippe is glowering, that would be a no.

"Oh," Hannah drawls. "You mean back to *Avalon*."

"Hannah . . ."

"Don't *Hannah* me, Philippe." She glares at him and he takes a step back, uncertain of the woman in front of him. "You don't get to do that anymore. I don't know why I even let you do that to me before." She tries to laugh but it comes out a strangled cry. "I mean, when you told me to trust you, I trusted you. When you told me things would be fine, I nodded my head. When you told me you were staying in the city because the commute was too hard—guess what? *I believed you.* Because you're my husband and because you said you loved me. And I loved you. But not anymore." Hannah feels a surge of power, of confidence. Philippe no longer looks menacing. Instead he looks pathetic.

He tries to take her arm but she shakes herself free from his grasp. "You should come over for dinner sometime," she calls to Janet. "I make a mean beef bourguignon!" She turns to Philippe. "I do it with a watercress and pear salad. Delicious."

Philippe sighs. Hannah sees the throb of his jugular and wishes she could do some kung fu, karate-chop move that would take him out. But she doesn't know kung fu. She doesn't know any sport really.

"Just go, Hannah." Philippe holds the door open, waiting for her to leave.

Instead Hannah walks over to Janet before Philippe can stop her. "I can't believe you're sleeping with him," she says. "You know he cheats on his wife, right?"

Janet avoids her and looks to Philippe instead. "Philippe . . ." she intones, her lilting voice carrying a hint of warning. When did Janet get a lilting voice?

Philippe quickly intercepts the two women. "Hannah, stop it." He puts his hand protectively on Janet's arm.

Hannah stares at him. Why does Hannah have to stop anything? She hasn't done anything wrong. She's the one who has something to say, who is in the right here. She's the jilted wife.

But as she looks at her husband and his lover in the back rooms of Symphony Center, Hannah feels her bravado slip away. She has every right to be there and yet it's clear who doesn't belong.

Hannah straightens up, praying that she won't cry, at least until she's out of the building. That she leaves with dignity. She doesn't say anything when she hears Philippe calling to her, lamely saying that he'll call her tomorrow. She says nothing at all, but holds her head high and walks out of the room.

"No, that is *not* a good idea." Julia is adamant about this point. They're back at the hotel, having raided the minibar. Jack Daniel's for Julia, a wine cooler for Hannah. "You cannot poison your husband."

She's pretty sure Hannah is just upset, but she also saw a flash of possibility, and it makes her nervous.

"*Ex*-husband," Hannah corrects with a vehemence. She's paging through *Joy of Cooking* in search of the perfect recipe. Julia wasn't surprised to see it in Hannah's bag, knowing that she carried the book with her everywhere so she could skim recipes while standing in line or waiting for the light to change. "Here, look! Philippe loves quail. Something about small defenseless game birds. I can do a Spicy Maple-Roasted Quail. He won't know what hit him." The look in Hannah's eyes is wild but gleeful.

"Stop!" Julia covers the page with her hand, forcing Hannah to look at her. "You're not thinking straight, Hannah."

"Of course I'm not thinking straight! I just walked in on my husband kissing another woman. In public!" Hannah slams the book shut, her eyes brimming with angry tears. "All my life, I've been the good girl. I studied hard, I practiced all the time, I ate my vegetables. I got a good night's sleep. I never snuck out, never partied, never disobeyed my parents."

Julia looks at her friend. "There's nothing wrong with doing the right thing, Hannah."

"But what's the point? I worked hard to become the best cellist I could be, and then I got hurt. I saved myself for marriage, and then my husband cheated on me. I tried to keep my body in good shape, and then Janet Vandesteeg goes out and buys new breasts!" Hannah takes a swig of her wine cooler then looks at the small bottle in disgust. "Look at me! I can't even get properly drunk! What am I, in high school?" She throws it in the trash and marches over to the minibar. She rummages around until she holds up a bottle of Smirnoff vodka. She unscrews the top and takes a sniff, then makes a face, her resolve faltering. "Ugh. I can't do it. This stuff is nasty."

Julia stretches out on the bed, gazes up at the ceiling. What would she do if Mark cheated on her? The thought is ludicrous—Mark isn't the kind of person who would do that sort of thing. At least, he used to not be. Julia isn't sure anymore, tries to remember the last time they slept together. It was a long, long time ago. She had asked him about it once and he said he didn't mind, that he understood, but did he really? Besides, she's the one thinking about moving on, about putting the past behind them, including their marriage. So why does it matter if Mark has slept with someone? Julia winces, uneasy, because even as she contemplates a life without him, she feels hollow at the thought of him with someone else.

Hannah is rifling through the mini fridge, testing each bottle of alcohol with no luck. Despite her agitation Hannah still looks elegant and beautiful, and Julia feels a wave of tenderness for the young woman. "Hannah," she says. "What are you doing?"

"Trying to find something that isn't completely revolting so I can get myself into a drunken stupor." She holds up a bottle of whiskey and gives it a taste. "Ew."

"Who says you're supposed to end up in a drunken stupor?" Julia asks.

Hannah screws the cap back on the whiskey, dejected. "It just seems appropriate under the circumstances."

Julia rolls to her side. "Says who?" she wants to know. "Everyone's different. That's what they used to tell me in the beginning, that everyone grieves differently, but if you aren't going through the steps in the right order, and in the right amount of time, people start to think something's wrong with you. Everyone's got their own definition of what they think is appropriate under the circumstances. Forget them. You just need to do what's appropriate for you."

"I'm not like you, Julia." Hannah puts her hands over her face.

Julia stares at her. There it is again, another faint echo of Livvy. Livvy was always comparing them, because their parents were always comparing them. It used to irritate Julia to no end, because she didn't understand why Livvy didn't just ignore their parents and get over it. But now, to hear a woman as accomplished as Hannah compare herself to Julia—Julia who passed out in Madeline's house, Julia who is a bundle of raw emotions and clearly not quite ready to be out in the real world—she's beginning to wonder if she's been too hard on Livvy growing up. Or even now.

Hannah is crying, distraught at her own apparent failures as a person. Julia wishes they could rewind to the beginning, to a time pre-Philippe, pre–musical prodigy even, and start over. *Be yourself,* she'd tell the young Hannah, just like she told the young Livvy. But maybe even then it wouldn't make a difference. Even with our environment shaping us, we are born as we are. Julia sees this more and more with Gracie, who embodies her name. Grace. Julia never has to say, *Be yourself,* because Gracie always is.

"Hannah," Julia says gently. "My sister Livvy spent a lot of her childhood trying to do what she thought other people wanted her to do." Julia remembers Livvy polling her friends to see what kind of birthday party *they* thought she should have. "She tried very hard to be appropriate. It didn't work out so well."

"Why not?"

"Because Livvy is Livvy." Julia pushes a wisp of hair away from Hannah's damp face. "She came into her own her junior year when she made the varsity cheerleading team. Stopped apologizing for who she was, stopped asking permission. But she was still easily affected by what other people thought of her. Probably still is."

"Livvy is lucky though." Hannah looks up.

Julia smiles. "Really? How so?"

"Because she has you."

Julia opens her mouth to respond but doesn't know what to say.

"I'm not close to my brother, Albert. I never was—it's very hard to talk to him. He's a very angry person, especially toward my dad. The whole Chinese push-your-kids-to-excel thing didn't really work on him."

"Why? What happened?"

"Nothing happened. He did what my dad told him to do—got into Harvard undergrad, then Yale for medical school. He's the head of pediatric surgery over at Johns Hopkins. He married Lynn, who's an endocrinologist. They have two kids who are going through the exact same workup we did growing up. We see each other once a year but it's always pretty painful." Hannah makes a face. She sweeps the small alcohol bottles into the wastebasket, a look of satisfaction on her face when she hears them clink again each other.

Julia tosses her own bottle into the trash can, too. "Livvy and I don't talk anymore. We haven't in years."

"Because of what happened to your son?"

Julia nods.

"But you were close! Albert and I never even had that."

Julia picks at a loose thread on the bedcover. "It's complicated, Hannah."

Hannah doesn't disagree. "I bet she misses you, though. I would."

Julia drops her shoulders and gives a sigh. "Death is a big thing," she says simply. "It changes a lot of things."

Hannah nods, but she seems sad at the thought, and Julia doesn't want her to feel bad about something that no one can really do anything about. "Hannah, it is what it is. It's like you and Albert now, I guess."

"Oh God, I hope for your sake it's not. *Bleah*." She makes a face so comical that both women break out in grins.

"Whatever the case, you need to step back into your own skin, Hannah. Remember who you are and just take it all one step at a time."

"One step at a time?"

"It's an annoying truth. Nobody knows that better than me." Julia nods to the bottles in the trash can. "Anyway, you have too much class for that. You're not really a minibar kind of gal, Hannah. You used to play for the New York Philharmonic, *don't forget that*. Let those other gals drink themselves silly. You should be ordering room service instead."

Hannah brightens, considering this. "Room service. I'm pretty sure they have caviar. I can definitely see myself drowning my sorrows in some beluga. I haven't saved my money for nothing."

"Exactly." Julia grins.

Hannah walks over to the desk and looks through a large leather binder imprinted with the hotel's logo. "Oh," she exclaims. "They have a bath sommelier!"

Julia's never heard of this. "What's a bath sommelier?"

"Someone who actually prepares a bath for you in your room.

Listen: *Sink into your tub as aromatic fragrances surround you, tantalizing your senses, bringing you to a renewed state of relaxation . . .*" She looks up at Julia. "I could use a renewed state of relaxation right about now."

"Then I think you've found your vice. Let's order room service and I'll watch a movie while your bath sommelier gets you set up."

"A movie?" Hannah asks, looking worried. "Are you sure? We could probably get you a massage or a pedicure . . ."

Julia shakes her head, her hand already on the remote. Julia wouldn't mind a massage or pedicure, but she hasn't seen a movie in years. Not in a movie theater, not on TV, not anywhere. It's a secret, guilty pleasure; one she wouldn't—couldn't—let herself have back home. She'll choose a comedy, something funny, because she's still not ready for any serious drama—she's had enough of that. And if she's not tired after one movie, she'll watch another one. "Honestly? I can't think of anything more perfect."

A. A. Gilliland, 58
Bike Me! Shop Owner

"Hey, Double A! Are you finally going to join us or what?" There are three guys on bikes waiting for him in the parking lot, revving their engines, chrome pipes crackling.

A.A. shakes his head like he does every Saturday when he closes shop. "Nah, you go on." They heckle him a bit, poking fun until they get bored. Then they give him a farewell nod and roar out of the parking lot, earning a flood of disapproving stares from pedestrians walking around the tiny Avalon strip mall.

It's true that the guys do look like thugs with bandannas wrapped around their heads, a couple of tats, and the requisite black leather outlaw gear, but A.A. knows better. One guy, Bill, is an accountant. Another owns a pool-cleaning business. Another is a trust fund baby who got turned on to bikes by his ex-wife, a former exotic dancer. These guys can't tell a camshaft from a brake pad, but who is A.A. to judge? There aren't a lot of die-hard bikers in Avalon, so A.A.'s grateful for the guys going through a midlife crisis—it keeps his business afloat. More power to 'em.

A.A.'s best friend is Isaac, who goes by the nickname Iz. Iz built his own custom chopper with a shovelhead engine, and it's a work of art. Iz is one of those genius types, a mathematician and overall cool guy, the only fly in the ointment being that Iz still lives with his eighty-eight-year-old mother. Iz is a purist and can't stand the guys that ride the imported sports bikes.

"They do those damn stunts on the interstate," Iz complains. "They actually pop wheelies! And then they wave and expect me to wave back. It's embarrassing."

A.A. is more sympathetic. "Aw, come on. A lot of us started out riding metrics. Not everyone can afford a Harley."

"It's not just that. It's the kids on these bikes these days. They think they know everything. But they don't respect the road, and they don't respect the bike." Iz shakes his head in disgust, clearly put out. A.A. realizes with a chuckle that they're right up there with the old guys in the Caddys and the ladies in the boat-size Buicks, complaining about all the young whippersnappers and their bad manners.

At fifty-eight, A.A.'s straw-colored hair has turned an early gray. He keeps it tied back in a ponytail, which keeps it out of his face and basically makes his life a heck of a lot easier. He's been letting his mustache and beard grow out and doesn't mind that he looks bushy and a bit unkempt. He likes his "uniform": T-shirts and his black leather jacket studded with all his Harley badges and pins. He's a big guy, almost 6'2", broad-shouldered, a Scot on steroids. He's not on steroids, of course, he just has good genes, but he hears the guys whispering. He couldn't care less. He was raised by his grandmother from the age of five; she taught A.A. a thing or two, sometimes the hard way.

"Aye, you can't worry about what other people think," she'd declare, smacking her wooden spoon on the counter of the small house they shared. "They're all idiots, and if you spend your life trying to get into somebody else's head then you're an idiot, too." Then she'd tug on his ear until he'd yell, just to make sure he got the point.

So even though he looks like a walking cliché, A.A. is a man comfortable in his own skin. Let people say what they will.

It's six o'clock, and A.A. is ready to go home. He's not much for drinking or staying up late in bars, and he's lived on his own long enough to have developed some rituals he doesn't like interrupted. For example, on Sunday nights he does the books for the shop, which gives him a clear picture of what he needs to make in the upcoming week.

On Monday nights he does his laundry. He irons his pants and boxer shorts. Don't ask him why, but there's something about neatly pressed pants that he loves.

On Tuesdays he does his grocery shopping for the week.

Wednesday nights he does takeout and watches documentaries on PBS. He loves biographies and anything that has to do with war veterans. Once a month he'll rent a movie and watch that instead.

Thursday evenings are reserved for any repairs on his house or the two rental properties he owns on Madison and LeBell.

On Fridays he'll hang out with Iz, have dinner and maybe shoot some pool. He'll head home and get himself a good night's sleep because the next morning, rain or shine, he likes to ride.

There's one more thing A.A. does without exception. He does it every Saturday evening, starting at 7:00 P.M., and he loves it almost as much as he loves his bikes.

He bakes.

He knows the recipe for Granny's shortbread by heart (the key being real butter and brown—not white—sugar), and can turn out Eccles cakes, empire biscuits, scones, and Struan Bread without a thought. He's not intimidated by complicated recipes and doesn't mind investing the time to learn new techniques.

But today A.A. is experimenting, in the mood for something different. He got a bag of Amish Friendship Bread starter from his dentist and has already modified the recipe to include a symphony of dried fruit and nuts. Lately he's been trying to come up with heart-healthy recipes, so he's reduced the amount of oil and is using applesauce instead. He's going to use egg substitute in lieu of whole eggs and will skip the pudding mix altogether, trying a bit of ricotta and yogurt cheese instead.

He divvies up the starter per the instructions, figuring he'll give a bag to Iz, Bill, and the pool-cleaning guy. The divorced guy still can't cook for himself and A.A. doesn't want him tossing this in the trash.

He dusts two loaf pans with cinnamon, a touch of vanilla sugar, a pinch of nutmeg. He turns on the radio and whistles to "Smoke on the Water" by Deep Purple. If he had time for another hobby, he would learn the guitar. Maybe next year.

A.A. pours the batter into the pans, careful to scrape out every last bit with a rubber spatula. If it turns out okay, he'll take a loaf to the senior recreation center tomorrow during his lunch break. He goes there every week and they've come to expect a visit from him and some home-baked goods, as well. He'll have a cup of coffee and ask people about their week, help with any heavy lifting or whatever else might need to be done. If he has time he'll jump in for a quick game of cards or backgammon, maybe hold the yarn for Mrs. Pickering's knitting. And of course he can't leave without seeing the latest round of grandchildren pictures tucked in wallets and hanging from key chains.

He does the dishes while the bread bakes, his small kitchen quickly filling with the sweet smell of dried apricots and toasted pecans. The bread still has another thirty minutes to go before it's ready, so A.A. cranks up the music then settles into Granny's old wooden rocking chair with the latest issue of *Biker* magazine.

CHAPTER 17

"Mama!" Gracie launches out of Mark's arms and into Julia's the minute she walks through the door. It's Sunday evening and Gracie is already in pj's, her hair damp from her bath. "I missed you!"

"I missed you, too." Julia picks up Gracie, balancing her on her hip for a moment. She is surprised at how much she missed her girl. When did Gracie get so heavy?

Mark stands in the hallway, keeping his distance. Julia feels the guilt rushing back and then tells herself to stop. She's tired of the guilt.

"Hey," she says. She runs her hand through Gracie's hair, delighted when Gracie lets out a giggle. She smiles.

"Hey." Mark finally steps forward, gives her a careful peck on the cheek. An unexpected thrill runs through her at the touch of his lips, and she blushes. Mark doesn't notice but reaches for her bags. "Let me get that."

"Thanks." She gives him a grateful smile and it seems to unnerve him.

His voice is guarded as he asks, "Are you hungry?"

Julia tries to mask her disappointment. He doesn't ask where she's been, doesn't press for details, and she wishes he would. She knows it's a lot to ask given the way things have been—the way she has been. It feels like an impossible thing but she wants it nonetheless. She wants him to ask and she wants to tell him how she feels. About everything.

She wants to tell him that she had a good time in Chicago, that she watched three movies in a row and *laughed*. Hysterically for the last two—either the movies got better or it just became easier—and then she fell asleep in the early hours of the morning with a smile on her face.

What caught her by surprise was the unexpected desire for Mark to be with her. She had been relishing her independence, this sliver of life that didn't include her husband, and all she could think about was that she wished he were there, too.

He would have liked the movies. One was a romantic comedy with Jennifer Connelly, one of Mark's favorite actresses on whom he harbors a boylike crush. Another was a silly film with Will Ferrell, completely ridiculous but with just the right amount of funny to keep her giggling. The last one Julia doesn't even remember since she started nodding off, but every time she opened her eyes she found something to laugh about. It was with Ben Stiller or Jim Carrey or maybe both, and there was a funny love interest, Drew Barrymore perhaps. They bumbled their way through the movie, one mishap after another, so desperate to protect their own hearts from breaking that they put off their happiness until the very end.

And that's when it hits her. She doesn't want to wait until the end to see if she can find happiness again. Not only that, but she wants to find it with Mark.

"I saw a funny movie," Julia blurts out, catching Mark off guard. "At the hotel. The Fairmont. I went with Hannah, the cellist. Her treat, though I offered to pay. Her husband plays in the symphony but they may be splitting up since he's seeing the violist . . ."

Mark is nodding, taking this all in, trying to process it at the same time. Julia was in the city, too?

"She spoiled me," Julia says almost shyly. "I didn't mean for her to."

"You deserve it," Mark says and he means it. Julia deserves someone to spoil her, to take care of her. He wishes he could do a better job of it, frankly. He leads her into the kitchen where a large bowl of cut fruit is waiting.

Green grapes, red grapes, honeydew, cantaloupe, apples, bananas, orange sections. Julia used to love fruit salad—for both of her pregnancies it was all she would eat.

"Oh!" she says, surprised.

"It was our project for the day," Mark explains, glad to see she likes it. He scoops out a bowl for her, but not for Gracie who has already had two bowls and just brushed her teeth. Gracie reaches for a green grape and pops it in her mouth anyway. Oh well.

"Did you have a good time?" Gracie asks her mother. She's brimming with excitement, much too wound up to go to bed even though it's late. "I had a great time!"

"You did? What did you do?" Julia eats a spoonful of fruit. She looks genuinely interested and it makes Mark's heart ache with happiness to see Julia so engaged with Gracie and, at the same time, so relaxed around him. He always suspected that Julia came to life when she was alone with Gracie, but whenever they were all together it was always more stilted, more reserved. But now, for whatever reason, Julia has let down her guard and they are all here together, in this moment, happy. Mark doesn't want it to end.

"We made a birdhouse for Troy." Gracie is glowing. "He loves it, he's so happy! And we made paper dolls. I only colored princess gowns. I brought them home so you could see."

"Brought them home from where?" Julia asks. She looks at Mark, a smile still on her face.

Mark is perched on the stool next to her, his own bowl of fruit in front of him, untouched. He shifts uncomfortably, wishing he'd stepped in earlier to steer the conversation to something else but it's

too late. He thought he'd have more time to come up with an explanation about yesterday, hadn't expected Gracie would bring it up so
quickly. He's helpless as Gracie talks on, filled with dread for what's
to come.

Gracie is happily crunching on an apple slice. "From Aunt Livvy's
and Uncle Tom's. Did you know they used to have a dog? Patches.
They had to give him away but they have pictures everywhere. Aunt
Livvy really misses him."

There's a still silence in the room. "Patch," Julia says slowly. The
smile falls from her face. "The dog's name was Patch."

"Oh. Well, Aunt Livvy's going to paint one of her bedrooms,"
Gracie continues. "She says I can help. We're going to stencil." She
pushes through the fruit in the bowl, reaching for another grape.

"Don't use your fingers," Mark tells her. He starts to pick out the
grapes for Gracie, one by one, aware that Julia has turned to look
at him.

"When did Gracie see Livvy?" The edge is back in Julia's voice.

Mark clears his throat, doesn't look at her. "Yesterday. We ran
into Livvy at the grocery store then something came up with work
and she offered to watch Gracie for a few hours . . ."

"You left her with Livvy?" Julia gets up and scoops up her daughter just as she's about to reach for another grape. "Without even
checking with me? Without asking me?" She chokes out the last question before storming out of the kitchen.

Gracie is startled, casting an alarmed look at Mark. He hurries
after them. Julia is taking the stairs two at a time.

"Julia, it was an emergency," he says. "There wasn't enough time
and I didn't know where you were. *We almost lost a major client.* Not
that it would matter to you, but this is a big opportunity for me. For
us. We'll get our pick of projects after this, we won't have to work so
hard or scramble for jobs. It'll give me more time with Gracie and to
help out more around the house . . ."

"Why? Because I can't do it?" Julia spits out the words as she
kicks open Gracie's door. The door hits the wall and bounces back,

scaring Gracie and making her cry. "Because I'm such an incompetent mother, a lousy housewife?"

"I never said that. We shouldn't talk about this now . . ."

"Well, when, Mark? When is it ever a good time? It's never a good time for you or for me. You complain that we never talk, so let's talk!" Her anger scares him. Julia sits down on the edge of the bed and holds Gracie, bouncing her in her lap.

Mark tries to reach for his daughter, who's bawling now, but Julia bats his hand away, glaring at him. "Leave," she says.

Mark has had enough. "The hell I will." He's not going to leave Gracie and he's not going to let Julia dictate the terms of their relationship anymore. Come what may, he's had enough.

Maybe because it's late, or maybe it's because kids shut down in moments of distress, but Gracie soon falls asleep in Julia's lap, still sniffling, her cheeks wet. Julia holds her a few minutes longer, then gently eases her into the bed and pulls the covers over her.

She brushes past Mark on her way out. He closes Gracie's door with a click, then follows Julia into the kitchen where she's taken out a roll of tinfoil and has begun to cover the bowl of fruit.

"How could you, Mark?" Julia rips the foil against the serrated edge of the box. It makes a violent, angry sound.

Mark is fed up with Julia's crazy emotions, with this wild rollercoaster ride. "How could I what? I left Gracie with your sister for a few hours. She had a great time. They both did! What's wrong with that?"

Julia gestures to the class roster on the fridge. "She could have gone with anyone on this list, Mark!"

"No, she couldn't, because I didn't have the list with me when I was in the store, and Livvy was right there."

"Livvy? Come on, Mark!"

"Julia, I wasn't worried about Gracie or Livvy. On the contrary, I was worried about *you*, about what you would say, how *you* would react!"

"Obviously not that worried, seeing how you did it anyway." She opens the fridge and shoves the bowl inside. She slams the fridge door so hard the whole thing shakes.

Mark and Julia stand in the kitchen, the air charged and dangerously electric. Mark realizes that they're at an impasse, that they may never get past this, and he can't do this anymore.

It's not even a matter of whether or not he wants to—he just can't. He slides onto the stool, his shoulders slumped in defeat. He feels completely sapped of energy, completely drained. "What do you want me to do, Julia? I'm doing the best I can. I'm sorry that it's not good enough." It comes to him that it will never be good enough. Ever. He's suddenly overwhelmed with sadness.

Julia leans against the refrigerator door, closes her eyes. There's a long pause. Then she asks, quietly, "How was she?"

"What?" Mark looks up, resigned. "Oh, fine. She didn't want to come home, she was having such a good time. I think they went out of their way to make sure it was fun for her . . ."

"No," Julia says. "I mean Livvy. How was she?"

"Oh." Mark sighs. "She looked good. Older."

"Wiser?" Julia can't resist. It slips out, and with it, a smile.

Mark gives a sad chuckle. "More tired. I think they're having financial troubles."

Julia looks perturbed. "What do you mean?"

"At the grocery store Livvy had a small accordion file stuffed with coupons. And a shopping list."

"A shopping list?" Julia almost looks amused. They both know this isn't the Livvy they used to know and yet she's the same person Mark remembers. "Maybe she's just more organized," Julia suggests.

He doesn't know and at the moment he really doesn't care. "Maybe."

Julia sits down next to him and they sit side by side for a long time. Finally Julia asks, "Are you unhappy, Mark? I wouldn't blame you if you are."

Mark doesn't know what to say at first. He has moments of happiness and moments of unhappiness. But most of the time he's in that gray area in between. Happily discontent? Unhappily content? Instead he says, "I just know that I love you, and it hurts me to see you hurting and not being able to do anything about it." His voice breaks.

Julia reaches over and touches his hand. Mark holds his breath, resists the desire to take her hand in his, to run his fingers over hers. Sometimes it's just better to wait.

Julia turns Mark's hand so his palm is facing up, tracing the lines like a palm reader. He remembers their honeymoon, when all they could afford was four days in California, in Santa Cruz. There was a palm reader on the boardwalk, and she charged ten dollars to read their palms. He doesn't remember what she said, he was too busy gazing at his new wife, but he remembers the lines. There are four.

The head line. The life line. The fate line. The heart line.

Now he folds his fingers, holding Julia's hand in his own. She doesn't jerk away, but instead places her other hand on top, and Mark does the same. They stay this way for a long time.

Madeline frowns as she looks through her tea inventory. She needs to order some more Darjeeling and English Breakfast. She is going to add a Rooibos tea from South Africa, a red bush tea that is caffeine free but has more antioxidants than green tea and a sweet, nutty flavor. She's almost out of jasmine and probably has two weeks' worth of Earl Gray, one of her most popular items. She's also low on her tisanes like chamomile and peppermint.

Madeline is and always has been a big believer in the healing power of tea. She knows there are die-hard coffee drinkers out there, and while she doesn't mind a cup of coffee herself every now and then, there is something special about a good pot of tea. Brewing it properly requires a tiny bit of technique, patience, and an appreciation for subtlety. Madeline thinks of the Japanese tea ceremony she witnessed in Saratoga. It was one of the loveliest things she'd ever seen, the precision, the deliberateness, the inner quiet. She knows that tea has been revered around the world, that it's more than just a simple beverage. There are all sorts of customs surrounding tea, books full of tea etiquette that span the globe, not merely reserved for one culture or economic demographic. It seems that each culture has found a way to make tea its own. She loves that.

Madeline resumes checking her inventory. Last on the list is her house blend, a fragrant combination made predominantly of lemon peel and rosehips. That's her special tea ritual, she supposes, the gathering and mixing of her own blends in the quiet hours of the day when she's not cooking. She's thought of offering a class on making your own herbal infusions to help encourage more bulk sales, but that's just one more thing to add to her growing list of good intentions.

The bell rings over the door and Madeline glances up. It's not quite seven in the morning. She unlocks the door and turns the sign about half an hour before she's officially open, knowing that a few customers have to grab their tea and scones to go before a long commute. She knows them all by name and has come to think of them as her children, even the grown men who have families of their own. She's delusional, she knows. She's just projecting her own wishful thinking onto the town of Avalon. She tucks a pen behind her ear and pushes her notebook to the side.

A girl in her twenties walks in tentatively, her arms filled with several small boxes. Her hair is dyed black and spiked with gel. "Are you the Amish Friendship Bread lady?"

Lord, Madeline prays that doesn't become her nickname. It's right up there with Crazy Lady, Pigeon Feeding Lady, Cat Lady, and all the rest. "You can call me Madeline," she says.

The girl drops the boxes onto a table with a heavy thump. Madeline counts six boxes in total. "My name's Connie," the girl says. "I used to work at the Avalon Wash and Dry. A lot of my customers were doing this bread and it kind of grew into all this"—she waves at the boxes—"and I can't keep this there anymore. I tried the library, but they won't take it. I wanted to put it someplace where people could come and look up a recipe or find an answer to a question, you know?"

Madeline is intrigued. She pulls one of the boxes toward her and motions for the girl to have a seat. She removes the lid and gives a whistle at the cards stuffed inside. She pulls one out for a tropical variation with pineapple and coconut. A quick peek into the other boxes reveals more of the same—recipes and tips, all neatly organized. To say she's impressed would be putting it mildly—Madeline knows it takes a certain kind of mind to pull this off. "Did you do this?"

The girl nods. "So can you take them? I'd keep them in my apartment but that'd kind of be weird and my landlord would complain if people were coming and going. He still hasn't fixed my bathroom sink—I have to use the kitchen sink whenever I brush my teeth." Her eyes glance behind her, into the entryway. "But it'd be nice here. It might even help with business, get more people into your place. I mean, not that you need any help." A look of worry crosses Connie's face, as if she might have offended Madeline somehow.

It takes a lot to offend Madeline these days, and she gives Connie a reassuring smile. "I can use all the help I can get."

"So would that be okay?"

Madeline doesn't see why not. There's plenty of room in this house for a few boxes. "Sure. You can put them out in the foyer, or maybe over in the sitting room across the hall. No one uses that room much, and people can sit if they'd like to."

Connie reaches into her bag and pulls out a stack of brand-new index cards and pens. "I brought these. In case people wanted to copy down recipes or something."

"That's very thoughtful."

Connie just shrugs. "Do you want me to put everything in the other room?"

Madeline nods with a smile and Connie quickly picks up everything and heads for the sitting room. When she returns a few minutes later, she's holding a dust rag in her hand.

"I found this near a lamp," she tells Madeline. "It looked like you were in the middle of dusting the room, so I just finished up for you."

Madeline doesn't even remember dusting the sitting room. Last week, maybe. "Oh, thank you. I can take that."

"I can put it in the laundry room for you. Or I can rinse it for you by hand."

"What? Oh, that won't be necessary." Madeline takes the rag. Despite Connie's edgy appearance, Madeline's taken by her thoughtfulness, her politeness. "You're very sweet, though."

"It's not a big deal." Connie looks around the parlor, as if for the first time. "This is a nice place you've got. You serve tea here?"

"And breakfast and lunch. Baked goods throughout the day." Madeline gestures to the loaves of Amish Friendship Bread cooling on her counter. "You can have a loaf, if you'd like." Her starter was starting to get out of hand so she baked several bags at once.

Connie immediately brightens. "Thanks. I've kind of gotten used to eating it for breakfast but I haven't had one in a while." She takes her time choosing a loaf. "This one looks good."

Madeline peers over at it. "That's an apple cinnamon raisin."

Connie gives a happy sniff. "Yum. Thank you."

"You are quite welcome."

The bell over the door tinkles and several women walk in. "I'm *starving*," one of them says to no one in particular. One of her friends nods in agreement.

"Oh dear," Madeline says, suddenly flustered. She can't believe she's so unprepared for the day again. It's been like this a lot lately, her daily tasks creeping up on her so quickly that she can't really afford to take a moment off lest she forget something. She goes through her must-do checklist aloud as it helps her remember what needs to be done, counting the items off on her fingers. "I have to get the hot water on and put a Shepherd's pie into the oven. And I need to scoop out the butter for the tables and fill the water pitchers . . ." She frowns, debating what to do first.

"Do you need help? I'm not doing anything today." Connie wrinkles her nose. "I'm actually looking for a job. But I'd be happy to help you, for free." She holds up the loaf and smiles. "Well, not exactly for free since you gave me this, but it would be like an exchange."

An exchange. It's a lovely idea, very Californian, and Madeline certainly needs the help. Connie seems qualified enough, and spirited, too, which Madeline likes. But she should probably do a proper interview, request a résumé, check references, that sort of thing. Of course the big question would be when? She doesn't even have time to put an ad in the paper.

She stops herself—what a thought! *This is Avalon,* for goodness' sake. Plus there's the fact that Madeline already likes this girl, who seems if anything to be overqualified for this job. Madeline recognizes competence beneath the black T-shirt, blue jeans, and dirty sneakers.

"Let's do a trial," Madeline suggests, thinking quickly as she gestures for the customers to seat themselves. "Today and tomorrow. Six hours each day, plus thirty minutes for lunch. I'll pay you twelve dollars an hour plus a bag full of whatever is left over. If you get any tips, you can keep them. What do you say?"

Connie's mouth opens and her eyes shine. "Are you serious?"

Steven always said it was important to pay people well, that it was cheaper to invest in the people you already had. Madeline doesn't have time to haggle over a few dollars. If it works out Connie will be worth that and more. "I'm serious. Now go wash your hands and grab an apron from the kitchen. Make sure the oven is preheated to three hundred fifty degrees. It's been baking at four hundred for most of the morning and needs to cool down for the pie. I'll take the orders and then come back and help you."

Connie is already scurrying to the back, tugging at her T-shirt and smoothing her hair.

Well, this day has certainly become interesting. Madeline turns to the first table, a smile on her face. "And what would you like today? We have a special . . ."

Edie is suddenly deluged with every baby sample known to man. Baby wipes, baby formula, baby diapers, baby rash cream. Her mailbox is stuffed with catalogs for maternity wear, stretch mark creams, birthing tubs, baby furniture. She would never willingly sign up for all this. The culprit, again, is clear.

Livvy.

"This is a good idea," Richard says, pointing to something in one of the catalogs. "Instead of gifts, you ask people to give you items to

put in a time capsule for the baby to open on her sixteenth birthday."
He carefully folds the corner of the page and Edie expects it'll arrive
in the mail sometime next week. It's basically just a box with some instructions and party ideas. It's a complete scam, this whole baby business, but Richard has fallen for it hard.

"It could be a boy," she says.

"It could be," he agrees. "But it isn't."

They're going to have the ultrasound today. Richard is anxious to
confirm a due date and Edie is just plain anxious. In the back of her
mind she thinks that this could still be some kind of cruel joke, that
she's not really pregnant after all. If that turned out to be the case,
that would be good, wouldn't it?

"Edith Gallagher?" The nurse glances around the waiting room
and smiles when Edie raises her hand and stands up. Richard is quick
to follow, quick to hold the door open. The nurse is immediately
charmed.

"This is my . . ." Edie doesn't know what to call him anymore.
"Boyfriend" suddenly seems too flimsy, too fourth grade.

"Soon-to-be-fiancé," Richard supplies firmly. Edie manages a
weak smile as the nurse clucks her happy approval. She checks Edie's
weight, takes her blood pressure, does a urine test for good measure.
Then she hands Edie the detestable paper gown and pats the table
next to the ultrasound machine before closing the door with a soft
click.

"Do you want me to leave while you change?" Richard asks, unsure. He's a doctor but they've never been to a medical appointment
together and he suddenly seems nervous.

Edie points to the chair as she shrugs off her shirt. "You got me
into this—you're not going anywhere. Now sit, please." She tries to
cover herself with the paper blanket.

The OB/GYN is a woman, Dr. Briggs, and she seems delighted to
meet them. "Your first baby?" she asks.

They both nod. When Dr. Briggs finds out Richard is a doctor, the
conversation instantly swerves to medical talk—his area of expertise,
where he went to school, how he likes having his own practice. She

doesn't even give Edie warning before she squirts the cold gel onto her abdomen, making Edie yelp.

"Sorry!" Dr. Briggs looks apologetic and turns her pearly whites onto Edie. "So, let's see how far along we are, shall we?"

The screen is murky and looks like an underwater sonar. Edie strains to get a better look but Dr. Briggs has a frown on her face. She lifts Edie's chart and then runs the transducer over Edie's belly again, pressing a bit harder.

She glances at Richard who looks worried, perplexed. *Oh God,* she breathes. *Something's wrong.* There's an unexpected lump in her throat. She has to force herself to ask the question. "Is everything okay?"

"Everything is great." Dr. Briggs flips a switch on the machine and suddenly the room is filled with a fast rhythmic thumping.

A heartbeat.

"Wow." Richard's eyes are shiny as he turns to hold Edie's hand.

Dr. Briggs turns the monitor so Edie can get a better look. Edie gasps. It's a baby, curled up in a fetal position with a nose and fingers and toes. Arms waving, legs moving. A flicker of a heart beat, nice and steady.

"I didn't think it would look so clear," Edie stammers, shocked. She wasn't expecting this. She was prepared for stubby limb buds and big eye sockets. A bean. On the Internet everything looked alien, hardly worth bonding with. But this? This is a baby. A real live baby. *Her* baby.

"It's clear because you're fifteen weeks," Dr. Briggs says. "You're already out of your first trimester. Lucky you."

Now Richard looks shocked. "Fifteen weeks?"

"Give or take a couple of days. Which means we need to get blood work and a whole battery of tests to catch up, but so far everything looks good. Real good." Dr. Briggs reaches down and hands them a string of printouts from the ultrasound. "I estimate your due date to be around November second."

Edie just stares at her. November second? That's barely six months. She's not ready to be a mother in six months. She was supposed to get nine months. Nine!

"But I'm not even showing," Edie points out, looking down at her stomach.

"First baby," Dr. Briggs said. "I didn't show until just past my fifth month. Everyone's different, but you'll pop out soon, don't worry." She asks something about sex.

"No!" Edie says, alarmed. Sex is the last thing on her mind, and Richard will be lucky if he ever gets any again. "We're abstaining after this."

Dr. Briggs laughs. "No, no, Edie. My question is: Do you want to find out the sex? Of your baby?"

It takes Edie a moment to process the question. "We can do that?" she finally asks. Her voice sounds hollow, a swooshing echo in her ears. "Already?"

"It's early, but we've got a perfect view right here." Dr. Briggs gestures to the screen. "It's pretty obvious what you're having."

Richard and Edie look at each other. They haven't had this conversation yet. "I don't know," Richard says. He looks completely bewildered. "Er . . . um . . ."

Edie can't believe he's been reduced to this. She's never known him to be anything but confident, and he's never at a loss for words. "Let's find out," she decides for them.

"Are you sure?" Richard is completely indecisive. "I mean, wouldn't it be more fun if we found out on the day of?"

Edie's been told she has a high tolerance for pain, having limped around for days with a sprained ankle and broken toe, but she's not so sure how this labor thing is going to go. She is secretly relieved that she has the option of an epidural, just in case.

"Maybe for *you*," she says. "But not for me. I kind of think I'll be a bit preoccupied."

"We can write it down on a piece of paper and you can decide later if you want to open it," Dr. Briggs suggests, but Edie isn't having it. She wants to know now.

"If you're not sure, you can step out of the room, but I want to find out." Edie feels jittery and impatient now that she knows they can find out if the baby is a boy or a girl.

"I don't want you knowing and me not knowing." Richard is almost petulant. "Fine. Let's find out."

Dr. Briggs gives Edie a sympathetic look and Edie almost smiles. "Okay." Dr. Briggs puts a little more gel on Edie's stomach and glides the transducer over her abdomen once again. "Oh, uh-huh. See that? Between the legs?" She points to something on the screen.

Both Richard and Edie squint. "I don't see anything," Edie says, frowning.

"Exactly. You're having a girl. Congratulations." Dr. Briggs grins at them and hands Edie a paper towel to wipe her stomach.

A girl. Richard actually staggers and has to sit down.

"Oh God," Edie says, the blood pounding in her own ears. "Please tell me you're not going to faint at the delivery." What happened to her big macho Peace Corps doctor boyfriend?

"I'll get you some water," Dr. Briggs says, slipping out of the room. "Take your time."

Edie wipes the gel off her body and sits up. "Richard, are you okay?"

He looks at her, his face radiating happiness. He gets up and crosses the room, taking her in his arms and starts kissing her—her face, her hands, her fingertips. "You are incredible, you know that?"

"Why, because I'm so clueless about my own body that I didn't even know I was pregnant?" And not just pregnant, but *fifteen weeks* pregnant. It's still sinking in.

"She was perfect. Did you see her? Perfect." He kisses Edie some more. "Just like her mother."

Uh-oh. One part of her wants to roll her eyes, and the other part has already melted into a puddle on the floor. Edie has just caught a glimpse of her future, and it's clear that while caffeinated nights and stints to third world countries may be coming to an end, it's being replaced by something that she hadn't quite seen until now. Breakfast in bed. Fingerprints on the wall. Cartoons instead of documentaries on public television. And a doting, loving father and future husband.

Gloria Hugel, 56
Fortune Teller

It's not easy making money in this town. It's better than Conroy, the last place Gloria lived, though that's not saying much. The people there were small thinkers; they couldn't appreciate her gifts.

Here, in Avalon, Gloria has a few regular customers. She's launched a website and people are starting to call her from around the world. She's thinking about writing a blog, too. A lot of other psychics are doing it, but she needs to take a few more computer classes from the community college before she can pull that off.

Her 2:00 P.M. appointment is sitting in the living room. Gloria is putting the final touches on her presentation—large silver hoop earrings, hair pulled back in a bandanna, dark mascara and eyeliner. She doesn't consider it deceptive as much as inventive—the client is usually expecting a psychic to look a certain way, and it just goes so much faster if she dresses to stereotype. Walmart had a rack of plain black dresses that fit her ample frame perfectly, so she bought seven, one for each day of the week. Less laundry.

Gloria pulls a shawl over her shoulders. Checks herself in the mirror, then steps out of the bedroom.

"I am Miss Gloria." Gloria sweeps in and takes the woman's hands magnanimously. She leads the woman to a card table that's set up in the middle of the living room, amid glowing candles. A crystal ball is perched nearby, as is a stack of worn tarot cards. Gloria doesn't need any of that, but it adds to the ambience.

The woman is young, clearly a homemaker, clearly a mother of young children. A toddler and a baby. Gloria doesn't need to use her powers to figure that part out—the smear of pureed peas on the woman's top and Magic Marker stains on her jeans are telling enough, plus she has a huge diaper bag slung over her shoulder. By the way the woman is anxiously twisting her wedding band, Gloria would wager that she's here to talk about her husband.

The woman is nervous. "I've never done this before," she says. "I'm not sure what I should do . . ."

"Just relax," Gloria croons. She lights a candle on the table, a sandalwood-patchouli-scented pillar that she picked up at Bed Bath & Beyond when she was in the city last. On clearance.

"So you've done this before?" the woman asks.

"I'm a seventh-generation clairvoyant. I'm also an empath. What's your name?"

"Lenora."

"Lenora . . ." Gloria breathes her name and closes her eyes. An image forms almost instantly. She sees a carnival, an amusement park of some kind. Cotton candy, games on the boardwalk. A man in uniform. Army, no, Navy . . .

"I should tell you," Lenora interrupts with a whisper.

"One moment . . ." The image wavers at the interruption but Gloria opens herself up again and it comes flooding back. She's not sensing this is present day, but in the past . . . a father, maybe, or perhaps a grandfather, with a message for Lenora . . .

"I can't exactly pay," Lenora whispers.

The image disappears and Gloria opens one eye. "I'm sorry?"

Lenora looks embarrassed. "I just thought I should tell you that I can't exactly pay, you know, in cash."

Gloria breathes a sigh of relief. "I take Visa, MasterCard, and American Express."

The woman shakes her head and reaches into her diaper bag. She pulls out a Ziploc bag and hands it to Gloria.

"I know it's not much, but it's the starter for Amish Friendship Bread and it's absolutely wonderful . . ." Lenora tries to explain.

Gloria looks at the bag with masked distaste. She really doesn't like to barter her services, because unless she's doing a reading for her landlord, trades don't pay the rent. Plus whatever is in this bag is just revolting.

"I'm sorry," she starts to say, handing the bag back to Lenora, when an image suddenly whooshes in and knocks the words right out of her mouth.

Rain. Rising water.

"Hello?" Lenora is looking at her nervously.

Gloria's eyes fly open and she clutches the bag, startling Lenora. "Fishes and loaves," she says. "Fishes and loaves."

CHAPTER 18

❀

The town of Avalon is overflowing with Amish Friendship Bread. It seems that every other person (and their cousin or neighbor or aunt) has a bag of starter to share. Bake sales, cake walks, book clubs, and birthday parties serve some variation of Amish Friendship Bread in the form of cakes, loaves, muffins, brownies, cookies, even cinnamon rolls. People aren't getting tired of it exactly—just concerned that the amount of starter might soon outnumber the population of Avalon itself.

Today, the rain is pouring down relentlessly. The weatherman has predicted heavy rains all week, with flood warnings in certain counties. Word has quickly spread that Connie's recipe and tip cards have moved from the Wash and Dry to the tea salon, so right now Madeline's sitting room is clogged with at least fifteen women, their voices jumbled as they burrow through the boxes or compare notes.

The wicker "Spare and Share" basket is spilling over with bags of starter in various cycles. The Spare and Share basket was Connie's idea. Connie was also quick to notice that sometimes the women brought in their loaves of bread to swap and compare, and while Madeline doesn't mind, Connie doesn't want Madeline to lose any business. So she came up with an unofficial BYOB—Bring Your Own Bread—policy. She set out a self-serve tea station in the sitting room and found an old letter box to double as an honor box. She printed a small price list and put it in an antique frame with a suggested "donation" of $2.50 per cup or $5.00 for all the tea you could drink. She also wrote the daily special and a couple of their most popular to-go items on an old chalkboard and propped it up nearby. The letter box was always stuffed with cash by the end of the day.

"Wow," Hannah is saying as she cranes her neck from the tea room to get a better look. Their visits have become more frequent since Hannah and Julia's return from Chicago.

"I know." Madeline keeps her voice low even though she is delighted. Beyond delighted. The constant gaggle of women coming and going has made Madeline's a bit of a hot spot, and business is thriving. And while she looks forward to her regular visits with Julia and Hannah, there's something to be said about having someone help with all the heavy lifting—literally and figuratively. On slow days she has someone to talk to, someone who wants to see the tea salon be a success almost as much as she does.

"I'm so glad you have someone good to help you," Julia says. Some of the women coming in know Julia and offer friendly exclamations but Julia is cautious in her greetings, preferring to stay in the dining area with Madeline and Hannah. Madeline understands this and knows that while some of these women are just casual acquaintances, Julia has clearly distanced herself from most of the people she knows in Avalon.

But now is not the time to mention anything, and Madeline knows that timing is everything. She herself wasn't in a position—much less interested—to listen to anyone's advice when she was still finding her way out, and she doesn't want Julia to feel like she's lecturing. Julia's doing the best she can, and Madeline sees that and knows that, in itself, isn't easy.

She fans herself, trying to create a breeze with the new menus Connie has printed up. The ovens have been working nonstop and the kitchen is so warm it's taking her longer to cool herself down these days. "I tell you, that girl is a godsend. I feel like I'm helping her rather than the other way around. She has the energy of a hundred men—or women."

"Ah, youth." Julia gives a wry smile. She gives Hannah a nudge. "You young kids make us old folks look bad."

"Hey, I'm not *that* young," Hannah protests, her chin tipped upward in a touch of genuine defiance. She gives Julia a nudge back. "And you're not that old."

Julia grins. "Fair enough." She picks up a table tent with the daily special printed on it. There's also a "Tea of the Week" special to encourage people to buy loose tea or bags as gifts, and an inspiring quote. "I like this," she says. " 'My friends are my estate.' Emily Dickinson."

"That's Connie for you," Madeline says. She reaches over to another table and plucks the sign from there. "Each table has a different friendship quote." She hands the table tent to Hannah.

" 'The ornaments of our house are the friends who frequent it,' " Hannah reads. "Ralph Waldo Emerson. I'm going to copy that and put it in my wallet."

"I don't know where that girl gets her ideas from," Madeline continues. "Did you know that she ordered a self-inking stamp with our name and address? She stamps it on all of the blank index cards so that when people write down recipes and take them, they'll always be reminded of us. It's so much better than a regular business card! And the women adore her."

Connie chooses to walk by at that moment holding an empty cherrywood cigar box. The three women quickly hush themselves while giving her wide, encouraging smiles. Connie arches a suspicious eyebrow as she adds a fresh selection of tea bags to the box, but doesn't say anything and quickly returns to the sitting room.

"Oh, dear, she probably knows we were talking about her." Madeline sighs as both Julia and Hannah burst out laughing.

"I think she knows we're pretty harmless." Julia says. "And possibly a little crazy, too."

"Insane," Madeline amends. "Certifiable."

Hannah smiles along with them but then picks up a dessert spoon and rubs the smooth curve with her thumb. "Philippe wants a divorce. The papers came today."

The mood instantly shifts. "Oh, Hannah." Julia takes her hand and Madeline jumps up to offer a hug.

"In retrospect it's so obvious. I think he actually pushed us to come to Avalon so he could buy a house and stick me in it, keep me naïvely unaware until he knew what he wanted to do. I was such a fool for believing his whole story about wanting to live in a small town, that it reminded him of his village in France, blah blah blah." She looks disgusted with herself.

"Don't blame yourself," Julia tells her. "You didn't have any reason not to believe him."

Hannah wrinkles her nose, unsatisfied. "Looking back, I know there were signs. I just chose to ignore them."

"Think of it more like a timing thing," Madeline suggests kindly. "Everything unfolding as it needs to. You were doing the only thing you knew to do at the time."

"But I could have just saved myself the heartache if I hadn't gotten married in the first place," Hannah says. "Why put myself through all this, even subconsciously, if I'm just going to end up with a divorce? I mean, really! I think I can do without this part."

"True, but then you wouldn't have ended up in Avalon and we wouldn't have ever met you," Madeline points out.

Julia interrupts. "I don't know. That's exactly the sort of thing that people used to say to me, and I hated it." She quickly takes Madeline's hand to let her know she doesn't mean to offend her, and continues. "Someone who has never lost a child would say to me, 'Well, at least he's in a better place,' or 'All things happen for a reason.' But what do they know?

"My son's death should not be so easily explained. What is the real reason a ten-year-old boy has to die? That Gracie has to grow up never knowing her older brother? So we all become better people?" Julia shakes her head. "I *hate* being a better person. I don't want to be a better person." She says these last words bitterly, angrily blinking back tears.

Madeline holds Julia's hand tightly and looks her in the eye. She understands this, she really does, but she wants Julia to understand one thing, something that once filled her with despair and, at the same time, saved her.

"Dear Julia," she says quietly after a long pause. "What other choice do we have?"

Edie walks past the open doorway of the dining room, unsure of what to do. She's just spent the past hour talking with the ladies in the sitting room, sipping tea and gathering history. She's done it every day for the past week and found herself enjoying the chitchat, the conversation, the company.

But this morning she woke up and saw an email from one of her classmates. They were shortlisted for the Hillman Prize for an article on illegal immigrant detention. It was enough to remind Edie that she was there for a reason, and that it was time to get back to work.

She and Livvy have been meeting regularly to talk about Amish Friendship Bread. Livvy, despite her enthusiasm, is somewhat lacking in her note-taking and research skills, but it's still been a big help and Edie is grateful for it. Edie feels ready to write the article, to see if she can stir up some bona fide interest in Avalon and the Amish Friendship Bread insanity that has taken over their town. Edie recognizes that there is a certain charm in the story, but so much of it is dependent on revealing the players involved, to putting names and faces to certain Avalonians. Based on Livvy's notes and the dates of the recipes in the boxes, the earliest person to have the starter was Madeline Davis. That would have been sometime back in March, just about three months ago.

Edie's own bag of starter met a disastrous end. She'd left it in a cupboard in the kitchen, unable to stand looking at it, and then promptly forgot about it. It was Richard who heard an odd knocking from inside a couple days later.

When they opened the cupboard door, a fully inflated Ziploc bag jumped a couple of centimeters toward them, tipping over an almost empty plastic container of thyme. Edie screamed and Richard had plucked the bag out, only to have the whole thing pop open and explode over the cupboard and the two of them.

Once Richard had gotten past the shock, he couldn't stop laughing. Batter was dripping from his hair and shirt. Edie, on the other hand, was furious. It took a container of Clorox wipes and half a roll of paper towels to get everything cleaned up.

The smell of fermenting batter made her want to throw up. No, correction: She *did* throw up. Morning sickness, it seemed, was not reserved for the first trimester.

Fortunately Edie had a clear enough head to take a few pictures of the mess in their kitchen and already has the perfect caption: WARNING: THIS COULD BE YOU—STARTER CRAZE EXPLODES IN AVALON, AND IN ONE REPORTER'S KITCHEN.

Edie pretty much has the story written in her head, but the one thing she hasn't been able to put together is the Madeline piece. She hasn't figured out where Madeline got the bread from, and she's put off interviewing Madeline until today. For some reason she thought Madeline would be younger, a roly-poly woman in her fifties wearing a gingham apron—Livvy made her sound that way, at least. Edie should have known not to make an assumption until she could see for herself. Now she feels a twinge of discomfort at pointing to Madeline as the instigator of all this Amish Friendship Bread hoopla. Edie has to remind herself that she's a reporter who's just reporting the facts. It's nothing personal.

There's the sound of someone clearing their throat, and Edie jumps.

Connie, the punky girl who works at Madeline's, is cutting her eyes at Edie, clearly disapproving. Edie knows it looks like she is eavesdropping on the women's conversation, but she wasn't, at least not intentionally. She was going in to introduce herself to Madeline and it was clear the women were in the midst of a private conversation. If anything, she was being respectful.

Connie's voice is loud as she glares at Edie. "Madeline, I have some to-go orders. Do you want me to fill them?"

The three women look up and Madeline quickly puts on a welcoming smile. One woman with short strawberry-blond hair turns away and looks out the window. The Asian woman with dark hair just stares at her hands.

"What? Oh no, you keep working your magic with the ladies. I'll take care of this." Madeline comes over to collect the orders from Connie and gives Edie a sweet smile as she does so.

Edie feels her resolve faltering. Lately she's been at the mercy of pregnancy hormones, crying at commercials for flu medication and then almost bursting into tears when someone cut in front of her on the road. She bought a "Baby's First Year" scrapbook at the last meeting and has found herself weepy over the pink bootie die cuts and soft polka-dot ribbons.

Edie suddenly isn't sure if she can do this. She doesn't want to get attached to Madeline, feel sympathetic because of her age or her seemingly kind demeanor. She needs to stay objective, to finish what she set out to do. The Amish Friendship Bread story is quirky enough with plenty of soap opera antics to get picked up on one of the wires, provided Edie writes it right. And soon.

Connie is pretty good at sizing people up, and there's something about the young woman with wire-framed glasses that Connie doesn't trust. Her name is Edie something or other and she's been coming every day for the past few days. She always has a ton of questions, and every now and then Connie sees her jot something in a notepad. Connie doesn't want her harassing their customers, but the women don't seem to mind, enjoying any opportunity to talk about their lives and when they first started baking Amish Friendship Bread.

"I think it was in April . . ."

"March. Right after St. Patrick's Day."

"Two weeks ago. Doris Donald left a bag on the windshield of my car. Didn't even have the courage to ask me to my face if I wanted it!"

"I'm on my third starter, so maybe a month?"

"A little over six weeks . . ."

Connie doesn't know why Edie is so interested, especially since she's never baked the bread herself and refused on several occasions to take a bag of starter home from the Spare and Share basket.

Now, Madeline is shaking her head in admiration as she reads through the orders. "Connie, this practically rivals the business we did at lunch. You're a marvel!"

Connie blushes, embarrassed by the praise, and forgets that Edie is standing next to her. She loves working at Madeline's, and Madeline has practically given her carte blanche to do whatever she thinks is appropriate to help the business and offer good customer service. Connie not only feels useful, but needed. It's a good feeling.

She knows she should say thank you, but instead she changes the subject, wanting to get the attention off her. "I was thinking that maybe we could offer an end-of-the-day meal replacement special. We'll post it on the board along with everything else, and people would have to get their dinner orders in to us by eleven A.M. That'll give us enough time to get everything ready and we won't have to scramble at the last minute like this. If they don't get it in, we don't fill the order." Connie knows Madeline loves the work, loves that people love her food, but it's 3:00 P.M. and now Madeline has to go back into the kitchen after the end of a long day. Madeline is usually up at 4:30 A.M. getting everything ready. Connie doesn't even show up until two hours later.

"I don't mind the scrambling," Madeline assures her, but Madeline does look peaked. She lets out a long breath as she looks through the orders again. "But maybe you're right. We can talk about it some more this weekend. In the meantime, let me get going on these."

"I'll help." Hannah, the musician, stands up and comes over to join Madeline. "I need to get my mind off things."

Madeline puts a motherly arm around Hannah's shoulders. "I'd love to have you in the kitchen with me." They're about to walk away when Connie sees Edie step forward.

"Hi, excuse me? My name is Edie Gallagher and I'm trying to learn a little more about Amish Friendship Bread." She extends a hand to Madeline who shakes it. "I was looking through the recipes and it looks like you were the first person to start making Amish Friendship Bread in Avalon. Back in March?"

"Has it only been since March?" Madeline seems thoughtful. "I suppose the date is right, but I'm not the first person. I got my starter from this young lady here, Julia Evarts." She nods to the woman still seated, the woman with strawberry-blond hair. Connie tries to mind her own business and not pry, but she knows that Julia Evarts is the mother of the little boy who died a few years back.

Edie quickly turns to Julia, fake exuberance oozing everywhere. Connie wants to gag. "Oh, really? Well, um, that's great! Do you mind if I talk with you for a bit?"

The woman hesitates for a moment before shaking her head. "I'm sorry, but I actually have to go." She starts to gather her things.

Edie persists. "Can I just ask where you got your starter from?"

"I actually don't know," Julia says. "It was on our porch when we came home one day. It was the starter plus several slices of the bread. Gracie found it first." She smiles at the other women who are beaming at the mention of Julia's daughter. "We were supposed to save the last slice for Mark, but I ate it. So we didn't have a choice but to wait ten days and bake the bread ourselves."

"Mark is your husband?" Edie is edging a bit closer now and Connie intentionally bumps her, as if to say, *Don't come any closer.*

Julia is nodding.

"So you never found out who gave you the starter?" Edie asks.

She gives a noncommittal shrug. "I suspect one of my neighbors but no one has said anything to me about it."

"Interesting. Do you think I could interview your neighbors?" The look on Edie's face is hungry. Connie wants to shove her out the door.

Julia stands up, slinging her large tote bag over her shoulder. "I'm sorry, but I'm late picking up my daughter." She gives Hannah and

Madeline a quick kiss on the cheek before pushing past Edie and leaving.

"And we should get started on those to-go orders," Madeline says briskly. She nods for Hannah to follow her into the kitchen and Connie waits a beat before heading back to the sitting room, throwing one more look of warning Edie's way.

Edie is suddenly alone, the women having evaporated before she could ask another question. She knows she came on too strong, but that's no reason to give her the cold shoulder. And Connie is one level up from a thug. Amish Friendship Bread thugs. Right here in Avalon.

It doesn't matter. Now that she knows where it's all originated from (and from Julia Evarts no less!), Edie knows exactly how to frame the story. She's starting to feel tired and wants to go home and crawl into bed, annoyed that this pregnancy has completely sapped her energy by mid-afternoon. She snaps a quick picture of the empty tearoom then hurries out the door.

FRIEND OR FOE? AMISH FRIENDSHIP BREAD CRAZE TAKES OVER SMALL ILLINOIS TOWN

Reported by Edith Gallagher

AVALON, ILLINOIS—In a small Illinois town boasting a modest population, word of mouth is oftentimes the quickest and most effective way to spread the news. Now, only one thing threatens to travel even faster: Amish Friendship Bread and its ubiquitous goopy starter, complete with detailed instructions.

By now you or someone you know has been a victim of the Amish Friendship Bread craze that has swept through America since the mid-1980s and made a recent resurgence in northern Illinois. It goes like this: Someone gives you a plastic Ziploc filled with fermenting batter called "Amish Friendship Bread" (incidentally, there seems to be no corroboration on the part of the Amish for actually coming up with this recipe). You give it a little love by squishing the bag daily, adding a few ingredients (flour, sugar, milk) on day six. By day ten, you add those ingredients again, split the starter into three new baggies, and bake with what's left over. Then you get to find three friends who naïvely agree to take a bag of starter, not knowing that in ten days they'll be hard-pressed to find three friends of their own to pass it on to.

What's the harm, you may say? Well, picture this: One person keeps a bag and passes three more to friends. All four people do the same, and so on and so on. After three "generations" (approximately one month), there are sixty-four bags of starter floating around out there. After four generations: 256. Six generations: 4,096. And by ten generations (approximately three and a half months): 1,048,576. You don't even want to know what happens after fifteen generations.

Amish Friendship Bread is an excellent example of how epidemics get started. In a digital age, it's incredible to see viruses spread the old-fashioned way. And all in the name of friendship.

"Oh, I'll head in the opposite direction if I see anyone coming my way with one of those Ziplocs," says Sue Pendergast, the organist at Avalon United Methodist Church. "I don't mean to sound unchristian, but I find it very presumptuous of people to assume that I have time to do all this work to make what amounts to a simple quick bread. It's just not worth the trouble."

Eleanor Winters agrees. "I heard that Martha Stewart had trouble figuring it out. If she had trouble, what hope is there for me?"

As simple as the instructions may be, there are a few things you should be aware of. You cannot use metal utensils when mixing the batter as it will interfere with the fermenting process. According to Dr. Roland Fetters at the University of Chicago, the starter contains acids that will cause the metal to dissolve into it.

"It's a chemical reaction," Dr. Fetters explains. "It will not only contaminate the starter, but it will kill it." This small detail is responsible for the recent hazardous materials scare at the Avalon Police Department, when Cora "Miss Sunshine" Ferguson was found carrying a bag of starter on her person. If you've ever seen the starter, you'll understand how it's not difficult to be suspicious of it. Ferguson's failure to elaborate on the substance resulted in a tri-county hazardous materials alert, costing taxpayers valuable time and money.

The other thing to be aware of is that you must care for the starter every day, which includes squeezing the batter and letting out any air in the bag, otherwise it could result in mold or a clean-up job that will leave you cursing the person who gave you the starter in the first place (see picture to the right).

Which brings us to the big question: How *did* Amish Friendship Bread make its way into this small town? No one is quite sure, but the earliest sighting harkens back to March of this year, on the porch of Mark and Julia Evarts. It was their daughter, Gracie, 5, who first spotted it, and while her mother claims to not know who gave her the starter, no one else recalls seeing (or eating) Amish Friendship Bread before that time.

The residents of the town of Avalon are certainly split on whether the phenomenon that began with Mrs. Evarts has been a boon or a burden.

"Friends don't give friends Amish Friendship Bread," says Earlene Bauer, the dispensing optician at the Avalon All Eyes Vision Center. "I throw it in the trash the minute I get a bag."

"I love the bread, but have the worst time sharing the starter with friends," sighs Pearl Kirby, an avid birder who spends her days looking for white-breasted nuthatches in Avalon Park. "One person actually stopped talking to me. I finally gave up altogether."

But Claribel Apple is quick to disagree. "I think the bread is a blessing," she proclaims. Apple spends her afternoons in Madeline's Tea Salon where she and a handful of other ladies gather to swap recipes and compare notes in a room designated specifically for all things having to do with Amish Friendship Bread. "There's so much negativity in the world, so many terrible things happening that can't be explained. Why not make the world a better place with a little love and friendship bread?"

Why not indeed? Provided you're not diabetic, a little friendship bread can go a long way. You can beat it, freeze it, thaw it, and it'll live on in perpetuity. You don't even have to bake it on the tenth day—you can bake it on the eleventh day or even the twentieth, provided that you're always feeding it. But for this reporter, I'm hoping the good people of Avalon will learn to be their own best friend and keep their starter to themselves. Or, better yet, Mrs. Evarts, come up with a starter for a pot roast dinner, and then we'll talk.

CHAPTER 19

❀

"Edie, how could you?"

Edie looks up from her computer, surprised. Livvy's face is red and she's angry, the day's paper clutched in her hand.

"How could I what?" Edie's inbox has been jammed with emails and her voice mailbox is full. The article wasn't picked up by any of the newswires, but the flood of local attention has pleased her nonetheless. She's obviously hit a nerve, which is one of the greatest compliments to a reporter in Edie's opinion. She's thinking about writing more articles on the subject, maybe a series on Amish Friendship Bread. "You didn't like it? It was supposed to a humorous lifestyle piece. Did you read the part about the pot roast? I've been craving pot roast, don't ask me why." She smacks her lips and can practically smell it. Maybe she'll have Richard do takeout again from the Avalon Grill.

Livvy throws the paper on her desk. "Edie, Julia Evarts is my sister. You blamed her for bringing Amish Friendship Bread to Avalon! None of the research I gave you said that!"

"I did some of my own reporting and that's what I found. It's not a big deal, Livvy."

"Not a big deal?" Livvy explodes. "Julia's going to think I had something to do with this, that this is somehow my fault."

Edie suppresses a smile as she glances at the headline again. She'd written the story in less than an hour. She had planned to make a larger statement about life and world peace and the like, but the words just flowed onto the page so she went with it, and she's glad she did. Edie can't remember the last time she had fun writing an article. She credits the pregnancy to vamping up her creativity about a hundred notches. "How is any of this your fault? You didn't do anything wrong, Livvy. It's just an article—these are just the facts."

"*I* know that, but Julia won't. She knows I work at the *Gazette*. She'll think I put you up to this!"

"So call her and tell her that you had nothing to do with it." Edie is about to head to the break room for another cup of coffee when she remembers that she's already met her caffeine quota for the day. Rats.

Livvy is pacing frantically. "I can't do that."

"Why not?" Edie knows the answer but she wants to hear Livvy say it. It's the only thing Livvy hasn't shared about her life. Edie pieced it together quickly between what Richard told her and what she found in the newspaper archives, but it's curious how it's never come up, as tragic as it is. In some way having this secret makes Livvy more human, makes Edie think that their friendship has a shot of going beyond these superficial lunches and bubble gum discussions.

But Livvy just shakes her head, the look on her face so pained that Edie feels a morsel of regret. No question this would have been easier if Julia Evarts hadn't been Livvy's sister, but what can you do? "Look, Livvy, I know we thought it had to do with that Madeline person, but Julia had given the starter to her. She says someone gave it to her, but I haven't been able to verify it. I don't expect to, either."

"Edie, my sister has been through so much already! She doesn't need to be back in the fishbowl again! I heard people in line at the bank talking about making her bake all the excess starter . . ."

Edie has heard that, too, but actually thought it was kind of funny. "Come on, Livvy. You know they're joking."

"I don't care!" Livvy's face is red. "I don't see why you couldn't have found the person who gave it to her and started from there instead . . ."

"I can't do that, Livvy, because I don't think there was anybody else." Edie says this gently.

Livvy stares at her. "What are you talking about?"

Edie blows out her breath. She didn't really want to tell Livvy this, but it's too late now. "No one other than Julia received a starter that week. Don't you think that's a bit odd? You yourself found a recipe for the starter on the Internet. It wouldn't be completely out of left field to assume that she started the craze herself."

"Julia wouldn't do that. Why would she do that?"

"I don't know. Attention? Think about it. You make the starter, dish it out to some friends, maybe some people you're hoping to get to know, newbies to town who don't know what happened five years ago. It starts up the whole sympathy thing again . . ."

The color drains from Livvy's face. "You're saying she did this to get sympathy? For Josh?"

"I'm just saying that people do things for all sorts of reasons. I mean, come on, Livvy. She hasn't talked to you for years! She's completely withdrawn. You think she started this whole thing to be friendly to her neighbors?" Edie reaches into a drawer and comes up with a bag of chips. "Dorito?"

Livvy pushes the bag away. "Edie, Josh was my nephew. He was in my care when he died." Her voice is shaking.

Edie looks at her, her gaze steady. "I know."

Livvy looks shocked but doesn't ask how Edie knows. She raises her chin. "Well, if you know, then I'd think you'd be a little bit more sympathetic toward me and my family. I thought you were my friend!"

"I am your friend. It's just an article, Livvy—this isn't personal."

"*It's personal to me, Edie!* You have no idea what it's like, to have the one person in the world who really knows you cut you off! How would you feel if Richard did that? Just stopped acknowledging you altogether, pretended you didn't even exist?"

Edie swallows. She hates seeing Livvy so upset, and at the same time she finds herself pushing back. She looks up at Livvy who is flushed, her fists clenching and unclenching. "Why didn't you tell me before, Livvy?" she asks quietly.

Livvy shakes her head, looks away. "What was I supposed to say?" she mumbles.

Edie feels something unfurling inside of her. Livvy has been a good friend to her, much more so than Edie had expected or maybe even deserves. Maybe she should have thought this through more carefully, considered other options. But it's too late now anyway.

"Julia just wants everyone to leave her alone," Livvy says, falling into the chair across from Edie. "Everyone, including me."

Edie sees something out of the corner of her eye. "Maybe not."

Livvy gives a wry laugh. "Trust me, I would know. Julia isn't interested in seeing anyone, and I'm the first person on that list."

"I think you might be wrong about that, Livvy." Edie nods down the hallway. "Because I think that's your sister standing in your office."

Julia looks around the bare bones of Livvy's office. It's small, crammed with a desk and two chairs, a generic print of a flower on the wall. There's a recent picture of Livvy and Tom, one that Julia doesn't recognize. Tom looks a bit older, bits of gray sneaking into his hair, but Livvy looks the same, all smiles, peppy without a care in the world. No surprise there.

"Julia?"

Julia turns to see Livvy in the doorway. "Livvy." She grasps the straps of her tote bag tightly, the skin around her knuckles white and taut. Seeing her sister close up has muddled her brain. She's actually here to see Edie Gallagher, the reporter who wrote the article, but found herself asking the receptionist for Livvy's office instead.

When Mark had reluctantly showed her the newspaper, it took Julia awhile to place the reporter as the woman from Madeline's the other day. Once she did it all made sense. The questions, the prying behavior. Didn't they have to disclose that they were reporters or get permission to use your name in the newspaper? Obviously not.

Julia decided to go to the *Gazette* to confront Edie, to let her know that she doesn't appreciate being made into a scapegoat. She's had enough of that, of people pointing fingers and finding yet another thing to whisper about behind Julia's back. Mark was supportive, almost amused by the way she stormed about, complaining about the lack of privacy, the insensitivity of people who should know better.

"You go tell 'em, tiger," he'd said, and Julia stopped long enough to grin. She was back on her soapbox, one she hadn't been on for a long time, and it felt good. Mark had a bemused smile on his lips. "God, I pity the reporter."

Julia ranted for a few minutes longer as she gathered her things. She was almost looking forward to a confrontation. Then she opened the front door and found the doorstep littered with anonymous bags of Amish Friendship Bread starter.

Mark came up behind her and stared, dumbstruck. "What in the . . ."

"This must be the equivalent of Amish Friendship Bread hate mail," she remarked to Mark, who promptly scooped it all up and dumped it in the trash. It seemed like a waste, but Mark made the point that they couldn't be sure what was in the baggies or how old the starters were. Plus, they weren't exactly left in a gesture of friendship.

"Maybe there will be drive-by starter shootings, too," Julia had continued, earning herself a glare from her husband. She could picture water guns filled with batter aimed at the house.

"This isn't funny, Julia." Mark was pissed. One of the bags was opened and some of the batter leaked onto Mark's hands. "Disgusting."

She knows it's not a joke but at the same time Julia has to admit that it *is* a little funny. After all, it's just batter. It's not like she's spreading the avian flu or something.

Both Madeline and Hannah had called, expressing their outrage over the article. Madeline said that both the sitting room and tea room were filled with indignant women threatening to petition the *Gazette*. Madeline and Connie had to ply them with protein ("Luckily I had a few quiches on hand . . .") to get them to calm down.

Now, Julia isn't quite sure why she's standing in Livvy's office, and even less sure of what to say.

Livvy licks her lips and walks quickly into the room. Julia can see that Livvy has small wrinkles around the corners of her eyes, some new freckles on her cheeks. The sun and Livvy don't always mix, and Livvy always forgets to put on sunscreen. Julia has that old feeling of wanting to give Livvy advice, but Livvy isn't a child anymore and Julia is no longer in a position to say anything.

She clears her throat. "You look good," Julia says, and she means it. Livvy has always been good with clothes, has always had an eye for putting an outfit together. She's wearing a sky-blue tailored shirt and slacks with heels, a chunky bracelet around her wrist. Livvy looks professional and, like Mark said, more grown up. Her usually wavy blond hair is straighter, falling neatly past her shoulders. Julia stares at her sister standing only a few feet away and resists the urge to step closer, to seal the gap between them.

"Thanks. You, too." Livvy doesn't look up. "You cut your hair."

Julia touches her hair—she's still getting used to it. "Yeah, it was a spur of the moment kind of thing."

"It suits you." Livvy sits down at her desk, pushes around some papers. She's obviously flustered. She avoids eye contact with her sister.

Julia remains standing. She wishes she'd planned this better. She always pictured a confrontation charged with emotion, one outburst after another. Accusations. Apologies. More accusations. She hadn't expected that it would be something else entirely, more warm and liquid, a desperate rush of longing that makes her want to burst into tears, to reach for Livvy.

But Livvy is looking everywhere but at Julia, clearly ill at ease.

Julia can't think of what else to say, so she says, "Thanks for watching Gracie the other week. She had fun."

"Yeah. I didn't know if you knew. I just . . . Mark seemed like he was in a jam . . ."

"No, it worked out fine. Thank you." Julia was surprised how it wasn't as big of a deal as she thought it would be, her anger dissipating so quickly it was almost anticlimactic. "I mean, I was surprised at first . . ."

"Julia, why are you here?" Livvy looks at her, her gaze steady. Wary.

Julia clears her throat, adjusts her tote bag on her shoulder. "Well, the article that came out this morning . . ."

"I didn't have anything to do with that," Livvy says. She's defensive—there's a touch of vehemence in her voice, a hard edge Julia has never heard before. "I helped with the research, but I had no idea Edie had talked with you. I'm in sales; not editorial." Livvy's message is clear: *It's not my fault.*

Julia suddenly feels weary. Part of it is her bag, which is stuffed with who knows what. She keeps putting things in and forgetting to take things out. Right now it feels like it weighs a ton. She drops the bag into the chair and perches on the armrest, grateful for the reprieve. "I know. I'm not really all that bothered by it, though I wish she hadn't printed my name."

"I agree. I already yelled at Edie."

"You did?" Julia hadn't expected that, and yet she's not surprised. She tries to smile.

Livvy gives a small nod, her eyes down. "It was completely inappropriate. But Edie's a reporter, and she reports. That's her excuse, anyway." She picks at something on her keyboard, a frown on her face, her eyebrows furrowed.

For a second, Julia feels like she's having an out-of-body experience. She's watching herself trying to have a conversation with Livvy and it's painful, strained. Livvy doesn't seem the least bit interested in Julia, and Julia hadn't expected that, hadn't even considered that such a thing could ever be possible. It's all backward, with Julia being the one desperate for Livvy to see her, to say it's okay. All the rage and fury Julia has carried around have transposed into a thinly veiled shimmer of resentment from Livvy, as fragile and brittle as fresh ice on a pond. Julia has run out of things to say and can't move, afraid something might crack if she does.

Livvy regards her sister suspiciously. For five years she's done her best to stay out of Julia's way, to give her the space she's asked for. For five long years, Livvy had hoped—prayed—for an opening that would let her back into Julia's life.

But there was none. Julia hung up on her when she called, wouldn't answer the door if Livvy were knocking. Letters were returned unopened. An accidental meeting in the grocery store or post office resulted in Julia abruptly turning on her heel and walking out, leaving Livvy to navigate through the clucks and disapproving stares.

There were moments when Livvy's loneliness overwhelmed her. More than once she parked down the block from Gracie's Montessori school so she could watch Julia pick up her daughter, catch a glimpse of her sister, her niece. She would have said anything, done anything, to seal the rift between them. Anything.

But now she's not so sure. Maybe too much has happened. Julia has dealt her punishment and it's worked—Livvy feels punished, has felt every terrible feeling Julia has wanted her to feel. She's cried countless nights, has lost weight, hair, self-confidence. Tom talked about moving but Livvy wouldn't, wouldn't run from what she deserved.

But today, seeing her sister, Livvy thinks, *I've paid the price, Julia. In full.* She can't quite say it, but she can tell Julia senses it, too. Livvy doesn't know how it is she knows, doesn't even know how you can measure such a thing. All she knows is that it's over.

Julia fingers the strap of her bag. "So how are you?"

Is Julia lingering? Livvy shrugs, suspicious of Julia's intentions and at the same time wanting to burst out with the news that she's pregnant. The doctor gave them a due date of January 8. Livvy knows it's bad luck to tell people before passing the first trimester mark, but it's been hard. Edie turned out to be much further along in her pregnancy, and even though Livvy knows it doesn't make sense, she's envious that Edie will have her baby first. Livvy is anxious that something could go wrong, and just wants the baby to be born as soon as possible, healthy and happy. It's on the tip of her tongue to tell Julia everything, but she doesn't.

"I'm okay" is all Livvy says.

"And Tom? He looks good in the picture." Julia points to the framed photo on Livvy's desk.

"Oh, yeah. We took that last year. Tenth anniversary."

"It's been ten already?" Julia looks stunned. "I'm sorry I missed it."

What was Julia going to do, send a card? Livvy gives a shrug. "We just went out to dinner." An expensive dinner with expensive champagne that Livvy wishes they could take back. A simple picnic in the living room would have been just as good, maybe even more romantic.

Julia seems to be struggling for something to say. Livvy looks at the old canvas tote bag sitting in the chair, looking like it's stuffed with library books or bricks. The bag is faded and worn, but Livvy suddenly recognizes it. "Is that the bag we got in Evanston?" she asks. "At the lighthouse?"

Julia looks down at the bag as if seeing it for the first time. "I guess so."

It had been Livvy's idea to go. Josh had just turned eight, the minimum age for visitors at the Grosse Point Lighthouse. She thought he would love it so she proposed a road trip—her, Julia, and Josh. The husbands had to work and she convinced Julia to let Josh play hooky from school, a belated birthday present in which Livvy would do all the driving and take them to lunch at Merle's Smokehouse where a surprise birthday cake would be waiting.

Josh counted each of the 141 steps that got them to the top of the lighthouse, then gaped at the view of Lake Michigan.

" 'Built in 1873,' " he'd read. He turned to look at Livvy and Julia, his face awash in excitement. It was 2001. "That means it's almost a hundred and twenty-eight years old!"

They had been amazed at Josh's math, which wasn't one of his strong suits. And yet there he was, adding and subtracting years as they read through the history of the lighthouse, figuring out when the area was first charted, when the construction of the lighthouse finally began, the years of service of various lighthouse keepers.

When it was finally time to leave, Livvy bought them each a souvenir from the vendor stationed outside—a magnet for herself, a lighthouse snow globe for Josh, an oversized tote bag with vertical blue stripes for Julia.

"Really, do you think you'll have enough room for all your things?" Livvy had joked as she paid.

"There's nothing wrong with having a little extra storage," Julia said defensively. Livvy could see that she was already in love with the bag. "We can take it with us on future road trips, right, Josh? Maybe visit some more lighthouses around the lake?" There was something like 116 lighthouses in total.

Josh had pumped his fist in the air. "Can I skip school again?"

Julia laughed. "We'll see."

"I can come, too, right?" Livvy had asked, a bit anxious that she might be left out. After all, this had originally been her idea.

"Of course!" Julia put her arm around Livvy's shoulder, gave her sister a happy squeeze. She had looked Livvy in the eye, her voice lowered just out of earshot from Josh. "Thank you, Livvy." The look on her face was full of gratitude.

Livvy had flushed with joy from the compliment, of knowing that she had done something good, something right. But then life got busy and Livvy had to get a job, and they never had a chance to do another trip.

Livvy stares at the bag, wondering what Julia could possibly have inside and why she's still dragging it around. The old Julia would have donated it ages ago. "Do you want me to talk to Edie some more about the article?" Livvy asks, turning her attention back to the matter at hand.

"What? Oh, I don't care." Julia rubs at a smudge on the edge of Livvy's desk. She gives a halfhearted shrug. "It's not a big deal. Turns out it's been a lot of fun doing it. Who knew?"

"Yeah." Livvy thinks about what Edie told her earlier about her sister starting this whole thing by herself. She's sure Julia wouldn't do such a thing and yet, seeing Julia and her ridiculous tote bag, Livvy finds herself wavering in uncertainty. "Julia, do you think it's weird that you were the first person in Avalon to do this whole Amish Friendship Bread thing?"

Julia seems surprised by the question. "No. How could I be the first person?"

"Well, no one else seemed to have it before you."

"Well, obviously somebody did, because they gave it to me. That's the whole point of the bread—it just keeps getting passed around."

Livvy presses, unconvinced. "But don't you think it's strange?"

"Why is it strange? Whoever gave it to me was just trying to be nice."

"But *who* gave it to you?" Livvy knows she should probably let it go, but she can't. She wants to know. "Has anybody said anything? You know, like 'Hey, did you get the friendship bread I left on the porch?'"

Julia stiffens, frowning. "No."

"How come? I mean, aren't you the least bit curious? I would be. I'd be asking everyone. I'd want to know. Don't you want to know? Did you try asking around?"

Julia picks up her bag and hefts it on her shoulder. She looks at her sister, and the openness that was there when Julia first walked into her office is gone. "No, I didn't ask around, because it doesn't matter. *It's not news, Livvy.* It's just friendship bread. And you can tell your reporter friend that."

Livvy's mouth falls open. "I'm just saying that it doesn't make sense." It sounds lame, flimsy, even to her own ears.

Julia walks quickly to the door. She pauses, then says quietly, "You should know better than anyone that I've given up trying to make sense of things."

Livvy wishes she hadn't said anything. Julia's right—it *is* just bread. "Julia, wait! I'm sorry."

Julia turns for a moment and for an instant her face is filled with regret. "I know. Me, too." Then she walks out of Livvy's office.

Madeline is making a peach cobbler and tucking pats of butter into the mixture. She sprinkles brown sugar on top and then promptly covers it with foil and slides it into the oven.

"So thirty-five minutes?" Connie's hand is on the timer, a funny little chicken timer that Madeline picked up at a garage sale.

Madeline nods. "We'll peel the foil off after twenty." She begins to wipe down the counters.

"I can do that, Madeline." Connie sets the timer and puts it down, then takes the rag from Madeline. She scrubs the counter quickly and efficiently, scooping crumbs into the palm of her hand. She dumps them into the sink and rinses the rag with soap, then hangs it on the rack to air dry. "What else do you need me to do before we open?" She's bright-eyed and full of energy, and Madeline envies her.

It's funny, because Madeline never craved youth the way some women did. In California she saw it a lot. Up north, where people did yoga, pilates, hiking, kayaking, anything and everything to keep their bodies fit and trim, and then down south, where plastic surgery took care of unsightly cellulite and flabby underarms with the swipe of a knife. She doesn't mind the gray or the wrinkles, not even her failing eyesight. But it's the energy that she misses, the seemingly boundless well that young people take for granted. By the time you come to appreciate it, your time has passed and you're sitting at the kitchen table watching somebody less than half your age do all the work.

"Let's see." Madeline has to force herself to think hard. In a way, she misses the early months when business was slow. She had plenty of time to relax and think, even read. She'd cook at her leisure and could afford to give generous portions. Now, they risk running out of food by the end of the day. She gave Connie a raise and brought her on full-time and they've been talking about hiring someone to help

Madeline in the kitchen. "I know we're running out of eggs so we should probably call Ollie and see if he can bring up a couple of flats. If not we'll need to buy from the store. The herb garden out back needs to be weeded . . ."

"I did that yesterday. I ran out there during my break and got most of it done."

"Connie," Madeline reprimands her even though she's secretly pleased—she loves Connie's initiative and gumption. "Please tell me next time. You should relax during your break. You do so much as it is."

"I don't mind, Madeline. Really." Connie is eager to please. "What else?"

Madeline flicks on the light for the walk-in pantry and browses the shelves. "It looks like we definitely need to do a run to the store. I'm low on canola oil and applesauce. There are also two packages in the foyer that need to be dropped off at the post office. They're already sealed and addressed."

"Oil and applesauce. Eggs if Ollie's out." Connie takes out a small notebook from her back pocket and turns to a fresh page. She insists on keeping the shopping list in a notebook so they can better track their food costs. She's also been testing several accounting software packages and is trying to convince Madeline to invest in one that will process their credit card slips as well, but Madeline's not sure it's worth the trouble. "And I already dropped those packages off yesterday on my way home from work."

Madeline beams as she brings out a large bag of dark chocolate chips. "You must be some kind of mind reader. Thank you, Connie."

"You're welcome. Oh, and I mailed your letter, too."

Madeline is pulling open the bag and it gives easily, sending a shower of chips over the kitchen floor. "What letter?"

Connie is already on her knees, cleaning up. "The letter sitting on the table in the sitting room. It was next to the old Victorian writing box that Mrs. Ramirez was looking at yesterday. She says if you ever want to sell it, she'll buy it."

Madeline feels her body temperature plummet, like the time

she was taking a shower at that earthy retreat in Bolinas and the hot water got turned off. "Was it addressed to Benjamin Dunn?"

"I don't know. I think so. In Pennsylvania?"

Madeline stumbles for the closest chair and sinks into it, then puts her face in her hands. Her heart is pounding in her chest.

"Was I not supposed to . . . did I do something wrong?" Connie dumps the chips into the trash and hurries to Madeline's side. "I'm such an idiot! I totally should have asked you first. I thought you had left it there by mistake . . ."

Madeline has a pretty good idea of what happened. She'd been keeping the letter in the walnut writing box all this time, and the increased traffic in the sitting room had gone right over her head. She hadn't thought to take the letter out and put it somewhere safe. Mrs. Ramirez must have taken it out as she looked through the box.

Connie is still berating herself, and Madeline puts a hand on her arm to stop her. "Connie, it's all right. I should have moved it from the sitting room. I just didn't think."

"Is it going to be a problem? Because I can take full responsibility for this, Madeline. I'll tell them it was my fault." Connie's trying not to cry. Madeline is filled with compassion for this sweet girl, this young woman.

She smoothes Connie's choppy hair. She'd look so pretty if she got a good haircut, maybe changed her wardrobe or put on a little makeup. They don't talk about Connie's family much—Madeline can tell it's a sensitive subject and she's following Connie's lead. She sees Connie working hard to make something of herself, anxious to look forward instead of back. Perhaps she should do the same. "It's nobody's fault," Madeline assures her.

So the letter is finally on its way to Ben. This should be interesting. Madeline no longer feels panic, but a little flutter of hope. Maybe he'll call. Maybe they can meet up somewhere, like Chicago or Philadelphia. She'll fly out to see him if necessary. If he needs help, she wants to give it. Maybe he'll want to come to Avalon and see the tea salon. She doubts he drinks tea, but that's okay. There are other places they can go, too.

"Is there anything else you'd like me to do, Madeline? I won't do anything else without checking with you first." Connie looks miserable. "I'm such a dummy."

"Don't be ridiculous," Madeline tells her. "On the contrary, I think you're one of the smartest girls I know. And between the two of us, I'd put my money on you. Now I'm going to make some double chocolate chip cookies. Want to help? Good. Then help me up."

Oma Frank, 68

Part-Time Receptionist, Dental Office

Oma Frank does not believe that things happen for a reason. There's good luck, there's bad luck, and there's not a whole lot in between.

Her husband, Norman, is the exact opposite. A retired school-teacher, Norman believes that every action and reaction is purposeful. The two of them would debate over dinner, comparing stories and bits of gossip from the day.

Oma: "Poor Maureen Nyer just lost her job at the hair salon. I tell you, this economy is putting good people out of work, and we're going to pay for it as a country. It's a tragedy."

Norman: "Didn't Maureen want to quit that job? I recall her wanting to spend more time on her crochet work. You said she makes some of the best afghans and baby bibs in the county. At least now she'll have time to get some projects done, maybe even sell them for some good money. Lucky woman!"

Or,

Oma: "They're going to have to pull out all of Mr. Gilbert's teeth. He has periodontal disease something awful. Dr. Tindell had me deliver the bad news. Poor man was almost in tears."

Norman: "That is a shame. Hopefully they'll be able to fit him with some dentures that will be comfortable in his mouth, maybe give his gums a chance to heal. We all need healthy gums. Good thing Dr. Tindell caught it when he did!"

It usually went like this. Oma didn't mind so much, and it was part of what kept their marriage lively. This year they'll be married forty-five years. Now that's good luck.

But as Oma stares at the fifth bag of starter dropped off by some well-intentioned neighbor, all she can think is this:

What lousy, bad luck.

Norman, of course, is delighted. "More Amish Friendship Bread!" he crows. He loves it, especially the coffee cake variation Oma does with a streusel topping and cream cheese spread.

Oma takes the bags, marches into the house, and throws them in the freezer. She slams the door closed. "Norman, I am not baking any more!"

"Aw, come on Oma," her husband tries to coax. "You make the best Amish Friendship Bread I've ever tasted. And I'm not just saying that." Norman catches his wife in a hug. "It's almost as delicious as you." He nuzzles her neck.

Oma loves that Norman is still so amorous with her, but she will never admit it. "Norman Frank, you stop that!" She pretends to struggle to break free. She finally jerks the freezer door open to salvage one chilly starter. "Fine. I'll make one bag: two loaves."

"Two?" Norman looks disappointed. "It'll be gone by this weekend. Can't you make extra?"

"Norman Frank . . ." Her voice carries a hint of warning.

"Two would be wonderful, dear." Norman flicks on the television to catch the morning news.

Oma gives the bag a squeeze before putting it on the spare cutting board on her counter. "You know there's rumors that this all started with that woman whose son was killed by the bees."

Norman cranes his neck to look at her. "The Evarts boy?"

"Yes. That's what they're saying. All roads lead back to her it seems. I have a mind to take these bags and leave them on her doorstep!" She'd heard that people were doing that and while Oma doesn't approve, she can certainly see a certain satisfaction in it.

Norman turns off the television and leans back heavily in his chair. He'll never forget that day. "It wasn't bees," he says.

Oma is checking her pantry and writing up a shopping list. "What?"

"It wasn't bees. It was a wasp. A yellow jacket." He had been driving by when he saw the boy buckle on the front lawn. The wasp had been gone by the time he reached him. The boy couldn't speak, and no one knew what was wrong until his aunt came out of the house. If they'd known earlier, maybe it would have worked out differently.

Norman shakes his head and sighs.

Oma notices her husband's somber demeanor. "It is a shame," she says quietly. "He was ten, right?"

Norman nods. They don't have children of their own—something to do with Oma's ovaries—but the Evarts boy looked just like the sort of grandson he'd like to have. He had stared at the boy's picture at the memorial service, so different from the boy lying at his feet. He had felt helpless, wishing he had been there a moment earlier, and at the same time, not knowing what else he could have done.

Oma looks at her list. More flour, more sugar, more cream cheese. She could probably stand to have another jar of cinnamon, too. She turns to look back at Norman, who looks sad. And old. Oma doesn't see her husband like that, doesn't see herself that way, but right now that's exactly how he looks.

Old.

Oma knows that the death of the Evarts boy five years ago shook Norman up good. But still he held tight to his belief that, somehow, a divine reason would be revealed.

So far, there has been nothing. But Oma doesn't say anything.

She checks the ingredients one more time. She's a simple cook, she knows exactly what she needs and the precise quantities. It's perplexing as to why she's going through this list again.

When the reason comes to her, Oma pauses. She crosses out the old quantities and slowly writes in the new. Then she goes to the freezer to rescue the rest of the Amish Friendship Bread starters.

CHAPTER 20

❀

If you were to look at the town of Avalon on a map, you'd see that it runs along Leaf River, a tributary of the Rock River which, in turn, is part of the Mississippi River watershed. Flash floods and heavy rains are common occurrences in northern Illinois, and Avalon has had its fair share of torrential thunderstorms and rising water. Many of the residents still remember the floods of 1996, when the river spilled over sixteen-foot levees and flooded neighborhoods. The governor had declared the county a state disaster area and flood waters kept students out of school for two weeks.

Now the rising water has the town concerned again. Heavy rains have been pushing water into all the neighboring counties and high winds have knocked down trees and tree limbs, causing many homes to be without power.

Mark stares out the living room window. Rain is streaming down the window like a waterfall, completely obscuring his view of the yard or road. "God, what rotten luck." Their follow-up meeting with Bruno Lemelin is scheduled for today.

Mark sees Julia walk by with several plastic mixing bowls to put under leaks in the upstairs bathroom. He knows that Gracie is camped out in front of the TV, snuggled inside of a sleeping bag. Julia has taken out all of the camping and emergency gear, just in case.

His cell phone rings. It's Vivian.

"Why is the office closed?" she demands. "No one's here."

"Because we called everyone early this morning to tell them to stay home." He and Victor made the decision shortly after dawn when it became clear that the roads were starting to flood. "Didn't Dorothy call you?"

"She did, but I thought it was optional."

"You need to get back home and stay inside," he tells her. "I'm about to call Lemelin to postpone the meeting."

"Postpone the meeting? Mark, I have worked my ass off these last three weeks—we can't just throw it all away! You know he's talking to other firms."

Mark is aware of all of this—Vivian wasn't the only one working around the clock. "I know, Vivian. But no one should be out in this weather. I doubt Lemelin will even show up."

"Oh, he'll show." Mark detects a snicker in her voice. "Guys like him always show. And they expect everyone else to, too." Vivian's meaning is clear: If Mark had any balls, he'd be in a car en route to Chicago right now, weather be damned.

Mark looks outside again. The sky is dark. Troubled.

"Let me call Lemelin," he says. "In the meantime, you need to get back home." Vivian is still protesting when Mark says goodbye and disconnects.

Mark dials Lemelin's number but it goes right to voice mail. Well, of course. Only a madman would be out in this weather. He leaves a message, telling Lemelin to please call when he gets a chance.

A crack of lightning makes the house lights flicker, and there's a squeal of alarm from Gracie. Julia rushes in, cuddling up to Gracie, who seems more excited than scared.

"I should have gone shopping yesterday," Julia says over the top of Gracie's head. "I thought about it, but then I didn't. We don't have a lot of food in the house."

"I'm sure it'll be fine," Mark assures her. "Let's go look. Come on, spark plug." He scoops up Gracie.

They troop into the kitchen. Mark deposits Gracie on the counter then goes through the cabinets taking inventory. Julia's right: There's not much. This could be a problem if the weather continues this way or worsens.

Mark opens the last cabinet door and a barrage of starter-filled Ziploc baggies tumbles out. They fall into his arms, then spill onto the floor. Each bag is marked with different dates in permanent pen. There has to be at least twenty bags.

"Well, at least we have plenty of Amish Friendship Bread starter," he jokes as he starts to put them back. The scary thing is that all these bags are just Julia's. He's been disposing of the anonymous ones that are still being left on their doorstep. "If we don't lose electricity, you can bake and keep us well stocked in bread and muffins."

"I should just pour this all down the sink," Julia says as she helps him. The bags aren't cooperating, not wanting to be stacked on top of each other, slipping out of their grasp. "I've run out of people to give it to, especially since the article came out." She passes a bag to Gracie who immediately starts to give it a squeeze.

Mark hears the disappointment in Julia's voice. "We'll figure it out," he reassures her. Mark knows how important the Amish Friendship Bread is to her. It's become a ritual for their family, the squeezing, the baking, the discussion of what to make next. If it were up to him, he'd tell couples to forgo marriage counseling and try friendship bread instead. "We just need to cut back. Didn't you say you could freeze this stuff?" He goes to the freezer and opens it. "Oh."

Julia comes up behind him. One whole shelf is filled with frozen starter. She reaches out and closes the freezer door with a shake of the head. "I obviously have an Amish Friendship Bread addiction. They need to come up with a twelve-step program for this stuff."

Mark starts to laugh—he can't help it. It's contagious, and Gracie bursts into giggles. Even Julia cracks a smile.

"Okay, laugh it up, you two." Julia goes back to the cupboard and checks the dates on several bags of starter before pulling two out. "I think you're going to be right about the electricity. I may as well see if I can bake a few loaves now, just in case."

"Can I help?" Gracie asks.

Julia smiles. "Of course. Turn off the TV first."

Mark helps Gracie down and she races out of the kitchen. Julia turns to him, the look on her face suddenly shy. "Would you like to help, too?"

Mark would love to help, but at that moment his phone rings. He sees Lemelin's name flashing in the display. "Sorry, I have to take this. I'll be right back." Julia gives a halfhearted shrug as he walks away.

Lemelin's voice is cheerful. "Mark, my man. Sorry I missed your call. Enjoying this lovely weather?"

Mark is encouraged by Lemelin's casualness. At least he knows the weather sucks. "So long as I don't lose electricity, I'm good."

"Ditto, ditto. I like to keep my restaurants open. People still have to eat, right?"

Right. Mark clears his throat. "I called to see if we can reschedule for next week. The roads here are starting to flood."

"Really? Vivian didn't mention that when we talked."

Does Lemelin not watch the news, not look out the window? He's either clueless, careless, or Chicago has just been airlifted to Hawaii. "Well, we just made the decision."

"In the past ten seconds?" Lemelin chuckles. "Interesting, seeing how I just got off the phone with her."

Mark frowns. "You just got off the phone with her?"

"Not even a minute ago—that's why I missed your call. She said she spoke with you, said she was already on the road but you might not make it. What's going on, Evarts?"

Evarts. Lemelin's calling Mark by his last name—that's not a good sign. "Just some crossed wires, Bruno. I'll sort it out with her."

"Sure." There's a pause. "So I'll see you in bit? We can have a good meal, talk business."

Mark can sense that this is not so much an offer as a request. Lemelin knows Mark is trying to cancel but he's not going to let him go without a fight, or at least make Mark feel like a complete wimp.

Maybe he is being a wimp—maybe he should bite the bullet and go. Try, at least. But a glance out the window tells Mark that would be insane. "Thanks, but I think rescheduling makes more sense. What about next Tuesday? Same time?"

"Hmmm, next Tuesday," Lemelin balks. "I'll have to get back to you on that. I don't have my calendar in front of me."

Lemelin's backing out. Mark can feel it. He glances out the window again. Even if Avalon doesn't flood, there are two counties between him and Chicago. The closer he gets to the city, the worse the weather. It's always that way. He'll be stranded, and then Julia and Gracie will have to be here alone. Lemelin is single, thrice divorced. He spends all his time in his restaurants because he has nowhere else to go. He's got nothing to lose.

"Hey, I'd love to be there," Mark says, feigning regret. Lemelin is a guy's guy, but Mark knows he has a thing for Vivian and tries to appeal to Lemelin's soft side. "But the weather sucks and I don't think anyone should be out in this weather, least of all Vivian."

"Vivian?" There's a pause, a beat, and then a snicker. "You don't have to worry about Vivian, mate. That girl can take care of herself—I'm not worried about her. You, on the other hand . . ." He trails off, letting Mark fill in the blanks.

Mark is about to offer up another excuse when he realizes it's futile. He'll be doing backflips for Lemelin forever, and Lemelin doesn't care if Mark does it at his own expense or at the expense of his family. Mark is an architect and a damn good one. He's given Lemelin plenty to go on, a ton of great ideas that he knows Lemelin will use. But Mark is no longer interested in being someone's paid companion or lackey.

Not even for the project of a lifetime.

"If you want to meet next week, I'll have Dorothy call and get it on the calendar," he says.

Lemelin's voice is flat. "I don't think that will be necessary."

"Then good luck to you, Bruno," Mark says. And he hits END on his cell phone.

Mark can't believe he just let the Lemelin project go. But on second thought, he thinks that maybe Vivian was right, that they'd already lost it weeks ago. They held on to the hope that they could change his mind at the last minute, but Mark thinks both he and Vivian know the truth inside. It's easier to kid yourself into thinking that you still have a shot.

He dials her number to tell her the news. There will be other projects, other opportunities that will be much less of a headache for both of them.

"Hey there," she says cheerfully. He can tell that she's toked up on caffeine, running on adrenaline. "I'm on my way to Chicago. The streets aren't so bad."

Vivian doesn't know the first thing about flash floods, but Mark does. "I canceled the meeting, Vivian."

"What? But I can go, Mark! I'll be there in an hour, hour and a half tops."

"Vivian . . ."

She continues, unabated. "I can represent Gunther & Evarts, I know what Bruno wants to hear. I can close this deal, Mark. I have everything with me—"

Mark frowns, not comprehending. "What do you mean, you have everything with you? I have the plans and final bid proposal right here with me." He glances over at his desk and sure enough, there they are.

Vivian lets out an impatient sigh. "Look, don't be mad but I made a copy of everything yesterday because I wanted to show it to a girlfriend of mine. She has an amazing eye for color and had some fabulous suggestions about how we can tweak the fire palette to more of an orange than a red, which I didn't agree with before but when you couple it with the blue tones Bruno wants near the entry-way . . ."

Mark stops her. "Vivian, you can't go showing our work to some-body outside of the firm, especially if we're still bidding on a project."

"I know, Mark, but it was just a casual thing, nothing that she's going to charge me for or mention to anyone. I've known her forever and she's completely professional. I mean, my God, she works for Perkins Eastman—"

"Perkins Eastman?" Mark suddenly feels cold. Perkins Eastman is huge. They're an international firm, an architecture-interior-design-project-management-you-name-it kind of company. They play at a whole other level, and because of this Mark doesn't see them as com-petition, though in this business, everybody is. And while he doesn't suspect they're bidding on Lemelin's project, you can never be too sure. Either way, it's a conflict of interest and a massive breach of company policy for Vivian to show their work to anybody outside of the firm, much less a potential competitor. He's stunned that she would do this, that she doesn't know better. And then it occurs to him that maybe she *does* know better, but just doesn't care.

Mark closes his eyes. Victor had warned him of exactly this sort of thing, of how Vivian's ambition exceeds her actual authority in the firm. She's not a partner at G&E, not even a principal. His admira-tion for her savvy may have colored his objectivity, but it's becoming clearer by the second what's at stake.

Vivian must be sensing that something's wrong, because there's a shift in her tone. "Mark," she says softly. "I just thought that under the circumstances it would be good to talk to someone else in the in-dustry, you know? Somebody who plays with the big boys all the time, who knows what clients like Bruno want. I don't want to lose this project . . ."

"You don't want 'us' to lose this project, you mean." His voice is wary.

"Right. Us. Of course. You know that's what I meant." She gives an uneasy laugh. "Look, it doesn't really matter, Mark. The point is I have everything we need. I'm confident I can close this deal—*for us*—even if you can't make the meeting. I have it all under control. It's not a big deal."

"Actually," Mark says. "It *is* a big deal, Vivian."

There's a stunned silence. Then, "Mark . . ."

"No," he says firmly. "I appreciate your enthusiasm, Vivian, but . . ."

"You appreciate my enthusiasm?" She says this with disdain, her softness suddenly a hard edge.

Mark grits his teeth. He's usually good with this sort of thing, but Vivian has a way of turning everything upside down. That night in Chicago it took four hours and a good meal before she sobered up. She'd been running on empty all day, forgoing meals and pushing herself past her limit. During dinner he heard everything, all her unhappiness, all her insecurities, but Mark was okay with that part. If anything it showed her humanity, how she was just as fragile as the rest of them. But he also realized that Vivian was hungry—for love, for success—and Mark isn't the person who can help her get those things.

He knows it's his own fault he let things get personal, that somehow it's preempted their professional relationship and obscured the small detail that Vivian does, in fact, report to Mark. But things have just been taken to a whole new level now that Vivian has crossed the line in a very big way. Mark knows what Victor will say, that even though the Lemelin project was already lost, there's no telling if she will do something like this again. Even Mark isn't sure she wouldn't do this again. He feels sorry for what he's about to do, because he knows she's just trying to find her way in the world and he wishes he could help. "Vivian . . ."

"Don't 'Vivian' me, Mark." Her voice is biting, caustic. "I'm not Julia—you don't have to talk me down from the ledge. I'm sick of you being such a nice guy, Mark!"

And that's enough. He can't believe he's putting up with this. His empathy has dissolved into annoyance, and it's directed at himself more than anyone else. Mark wonders why he didn't see it before,

why he didn't clue in sooner, but he's had enough of this crazy rollercoaster ride. He wants off. And lucky for Vivian, he's not going to
bother being a nice guy about it.

"Vivian . . ."

"What?"

"You're fired."

It takes Mark an hour to update Victor and Dorothy, to call the security company that codes their electronic keys and have them revoke
Vivian's access to the office immediately. He calls Lemelin to tell him
the news, that Vivian no longer works for G&E and that she is not
authorized to talk to him on behalf of the firm, and that they are no
longer interested in pursuing the project. He speaks to their HR person who tells Mark to document everything, which he spends the
next hour doing in meticulous detail.

Whether she was hoping to impress him or was looking for a way
to bolster her own career and portfolio, Vivian has overstepped her
bounds. She's smart, talented, and extremely gifted, but she needs to
be with a firm in the city, one that can match her drive and ambition.
Or go out on her own. Mark has no doubt she'll make her mark one
way or the other. Whatever Vivian ultimately decides to do is up to
her, but she can't work for Gunther & Evarts anymore. This much is
clear.

When Mark joins his family in the kitchen a few minutes later, the
warmth of the oven and smell of sugary cinnamon envelops him. A
few loaves are already cooling on wire racks and another set of pans
is about to slide into the oven. Julia smiles at him and Gracie is sprin-
kling raisins into a mixing bowl. He forgets about the rain, about
Vivian, about Lemelin, about being the best architect in the world. Instead, he sets his sights on his wife and daughter and holds his hands
out to help.

CHAPTER 21

❀

"I have a bunch of packages for you." Jamie Linde stands on the porch in a UPS-issued rain slicker. Water is dripping from his face but he's smiling, and Hannah feels her heart give a little flutter as it always does when she sees him. "I can cover them in plastic so they don't get wet. Or I can back the truck up the driveway."

Packages, plural. Hannah tries to remember what she ordered. She's been shopping online quite a bit, buying new appliances for her kitchen—a food processor, a juicer, a tabletop grill—plus a host of new utensils. So far her favorite is the silicone bakeware. There's something about the soft, flexible pans that Hannah loves. Her loaves of Amish Friendship Bread just slide out with a simple twist, perfectly and evenly baked. Cleanup is a breeze, too. Why can't everything in life be this easy?

"Whatever is simplest for you," she tells him, feeling bad that he has to work in such bad weather. There are only a few cars out on the street and the wind is howling, whipping rain sideways. She slips on her shoes.

He peers at her driveway. "Do you want to open your garage door? I can bring them right in."

"How many packages are there?"

Jamie is already heading back out into the rain. "About ten."

Hannah goes through the house and opens the garage door. Jamie is already there, the UPS truck almost touching the eaves. He brings out the first box and walks it into the garage, placing it by the door to the house. "Here's the first one."

Hannah looks at the addresses which have been scrawled across the top of the box with a fat permanent marker.

From: P. de Brisay, 540 North State Street, #843, Chicago, IL 60610.

To: Hannah Wang, 11248 First Avenue, Avalon, IL 61798.

Hannah stares at the box. She thought Philippe was going to wait until the season was over in June before sending back her things, but apparently that's too long. Hannah shouldn't be surprised—once Philippe makes up his mind, he's impatient to get it over with, to move on—but she wasn't prepared for the shock of seeing her own name again, suddenly separate and disconnected from his. It's amazing how someone can cut you out of their life by simply taking their name back.

She hasn't been Hannah Wang in years, not since she married Philippe. Her father had been against her changing her name, even her agent was against it, but Hannah wanted to change her name. She loved how Philippe would chant, "Hannah de Brisay, Hannah de Brisay," with so much pride and joy. He practically sang it out to everyone in the first-class cabin when they were on their honeymoon, he was so proud.

"Are you okay?" Jamie is ferrying in boxes of different sizes and shapes, miscellaneous cardboard boxes that Philippe picked up from Costco or at the back of some warehouse.

Hannah doesn't say anything but tugs at a single strip of flimsy packing tape that holds the flaps together. It comes off easily, making her marvel at the fact that the box didn't burst open during transit.

Inside is a jumble of her things from the apartment. Clothes, books, toiletries. The lid for her shampoo is loose, and it's leaked all over everything, even the cashmere throw Philippe gave her for Christmas. Hannah tries to scoop some of the shampoo back into the bottle, but finally gives up and drops the whole thing back into the box.

Jamie wrinkles his nose. "Wow, that's too bad. People don't always pack things well and things can open along the way. Smells nice, though."

Hannah smiles at him gratefully, touched that he noticed. That's exactly why she bought the shampoo, a milk and rose variety from Fresh. But Philippe didn't care.

"Thanks, Jamie. Do I need to sign anything?"

"Nope. Sender didn't request confirmation."

Hannah feels a twinge of rejection again that Philippe couldn't even be bothered to make sure she got everything. "Oh. Well, okay." She surveys the other boxes and dreads opening them. Maybe she shouldn't. She can't even remember what she had in that apartment. Maybe she should just donate everything sight unseen and move on.

"So." Jamie casts his eyes around the almost bare garage. There aren't any tools or lawn equipment, none of the usual things that you might find. Philippe was never one for manual labor, nor would he risk his hands, which are insured by the CSO. They have a gardener who comes twice a month. "Are you renting this place?"

"No, we bought it." Hannah closes up the box and pushes it away.

"Oh. Right. Your husband is a musician, too?"

"He's a violinist with the Chicago Symphony Orchestra. We're separated, though. We're getting a divorce." She opens up another box and sees a jumble of sweaters.

Jamie doesn't look surprised, his face sympathetic as he points his chin to the empty spaces around them. "I figured. It doesn't look like there's a man around here. I'm sorry."

"Me, too. He's sleeping with the violist." That was totally unnecessary—Hannah wants to clap a hand over her mouth. But then she thinks, *I don't care. I'm glad he knows.* She nudges another box with the edge of her ballet flat, wonders what's inside.

Jamie grimaces, makes a face. "He must be mad. I'd take a cellist over a violist any day." He says this with so much authority that Hannah smiles, charmed. There's a flash of lightning followed almost immediately by another rumble of thunder.

Jamie glances outside. "I should go. You're my last delivery—they want us to head back because of the weather. There's major flooding in Laquin but Barrett is hit the worst." Barrett and Laquin are small towns neighboring Avalon.

"Oh, wait," Hannah says, jumping up. She hurries into the house where she wraps a couple of potato croquettes, still warm from the pan. She returns to the garage and hands them to him. "I just made them."

Jamie accepts them gratefully. "Wow, these look amazing. Thanks—I was starving. I skipped my break because I wanted to finish my route early." His eyes dart outside, where the sky is dark and menacing. "I know this may not be great timing for you, but would you be interested in going out sometime? Not like a date, because you're still married, but maybe for dinner or something? Do you like Italian?"

Oh, Hannah would love to go out to dinner with him. Jamie is tall and handsome and incredibly sweet. It doesn't hurt that he has a great body, either, which is easy to see in his trim UPS uniform. And it's clear that he likes her. Hannah misses that part the most—having someone to dote on her, someone who thinks she's the greatest thing since sliced bread.

"Thanks, but I probably shouldn't . . ." Her voice trails off, disappointed.

"Right." Jamie is quick to nod, embarrassed.

Hannah bites her lip, frustrated. God, she wants to. She *wants* to go out with Jamie, wants to know more about him, wants to see what they have in common. But it's too soon, isn't it? She should probably finalize the divorce, have a period of aloneness, of independence. "It's just that everything is so messy with my husband right now . . ." She stops.

How much more aloneness does Hannah really need? How exactly is she supposed to quantify that? Is it like a period of mourning? Because the more she thinks about it, the more she's noticing something else entirely. She's spent a good part of her life being alone, maybe not physically, but emotionally, and she's not interested in living like that anymore. Her marriage is over, her professional playing career is over. And while there has been so much sorrow around these losses, there is something new in its place.

Freedom.

Freedom to make mistakes, freedom to live life messily. That's what Madeline and Julia said, right? *Life is messy.* Their friendship, like a breath of fresh air, has swept away the cobwebs from the dark corners of her life, has shown her that while aloneness may have its place, friendship—and love—offer so much more.

"Well, I just thought I'd ask." Jamie runs a hand through his hair, mussing it up, and Hannah loves how it makes him even more handsome. He smiles politely then turns to leave.

"Wait," she says. She reaches out and touches his arm, lightly, and isn't prepared for the sudden flash of heat that runs through her, causing her body to tingle.

Wow.

"Not a date yet, but maybe we can meet for ice cream sometime," she proposes. "How about next week?" She's had enough of the fancy dinners and elaborate dates—she wants to do something fun for a change. Something that doesn't require a lot of planning or coordination, or having to have her hair done or a special outfit picked out. She's been wanting to go to the ice cream parlor near her house and she likes the idea of sitting with Jamie in a place filled with the wild cacophony of school-aged kids, sharing a sundae or ice cream float.

"Ice cream?" Jamie says this with such a look of amusement on his face that she can't help but laugh. "Okay. But you have to stay on your side of the booth." He says this playfully but Hannah hears the flirtatious undertones, can see that he's already trying to figure out how to woo her. She prays he isn't the kind of guy who will smash her heart into a million little pieces, because she can already feel herself falling for him. Or maybe it's too late and she already has, and she just needs to let it go.

Hannah is full to bursting, radiating a happiness she hasn't felt in a long time. She presses her lips together to keep her smile in check. "I'll try my best."

Jamie grins back, pulls the hood back on his head. "Great," he says. "I'll call you next week. Stay dry, Hannah."

"You too. Bye, Jamie."

She watches him dash into the rain and into his truck. The brake lights flash, and then he's gone.

"Well, it's official." Tom walks in the front door, drenched to the skin, and drops a box into a corner. "They let me go."

"Oh, Tom." Livvy hurries over. They knew this was coming. The company cut 150 sales reps from across the country since abandoning plans to release their latest drug, some pain pill that obviously didn't work or had too many side effects. "Like death," Tom had snorted bitterly when the firings first started.

Livvy wants to hug him but he's sopping wet. Plus he doesn't really look like he wants to be touched. "Can I get you something to drink? A beer?"

"I'd like some coffee, actually." Tom peels off his clothes right there in the entryway until he's clad in only boxers and socks. "They should have just sent an email. It was completely pointless to make us drive out in this storm to give us the ax in person."

Livvy tosses him a fleece throw from the back of the sofa and scoops up his clothes. "I'll put some coffee on. And Mrs. Lowry stopped by to give us a loaf of that Amish Friendship Bread. Can you believe it?"

Tom wraps the throw around himself then pads into the living room. "Did you have it tested for poison?"

"Tom." But Livvy is smiling, having had her own suspicions as well. "I actually invited her in and we each had a slice. You'll like it."

"Maybe she's in cahoots with Julia."

Livvy doesn't say anything. In the past she appreciated the small jabs at Julia, at Tom's attempts to stay loyal to his wife. But now she feels remorse at hearing Julia's name, at their inability to make things right again. It's no longer vengeful or funny, just sad.

Tom picks up the remote but then puts it back down and settles onto the couch. He look around, gives a shiver. "We need a fireplace."

Livvy goes to the thermostat and turns the dial. "I'll turn up the heat." The lack of a fireplace in the house is the one thing that bothers Livvy. The house is relatively new and has everything else, but the real estate agent said the previous owner had run out of money before they could put a fireplace in, and Livvy and Tom couldn't afford to put one in, either. She longs for the sound of a fire crackling and popping, the smell of wood burning. S'mores. That's really what it is. She wishes they could make s'mores in their living room, as silly as that might sound.

In the kitchen Livvy hums as she cuts several fat slices of the bread and puts them on a plate. She makes a pot of coffee and chooses a container of nonfat yogurt for herself then gets one for Tom, in case he'd like one, too. She's read about how husbands will sometimes gain sympathy weight, and she hopes that won't happen to him. Both of his parents are a little on the heavy side. She puts everything on a breakfast tray with a nice cloth napkin and carries it out to him.

"You're in an awfully good mood for someone who just became the primary breadwinner," Tom notes as she puts the tray down in front of him.

Huh. She hadn't thought of that. Still, it's not like they were blindsided by the news. "I guess I figure there are worse things that could happen." She breaks off a corner of the bread and pops it in her mouth. *Mmm*. She could eat this all day.

"We could lose the house, Livvy." Tom is serious. He adds some cream to his coffee.

"I know." The thought's occurred to her several times over the past month. "Maybe we should sell."

Tom stops stirring his coffee. "You'd sell the house? I thought you loved this house."

She does. Lack of fireplace aside, it's her dream home. It was a stretch for them to get it in the first place and it's mortgaged to the hilt, but she wanted it so they got it. She always pictured it filled with family and laughter, but it's still just the two of them and all this extra space only serves to echo their loneliness. The truth is that they would probably do fine in a smaller place, even with the baby coming. Livvy has no idea what they'll get for the house but prices have appreciated since they bought it, even if it is a buyer's market right now. There are a lot of nice features and they've done a good job of keeping up the place. "If we can sell it we can pay off the mortgage and maybe look at something more affordable. It can still be nice." The idea of having a smaller, more manageable mortgage payment is very appealing. And there's nothing wrong with having a smaller house. It'll be cozier for all of them.

Tom nods in agreement, sipping his coffee slowly. "If we want to do this, we should probably do it sooner rather than later. I don't want to get behind on our mortgage payments and lose the house altogether." Livvy sees his eyes dart toward the garage, probably remembering what happened with the BMW.

"Do you think we'll have a problem selling the place?"

Tom shrugs. "I don't know. But we'll probably have better luck selling it than me trying to find a job in this economy. Nobody's hiring." He takes a bite of the Amish Friendship Bread, his eyes registering surprise. "Hey, this isn't so bad."

"Told you." She takes another little piece for herself. She doesn't know if she'll be able to wait ten days before she can bake her own bread. She could eat it morning, noon, and night.

Tom stares into his coffee mug. "I've been thinking I should sell my golf clubs, too."

"Really?" Livvy stares at him. Tom loves golf.

"Yeah. Well, okay, maybe not my clubs, but I think I should let the golf membership go." He gives her a sheepish grin. "I can only play a few months out of the year and there are lots of good muni courses around. I shouldn't have bought it in the first place."

Livvy doesn't know what to say.

"I figure that I won't be playing much anyway. Any free time I have I want to spend with you and the baby." Tom pats the space next to him.

Livvy scoots over and burrows into the crook of his arm. "Tom?"

"Mmmm?"

"Do you think . . ." Her voice drops to a whisper. "Do you think I'll be a good mother?"

Tom looks at her and she knows he knows what she's thinking. "Livvy," he says. "I *know* you'll be a good mother."

She swallows. "Even after . . ."

"Even after what happened," he finishes for her.

Tom wraps the blanket around them—all three of them, if you include their little bean in utero—and they continue to talk quietly and eat as the rain falls steadily against the house.

"Stupid mother—" Edie closes the lid of her laptop angrily.

Richard walks into the bedroom and frowns at Edie sitting up in bed. "You're supposed to be lying down. As in completely horizontal." Richard puts a tall glass of water next to the bed stand and picks up her laptop. "Drink."

Water, water, everywhere. It's pouring outside, a hazardous weather outlook according to NOAA, the National Oceanic and Atmospheric Administration, home of the National Weather Service. Rivers across the northern part of the state are flooding. Heavy thunderstorms are rolling through the area with nonstop rainfall. Residents of nearby towns have been evacuated and there's reported damage to almost two hundred homes. Avalon, while wet, seems to have been spared.

"Since when did you become such a medical Nazi?" Edie grumbles, but she obediently takes a long sip of water.

"Since you were diagnosed with preeclampsia and the doctor put you on bed rest." He folds back the covers and nudges her to lie down.

Edie sighs. "Oh, right." She scoots down under the covers and lets her head fall back on the pillow.

Her last prenatal appointment with Dr. Briggs revealed hypertension and excess protein in her urine. Add to that the occasional dizziness and the nausea and vomiting (turned out it wasn't morning sickness after all) and hello, preeclampsia. The only cure for preeclampsia is to have the baby, which is not a possibility since Edie still has twenty weeks to go. So Dr. Briggs has put Edie on bed rest until it's time for the big day. As much as she's dreading labor, being put on bed rest feels like a prison sentence.

"It's not uncommon, unfortunately," Dr. Briggs told her. "It happens with first pregnancies and women over forty."

"But I'm thirty-six."

Dr. Briggs lifted her shoulders as if to say, *What can you do?*

"Patrick hired another reporter," Edie says as Richard plumps a pillow. "I just saw her byline. *Lori Blair.* What kind of name is that? She doesn't even have a degree in journalism. She was a poli sci major from some community college. Her last job was working at the Avalon Book Nook."

"How do you know?"

"I Googled her and found her on Facebook." Edie pulls the covers up to her chin. "She's also on mySpace and is a food reviewer on Yelp."

Richard zips up her computer case and puts it to the side. "That's being a bit obsessive, don't you think?"

"She also self-published some book about how to bond with your dog." Edie rolls her eyes. "It's four ninety-nine. You can buy it on Amazon. Amazingly she got ten reviews from . . ."

"Edie." Richard interrupts and gives her a look.

"What?"

"Stop stalking the new hires at the *Gazette*."

Edie rolls over onto her left side, her back to him. "I'm not stalking. I just wanted to find out why he hired her. She's not a freelancer. Her byline says Staff Reporter."

"You didn't want to be on staff," he reminds her. "You wanted your freedom. And Patrick's got to figure out some way to get the news out while you're laid up, Edie."

"I'm not laid up. I'm working from home."

"Fine. Tell yourself that if that makes you feel better. But we both know there's only so much you can do from bed, Edie. Patrick knows that, too." Richard rests on the edge of the bed and hands her the water glass. "Drink up. You're only on your third glass of the day."

Edie downs the water and hands the glass back to him. "I could really go for a plate of chili cheese fries. With a side of chili cheese fries. And topped with some chili cheese fries." She pouts, frustrated.

"Hold on just a few more months and then I'll make them myself if I have to. I am also going to make a bunch of meals before the baby comes so we can have something ready in the freezer. Let me know if you have any special requests, otherwise I'll just make your favorites."

Edie feels a swell of emotion. It's her damn hormones, but it doesn't help that Richard is so sweet. She knows that he would have the baby if he could, sparing her all of this. She watched four babies being born while living in Benin, and while the women were all remarkably calm and focused, Edie doesn't feel quite so confident herself.

"I'm going to have to go in about an hour," he says. Richard is part of an ad hoc medical relief team circulating through the county, helping hospitals and clinics that are trying to manage the influx of patients and flood-related crises. "Are you going to be okay?"

"Yeah, I was thinking about hitting a couple of bars, but maybe I'll just stay put."

"Smart-ass." He leans over and gives her a nice long kiss that takes her breath away. "I have something for you. Hold on." He winks and bounds out of the bedroom.

She stares after him. What's going on? He's not going to . . .

No. Oh God. She's not ready. She hasn't showered in two days! And she has the worst case of bed head from having been horizontal for the past week. Knowing Richard, there's probably a camera somewhere for the obligatory self-portrait. There's no way he would propose without getting evidence of it on film.

Richard returns holding something large wrapped in brown paper. Unless he put it in a really big, flat box, it's obviously not a diamond ring. "Okay, are you ready?" he asks, grinning.

Edie's confused, but nods.

Richard tears back one corner and Edie sees a flash of color. He pulls back the rest of the paper and she instantly recognizes the wide swath of purple, white, and red—a Mark Rothko print that she loves to see every time they go to the Art Institute in the city.

"You bought the poster?" she gasps. She props herself up on her elbows, anxious to get a closer look.

"I bought and framed it." He rips off all of the paper and leans it against the wall. Then he disappears and returns with two more, one with squares of orange and yellow and another of a green rectangle divided by a blue stripe. "Where do you want them?"

"Are you going to put them up in here?" She claps her hands, beaming. Their walls have been bare for so long, a function of neither of them having time or interest in doing more than was necessary. Personally, Edie thinks that home décor is way overrated. So why then is she so happy?

Richard looks proud of himself. "I figured we should make the bedroom as comfortable as possible for you, so we can put them wherever you like. And . . ." He disappears again and returns with another large box, this one square in shape. It's a package addressed to her. "I'll help you open it if you lie down again."

"But I'm only up on my elbows!" she protests.

"Down." He waits until she's flat on her back again before cutting through the tape with a penknife. He removes some wadded up paper and then holds up a brightly colored throw pillow that instantly reminds Edie of Africa. "They're from Malawi. It's traditional potato printing on mud cloth." He tosses it to her and it hits her lightly in the face, making her laugh. He reaches into the box and pulls out another one with colorful glass beading. "Xhosa appliqué. I thought they'd look nice on the bed."

"Where did you get them? I'm assuming you didn't go to Cape Town to pick them up."

"I found a place that sells them online." At Edie's raised eyebrows Richard adds, "It's a fair trade organization that buys their products through African Home. Fifty percent of the profits benefit an orphanage in Malawi."

Edie gives him a happy smile. "I love you." She catches the other pillow as it sails in her direction. "Come here so I can kiss you."

"In a minute. I'm not done." Richard steps outside of the bedroom again and returns a second later with an armful of books. "I took the liberty of buying all of the books and music CDs on your online wishlist at the Avalon Book Nook, because I know how important it is for you to support the independent booksellers."

"Well, that was before I found out that Lori Blair worked there."

"But she doesn't work there anymore, remember? She took your job." He comes over and piles everything on the bedside table.

Edie gives him a teasing pinch. "Not funny."

He holds up three red envelopes. "And I finally bit the bullet and bought a Netflix membership. I figured you can go online and build the list of movies you want to see. I reserve the right to get a couple of action films and the last season of *Dexter*."

"I should probably be worried about that last one, but I'll let it pass."

Richard grins mischievously. "In the meantime, I got a foreign film from Sergei Bodro, the latest documentary from Michael Moore, and some indie film that got rave reviews at Sundance last year." He walks over and puts them on top of the TV. "Maybe we should get one of those multi-DVD players so you can load everything up instead of having to get up and down." He mulls this over as he slides one of the movies out of the envelope.

Edie flips through the books, deliriously happy. Or is it the hormones again? Oh, who cares? She wants to remember this moment forever. "Richard, you are too good to me."

"It's true, I am." He grins. And then he knocks a hand on the side of his head. "Oh! I almost forgot." He disappears once again.

Edie lies back and holds one of the Malawi pillows in front of her. Gorgeous. Everything that Richard is doing is so incredibly thoughtful, though he's that kind of a guy. She hears Richard whistling as he comes back up the stairs. This is all really just perfect.

She pauses. *Too* perfect.

It dawns on her that maybe her gut was right, that she's being set up. Richard is going to ask her to marry him tonight. But why tonight? What's the occasion? She tries to think of when they first met, their first kiss, when they moved in together. Her birthday? His birthday? Valentine's Day? Wait—next month marks their one-year move to Avalon. Was it on a Tuesday? Edie groans. What is Richard up to?

She knows she's overthinking this but she doesn't want to be surprised. Edie hates surprises. He needs to give her warning first. Twenty-four hours minimum. Obviously she's going to say yes (they both know this), but he has to warn her. She made him promise that he would, and he agreed. So why is she so worried?

"Ready?" Richard peeks his head in the doorway, making Edie jump.

"No!" She tries to think of something—anything—to put him off. "Richard, it's really not a good time to . . ."

His brow furrows as he holds up a large takeout bag. "Are you sure? I thought you were hungry."

Oh. Edie feels a flush creep up her neck. "No, right. I am."

He comes over and pulls out two containers. "Low fat, low salt, all natural. In this one, a green salad with cottage cheese, every vegetable under the sun, a side of tofu, a sprinkle of flax seeds. In this one, steamed trout and crushed new potatoes." He grins, knowing he did well, even by Edie's standards.

"Wow." She opens the salad container and plucks a cherry

tomato. She feeds it to Richard and nabs a cucumber slice for herself. "Where did you get this from?"

"From that tea shop place. Madeline's. They have takeout in the evenings. But she did this kind of special for you."

Edie feels a twinge of guilt. She knows Julia is good friends with Madeline. "Why did she do that?"

"Because I told her you had preeclampsia and needed to be on a low-salt diet. She sends her best wishes. Oh, and this." He holds out a mini glazed lemon poppy-seed bundt cake. "Dessert!"

Now Edie really feels guilty.

"She says she cut out a lot of the oil and sugar and used a salt substitute. She gave us six of these cakes—said it freezes nicely. It's one of her Amish Friendship Bread recipes and she didn't charge me for it. Said it's a gift."

Giving Madeline their firstborn will be easier than the thank-you note Edie's going to have to write. She's definitely going to need some fortitude with this one. "I think I'll start with dessert."

Richard places the food on the small TV tray he brought upstairs. "I figured you would. Would you like some tea to go with that?" He pulls a fork and napkin out of the bag and hands it to her.

"No, thanks."

He reaches into the bag again. "What about a diamond ring?" He brings out a midnight blue velvet box and opens it, revealing a sparkly diamond solitaire in a simple six-prong platinum setting.

Edie freezes. The fork is in her right hand and the cake is literally en route to her mouth.

Richard just smiles. "Great. I'll take that as a yes." He grasps her left hand and slides the ring on gently. It's a perfect fit. He leans over to give her a kiss, not bothered by the fact that she's still speechless. "And, not that you need to ask, but it's a blood-free, conflict-free diamond from Canada."

Edie's eyes fill with tears. "Richard, I love you."

He gives her a kiss and looks her in the eye. "I know, Edie. I love you, too, which is why we're going to get married and live happily ever after." He grins, clearly pleased he's succeeded on his mission to surprise her. "I have to run. See you later tonight. I'll clean up everything when I get back, so don't worry."

"But, but . . ." The ring sparkles and catches the light, sending small rainbows here and there. It is a very nice ring and Edie stops to admire it, then catches herself. She forces herself to give him a stern look. "But I thought you'd want to propose on a special day—you're always into that. And you promised to warn me, by the way!"

Richard brings out his cell phone, checks the display. He pauses at the doorway. "Oh, that. That didn't count because I was under duress and you know my position on coercion. And, for the record, today *is* a special day, Edie." He holds the phone at arm's length, the small camera lens pointed at the two of them.

She racks her brain but is still coming up empty. "It is?"

"Smile." There's a click as his cell phone camera captures the moment. "It's the day we got engaged." He winks and then disappears.

CHAPTER 22

The rain has stopped, the troubled skies finally making room for little patches of sunshine. Everyone in Avalon is silently relieved, having
held their breath over the past couple of days. The high waters have
receded, but they've left a trail of debris and damaged homes in
neighboring counties across northern Illinois.

"We were lucky," Julia tells Hannah and Madeline, who haven't
really been through this kind of weather in a town that doesn't have
resources like a major metropolitan city. Julia's been listening to the
news reports and checking updates online, knows it could have easily
been Avalon under a foot of water.

She was grateful to be tucked into their sturdy house with Mark
and Gracie while the storm raged, and there was a moment when
Julia looked at the two sleeping bodies next to her and thought, *I
want to be free*. Only it wasn't the freedom she had toyed with before, that singular independence that excluded Mark and Gracie. It
was a freedom that *included* them. She wanted to be free to love

them, to be with them, to experience the rest of her life with them by her side. *This is what I want,* she thought as she closed her eyes. *I choose this.*

Now Julia drums her fingers on the table as she tells them what she knows. "There are hundreds of displaced families. I know the school gyms in Barrett have all been converted to emergency relief shelters. I don't even know if they've restored electricity in some places."

"It's just terrible," Madeline agrees. "I know they're collecting donations for flood victims. I was thinking maybe I could do a canned food drive to help out. Maybe a thirty percent discount if you donate a can or two?"

"There are requests for other items, too," Julia says. She fishes in her purse for a piece of paper and pen. She begins to write. "Organizations are asking for blankets, clothing. Things for children and infants, like diapers and formula. Toys. Books."

"I've been thinking about how I can help, too," Hannah says. "I spoke to someone at the Red Cross who thought it would cheer people up if I played some music. So I'm going to take my cello over tomorrow to play for the families, to help them get their mind off things." She gives a shy smile. "I know it's silly, but I haven't played for anyone in such a long time. I'm actually looking forward to it."

"Well, I'm coming, then," Julia informs her. "I wouldn't miss this for the world. I'll take Gracie out of school for the day and we'll go over and help however we can."

"Count me in, too," Madeline says. "Let me check with Connie to see if she'll be okay holding down the fort on her own tomorrow. I think she's in the sitting room with all the ladies." She gets up and heads across the hall.

"I've been thinking," Hannah says, stirring honey into her tea. "If you and Gracie are serious about lessons, I'd love for you to be my first students."

Julia regards her with surprise. "You're definitely going to stay in Avalon?" She figured Hannah would return to New York. With her marriage over, Hannah has little reason to stay in Illinois, much less Avalon.

Hannah nods. "There's no place else I need to be, so why not? The house is paid for, I have more than enough money to take care of myself here. But if I move back to the city, *any* city, I'll have to figure out something else to make ends meet. Why put that kind of pressure on myself? I'll have to work harder just to maintain the kind of life I'm living now—and what's the point of that?"

Julia just smiles. She loves hearing the certainty in Hannah's voice, the confidence. Her whole demeanor has shifted, and she notices that while Hannah is sitting up straighter, taller, she is relaxed and more at ease.

Hannah continues, eyes bright. "If I need anything from the city, I can just go there and get it. But I like the idea of Avalon being home. I like this neighborhood, I like my neighbors. *I like it here.* Plus I've already had quite a few requests to teach. If I get some private students and manage my money well, I'll be able to do more things that I may not otherwise be able to do. Like teach music pro bono at the public school. I want to help them get some good-quality student instruments, give more children a chance to play."

"I think that's wonderful." Julia leans over to give Hannah a hug. Hannah's friendship has become so important to Julia that no matter where Hannah ends up, she knows they'll stay good friends. But this, of course, is so much better. "I'm so happy you'll be staying."

"Me, too."

They hear Madeline's voice calling to them. "Hannah and Julia, can you please come join us in the sitting room?"

Hannah and Julia exchange a curious glance but get up and cross the hallway. There are about twenty women gathered in the sitting room, sipping tea and munching on sweets. They titter excitedly when they see Julia, who's become somewhat of a celebrity and a hero to them, and Hannah, too, who actually is a celebrity of notable fame.

Connie is holding one of the Spare and Share baskets, which is spilling over with bags of starter.

"Well, the good news is that Connie can cover for me tomorrow," Madeline tells them. "The bad news is, our starter runneth over."

"There are three more baskets over there," Connie says, pointing with her chin. "But the bags in these baskets need to be used or divided today. I think I counted twenty-five bags."

"So we've been talking and here's what we're thinking," a woman says. It's Irma Fagen of the Avalon Gutter, Avalon's lone bowling alley. "Each bag will yield two loaves plus three more baggies, right? Rather than divide the starter, we'll bake with it. So we'll each end up baking eight loaves if we take a bag."

"I still have starter at home," Julia says. "I was going to bake tonight. But I don't think I have room in my freezer for sixteen loaves."

"Exactly!" This voice belongs to Claribel Apple. "Which is why we think we should do a Bake and Take."

"A Bake and Take?"

"Yes! We gather up all our starters, bake our loaves or muffins, then take them over to Barrett tomorrow for the families in need. We can serve it with coffee or tea at the civic center."

"I'll donate the tea," Madeline immediately volunteers. "And my ovens are open to anyone who wants to use them."

There's a murmur of assent as the women discuss the plan.

"I have a minivan we can use to transport the loaves over," someone says.

"Me, too," comes another voice.

"I'll call over now to see if it'll be okay," Connie says, putting the basket on the ground. "So how many loaves do we think?"

The women do a quick count. Some have starters that are ready to use, others including Madeline have extra frozen in their freezer, which will take a couple of hours to thaw. Nobody minds baking round the clock, so when all is said and done, over one hundred loaves of Amish Friendship Bread have been pledged.

"I'm going to call my daughter," Jessica Reynolds announces, pulling out her cell phone. She's in a wheelchair, her body debilitated by lupus, but not her spirit. On her good days, her afternoons spent at Madeline's are the highlight of her day, making her happier than she's been in years. "She can help us get the word out, maybe put a sign up near the takeout windows asking people to help bake and donate their loaves."

"Is she allowed to do that?" someone asks.

"She owns the McDonald's franchise for Avalon—I would certainly hope so. And I think, under the circumstances, what with the governor having declared a state of emergency and all, it will be okay. Hello, Debbie?" Jessica turns away to speak with her daughter.

Connie is on the phone, talking with a Red Cross relief coordinator and jotting notes on a piece of paper.

"Okay," she says, hanging up. Her face is flushed. "I just spoke with the regional executive director who's overseeing the mobile feeding and food distribution for shelter residents and flood victims. She says that they'll take whatever we can bake. They have a lot of community volunteers helping, too, and she thinks they'll appreciate whatever we can bake for them. They've asked us to come to the Civic Center where they'll help us distribute all the loaves."

"I'll check with Gracie's school," Julia says. "I think almost all of the teachers and students were baking the bread at home. Some of them might still be doing it."

"Debbie is going to print out signs right now," Jessica Reynolds tells the group, triumphantly snapping her cell phone closed.

"I know Bernice Privott will put something up by the circulation desks at the library," Helen Welch says.

Suddenly all the women who have cell phones are using them, calling anyone and everyone they know who might have some starter and be willing to bake. Julia looks around at the busy women and feels a surge of energy. Rather than wanting to slink away, she feels just the opposite—she wants to be a part of this wonderful, chaotic moment. She grins, then reaches into her purse for her cell phone to call Gracie's school.

"This is becoming quite a production." Madeline cocks her eyebrow as the room bursts into a frenzy of activity accompanied by the occasional triumphant shout that another person is on board.

Connie drapes an arm around Madeline's shoulder and grins. "Don't worry. I'll keep track of everything. We should log who's baking what, and then use the sitting room as a central drop-off point. We'll open the kitchen to six people—everyone else can bake at home." She glances around the room. "There are probably ten more regulars who aren't here right now. I'll have someone give them a call."

"Is this going to be too much for you?" Madeline asks. She doesn't mind any of this, but she doesn't want Connie doing more than she already does. "We're going to be up all night by the looks of things."

"I don't mind," Connie assures her. "I pull all-nighters all the time. The only difference is that I'll be here instead of at home."

"Stay in the Savanna room," Madeline tells her, calling the rooms by the names given by the previous owners. "So you can catch some shut-eye every now and then." The Savanna room is a small suite with a private bath and balcony.

Connie beams. "I love the Savanna room," she says. Connie has helped her straighten the rooms before, and Madeline knows it's her favorite room.

"Good, then it's settled." Madeline is more at ease knowing that Connie will be comfortable. "I'm going to go defrost my starters and get the ovens going."

She passes Julia in the hallway, who tells her, "Gracie's teacher is going to send a letter home with the students. And she says she can bake tonight, too. I'll go tell Connie." She gives Madeline a pat on the arm and hurries back into the sitting room.

The chatter of the women in the sitting room seems to have gone up several decibels, making Madeline smile. There are more happy people here than in any home she's lived in. She thinks of the dinner parties, the casual get-togethers, the endless company functions. She remembers how forced it was at times, at how her eyes would discreetly slide to her watch so she could count down the minutes before people would go home and put them all out of their misery.

But here, in this small, unassuming little town, resides an abundance of people—good people, simple people, people with large and generous hearts—that she has had the pleasure of knowing and calling her friends. It's so unexpected and overwhelming. It hits her all at once, filling her with an unspeakable joy. And yet . . .

Madeline moves to the privacy of her kitchen where she knows it will only be quiet for a few minutes more. Things have gone better than expected in so many ways and at the same time it's not enough. Or maybe, she concedes, it has nothing to do with the tea salon, with its modest success, with these women she's surrounded herself with. It has nothing to do with them but everything to do with her, with Madeline.

She clears the counters to make space for the women who have volunteered to bake that afternoon, laying out fresh dish towels, measuring cups, flour. Despite the company of friendship we still have ourselves to reckon with at the end of the day. Wise words that Madeline has shared before but needs to remember for herself. She can't force her hand with Ben, but he is her family and she wants him, regardless of what condition he's in, to be a part of her life. That's really it, she realizes. That's family in a nutshell. You take them as they are, and you love them, no matter what.

By nightfall Madeline's Tea Salon has become the equivalent of Grand Central Station with people coming and going. Julia has only left twice, once to get Gracie from school and then again to pick up her own bags of starter and extra baking ingredients from the store.

Julia hadn't intended to stay for so long, but once word got out (Connie dubbed their effort "Operation Friendship Bread"), things started happening quickly. It was clear that Connie was going to need some help. Julia was soon coordinating, helping Connie track people, donations, friendship bread starters and loaves.

Connie peeks her head into the tearoom where Julia is working on Connie's laptop and portable printer. "Julia, the loaves are starting to come in."

"Here." Julia hands Connie a sheet of round stickers and a clipboard. She's created a numbered sign-in sheet, up to two hundred.

"Have people sign their name and give us their phone number. Write down the number of loaves they're donating. Then write their number on the stickers and put them on all their loaves." Julia's thought about this and she thinks it's important to have some quality control, to be able to track who made the bread in case there are any problems. It will also let them thank everyone who's contributed to the effort, maybe even do one of those nice ads in the paper where you list all the volunteers. Would the *Gazette* let them have the space for free? She could call Livvy to find out, since Livvy is in sales and might even be the one who Julia would need to talk to about this anyway.

Or maybe she'll just wait until later, when things are less crazy.

Connie thumbs the hallway where there's a steady flow of people coming in and out. "What about having more people come with us to help out tomorrow? Should I ask people as they come in?"

Julia's already considered this. She fishes around the papers on her table until she comes up with a volunteer sign-up sheet. "Here." She noticed people lingering as they wait for their loaves to come out of the ovens, eager to help in any way they can.

"Great." Connie grins. There's a nervous energy in the air, but like Julia, Connie seems to be thriving on it. "Oh, and our boxes for canned goods are already full. I'm going to move them into the garage and put some new boxes out after I sign in all these loaves."

"Don't move them, Connie!" Julia warns her. "They're too heavy."

"Oh come on, Julia," Connie scoffs. "I've lifted heavier things before. It's not a big deal."

"No." Julia is firm about this. She doesn't doubt that Connie can do it, but she isn't taking any chances. Connie is more valuable than she realizes, and Julia doesn't want her to get hurt. "I'll call Mark and have him come help. He needs to get Gracie anyway."

Julia glances at the clock—it's almost eight o'clock. Gracie had been abuzz with excitement like everybody else, trying to help but providing comic relief more than anything. Hannah took her home to pick up the cello and for the past couple of hours there have been strains of music and laughter coming from the sitting room.

Julia picks up the phone to call Mark, pointing down the hallway when someone walks in holding up four loaves of Amish Friendship Bread. "Hey," she says when he answers. "It's me."

"Hi, me."

Her face breaks into a smile even though she's trying to stay serious. "Things are starting to pick up over here and Gracie should probably get home to bed. We also need your help with some heavy lifting."

"Hmm. I might have to charge you for that."

"Mark!" She stifles a giggle.

"I'm almost home. Give me a few minutes to change and then I'll head over. Did you and Gracie have a chance to eat?"

Julia types into her laptop. "Mark, I'm at Madeline's. There's enough food here to last us the week."

"I'm glad to hear it because I'm starving. See you soon."

It's not until she hangs up that Julia realizes she's just been flirting with her own husband.

"Hey, Julia." Hannah steps into the room, a huge grin on her face. "I think your daughter is going to be a natural on the cello."

"Really?" Julia leans back in her chair, wanting to hear more.

"She was watching me practice and then I let her hold my bow. She held it perfectly. We played a couple of notes together, and then we played a concert-worthy rendition of 'Twinkle, Twinkle, Little Star.' Ten times. She was pretty disappointed when we stopped, but I think she's hooked."

Julia beams. "So when can she start?"

"Next week if I can get my hands on a quarter-size cello. I have a full size for you if you want to start next week, too."

Julia does want to start. She probably doesn't have any propensity for music, but she wants to try, anyway. "That's a yes for both of us. Where's Gracie now?"

"She was nodding off so I put her to bed in one of the rooms upstairs. The Thicket room. She's completely worn out."

"It's from all the excitement." Gracie was chattering nonstop with everyone from the moment she arrived. "Thanks, Hannah."

"You're welcome. She's adorable. And I really think we'll have fun." Hannah casts a look around. "Connie looks mobbed in the sitting room. I'm going to see what I can do to help." She lets out a yawn.

"You need your sleep, Hannah," Julia reminds her. "You spent the whole afternoon in the kitchen with Madeline and you're performing tomorrow. Connie and I can get some of the other volunteers to help with everything else."

"Okay." Hannah gives her a sleepy smile. "Then I'm going to head home. I'll see you in the morning."

"Sweet dreams."

Hannah waves as she walks out the door. Madeline emerges from the kitchen, a light dusting of flour on her face. "Was that Hannah?"

"She's tired so I told her to go home. She needs to be in top shape for tomorrow." Julia pulls out a chair for Madeline, who looks spent. "I think maybe you should call it a day, too."

"No, sir, there's still too much to be done." Madeline pats her apron, sending up small puffs of flour.

"There will always be something that needs to get done," Julia says. "We just need to do the best we can. You've been up since early this morning. Go and get some sleep. Oh, and Gracie's in one of the bedrooms upstairs. The Thicket room, I believe. I hope that's okay."

"Of course it's okay. I'm glad she and Connie will be making use of those rooms. I feel so wasteful having them, it feels good to have people using them." Madeline closes her eyes with a happy sigh.

"Well, I have a list of people who have volunteered to bake." Julia's eyes skim down the computer screen. "I can probably get a couple of them to come over tonight and give you a reprieve. Everyone else is baking in their own home and bringing the loaves over as they're ready. We'll plan on heading out at about nine A.M. . . ." Julia stops.

Madeline is snoring—she's fallen asleep. Her face is slack and her mouth is open as she takes short, shallow breaths. Julia watches her for a moment, overwhelmed with a tenderness that feels almost maternal. Madeline, who's opened her home and her heart to Julia, suddenly looks frail and vulnerable, and Julia feels fiercely protective.

She quietly pushes back her chair and stands up, then gently drapes Madeline's arm over her shoulder and eases her up. "Nice and easy," she says softly, wondering how she's going to get up the stairs with Madeline.

The look of relief and happiness on her face is palpable when Mark walks into the room, a small bouquet of flowers in his hand.

Mark is still flying high from his meeting with the levelheaded developer of Bluestem Estates, a cluster of eighty homes to be built in three phases. They want to make it green and keep it simple, with innovative materials and design. Losing Lemelin was certainly a disappointment, and Vivian's absence will be felt as well. Replacing her won't be an easy task, but in the end both Mark and Victor agree that they can do without the drama. Let the high flyers build those castles in the sky. Focusing on good, solid projects is more than enough for both of them. Mark gets that now.

He glances at his dashboard and sees that it's later than he thought. Everything is upside down with the weather and flooding of the past week. It's a strange thing to think how life is continuing on like normal for some people, while others have been displaced from their homes, their daily lives crashing to a halt.

On the drive over, Mark goes over the details of the Bluestem project, his ideas already flowing. Ted Morrow has certain things in mind but is otherwise leaving it to Mark to come up with something creative that'll work within their objectives and budget. Mark knows that buildings consume about 65 percent of electricity, and construction of new housing projects can generate hundreds of millions of tons of waste. Going green means that the houses will not only be more efficient for the end user, but for the environment. He knows it's an overused buzz word, but Mark figures they'll be able to cover a lot of ground just by incorporating environmentally friendly building materials and ensuring that the water and energy systems are efficient. They can design the homes in an innovative way that will minimize the building's environmental impact while still keeping the homes comfortable and functional. It's a different sort of challenge from the glitz and glamour of an upscale, luxury restaurant, but one that could have a much longer term impact on his business and the community that they live in. As far as Mark's concerned, that's not too shabby.

He stops to refill his gas tank at the Avalon Mini Mart. When he goes inside to pay, he sees a bucket filled with wildflowers. He doesn't even ask the price, just picks the bunch that reminds him most of his wife—wild, lush, and beautiful.

When Mark arrives at Madeline's a few minutes later, he's astounded by the number of cars overflowing from the parking lot and lined up and down the street. It takes him awhile to find a parking space. Avalon is a sleepy town that shuts down at 6:00 P.M. Here it is, almost 8:00 P.M., and you'd think it was a frat party with all the people coming in and out.

He holds the door open for a pair of women, then steps inside. He hasn't been inside Madeline's before, but he knows the building well. It's not on the historic registry but it's modeled after the classical revival style of the 1900s that dots the town of Avalon. He likes that the house has its own personality but carries a certain warmth and charm. He's only spoken to Madeline once on the phone, the night that Julia fell asleep and stayed until midnight, a night they never really talked about. In the past he would have pushed for an explanation, but he's okay to wait now, to let Julia share what's on her mind whenever she's ready. He thought then that he was at the end of his rope, but it turned out he still had a few more feet left.

He's curious to meet Madeline, whom he's heard so much about. He's seen her picture in the paper. She was kind but firm on the phone, telling him that she didn't want him to worry but that it might be a good idea to let Julia sleep. She had the kind of voice that made it difficult to argue, and he pictures her as a kind of tough woman wielding a rolling pin who doesn't take kindly to being challenged. But when he steps into the tea salon, he sees Julia supporting an older woman who looks exhausted. Julia is relieved to see him, and he gets there just as she's about to buckle.

"She's out," Julia whispers as Mark gently scoops Madeline in his arms. "I just want to put her in bed."

"Where?"

"Upstairs. Follow me. We'll go up the back stairs to avoid the crowd."

Mark follows his wife, holding Madeline carefully. She's so much lighter than he expected. "Where's Gracie?"

"Asleep. I say we just leave her be. I was going to keep her out of school tomorrow so she could go with us to Barrett anyway. I figure there will be more educational value helping out the Red Cross than making play dough and counting beads." Julia's voice is tired, but serious.

"I agree, although someone's got to count those beads." Mark's voice is equally serious.

Julia stifles a laugh, not wanting to wake Madeline. Mark just grins as he carries Madeline up the stairs.

"Hannah's going to be playing her cello tomorrow and I don't want Gracie to miss that, either," Julia continues in a whisper. "Gracie can't wait to start lessons. Hannah says she can start next week."

"Gracie's taking cello lessons?" It's the first he's heard of it.

Julia opens a bedroom door and motions Mark to come inside. She pulls back the covers and he gently lays Madeline on the bed. Julia slips off Madeline's shoes then tucks her in. Madeline mumbles in her sleep, "Apple crisp . . . vanilla hard sauce . . . need two elbow pipe fittings . . ." then rolls over and lets out an indelicate snore.

Julia motions Mark to step outside. "I thought I told you. I'm going to take lessons, too."

This is news to him but he loves it. "I definitely would have remembered that," he tells her. "Should I get my trumpet?"

Julia closes the door to Madeline's room. "Are you making fun of me?"

"Of course not. I just think you should consider a trio. Two cellos and a trumpet. We could make money on the weekends. I'm pretty sure we'd be the only one of our kind."

She gives him a playful swat.

At the door for the Thicket room, Julia puts her fingers to her lips and cracks the door so Mark can get a peek. Inside Gracie is sprawled out on the bed in a deep sleep, the covers kicked to the side. "I have her pajamas in the car," Mark says. "Should I change her?"

"No, let her sleep." Julia tiptoes inside and drapes a heavy afghan over her daughter. "We can check on her later."

Mark follows her down the front stairs. "I also brought a change of clothes for you. Your sweats and that blue shirt you like. I thought it'd be more comfortable in case you decide to pull a late night."

"A late night? I'll be here *all* night. But thanks, I appreciate that."

"You're welcome."

They stand at the bottom of the landing, suddenly embarrassed and a bit uneasy.

"So . . ." says Julia.

"So . . ." Mark repeats. He clears his throat, then gazes past her into the sitting room. "It looks pretty busy in there."

"It's nuts," Julia agrees. "We have three hundred loaves and counting. I think we're going to hit five hundred by daybreak."

"Wow. That's a lot of Amish Friendship Bread."

Julia grins. "Never underestimate the power of one bag of starter."

A young girl with black hair dressed in punk gear emerges from the room, a pencil tucked behind her ear. She's covering the mouthpiece of the phone and calls up to Julia. "I just got a call from Dora Ponce. Her husband is president of the local Rotary and she got him to ring every Rotarian in the county to see if any of their wives had any starter and would be willing to bake. She has one hundred and twenty loaves for us."

Mark raises his eyebrows, impressed but a little concerned. He has a feeling things are going to go much faster than Julia realizes.

"Uh, okay, Connie," Julia says to her. She glances at Mark. "Tell her thank you, and to bring them over whenever she's ready."

Connie nods and gets back on the phone.

"I think you're going to hit five hundred by nine P.M.," Mark tells Julia.

Given the way she's chewing on her lip, she's obviously thinking the same thing. She looks at him and asks, "What do you think I should do?"

It takes Mark a moment to realize that she's asking for his help. Julia hasn't asked for his opinion about anything since Josh died. She's always made up her own mind, and he'd be lucky if she even informed him, much less consulted with him. He thought it had come to the point where his opinion didn't matter anymore, at least not to Julia.

He quickly thinks. He has no idea how many people have starter or who will still be baking as the night gets later, but he has a feeling Julia will need to be prepared.

"You need more bodies," he says. "You're going to need people to help you inventory all the loaves as they come in, and then figure out how to transport everything from Madeline's to the cars or trucks or whatever you're using. You're going to need boxes. You need to have available drivers and people to help unload in Barrett. Then enough people to help slice and serve. I assume the Red Cross has people, but they're going to be very busy doing other things. You don't want to create more work for them if you can avoid it."

Julia is nodding as she listens, deep in thought.

Mark continues. "If this ends up being something that goes on all night then you're going to have to work in shifts. People will need sleep. Better to err on the side of caution and have too many people than not enough."

"You're right. I'd better make some calls." Julia is all business now, and heads for her computer. She pauses before turning back to look at her husband, the look on her face suddenly shy. "I don't suppose you'd be able to stay, would you? I mean, I know you have work tomorrow . . ."

"I'd love to stay," he says quickly. This is new territory for them, and he doesn't want to blow it. "Did you say you had some heavy lifting for me?"

"There are several boxes in the sitting room. Connie will show you. She's the girl with the spiked hair . . ." Julia gestures to her head and grins.

"Right. I'm on it." He turns to the sitting room.

"And Mark?"

His heart is beating so hard he's sure she can hear it. "Yes?"

"Thank you."

CHAPTER 23

It took less than three hours from the moment the women decided to bake for Barrett for word to spread around Avalon.

Russell Rogers' wife called him on the golf course just as he was finishing up his round. It had been a lousy back nine, and he just wanted to hit the club bar and unwind, mulling over his pathetic score card.

"You have to go to the store," she told him. *"Now."* She gave him a list of ingredients and an absurd quantity.

"Jumping Jehoshaphat," he had muttered as he shoved his putter into his bag. "Woman, this is not a good time."

"This is the perfect time, Russell. Don't think I don't know that you've snuck out to play some golf. And with all the tragedy that's happened because of the flooding!"

Well, that would explain why the course was so damn wet. Still, it should have drained better.

"I need you home in an hour. The ladies from my knitting circle are coming over and we're baking for Barrett. Don't be late." She hung up the phone.

In the store, Russell finds a small mob in the baking aisle. He is reaching for what looks like the last bag of flour just as a young girl steps in front of him smiling sweetly.

"That's my bag," she informs him. Her name is Winifred Leary, and she's six.

"Well, how come it's not in your cart?"

"It's too heavy. I'm waiting for my sister to come help." She puts a proprietary little hand on the top of the bag.

Russell glances around. "Well, where is she?"

"Getting the milk."

The last thing Russell needs is to catch heck from his wife. "I'm sure they'll be bringing more out. How about I take this one and you ask that nice man over there for another one?" He points to the pimply teenager wearing the store's logoed shirt and obligatory visor, fielding questions.

"Are you baking for Barrett?" Winifred asks.

He's not, but his wife is, which is pretty much the same thing. "Yes," he says, squirming a little.

"Oh. Well, me, too."

They stand there at an impasse. Russell knows this little girl can probably outstare him and, if need be, outlast him. What's taking her sister so long?

"Folks, I'm sorry, but there's no more flour in the store." The young clerk looks nervous making this announcement. "But we just called over to the Pick and Save and they have plenty."

Russell doesn't have time to go to the Pick and Save. "Let's make a deal," he finally says. "I'll buy you a candy bar and you give me this bag of flour. We both win."

Winifred acts as if she hasn't heard him. "I think we should share it. We're both making Amish Friendship Bread. So we can split the bag."

Now Russell is confused. How are they going to do that?

"We can get a plastic bag at checkout. Deal?" She holds out her little hand.

Russell doesn't know how his wife is going to feel about a bag full of loose flour, but what choice does he have?

"Deal." They shake on it, then Russell puts the bag into his cart and they go off in search of Winifred's sister.

Ervin Holder usually works in the produce department at the Pick and Save, stacking fruit, picking out old ones, cutting up samples. But when no one answered the call for assistance on aisle six, his boss told him to go out and help, so that's what he did.

Ervin is shocked by the number of people blocking the aisle, grabbing items off the shelves. At first he thought that maybe something had happened and people were stockpiling, only they seemed to be stockpiling items in the baking aisle, not water or toilet paper like the week before when Avalon threatened to flood.

"The PTA is gathering to bake Amish Friendship Bread for Barrett," Cordelia Gutierrez informs him now. She's president of the parent-teacher association at Avalon High School, where she has two teenage boys. "I need ten five-pound bags of sugar. Do you have more in back?"

"Er, I can check . . ."

Bridget Gholston, a beauty technician who works at Naughty Nails, calls to Ervin from the pudding section. "Are you out of French vanilla? I really prefer French vanilla over regular vanilla." Her electric blue manicured nails click against the empty space on the shelf.

Lila Schneider looks into her own cart filled with boxes of Jell-O pudding. "How does the French vanilla differ from regular vanilla?" she asks.

"It has a stronger vanilla flavor," Bridget explains. "It's also darker in color, but you can't really tell once the loaves are baked."

Lila considers this. "And do you still use the vanilla extract?"

Bridget nods. "I even add an extra teaspoon. Men love vanilla, you know." She offers a knowing smile and a wink, making Lila giggle.

Mona Coulson sniffs. She heads the women's Christian ministry for Avalon First Baptist, and she knows exactly who Bridget is. "Well, we're baking Amish Friendship Bread for Barrett." The way Mona says "we" means to incorporate everyone but Bridget.

Bridget gives her a sweet smile. "Well, isn't that nice? So am I."

The two women glare at each other over Lila Schneider's shopping cart.

Lila's eyes cut uneasily between the two women, realizing that she's caught in the middle. She attempts to edge her cart out of the way but she's blocked on either side by Mona or Bridget. "Um, excuse me . . ."

Bridget puts a hand on Lila's cart. She gives Mona a hard look. "Now I know you wouldn't be insinuating that a heathen like me can't bake bread for Barrett. Are you, Mona?" Bridget knows Mona well. Aside from seeing her picture in the newspaper every Christmas under the special "Church Round-Up" section, she and Bridget used to be best friends in high school.

"I'm just saying that some of us are focused on how we can help the greater good, and not thinking about how to get a man in bed."

Bridget's eyes flash. "First of all, Moan-uh, I am baking bread for the greater good and since half of that greater good is of the male persuasion, I'm sure they won't mind a little vanilla to calm their spirits. The women, too."

"Vanilla *is* a calming scent," Lila interjects. "It's very relaxing. I have a few vanilla-scented candles at home . . ."

Bridget holds up a hand, silencing Lila. "And second, I don't have to think about how to get a man into bed; I *know* how to get a man into bed. Unlike some people." Bridget smirks.

Mona's mouth falls open. "What . . . I . . . you . . ." she sputters.

"And third, I'm not doing this because I have some immature need to be recognized as a holier-than-thou person when we all know the truth!" Bridget says this last bit with flourish, crossing her arms and giving Mona a knowing look.

Mona snaps her mouth closed, her cheeks flaming red.

"I don't know the truth," says Roy Banes, a mechanic who's

helping his wife with the shopping and has been watching this little incident unfold with interest.

"Me, either," adds Wiley Brown. Wiley drives a water truck for the county.

Patsy Jones isn't rooting for any one particular woman, although she has done a few church bake sales with Mona and the woman is annoyingly condescending. After all, we're all God's children—Bridget, too, even though she works in a store that clearly promotes the objectification of women and sin—but Mona acts like she's the chosen favorite.

"Me, *neither*," she corrects Wiley, and then wants to bite her tongue because it sounds as if she wants to know, too, which she doesn't. But if something is going to be said, well, it's a public place, isn't it? And she hasn't finished her shopping yet.

"This is ridiculous." Mona's nostrils flare. "Nobody here expects to believe you, Bridget, as they are all good folk who aren't interested in malicious gossip."

Bridget doesn't say anything, a look of utter satisfaction on her face as she watches Mona squirm.

"So? What is it?" Roy demands impatiently. "We don't got all day." His wife swats his arm, but she isn't exactly dragging them away, either.

Bridget arches an eyebrow. "Well, Moan-uh, what's it going to be? Think you can lighten up on your 'I am better than you' attitude or do I need to tell these good people what transpired—or, rather, what *didn't* transpire—between you and our gym teacher, Mr. Grabowski, when we were in the tenth grade?"

There is a collective gasp among the shoppers.

"Bridget Avery Gholston, you promised!" Mona's voice is shrill. "You swore you'd never tell!"

"What, are you kidding me?" Bridget stares at her in genuine disbelief. "You're kidding me, right? We're forty years old, Mona! You haven't spoken to me since we were eighteen. You ignore me at reunion, or whenever you see me on the street. And we were best friends!"

"That's not very Christian," Patsy comments.

"And I *still* haven't told your secret. After all these years. Have I?" She spins around to the crowd. "Have I?"

They all shake their heads, acknowledging that, indeed, Bridget has not yet told Mona's secret.

"But she slept with him, right?" comes Wiley's guess.

"No, she didn't!" Bridget snaps.

"Well, then, did she . . ."

"I didn't do anything," Mona says loudly. "He didn't want to. Wouldn't." She glares at Bridget. "Happy now?"

Bridget studies her fingernails. "No, not really. An apology would be nice. For all of those years of snubbing and putting up with your condescending crap."

Mona casts her eyes to the ceiling, her lips pursed.

"Aw, come on," Roy says. "Apologize. Some of us would like to watch a little TV this afternoon." His wife elbows him in the ribs. "Ouch! I mean, make Amish Friendship Bread for Barrett." He rubs the sore spot.

"Come on."

"Say you're sorry."

"Apologize."

"It *would* really be nice if you said sorry," Lila finishes meekly. Even Ervin the clerk is nodding his head in agreement.

Mona blows out her breath, fidgeting in place. "FINE."

Bridget taps her foot. "I'm waiting."

"I'm . . . sorry, Bridget, for not having had a very Christian deportment toward you all these . . ."

"Oh, for Pete's sake, Mona!" Bridget looks exasperated.

"OKAY! I'm sorry for being so mean." The words come out in a rush, almost like a sigh of relief.

There's a titter of approval as everyone breaks into a smile, including Bridget.

"See, that wasn't so bad, now was it?" Bridget grins. "A few tears would have been nice, but that's okay. I'd take an invitation to bake with you this evening, too, but I'm afraid I already have plans."

Mona looks relieved.

Lila looks like she has actual tears in her eyes. "I'm so glad it worked out!" she cries.

Mona shoots her a look but Bridget gives Lila's hand an affectionate pat. "You are such a sweetheart, but your cuticle beds are a mess. Why don't you come in next week and we'll get them fixed up nice and pretty? Maybe help you do a little shopping, too. We just got in a shipment of silicone rabbits. Do you know what they are?"

Lila shakes her head. She pushes her cart after Bridget as the two head for checkout, leaving Mona to look up toward the Pick and Save ceiling, annoyed but her heart a little lighter.

Wiley Brown watches the women check their shopping lists, all grabbing the same things off the shelves. Flour, sugar, boxes of Jell-O instant pudding. Their carts are already filled with milk and eggs, and there's a murmur of talk about "Amish Friendship Bread."

Wiley's just here because he has a thing for condensed milk. He takes it in his coffee and adds it to his soup. It works good in meatloaf and mashed potatoes, too. As a bachelor he's learned to cook for himself, and while he may not do anything fancy, he can feed himself well enough.

"What's going on?" he asks the woman next to him. She hands him a piece of paper and explains what it is. It sounds interesting enough, but he doesn't have that starter stuff, and either way it's clear he's too late in the game.

Cordelia Gutierrez senses his hesitancy. "We're gathering a bunch of people together at the high school cafeteria," she tells him. "Believe me when I say we have plenty of starter. Ingredients, too. What we need now are people to help mix and bake."

Wiley straightens up. He knows about the flooding in Barrett as part of his route goes through there. "I can mix and bake," he says.

"Well, if you want to spare us a few hours tonight, I'm sure it will be appreciated."

"Yes, ma'am. When should I be there?"

Cordelia glances at her watch and sees it's already five o'clock. "Now would be good, but we'll be baking all night."

He can swing past the deli and pick up some fried chicken, then head on over. He's relieved that he thought to take a shower as soon as he got home today. "I'll see you there," he says.

Rhea Higbee, a cashier at the Pick and Save, has been scanning the same things all afternoon. She's on break now, and rather than step outside for a cigarette, she calls her sister.

"Dawn, it's me," she says. "Something funny is going on over here . . ."

Travis Fields stands on the doorstep, fuming. "Now? Don't you think it's a little late to be canceling a date? I have reservations for eight o'clock!"

"Where, at the Pizza Shack? Or the sports bar over in Digby?" Dawn Perry says this sarcastically as she kicks off her heels and looks for her tennis shoes instead. She'll need socks, too. She goes through the basket of clean laundry in the hallway until she finds a pair.

"I thought you liked the Pizza Shack!" Travis is about to step into the house when Dawn stops him.

"I'm on my way out, Travis, so don't you be coming in." Dawn pulls off her dangly earrings and scrubs some of the extra makeup off her face with a tissue. She doesn't know why she bothers getting dressed up for these dates with Travis. Come to think of it, she doesn't know why she bothers dating Travis at all. It's a lousy way to kill time, that's for sure.

"Well, you should have told me." Travis is petulant. "It would have saved me the trip."

"What, the five minutes from the copy shop? You didn't even bother changing! And your hands still have glue on them!" She grabs a jacket from her closet. "Besides, I just found out. The whole town is pitching in."

Travis pouts, as if he hasn't heard her. "I was making notepads. The clinic ordered up a new batch of prescription pads. Twenty sets of one hundred sheets!"

"How nice for you," Dawn says. She flicks off all the lights in the house. She closes the door behind her and locks it. Travis still looks flummoxed, picking strings of dried glue off his fingers. She has got to start dating better men. "Now if you'll excuse me, I have to go help bake some bread."

"So you'll be okay?" Frances Latham tiptoes quietly down the stairs, her husband behind her.

"We'll be fine."

"I should be back in a couple of hours. More, if they need me. I'll send you a text message so the phone doesn't wake up the kids."

"Those guys?" Her husband, Reed, thumbs the kids' rooms where their three children lay sleeping—ages seven, four, and two. All boys. "They'll be out until morning."

"Good." Frances goes to lift the box of ingredients but Reed nudges her out of the way.

"Let me get that. I'll get the other one, too."

They go into the garage and Reed loads the boxes into the car. "Call if you need anything."

"I will. I'm just over at Madeline's, so I'm not far. I've left a few slices of Amish Friendship Bread for you on the kitchen counter."

"Thank you." Reed pulls his wife in for a kiss. Even after fifteen years, he loves her more than life itself. She's been baking all afternoon for Barrett, even with the two little ones clinging to her legs, doing her best to make it fun and include them. Now she's going over to some tea restaurant that's the designated drop-off spot to bake some more and help coordinate.

Reed admires his wife, always has and always will, but something about this day is making him see her in a new light. Frances is willing to go the distance—for their kids, for their marriage, for this town even.

He helps her into the car, then closes the door. She starts the engine and rolls down the window, giving her husband a quizzical look. "What?" Reed has a funny look on his face, like he's holding a secret.

"So you know all that information you've just been leaving around about adoption?" he says. "From China?" Articles and books about China adoptions have been strewn about their otherwise neat house for weeks.

Frances looks guilty.

"Well, I read it. All of it. And I think we should do it."

"What?" Frances breathes, grasping his hand. "Are you serious?"

Reed laughs. "Well, we should look into it at least. I mean, we should talk to the boys first and go to one of those informational meetings . . ."

"There's one at the public library in Rockport next month."

Reed grins. "I know, I saw. Now go—we'll talk about it later. I'll sign up for the information meeting tomorrow. Call me when you're heading back."

"I will." She kisses him hard. "I love you," she says fiercely. Her eyes are wet.

Reed is surprised to find his eyes are a little wet, too. He watches his wife's taillights as they disappear into the cool, crisp night. He was going to go through some papers for work, but maybe he'll get himself a glass of milk and some of the Amish Friendship Bread and look through the brochures one more time.

CHAPTER 24

By 10:00 P.M., there are six hundred and twenty-three loaves.

CHAPTER 25

By midnight, they have one thousand.

CHAPTER 26

And by 2:30 A.M., there are two thousand four hundred and nineteen loaves.

CHAPTER 27

At 5:17 A.M., they have four thousand six hundred and eighty-one loaves of Amish Friendship Bread.

And counting.

"Holy crap" is all Connie can say. She dozed off around 3:00 A.M. and woke up surrounded by a tower of loaves.

"Dale Hodge from the Pick and Save is bringing over more boxes for us," Mark says. He fell asleep once and his hair is mussed, but things have been going nonstop and he hasn't had a chance to fix it. He has the same look on his face as when Josh was born after thirty-six hours of hard labor.

"We have a little less than four hours before we need to leave," Julia says, surveying the scene around them. Volunteers are busy inventorying the loaves and snoozing here and there. "You don't think people are still baking, do you?"

Mark scrubs his head with both hands in an effort to wake himself up. He squints, then peers out the window. "I definitely think people are still baking." The front door swings open with a loud tinkle of the bell and a steady stream of people begin coming in, their arms full of loaves wrapped in plastic wrap.

"I'm putting on more hot water for tea," Connie announces. Then, a little guiltily: "And coffee."

"Oh my goodness!"

Everyone turns to see Madeline perched on the stairway, a look of shock on her face. She's dressed and looks perfectly rested, which is more than Julia can say for herself.

"Or I can just make tea," Connie amends quickly.

"I think Madeline is referring to the success of Operation Friendship Bread," Julia says. She goes over to escort Madeline down the stairs and begins to fill her in on the details. "It comes and goes," she explains. "We just had a bunch of people drop bread off. We'll probably get a few more waves before it's time to leave."

Madeline is shaking her head in wonderment.

"I can't believe it," she keeps repeating.

"I know. And it's just not the bread. We have blankets, clothes, toys, money. Everyone donated whatever they could. We're going to Barrett with everything we've got." Julia crooks a finger and beckons Mark to come over. He looks shy and a little nervous. Julia takes his hand. "Madeline, this is my husband, Mark."

"Mark." Madeline beams as Mark awkwardly shakes her hand then gives her a tentative peck on the cheek.

"It's nice to finally meet you," he says.

Madeline grasps both his hands in hers and gazes at him happily. "Likewise. And you all look like you need to eat something substantial. I'm going to head into the kitchen and whip up a couple of omelets. With roasted potatoes, too."

"Keep it simple," Julia advises. "I think it's going to be a busy morning."

Madeline dismisses Julia's comments with a wave of her hand, and soon Julia hears her talking to the three women in the kitchen who are still baking.

Hannah walks through the door, her cello in tow. "Ugh, I'm so glad I live just down the block," she says, grunting. Her hard case has wheels but it's still formidable against her slight frame. "Cars are parked all the way down to my house—I couldn't get out the car out of my driveway. I thought it would be easier to catch a ride from someone here."

"Don't worry, Hannah. You're a priority—we'll get you there." But Julia frowns as she looks down her list. They just don't have enough drivers. Everyone who can help is already doing so.

"Look who I found," Mark says.

Julia looks up and sees Livvy and Tom standing next to him. Livvy is trying to smile, but she's nervous, her eyes darting around the room, taking in the cacophony of frenzied activity. Tom is standing tall, his shoulders square, like a man trying to hold his own but expecting a reprimand. They were always the younger couple between the two, not just in age but in the way they saw the world—more reckless, less concerned with consequences, a spur-of-the-moment attitude that often drove Mark and Julia nuts. Now, however, Julia sees that the gap is no longer obvious. It's narrowed. They are here now, four adults bound by old memories and regrets, staring at one another shyly and somewhat ill at ease. They all seem to be waiting for Julia to react, to decide how this moment will go.

"Livvy," she says, finding her voice. "And Tom." It's all she says, but it's enough, and Tom steps forward and gives Julia an awkward kiss on the cheek.

"We're here to help," he says, clearing his throat. "With this bread stuff."

Julia is stunned. Tom was always the reluctant one, the last person to volunteer to help, the dinner guest who couldn't be bothered to bring his dishes to the sink or at least make a halfhearted offer to do so. Julia remembers how hard it was for Livvy to get him to take out the trash. He's such a lug of a guy, an unexpected match for her sister and yet perfect for her at the same time. By the way he has his arm protectively around Livvy's shoulders, Julia can see that things are going well for them, and she feels overcome by an unexpected happiness for Livvy.

"We would have come earlier but Tom couldn't wake me up," Livvy says, apologetic. "I've been sleeping like the living dead and it's been, well, never mind. What can we do? I mean, if you want our help?" Her voice is uncertain.

"Yes," Julia says instantly. She reaches out to touch Livvy on the arm. *"Yes."*

"Okay." Livvy gives her a small smile. A brave smile. "What do you need?"

What does she need? How does Julia begin to answer this question? But Livvy is talking to her about Barrett, and it's Mark who says, "Drivers, I think. Can you run loaves and other things to Barrett with us?"

"We only have one car now," Tom says. "The Pilot. Livvy can drive that and if there's anything you want me to do . . ."

"You can take my car," Mark says automatically, digging around for his keys. "Load it up and drive it over. I'm going to stay here and watch over the fort."

Tom accepts the keys and the two men grin at each other. "I missed you, man," Tom says.

"Me, too." Mark claps him on the shoulder. "Come on, I'll show you two where everything is."

Julia wants to talk with Livvy but it's a mad house. She offers a helpless shrug as Livvy trails after Tom, and Livvy grins back. *Later,* her look seems to say. Or maybe it's something else.

It's all going to be okay.

"Here comes another wave," Mark calls back to Julia.

From this point on, the parade of people doesn't stop. Faces both familiar and unfamiliar walk through the door, holding single loaves, bags of loaves, even boxes of loaves. Mary Winder and her Bunco buddies, Phyllis Watts, Roxy Hicks from the police station. Bernice Privott and Koji Takahashi hand Julia six loaves of bread, still warm from the oven. Clinton Becker brings his daughter, Juniper, who's helping Debbie Reynolds push Jessica's wheelchair. On Jessica's lap is a basket filled with Amish Friendship Bread.

Cordelia Gutierrez and Wiley Brown announce that they have five boxes of forty loaves each—two hundred loaves in total—in the back of Wiley's pickup.

It's not planned, but somehow Julia ends up greeting everyone, with Mark and Connie ferrying the loaves to the back. There are a couple of awkward moments with people Julia has avoided or who have avoided her, but those moments quickly pass, usually ending in a hug and a promise to catch up soon. This is not something Julia could have ever imagined—playing hostess, reconnecting with people from her past—but an encouraging smile from Madeline and Hannah is all she needs to keep going.

Connie offers to relieve her, handing her a plate of food, but Julia doesn't want to stop. The two women work side by side, thanking people and signing up drivers, until Sandra Linde and her son, Peter, walk through the door.

"Sandra." Julia feels her adrenaline-induced euphoria fade. Sandra looks gorgeous, wearing the look of a mother whose kids are finally starting to grow up. She can take care of herself now, she can get her hair done and get a decent night's sleep. Three boys are out of the house and only one is left. Peter, Josh's best friend, who is now fifteen.

"Julia." The two women stare at each other, unsure of what to say. At one time the two women were good friends, always carpooling or having play dates, comparing the latest scrapes and falls of their two boys. "Jamie told me he saw you on his UPS route. I've been meaning to call, but . . ."

"That's okay," Julia says. She doesn't blame Sandra for being hesitant. It's been a long time and Julia hasn't made it easy on anyone to stay in touch with her. "It's good to see you."

"You, too. You remember Peter?" Sandra instantly reddens. "Of course you do. Peter, say hello to Mrs. Evarts."

Peter is as tall as Julia. He's outgrown his lankiness, and he doesn't look like the wild mischievous child that used to tear through the house with Josh, wrecking everything in their way. He's become more man than boy, and she can't stop staring at him.

"Hi," he mumbles. He glances at Julia then his eyes dart away.

"Peter, you've grown so tall!" Julia says, forcing herself to sound cheerful. "I hardly recognize you."

"Thanks."

Sandra gives him a nudge. Peter holds out four loaves of Amish Friendship Bread and Julia accepts them with a smile, her eyes filling quickly with tears.

Sandra fumbles in her purse looking for a tissue. Peter looks so uncomfortable that Julia just wipes her eyes on her sleeve. "Oh, it's just been a long night. Thank you for coming by."

"Any time." Sandra grasps Julia's hands. "I mean that. Will you come see me soon? Or I can come see you. I miss you."

Julia just nods, tears spilling down her cheeks. Sandra embraces her, then loops her arm through Peter's and they leave.

Mark comes up behind her. "Was that Sandra and Peter?" he asks.

Julia nods.

"Wow." Mark is blinking rapidly, a strangled look on his face.

Madeline is behind them and touches them both on the arm. "It looks like we have a short lull," she says gently. "Why don't you two take a break, maybe check on Gracie?"

They both manage a nod, then Mark slips his hand into Julia's. They head up the stairs to Gracie's room.

"He looks so different," Mark is saying. "But the same. You know?"

"He's bigger . . ." Julia tries to say, but the words get stuck in her throat. She feels the sudden weight of each step, of her legs turning to jelly. That old, familiar feeling of endless despair and unhappiness, of utter bleakness and hopelessness, is back. Julia thought she had left it behind or that it had evolved into a quieter numbness, but she was wrong. It's still here, residing in her bones, her blood, her breath. It isn't going anywhere. She used to think it was unbearable—now she knows it is.

And then she senses Mark's hand in hers. The feel of the curve of his palm as he gives her hand a ferocious squeeze. She looks at him and sees it in his eyes, too. That same wish. In every moment since they lost Josh, Mark has been dying alongside her. They are living, yes, and they are alive, but each day without their son is a mini-death, a small stab that threatens to destroy them altogether.

At the top of the landing, she breaks down, and Mark gathers her in his arms. They rock and cry, holding each other tightly.

"Are there any more of those chocolate fudge bars?" Edie hollers into the baby monitor.

There's a crackle of static.

"Richard, did you hear me? ARE THERE ANY MORE OF THOSE CHOCOLATE FUDGE BARS. Over."

Richard appears in the doorway, an irritated look on his face. "Edie, I told you. The baby monitor is not a two-way walkie-talkie. I can hear you, but you cannot hear me. And you don't have to yell— it picks up every last sound."

"Really?"

"Really." He enters the room brandishing two fudge bars. "The last two. I'll go out and pick up another box after work."

"It has to be the Tofutti. Fat free, sugar free . . ."

"Edie, I know." Richard peels off the paper wrapper and hands a bar to her. He does the same for himself then settles next to her on the bed, clicking on the remote for the morning news.

". . . and in times of great need, we find that there are always those who are willing to lend a helping hand. In this case, a community. Folks from the neighboring town of Avalon have gathered here today to share Amish Friendship Bread with the families and volunteers of Barrett, a town still reeling from the devastation of last week's flood."

"Richard, turn it louder!" Edie struggles to sit up.

Richard points his fudge bar at her. "Lie down or I turn off the TV, hide the remote, and confiscate your fudge bar."

"But . . ."

Richard holds the remote beyond her reach. *"Now."*

Disgruntled, Edie lies back down.

Richard turns up the volume and the reporter's baritone fills up the bedroom. He's standing outside the Barrett Civic Center and pointing down the road to a string of cars. "Residents of Avalon are caravanning here today to partner with the Red Cross and other relief organizations to offer friendship and support to the town of Barrett. A reported seven thousand three hundred forty-two loaves of Amish Friendship Bread are currently being distributed inside the civic center. Now, Amish Friendship Bread isn't bread bread, but more like a cake, like a banana bread . . ."

"This is my story! He's reporting my story!" Edie gives Richard an incredulous look.

"Edie . . ."

The reporter is still talking as he walks inside the civic center. ". . . Hannah Wang de Brisay, an accomplished cellist who used to play with the New York Philharmonic, is entertaining the crowd as the generous folks from Avalon continue to pass out coffee, tea, and bread." The camera pans in on Hannah wearing a lovely black gown, playing her cello to a packed house. The camera then follows the reporter as he walks past a line of people and up to the head of the table. "Over here, Ms. Madeline Davis, owner of Madeline's Tea Salon, and partner Julia Evarts, are the brains behind this generous and creative effort."

Madeline pinks and fusses with her hair while Julia immediately protests, "Oh, we're not partners, just friends. And, uh, this idea really came from Connie Colls and all the women who gather regularly at Madeline's to swap Amish Friendship Bread recipes and tips, but the whole town pitched in to help bake and . . ."

The reporter nods, half listening, and turns back to the camera. "So there you have it. The ladies of the Amish Friendship Bread Club in Avalon and this"—the reporter holds up a Ziploc bag of starter while giving the camera a can-you-believe-it kind of look—"simple bag of starter are feeding the town of Barrett this morning. This is Alden Ortega, KGFO, reporting live from Barrett. Back to you, Kevin."

"That's my story!" Edie is furious. "I have boxes full of interviews, transcripts, research! Now everybody and their uncle are going to be writing about it!" The TV remote flies through the air. "Like G.D. Lori Blair!"

"Edie!" Richard grabs the remote and flicks off the TV. "We both know there is no way you would have been able to be in Barrett to cover that story for the *Gazette*. NO WAY. You're on bed rest, Edie, and you need to be okay with the world going about its business without you."

"But Richard . . ." Edie starts to cry. She buries her face in a pillow. "This was *my* story, *my* feature! I was going to do a follow-up . . . a series . . ."

"Edie . . ."

"What am I going to do now? *I haven't done anything with my life.* Now I'm going to have a baby! I'm going to be a terrible mother, we both know that. I'm a reporter, I'm supposed to be writing and interviewing people . . ."

"Sweetheart, listen to yourself." Richard takes their ice cream bars and puts them on a napkin. "Why can't you leave room for the possibility that you're going to be a great mother as well as a great reporter? And that for reasons beyond your control, right now reporting has to take a backseat?"

"But I don't want it to take a backseat! Why can't I do both?"

"You can do both. Just not in the way you think. Things are different now, Edie. We both know you can't be running around like you used to, at least not for a few more months. And by then, you'll have a baby in tow."

"Great. How is that going to work?" Her voice is muffled.

"They're called baby carriers, and seeing how you used to lug fifty pounds in your pack when we were in Benin, I doubt you'll have any problem with an eight-pound baby." Richard pulls the pillow away from her face and brushes a wet strand of hair aside. "Don't be sad, honey."

Edie sniffs. "I'm not sad, Richard. Honest, I'm not." She gives him a brave smile.

"Well, what is it, then?"

"It's just . . . I'm just . . . I'M JUST SO SAD!" She starts bawling again and grabs the pillow back from him.

Richard is sympathetic. "I know it was hard for you to see that news report."

Edie pushes the pillow aside. "It's just . . . *seven thousand loaves?* I mean, that's insane! And they went to Barrett? You know how that makes me look? Like a heartless schmuck."

"You don't look like a heartless schmuck."

"Yes, I do. My article basically branded Amish Friendship Bread a public nuisance. And then I published letters complaining about how annoying the whole thing is. As a reporter, I'm supposed to offer a fair and balanced view. I didn't do that."

"Edie, it's just bread. Not some international peace treaty or something."

"But it's not just bread," Edie insists. "Don't you see? It's the town. It's the people. It's . . . Avalon." The fudge bars are a puddle of chocolate on the napkin. "Don't you see how incredible this is?"

"I'm not following you and now you're starting to worry me."

Edie reaches for a pad of paper and a pencil. "Go to work, Richard. And hand me back the remote, will you?" She lies obediently on her left side as she starts jotting some notes, her disposition suddenly calm and serene.

Hormones, Richard reminds himself as he hands her the remote and drops the soggy napkins into the trash. *It's just the hormones.* He's seen this plenty of times in his medical practice—pregnant moms who are happy one minute and then sobbing the next, and of course there's all the post-partum craziness he has to look forward to after the baby is born. He's told many an alarmed husband that it's par for the course and not to worry, but Richard is starting to feel a little concerned himself. He watches Edie hum happily as she writes and thinks, then thinks and writes. She looks up and blows him a kiss, waving him airily out the door as if everything is as right as rain.

Oh boy.

CHAPTER 28

Operation Friendship Bread was a success with eight thousand dollars in cash donations along with canned and household goods collected by Avalon residents for their Barrett neighbors. Over fifty men and women from Avalon spent the morning in Barrett, serving up slices of Amish Friendship Bread and listening to Hannah play her cello. It seemed as if they were able to feed the whole town with enough left over for seconds, even thirds.

When they all got back into their cars and drove back home, exhausted but their bellies and souls satisfied, they weren't prepared for the deluge of media trucks and cameras waiting outside Madeline's Tea Salon. The country, it seemed, wanted to get a look inside Madeline's to see the home of the Amish Friendship Bread Club. That was their new name, given to them by the media: The Amish Friendship Bread Club. Connie loved it, as did their regulars, and they each enjoyed their five minutes of fame as they were interviewed in front of the camera.

Business was good before, but now there are actually people waiting to get in. Connie is taking reservations and they even have a waitlist. Hannah has been coming in to help and Madeline is letting her take over more of the kitchen, setting the menu for the day and introducing new daily specials. They're booked out three months in advance after the last news feature gave a rave review of the tea and food served at the tea salon.

"A Small Town with a Big Heart" was how one newscaster put it, and the *Chicago Tribune* headed an article on Avalon with the title, "Need a Friend? Then Come to Avalon."

"This is good," Julia says now as she reads the article. "For all of us. For Avalon." Avalon had been suffering with the rest of the country, the economic bubble having burst a couple years back. But a little encouragement and a lot of tourism are going a long way. If Avalon wasn't the friendliest town before, it certainly is now. There is a regular crew of Avalonians going to Barrett weekly to help clean up and rebuild homes and schools, even though the media trucks are long gone. Julia smiles as she thinks of how proud everyone is, of what they've done and are continuing to do, and how proud she is to live in a town like Avalon.

Madeline and Julia are sitting in Madeline's backyard, under the shade of a ginkgo tree. Madeline is dressed in overalls, ready to work in the garden. It's a beautiful day. The summer sun is hot and the male cicadas are calling to their mates.

Madeline watches Julia stir some sugar into her iced tea. "So," she begins, clearing her throat.

Julia darts a glance at her, eyebrows raised. "Uh-oh—this doesn't sound good. Something on your mind, Madeline?" Her voice is teasing, but concerned.

Madeline tries to give Julia a reassuring smile, but can't. It's been on her mind for a while, and she's debated what to do, what to say. She's not even sure it will make a lick of difference, but she feels too much is at stake not to talk about it. Madeline isn't sure how to lead up to it, so she decides to get straight to the point.

"Julia," she says. "What is the situation with your family?"

Julia's face breaks out into a wide smile. "Mark and Gracie are doing great. We're talking about spending a couple of days in Chicago. There's an American Girl store on North Michigan and we've never been. We want to get her an early birthday present. And of course Mark wants to go to Wrigley Field to see the Cubs play. One of his clients has a box . . ."

"I was talking about your parents," Madeline says gently. "And your sister."

The smile falls from Julia's face. "Oh." She busies herself wiping the condensation off her glass.

"I wish I could say I wasn't the meddling kind, but we both know the truth of that statement." Madeline tries to get Julia to crack a smile and it works. A little. "I am just so happy for you, sweetheart—you have to believe this. I know it hasn't been easy these past few years and what happened was terrible, an awful, awful thing.

"What I'm about to say is because I know you have a huge capacity for love. Not just to give it, but to receive it. And I want so desperately for you to understand this. When I married Steven, I made the mistake of deferring to Ben. I let him push me away—if he didn't want to talk to me, I didn't force it. If he didn't want me to be around, I gave him space. It was such a struggle to be in a relationship with him—he just didn't seem to want me, and in my stubborn pride, it was just easier to give in.

"But what I've come to learn is that sometimes we push people away because we want them to come back to us. We want them to come and get us, to say they haven't forgotten about us. We want them to *show* us how much they want and need us. We want them to prove they love us enough to fight for us. You have two parents and a sister who are full of love for you, Julia. Can you let them back in, sweetheart? Can you let them know how much you still need them?"

For a while Julia says nothing, her head down. Madeline just waits.

"It's not that simple, Madeline." Julia's voice is a whisper. "I already told my parents I don't need them. I've made it clear that they failed me somehow by not being able to offer the right kind of support when Josh died. And when they moved to Florida, they took the easy way out. They left."

"Julia, there is no easy way out of something like this."

Julia closes her eyes. "So what am I supposed to do now? Ask them to forgive me?" She balls her hands into fists, her voice shaking.

"No, Julia. All you need to do is give them enough of an opening to come back in." Madeline reaches over and gently unfurls Julia's tight fists. "There is no right or wrong here. They did at the time what they thought was best, just as you have. And now here we are. What's next, Julia? I know Mark and Gracie are enough for a happy life—I see that in your eyes and I know that they love you deeply. But I also know that you can have so much more, and I want this for you. You deserve love, too, Julia. Not just from your parents, but from Livvy, too."

But at this Julia begins to shake her head. "No, no," she's saying. "It's just too late, Madeline."

"Why?"

"I've blamed Livvy for so long for Josh's death because I couldn't see . . ."

"Couldn't see what, Julia?"

Julia looks at her, eyes shining with tears. "I couldn't see that Josh's death was *my* fault. I'm his mother, Madeline, and I wasn't there to protect him." She begins to weep. "It was my job to take care of him. I failed him."

"No, Julia." Madeline's voice is firm. "It was nobody's fault. The most basic elements of our life—our birth and our death—*are out of our control*. People spend a lifetime trying to control these things but it's impossible. Even if we think we're calling the shots, we're not. It's the hard truth, Julia, and you don't have to like it, but you cannot fight it. No single human being has been able to.

"But we need other people, and it's a gift when the people who have known and loved us since childhood are still a part of our lives. Your parents, your sister. You have to be the one to start it again, Julia. Not because they may not eventually try, but because you can see now how much you really want this and you don't want to waste another minute not reaching for joy. To be surrounded by people who love you. It's an incredible thing, Julia. And I know you know this."

There's a long pause and Madeline doesn't say anything more, just makes room for the silence that she knows holds promise.

Julia wipes her eyes and looks up at the blue, cloudless sky. "When I saw Josh's friend the morning we were going to Barrett, I realized that's what Josh would look like now if he had lived. And it makes me so mad, so angry, that he won't have a chance to play football like Peter, or go to college, or fall in love. It's just not fair." Julia lets out a breath. "He was so beautiful, Madeline. Hair just like mine. A smile that would knock your socks off. He could get away with anything."

"I believe it."

Julia gulps. "When Mark and I were upstairs, I thought, 'Oh God, I'm never going to be able to go back downstairs.' In the past there was no way I could do it. But half an hour later, I was back downstairs, loading things up to go to Barrett. And I felt, well, not great, but okay."

Madeline just nods, taking Julia's hand in her own again.

Julia looks up and gazes at the sky, a perfect blue morning. "I remember so many nights where I was willing to do anything—*anything*—that would bring Josh back to me. I would have traded places with him in a heartbeat to give him a chance to grow up, to live his life, to find his own happiness." Her voice falters. "To not have had a moment of fear or aloneness when he died. I wish . . . I wish . . ." Julia takes a deep breath, lets out a sigh. Madeline knows Julia's been down this path so many times and each time the pain is still fresh, the anguish hitting her square in the chest, squeezing the breath out of her. "That's the worst feeling in the world. To want to do anything to make it better, to make it right, but you can't. You can't."

There is a long interminable pause as the women stare out into the garden. "Some things, perhaps, cannot be made better," Madeline concedes. "But some things can."

Julia is silent.

"Call your parents, Julia. Invite them home to Avalon. And go see Livvy."

It's a lot to ask, and Madeline knows this. But she also knows Julia can do it. When Julia manages a slight nod and there's a small smile, Madeline knows it's going to be okay.

They silently watch Connie talk to the gardeners and point to different spots around the grounds. Connie has managed their budget carefully so they can now pay someone to tend to the property, and it delights Madeline to see that this is finally happening—it felt negligent not to do more with what she had. They want to create more pathways and benches for people to sit on. They want to be able to accommodate more people and are figuring what they need to do to offer outdoor food service.

Madeline shields her eyes as she watches Connie explain what needs to be cut away and cleared. Connie turns at that moment and gives them a wave, her smile bright. Connie has been promoted to Tea Salon Manager, a title she proposed to Madeline, which Madeline readily accepted with a caveat: Should Connie ever choose to move from her dingy apartment above the Pizza Shack, Madeline wants her to know that she is always welcome to share the house with her.

"I know it's not a very hip thing to do," Madeline had said, not wanting Connie to worry about hurting her feelings. "But your landlord sounds like such an awful fellow and I wouldn't charge much rent at all. I understand that you probably spend too much time here as it is and might not want to—"

"Yes!" Connie had said breathlessly, throwing her arms around Madeline. "Thank you!"

She moved in the next day.

Now Madeline waves her over, pouring her a glass of iced tea. The three women continue to sit, enjoying the waning afternoon, their minds filled with their own thoughts. Hannah emerges from the house, untying her apron and collapsing next to them with a happy sigh.

"Strawberry rhubarb pie," she says. There's a smudge of flour on her cheek. "You're going to have to hurry if you want a piece." She turns her face to the sun and smiles. "I can't believe it was flooding last month. It's amazing how quickly the weather can turn."

Madeline couldn't agree more, and she offers a glass of iced tea to Hannah as she lifts her own in a toast. She looks at these young women who surround her, women who have a lifetime of joy and love waiting for them. Not just for them, but for Madeline, too. As unpredictable as life is, as much as it pains her to think that Ben is lost to her, Madeline remains optimistic. There's been no word from Ben, either because the letter never found him or he doesn't want Madeline to find him. She could do more, hire a private investigator or the like, but she tried that before without much success. Instead she says a small prayer for him at night, that he's safe and healthy and well, and that he's found happiness. She hopes that if he were ever to think of her again, that he would sense that he is always on Madeline's mind, and in her heart. He is the only piece of Steven she has left, and while that is important, it's not just that. Ben is the closest thing she's ever had to family, to having a child, and she can see now how much he really needed her, because she needed him just as much.

"All the more reason to make every moment count, girls."

Hannah, Connie, and Julia look at Madeline and nod. This moment has been hard-earned by each and every one of them, their lives having converged in this place, in Madeline's Tea Salon, in Avalon. They raise their glasses and toast one another, Madeline's words echoing in their ears.

When Julia pulls up to Livvy's house, she feels that familiar pinch in her gut. Even though she wasn't here when Josh died, she can't help but picture him on the lawn. She wants to look away, but she doesn't. Instead she steps out of her car, her arms filled with containers of food.

There's an unfamiliar car in the driveway. Perplexed, Julia rings the doorbell then peers through the windows.

The house is empty. The furniture is gone, the pictures taken down from the walls.

There is no one living in this house.

Julia feels a rise of panic, of dread. Something important has happened and she missed it. She has the feeling of having arrived a moment too late, a door closing.

Livvy is gone.

"Livvy," she whispers, and then finds herself calling her sister's name again. "Livvy!"

"What?"

Julia turns and sees Livvy walking around the corner of the house, wearing an old T-shirt and shorts. She's barefoot and holding a garden hose.

"Livvy!" Julia breathes. She feels a wave of relief and doesn't know whether to laugh or cry. "I thought . . . what happened to your things? Where's your car?" She resists the urge to rush forward and hold Livvy tight.

"With Tom. That's just a rental. It's a long story." Livvy tries to wind up the gnarled garden hose. "Tom got a job in Faberville. A really good job, so we're moving. He's already there."

There's a prickle in her chest—Julia never considered that Livvy might move, might leave Avalon, might leave her. "Were you going to tell me?"

"Yeah, sure. Of course. It's just that everything happened so fast, and I knew you were busy with this whole Amish Friendship Bread thing . . ." Livvy tosses the hose to the side. "I always meant to get one of those hose hangers to mount on the side of the house, but whatever." She gives the hose a frustrated kick.

Julia is about to say that she and Mark can help, but she sees it's too late. Not for everything, but for some things, that much is clear. She swallows, then holds up the containers of food. "I made chicken enchiladas for dinner and remembered you liked them, too, so I made extra for you and Tom. There's some Spanish rice, a salad, and dessert . . ." Her voice trails off.

Livvy hesitates but only for a moment. She steps forward and accepts the containers. "Thanks. I hadn't figured out dinner tonight so this is perfect."

They sit on the porch steps and Livvy opens the container with the enchiladas.

"The real estate agent is putting up the sign tomorrow," she says. She picks at a tortilla with her fingers. "I didn't want her to do it while we were still in the house."

"What about your job at the *Gazette*?"

"Huh? Oh, I quit. I mean, obviously. I'll find something else in Faberville. Eventually." One hand flutters absently to her stomach while the other picks at her food. "Sorry I don't have any utensils."

"Don't apologize. I made it for you—you can eat it however you want." Julia looks around. "Gracie said you gave Patch away. What happened?"

"Oh, he kept going over to Mrs. Lowry's yard, digging up her flower beds. He would jump the fence or find a way out, and it didn't seem fair to keep him chained up while we were at work all day. He was really lonely. We thought he should be with a family that had time to play with him, take care of him."

Josh loved that dog. "Patch was a good dog. Do you miss him?"

Livvy nods. "I do." She looks at the food. "This is good, Julia. Thanks."

Julia doesn't say anything, just picks up a leaf from the ground. "Faberville, huh?"

Livvy says, "Faberville's not too far away. Two hours if you drive straight through."

Faberville is easily a three-hour drive from Avalon. "Maybe the way *you* drive," Julia says. "You have a lead foot, if I recall."

Livvy laughs. "That's true, I do." She eats a little more, then makes a face. "Oh, the cheese is going to give me gas."

Julia doesn't remember Livvy ever having a problem with cheese. "Why?"

"It's just that with the pregnancy, dairy seems to wreak havoc on my digestive system." Livvy looks for the container with the salad.

Julia blinks. "You're pregnant?"

"Sixteen weeks tomorrow. That's the other nice thing about Faberville. They have a good hospital. We toured the family birthing unit, and they have private rooms and labor tubs—everything. And we're going to get a smaller house. Something more affordable than this behemoth. We're staying in a rental right now." She offers to share the salad with Julia.

The two sisters sit side by side, picking at bits of lettuce and diced tomatoes in silence.

Julia looks at Livvy's belly and there's a small paunch. You'd never notice it to look at her, but now that Julia knows, she feels that careful delicacy you have around someone who's expecting. She tries to remember what wasn't safe to eat . . . was it honey? Or was that just for the first year after the baby was born? Spicy food would always make Josh fuss when he was in utero. Tuna fish was something Julia ate in moderation because of all the reports of elevated mercury counts. She had avoided peanuts because she didn't want to risk either of the kids getting a peanut allergy. All of that seems inconsequential now. "So is everything going well with the pregnancy? Tests okay?"

Livvy nods. "They just did that AFP test to see if there are any genetic abnormalities. I couldn't sleep until they called me and said everything was okay. I was driving Tom crazy with worry." She catches herself and stops, then adds a bit meekly, "But everything came back fine."

"Good." Julia smiles. She knows Livvy is a natural worrywart, that people sometimes assume she doesn't care much about things, but really Livvy cares deeply about everything. She's more sensitive than people realize—more sensitive than Julia, that's for sure. Julia feels a rush of tenderness. She takes a chance and puts her hand on top of Livvy's and gives it a gentle squeeze.

Livvy starts, then relaxes, and offers back a small smile. But just as quickly Julia sees her sister's eyes fill with tears. "Livvy? Is everything all right?"

Livvy shakes her head, looks away.

"Livvy, talk to me. Look at me." Julia presses her palm against Livvy's wet cheek, turns Livvy to face her. Her sister's face is ashen.

"Julia?" she whispers. "What if I won't be a good mom?"

Julia feels her sister trembling beside her. "You'll be a wonderful mother, Livvy. I know you will." She holds Livvy's hand in both of hers. "*You will, Livvy.*"

"But a real mother . . . I mean, if I were a real good mother . . . I wouldn't have forgotten . . . I wouldn't have locked the car . . ." Livvy starts to sob, then buries her face in her hands.

Julia swallows hard. She's fighting back tears but loses, and she can't stop herself, either.

"Julia," Livvy says, crying. "I am sorry. I am so, so sorry . . ."

It's those words that slow Julia's tears, that give her a moment to gather herself together. Livvy had spent the whole first year after Josh's death apologizing, and Julia never felt like it was enough. How can you sufficiently apologize for something like that?

She thinks of her conversation with Madeline and realizes, *you can't.*

"Livvy," Julia says, and she takes her sister's hands—both of them—even though Livvy is still sobbing and her nose is running. "Livvy, it's not your fault."

"But I . . ."

"It's not your fault, Livvy. We can't control these things, even when we think we can. It's impossible."

"But if I had left the door unlocked or left him in the car . . ." Livvy starts to cry again. She falls into Julia, who wraps her arms around her sister.

Livvy's familiar smell makes Julia close her eyes. She wishes they could rewind time so they can start all over again. How nice it would be if they had done this earlier, had time to create a new history other than the one they've lived for five years. But that, too, is impossible. All they have is this moment, and what's ahead of them.

She pulls back and looks at her sister. Up close, Julia can see how Livvy's face has changed over the years, the slight wrinkles around the eyes, her laugh lines more pronounced. But she is still beautiful, and she is still Julia's sister. "I love you, Livvy. And I'm sorry I didn't come to you sooner."

This just makes Livvy start crying again. "I missed you," she says between sobs.

Julia kisses the top of her sister's head, inhales her sister's scent. "I missed you, too, Livvy."

Livvy sniffs and wipes her eyes. "Oh. It looks like I kind of used your T-shirt as a handkerchief."

Julia looks down and sees that Livvy has indeed used her shirt as a handkerchief, and she grins.

"So what now?" Livvy asks, and Julia can see that their roles have been restored, Livvy automatically turning to Julia for the answers.

"I don't know," she says honestly.

"You'll come visit, right? Help me with the baby when it's born?"

"Yes," Julia breathes. "I'd love that."

"Or you can come up sooner," Livvy suggests. "I hope you'll come up sooner. Come anytime."

"I will," Julia promises. "We'll all come. Gracie, too. She'll be so excited to have a cousin."

"She'll be a great cousin," Livvy agrees. She points to the last container sitting on the porch. "What's this?"

Julia grins. "Amish Friendship Bread."

"Of course." Livvy grins back as she pops off the lid. "Good thing I can afford the calories." She holds the container out to Julia, who takes a fat slice, and then Livvy does the same.

"Are you staying here tonight?" Julia asks.

Livvy nods. "Got my sleeping bag. I have to sign the papers tomorrow. I thought I'd be more sad to leave, but I'm excited, you know?"

Julia does know. And she knows she doesn't want Livvy sleeping on her floor alone.

"Stay with us," she says suddenly. "We have a spare room." They both know the spare room is Josh's old room so Julia quickly adds, "Or you can stay in Gracie's room. I have utensils at my house. You can have a proper dinner, a proper breakfast, and then meet with the real estate agent and head back to Faberville." She says this in a rush, and when she's finished, she realizes that she's holding her breath.

Livvy seems to be thinking about this, her head bent over the containers. When she looks up, her face is shining. "Sure," she says. "I'd like that."

THE START OF SOMETHING BEAUTIFUL
IN AVALON, ILLINOIS
Reported by Edith Gallagher

AVALON, ILLINOIS—For many residents in this small town in northern Illinois, Avalon has been the only home they know. Born and raised here, Avalonians are a content bunch, proud of who they are, proud of where they live, proud of what Avalon has become known for in recent months.

Friendship. Family. Community. And all thanks to a single bag of Amish Friendship Bread starter.

Google "Amish Friendship Bread" on your computer and be prepared to have enough reading for a week. It's a slice of American contemporary history, an edible chain letter that fills people with equal amounts of hope and dread. But for families in Barrett and Avalon, it's quickly become the epitome of what brings people—and towns— together.

Like warring neighbors, for instance. Martin Colon and the Padillas, Lester and Marsha, have lived next door to each other for sixteen years. Their children grew up together. Many summer evenings would find the neighbors sharing a beer or glass of wine on the lawn. But two years ago Martin's twelve-foot climbing wisteria caused subsidence of the Padillas' home, damaging the foundation and drainage pipes. The two families became engaged in a two-year legal battle over a repair bill totaling $7,500, which Colon refused to pay.

Fast-forward to this past May and cue Marsha Padilla and a bag of Amish Friendship Bread starter. Remembering her neighbor's birthday, Marsha felt compelled to bake and leave the bread with a kind note. Now the neighbors are in mediation and have agreed to share the repair bill, restoring not only the Padillas' foundation, but their friendship.

Chief of Police Craig Neimeyer says that Avalon's already low crime rates have dropped to almost nothing in the past two months.

At the local YMCA and senior recreation center, the number of volunteers have increased, much to the delight of our young and elderly residents.

School bullying and other classroom disruptions have also dramatically dropped.

"Avalon has always been a nice town," says longtime resident Octavia Stout. "But now it's more peaceful. People seem happier. It's a joy for me to say I'm from Avalon."

Doug MacDonald agrees. "My kids baked for Barrett. Normally they're fighting and disagreeing, arguing with me and my wife about homework, but it's like there's been a hiatus from all of that. We can sit down at the table and have a good meal together."

At Madeline's Tea Salon, an official room has been designated for the ladies who regularly make and share Amish Friendship Bread. Dubbed "The Amish Friendship Bread Club" by the media, this growing group of women has made it their ongoing mission to bake for families, organizations, and communities in need. They are currently providing loaves to women's shelters across the county, and are available to guide interested parties in starting club chapters of their own.

"I'm honored to have the club here, as I am to be a part of a community that has done so much for others," says Madeline Davis, owner. "The bread has touched my own life, bringing me good people that have since become good friends."

It is still a mystery as to how Amish Friendship Bread was initially introduced to Avalon, with the first known person being Julia Evarts. But according to Mrs. Evarts, she was "a lucky recipient of the bread just like everyone else." While this mystery may join the archives of life's unanswered questions, perhaps its origins do not really matter. What does matter is that the bread, and its starter, found its way to Avalon, and from it, something beautiful has been born.

CHAPTER 29

❀

"Why didn't you tell me it was going to hurt?" Livvy demands into the phone. It's the day before Christmas. Livvy looks out the hospital window and sees fat flakes of snow lazily making their way to the ground. The sky looks like it's full of fluffy feathers.

Edie laughs. "Because if I did, it would have made you crazier than you already were. I did you a favor."

That's probably true. Livvy had been making lists of everything that could go wrong with the delivery, emailing them to Edie on a daily basis. Still, a little warning would have been nice.

Livvy turns to look at Tom, who's cradling their new baby, a perfect eight-pound, ten-and-a-half-ounce little boy. Aiden Logan Scott. "Oh, and the stitches were fun, too. Thanks for the heads-up there. Doctor didn't realize until later that he didn't give me enough anesthetic." Livvy winces at the memory.

"What tipped him off?"

"Probably my screaming. But I'm good now. Just don't ask me if

I'll ever do this again." She says this dramatically, knowing that she sounds like those annoying pregnant women she always complains about, but Livvy has to admit that there *is* an odd pleasure in being able to say it at all, a roundabout way of announcing, *I did it.* Which Livvy still can't believe.

"Oh, you'll do this again," Edie says confidently. "Knowing you, you've already bought a double stroller."

Livvy reddens. "It was on sale," she protests. "Thirty percent off. And I need room for all my things."

Edie gives a chuckle. "Of course you do. We'll be up to see you next week, okay? Help you ring in the new year."

"Julia will be here, too. And my parents. Maybe I should just invite all of Avalon to Faberville to celebrate." She and Tom were talking about how, when they had the big house, no one ever came to visit. But next week they'll have more people crammed into their small space than she ever thought possible. It'll be crazy, that's for sure.

"I know I'm wasting my breath, but you need to be resting, not entertaining," Edie tells her.

Edie is wasting her breath, because having friends and family around her is the one thing Livvy wants right now more than anything. Aiden is only a few hours old, but Livvy wants him to know the people to whom he belongs, whose lives are already a part of his and will be forever. "So don't come then," Livvy says nonchalantly. She'll kill Edie if she actually agrees.

But Edie doesn't. "Ha ha, nice try. Hold on a second. *Richard, we have a diaper here!*"

"How is that beautiful daughter of yours?" Livvy wants to know. Miranda is two months old and looks just like a miniature Edie. Livvy can't wait to see what she'll be like when she grows up.

"Giving me a run for my money. She nurses constantly and doesn't want to sleep at night. Oh, and before I forget, Patrick has been asking after you. He wants to do a birth announcement in the *Gazette,* maybe even a short little feature story."

Livvy finds it amusing that Patrick seems to be taking such an interest in her *after* she's left the *Gazette*. "Who would be the writer?" she asks innocently. "Lori Blair?" Livvy actually likes Lori, but she likes teasing Edie more.

"Ha ha. You know it'll be me."

"Are you back full-time now?"

"Not exactly," Edie says. "But enough. I want to stay home with Miranda as much as possible."

Livvy can't believe her ears. "You're actually going to be a stay-at-home mom?" she asks in disbelief. She was certain Edie would be back at work, back in the thick of things.

"Don't be ridiculous," Edie scoffs. "Of course I'm not going to be a stay-at-home mom."

Livvy is grinning, enjoying this moment. "Edie, someone who stays home to be with their kids is a stay-at-home mom. Because you're a mom, and you're staying at home . . ."

"Yes, thank you, Livvy. I get it." Edie sounds grumpy. "Where's Richard? I think it's a number two." There's a pause. "Yep, it is."

"You could always change the diaper yourself," Livvy suggests.

"I could, Livvy, but Richard said he wanted to do all this so I don't want to deprive him of the experience." There's a wail and Livvy suspects that Miranda doesn't care who changes her diaper so long as somebody changes it now. "I have to go. Kiss Aiden for me, okay?"

Livvy looks at Tom, who is humming to their new baby as he sleeps in Tom's arms. "Don't worry, I will."

Leave it to Livvy to push her buttons even though she's several towns over. And the woman just gave birth!

So maybe the technical term is stay-at-home mom, but it's not like Edie is sitting around and watching back-to-back episodes of *Barney* or *Sesame Street*. During Miranda's naps she jumps on the computer to catch up on emails or do a little research. Granted Miranda's erratic sleep schedule and five-second catnaps mean that Edie can't get much done, but she's confident they'll get there.

Eventually.

The sleep-deprived stupor will pass and at some point they'll actually venture out of the house. Edie plans to try a few interviews with Miranda in the baby sling. It's a *kitenge,* a generous swath of printed fabric used by women in Kenya. It took a few tries for Edie to get it right, but now she is an expert and can get Miranda tied snug on her back or curled up against her breast in less than twenty seconds, leaving her hands free to do whatever needs to be done around the house.

Right now she's working on a story about higher incidents of leukemia and brain cancer for children living near electric power lines. She's writing about it because she wants to, because she thinks citizens and lawmakers and power companies should see what's happening to these children, these families. Maybe it's motherhood or maybe it's just a little more professional maturity on her part, but Edie is no longer interested in short, sensational stories that make it on the front page for only a day. Somehow she'd forgotten about something she realized when she was in the Peace Corps, about how the stories that made the most difference and had the greatest impact were the ones with the least amount of flash. There's something appealing about a quiet story that has depth, that has the ability to reach out and connect people for a long time to come. It's less about the story, Edie's learned, and more about the people. But, more important, it has to come from the heart and not the mind. Edie is still working on that one.

Richard walks into the room and sniffs the air, then scoops up Miranda and gives Edie a quick kiss before heading to the diaper-changing station. God, she loves her husband. She would have married him sooner if she knew how wonderful it was going to be. It always seemed like a small detail, mere paperwork since they were already living together and deeply committed. But the simple band on her finger reminds her of everything she has, and, more important, that she has someone to share it all with.

They stood in front of a justice of the peace and tied the knot the week before Miranda was born. It was cutting it close, but Richard was adamant that they get married before Miranda was born. So they did.

Never in a million years would Edie have figured that someone like Livvy would be her maid of honor, but Livvy stood next to her, weeping as if she were Edie's mother. Edie would have been more touched if she wasn't already having early contractions that had gone on for two days and would continue for another seven.

Edie's friendship with Livvy started in an unremarkable way, and then blossomed into something Edie has come to treasure. Edie knows Livvy should rest but she knows that Livvy is too geared up to relax, having just done one of the most incredible things in a woman's life. It hasn't even been five minutes before Edie picks up the phone and calls Livvy back. Livvy gives a whoop of delight and continues talking as if their conversation hasn't been interrupted at all, launching into graphic detail about how the epidural didn't work. Edie listens and smiles, knowing that the story might take as long as the actual event itself.

But Edie doesn't mind.

Hannah opens up *Joy of Cooking* and looks up the recipe for a tomato meat sauce. In the past she would have browned some ground beef and dumped in a jar of Prego, but she wants to learn how to do the basics right. It's what she tells her students, even the more experienced ones. If you don't get the basics right, none of the rest matters.

She reads the recipe and is delighted to see that it's not as easy nor as hard as she thought. There are enough steps so she knows she can expect a sauce that's complex and flavorful, but otherwise it's straightforward enough so that Hannah's not worried. She learns that the faster the sauce is cooked, the fresher and brighter the flavor, so Hannah chooses a wide skillet that will let the extra liquid evaporate quickly.

She takes her time dicing the pancetta, chopping an onion, and mincing garlic cloves. It's not exactly a traditional Christmas Eve dinner, but everyone is spending it with family and she's opted to go it alone. She had a few invitations, including one from Jamie and his family, but she feels it's important that she have this holiday on her own, her choice this time, not anyone else's. She'll see him after and they'll share a decadent trifle she's made with raspberries, white chocolate, and almonds. Then they'll drive around Avalon, looking at the lights and maybe joining in with the caroling. She wants to stop in and see Henry Tinklenberg and Joseph Sokolowski, her neighbors, and give them one of the holiday baskets she's made. She has one for the Krum family, too—a bottle of wine for Marion and her husband, some cookies and holiday poppers for their wild but hilarious twin boys whom Hannah sometimes babysits.

She heats the olive oil and cooks the pancetta until the fat turns to liquid and separates from the meat. Saint-Saëns is playing on the stereo, Concerto for Cello and Orchestra, No. 1 in A minor, Opus 33. It reminds her of the time she toured with the Philharmonic in Europe. In Amsterdam, the hotel they were staying in had a lovely reception waiting when they arrived. It had been a long flight and the musicians were starving. They descended on the banquet like locusts, even eating the display fruit and stuffing it into their pockets to save for a midnight snack. The waiters yelled at them in Dutch, and it wasn't until they had been sent to their rooms that they learned the reception was for a wedding party that was arriving right after them.

Hannah gently crumbles the meat of some sweet Italian sausages into the skillet. She's grateful to have plenty of good memories of her own, ones that don't include Philippe. Of course, there are some good memories there, too. Mostly of the early days, when they first met, the whirlwind daze that comes with first kisses and falling in love.

Her favorite memory is the time they were at the Hell's Kitchen flea market. It was a Sunday morning in July, and the heat was sweltering. By now she knew Philippe as the precise man he was, with his obsessive-compulsive tendencies, and it had crossed her mind more than once that he would either freak out amid all the sweaty bodies or demand that they leave. He did neither.

Instead, he found a table filled with children's alphabet blocks. As Hannah fanned herself, he spelled out JE T AIME, and then tipped her back and planted a long kiss on her lips, earning a cheer from the crowd. It was one of the most spontaneous, unexpected things he had ever done. It was moments like that when Hannah felt she could be with him forever.

She adds two cans of whole tomatoes, crushing the tomatoes with the side of her spatula. A little oregano, salt and pepper, a dash of sugar. A tablespoon of tomato paste. She lets it cook down, her kitchen filling with a sweet, fragrant smell. She'll add the slivered basil last, once the sauce is thickened and she's turned off the heat.

Joy of Cooking has become her bible, her guide to living. It's all the more precious because Madeline gave it to her, but also because she started reading—and cooking—in Avalon. Avalon is where Hannah finally came to understand who she really is, and what she really wants. What she is capable of doing.

She's a woman capable of being on her own, a woman capable of surviving a divorce. She's a woman who can pull together a goat-cheese-and-walnut soufflé, who can put the bow into the hand of someone who has never played the cello and help them make the most beautiful music. She's a woman who, at twenty-eight, has already accomplished more than most people will in a lifetime. But, most important, she's a woman who's learned not to take any of it for granted. And for that, Hannah is thankful.

"Gracie, we're going to be late!" Julia calls to her daughter.

Gracie appears in the foyer of Madeline's, lugging her small cello case. "The ladies wanted to hear me play 'Row, Row, Row Your Boat' one more time," she pants.

"Well, I'm sure Aunt Livvy will want to hear it, too," Julia says, taking the case from Gracie. It turned out that Julia didn't have much of a penchant for music after all, or for the cello at least, but Gracie has taken to it brilliantly. "But if we don't get on the road soon, you won't be able to play for her until tomorrow morning." She helps Gracie into her puffy coat, then slips on mittens, a scarf, and a woolen hat. The temperature just dropped another ten degrees and they're expecting more snow later tonight.

"That's okay. My fingers hurt anyway." Gracie flaps her hands.

Julia buttons up her own coat then pokes her head into the tea room. "Connie, we're heading out. Is everything okay here?"

"Everything's great." Connie waves. "See you in a couple of days."

"Did you tell Hannah we're going to miss our lesson tomorrow?" Gracie asks as they walk down the path to the car where Mark is waiting.

"Yes, and she says we can make it up next week, no worries." Julia opens up the door to the backseat and Gracie scrambles in. She pats the space next to her for Julia to place her cello case.

Mark is on the phone, his voice calm but an excited look on his face. "Sure, Ted. That sounds great. No, we are, too. Right. You, too. Bye." He hangs up, slipping his cell phone into the pouch on his belt. "That was Ted Morrow of Bluestem Estates. All the plans for the model homes were approved, and they're breaking ground next week."

The seat belt on Gracie's car seat is twisted but Julia stops wrestling with it to give her husband a smile. "Mark, that's wonderful! Congratulations." She knows how much this project means to him, and she's enjoyed hearing about its progress.

"Thanks." He drums the steering wheel happily.

Julia finally manages to get Gracie buckled in, planting a quick kiss on her cheek before closing the door. Livvy went into labor early—two weeks early, just like Julia did with Josh—and gave birth a few hours ago to a baby boy.

Tom sent over one picture taken with his cell phone, and both Mark and Julia are blown away by how much Aiden looks like Josh. He has a tuft of strawberry-blond hair, the same nose, the same cheekbones. But Aiden also has Tom's unfortunate forehead, which Mark noticed with a laugh.

"What, do you not remember how people used to tease Josh because he had your big ears?" Julia reminds him, tugging on one of Mark's ears.

Mark immediately scowls, cupping his ears defensively. "They're not big," he says. "They just have personality."

"A lot of personality," Julia adds, and yelps when Mark reaches over to tickle her.

Julia is about to slide into the passenger seat when she notices a couple—a small family, actually, since the wife is holding a baby in her arms—standing on the sidewalk outside of Madeline's, uncertainty etched on their faces.

"They look lost," Julia murmurs, watching them check a piece of paper before looking up at Madeline's again.

Mark checks his watch. "Julia, honey, let's go. I don't want to hit traffic."

"I know. Just a minute, Mark." Julia crosses the lawn, her boots crunching in the icy grass. "Can I help you?"

The man has a tumble of dark hair and a brooding look Julia recognizes from pictures. He's older, of course, but it's him. In his hand is a fat envelope that Julia remembers from that day in the tea salon. "I'm looking for Madeline Dunn," he says.

Julia swallows, her heart beating fast. "This is the place. I'm her friend, Julia Evarts."

The man nods as if he knows who she is but Julia can tell he's distracted. His baby girl looks tired and starts to wail, fussing in her mother's arms.

"It's been a long trip," he says, reaching for his daughter. "We've been driving all day. I live in Cleveland now, but the letter was sent to one of my old addresses in Pennsylvania. I'm her stepson, Benjamin Dunn." He glances uncertainly at Madeline's, clears his throat. He can see the throng of women through the windows and Julia can understand how it might be a bit intimidating.

The tea salon is officially closed for a special holiday gathering for the Amish Friendship Bread Club. Julia knows that Connie is the one who came up with the idea of an ornament exchange and potluck, giving Madeline and Hannah the night off. Hannah opted to stay home and Madeline declined to join the festivities. When Julia left her, she was sitting in the still quiet of her back sitting room, an afghan draped over her legs, a mug of hot tea in her hands. She was gazing at the snow-covered yard, at a small tree sparrow as it danced from one barren branch to another.

Julia leads Ben and his wife up the walkway. There's a beautiful, lush wreath on the door, and Julia turns the doorknob, wishing in some way that she could stay and see this moment unfold.

But this isn't her place, her long-awaited moment. It's Madeline's. Julia's place is with her family, with Livvy who is in Faberville with her husband and new son. Julia is anxious to get there, to gather her sister in her arms and gaze at this new soul who has found his way into all of their lives. They'll be there together: her, Mark, Gracie, Tom, Livvy, Aiden, and Josh. He'll be there because he is always with Julia, tucked inside her heart.

And so Julia opens the door and invites Ben and his family in, asking them to please wait while she makes her way back to Madeline's private quarters. Madeline is sitting there just as she left her. She turns to smile when she sees Julia. Julia touches her friend gently on the shoulder, her heart full of love, then bends down to whisper in Madeline's ear that someone special is waiting for her.

Rosa Ydara-Belair tucks a strand of curly dark hair behind her ear as she continues to shuffle through her father's things, sorting them into three piles: keep, give away, throw away.

Family photo albums and pictures: keep.

Her mother's jewelry and her father's watch: keep.

Clothes and shoes: give away.

Books and magazines: give away.

The jumble of random electrical equipment and scrap metal: throw away.

The thread-bare throw rugs and forty-year-old curtains: throw away.

Two telescopes, one set of binoculars, three cameras: give away.

Furniture, towels, and bedding: give away.

Television, stereo, video players: keep.

Her parents' wedding china: keep. Give away. No, keep.

Rosa holds up one plate with a sigh. It's a nice floral pattern and the dessert plates have a smooth scalloped edge. Her own china is a Lenox pattern with a simple blue and silver trim, more modern and a bit trendy, but she likes this nonetheless. Rosa stares regretfully at the collection of china, wishing she could take it but at the same time having no idea what she'd do with it. She debates saving it, but they already have so many of her parents' things to take back to Michigan.

Give away.

Rosa places each dish carefully between layers of bubble wrap. When she's finished, she frowns. Her husband knocks on the door frame of the living room, a large box in hand.

"We're almost out of boxes. I'm going to run to the store after I put this in the trailer. Do you want to come with?"

Rosa holds up a hand, her lips moving as she recounts the china. "They're missing a dessert plate. There's only seven, when there should be eight."

Jack shrugs. "So they broke one. Look at our china set."

That's true. Their service for twelve is more like a service for nine and a half.

"The real estate agent will be here this afternoon to complete the listing," Jack continues. "We should probably get something to eat first. I'm famished."

Rosa nods, stretching to relieve her sore back. Food sounds good right now. "In a minute. I'll meet you outside."

She runs the packing tape down the seam of the box and seals it, marking it with a pen for the Salvation Army. Then she picks up her father's will and reads it again, making sure she follows the short list of instructions he's left behind. His arthritis had gotten worse over the years, and she can barely make out his shaky handwriting. His savings are substantial, and he's been generous with her and the local astronomy club.

Outside, her husband is waiting in the truck. She climbs inside and he gives her hand a squeeze, knowing how hard this is on her.

"Excuse me!"

Both Jack and Rosa turn in the direction of the voice and see a woman with curly strawberry-blond hair hurrying toward them, a young girl running alongside her, holding a plate. Rosa recognizes them vaguely, having met them briefly before, but she can't remember their names.

"Hi, I'm sorry to bother you. I just didn't want to miss you before you left." The woman is slightly out of breath. "I'm Julia Evarts and this is my daughter, Gracie. We're neighbors of your parents. We were so sorry to hear of your father's passing. He was a kind man."

"Thank you." Rosa feels like crying again. "Thank you," she says again, not sure what else to say. What else is there to say?

"If you need any help with anything, please let me know. Anything." Julia reaches through the open window to gently touch Rosa's arm. "I wrote down my name and contact information, as well as the names and numbers for all the immediate neighbors. You probably already know this but I thought it might help to have it all in one place."

Rosa just nods.

"And . . ." Julia turns and motions to her daughter, who shyly holds up a plate. "We just baked this and Gracie wanted to share some with you. It's Amish Friendship Bread."

"Amish Friendship Bread?" Jack leans over Rosa to accept the plate, sparing Rosa the need to do anything. Everything, he knows, is hard for her right now. "We love it. Rosa makes it all the time. Thank you."

"Thank you," Rosa echoes, and forces herself to smile at them. She glances at the note stuck to the top of the plastic wrap.

I HOPE YOU ENJOY IT.

Julia and Gracie wave as Jack puts the truck in gear and pulls away from the curb. The vibration of the truck soothes Rosa, who hadn't expected to run into people who knew her father, hadn't expected that she would have to talk to anyone. Their kindness, as well meaning as it is, only reminds her that he is gone.

She had talked to her father just last week, and he had sounded fine. Two days later, he died peacefully in his sleep. It does comfort Rosa to know this, but still she wishes she could have hugged him one last time. The last time she saw him, he had protested the amount of food she'd brought. Roast chicken, beef stew, lasagna, casseroles, soups. She knew he loved her banana bread, and there was a round of Amish Friendship Bread circulating in her office for the umpteenth time, so she brought some of that. She had a bag of starter with her so she could bake while she was here, and on the day they left, he had asked her to leave a bag for him. Rosa was surprised, not figuring her father for a baker.

Her parents didn't raise her to have regrets, but she can't help it. She wishes she saw more of him. She wishes she had a chance to say goodbye, had a chance to hear him impart some wisdom that she could carry with her for the rest of her life—a final, lasting memory. More than anything she wishes he wasn't alone when he died. But Jack's job kept them in Grand Rapids, and her father refused to leave Avalon. Rosa knows it's because her mother is buried here. And now, her father is, too.

"I saw a place when we were driving in," Jack says. "It's not too far away. Want to try it?"

She offers a small smile. "Sure." She should be hungrier given all the work they've done, but she doesn't have much of an appetite. Still, she needs to keep her strength up. The last round of IVF worked, and Rosa is officially seven weeks pregnant.

Jack glances at her, then at the plate resting in her lap. He's thinking the same thing. "Maybe you should have a little something now since it'll take awhile to order and everything."

Rosa nods then peels back the plastic wrap. It's still warm, a comfort. She feeds a piece to Jack and then to herself, relaxing at the moist, familiar taste of cinnamon and sugar. She carefully tucks the plastic wrap back under the bottom of the plate, turning the plate over slightly as she does so. Her eyes widen when she sees what's printed on the underside, the last words.

Forget-Me-Not.

"Oh!"

Jack turns and sees Rosa staring at the plate, then at Jack, her eyes shining. "What?"

Rosa holds up the plate but Jack doesn't know what he's looking at, just some slices of Amish Friendship Bread on a china dish with small flowers.

"What?" he says again, confused.

She shakes her head, suddenly happy, her fingers tracing the outline of the flowers. She doesn't say anything else.

Jack is used to this, and he just reaches for his wife's hand, brings it to his lips for a kiss. "I love you, Rosa."

"I know." Her eyes are wet but she's smiling. Rosa leans against him and he hears her sigh, feels her body relax next to his.

It's a short drive to the lunch place, a quaint house with an engraved sign out front.

MADELINE'S TEA SALON

HOME OF THE AMISH FRIENDSHIP BREAD CLUB

Amish Friendship Bread
Recipes and Tips

AMISH FRIENDSHIP BREAD STARTER

Amish Friendship Bread starter is passed from one friend or neighbor to another, usually in a Ziploc bag or ceramic container. It's an actual sourdough starter, meaning that if you continue to feed it over time, it will become more flavorful and distinct. You can use the starter for loaves, muffins, brownies . . . even pancakes! If you haven't received a bag of Amish Friendship Bread starter but would like to experiment, here is the recipe for creating a starter.

INGREDIENTS
- 1 (0.25 ounce) package active dry yeast
- ¼ cup warm water (110°F)
- 1 cup all-purpose flour
- 1 cup white sugar
- 1 cup milk

DIRECTIONS
1. In a small bowl, dissolve yeast in water. Let stand ten minutes.
2. In a glass, plastic, or ceramic container, combine flour and sugar. Mix thoroughly.
3. Slowly add in milk and dissolved yeast mixture. Cover loosely and let stand at room temperature until bubbly. This is Day One of the ten-day cycle.
4. For the next ten days, care for your starter according to the instructions for Amish Friendship Bread.

BASIC RECIPE FOR AMISH FRIENDSHIP BREAD
Makes 2 loaves

This basic recipe has been circulating in the United States for more than three decades. I'm including it as it was given to me, minus the occasional misspelling. You don't have to wait an additional ten days to bake—on the day that you split the starter (Day Ten), you can bake with the remaining batter instead of saving a bag for yourself. If you plan to gift your starter, don't forget to include a copy of the instructions along with the dates for Day Six and Day Ten. You can download the instructions from our website, friendshipbreadkitchen.com.

NOTE: Do not refrigerate the starter. It is normal for the batter to rise and ferment. If air gets in the bag, let it out. DO NOT use a metal spoon or bowl for mixing as it will interfere with the fermenting process.

Day 1: DO NOTHING
Day 2: Mash the bag
Day 3: Mash the bag
Day 4: Mash the bag
Day 5: Mash the bag
Day 6: ADD to the bag: 1 cup flour, 1 cup sugar, 1 cup milk. Mash the bag.
Day 7: Mash the bag
Day 8: Mash the bag
Day 9: Mash the bag
Day 10: Follow the directions below

1. Pour the entire bag into a nonmetal bowl.
2. Add: 1½ cups flour, 1½ cups sugar, 1½ cups milk.
3. Measure out four separate batters of 1 cup each into four one-gallon Ziploc bags.

4. Keep one of the bags for yourself and give the other bags to three friends along with the recipe.

REMEMBER: If you keep a starter for yourself, you will be baking in 10 days. The bread is very good and makes a great gift.

Should this recipe not be passed on to a friend on the first day, make sure to tell them which day it is when you present it to them.

BAKING INSTUCTIONS:
1. Preheat over to 325° F.
2. Put the remaining batter in a bowl and add the following:
   3 eggs
   1 cup oil
   ½ cup milk
   1 cup sugar
   ½ tsp vanilla
   2 tsp cinnamon
   1½ tsp baking powder
   ½ tsp salt
   ½ tsp baking soda
   2 cups flour
   1–2 boxes Jell-O instant pudding (any flavor)
   Optional: 1 cup nuts and 1 cup raisins
3. Grease two large loaf pans.
4. In a bowl, mix an additional ½ cup sugar and 1½ tsp cinnamon.
5. Dust the greased pans with sugar/cinnamon mixture.
6. Pour the batter evenly into the pans and sprinkle the remaining mixture on the top.

7. Bake for one hour or until the bread loosens evenly from the sides and a toothpick inserted in the center of the bread comes out clean.
8. ENJOY!

SIMPLE AMISH FRIENDSHIP BREAD VARIATIONS

The following variations are made up of simple substitutions—feel free to make up your own! To make muffins instead of loaves, reduce baking time to 20–25 minutes. Fill loaf pans or muffin tins one-half to two-thirds full (if you have an eager new starter, I'd recommend only filling to one-half).

Banana Nut Friendship Bread
- Add 2 medium-size ripe bananas, mashed
- Use 1–2 boxes Jell-O instant banana-cream pudding
- Use 1 cup walnuts, chopped

Butterscotch Friendship Bread
- Use 1–2 boxes Jell-O instant butterscotch pudding
- Add 1 cup butterscotch baking chips

Double Chocolate Friendship Bread
- Use 1–2 boxes Jell-O instant chocolate fudge pudding
- Add ¼ cup cocoa
- Add 1 cup chocolate chips
- Omit cinnamon

Lemon Poppy-Seed Friendship Bread
- Replace vanilla extract with lemon extract
- Use 1–2 boxes Jell-O instant lemon pudding

- Add ¼ cup poppy seeds
- Add 1 tsp lemon zest

Pineapple Macadamia Nut Friendship Bread
- Reduce oil to ½ cup
- Add 8 oz can of crushed pineapple, drained
- Add ½ cup applesauce
- Add 1 tsp lemon zest
- Add 1 cup macadamia nuts, chopped
- Top with 2 tbs shredded coconut

Pistachio Cherry Friendship Bread
- Use 1–2 boxes Jell-O instant pistachio pudding
- Add ½ cup Maraschino cherries, drained and chopped (do not mix in batter but line bottom of prepared pan with cherries before pouring batter)
- Omit cinnamon

Pumpkin Cranberry Friendship Bread
From the kitchen of Stephanie Appleton
(makeitfromscratch.blogspot.com)
- Add ½ cup pumpkin puree
- Add 1 tsp ginger powder
- Add 1 cup dried cranberries, loosely chopped
- Add 1 cup walnuts, chopped

Zucchini Amish Friendship Bread
- Reduce oil to ½ cup
- Add 2 cups unpeeled zucchini, shredded—squeeze to remove excess liquid
- Add 1 tsp nutmeg
- Add 1 cup pecans, chopped

CHOCOLATE CARAMEL BROWNIES
Makes 18 brownies

INGREDIENTS

- 1 cup Amish Friendship Bread starter
- 3 eggs
- 1 cup oil
- ½ cup milk
- 1 tsp vanilla extract
- ½ cup sugar
- 2 cups flour
- 3 tsp cocoa
- 1½ tsp baking powder
- ½ tsp baking soda
- ½ tsp salt
- 1 box Jell-O instant chocolate pudding
- ¾ cup dark chocolate chips
- ½ cup semi-sweet chocolate chips
- 1 cup caramel bits
- ½ cup caramel bits to sprinkle on top

DIRECTIONS

1. Preheat oven to 325° F. Grease and flour 9" × 13" pan.
2. Combine the starter, eggs, oil, milk, vanilla extract, and sugar in a bowl. In a separate bowl combine the flour, cocoa, baking powder, baking soda, salt, pudding mix, both kinds of chocolate chips, and 1 cup caramel bits and make a well in the center. Pour the wet ingredients into the well and incorporate until fully mixed.
3. Pour into prepared pan and sprinkle remaining ½ cup of caramel bits on top. Bake for 45 minutes to one hour, checking for doneness. When a toothpick inserted in the center of the brownies comes out clean, remove to a rack to cool.

AMISH FRIENDSHIP BREAD PANCAKES
Makes 8–10 pancakes

INGREDIENTS
- 2 cups Amish Friendship Bread starter
- ½ cup nonfat milk
- 1 egg, yolk and white separated
- 2 tbs oil
- 1 cup flour
- ½ tsp salt
- 1 tsp baking powder
- 1 tsp baking soda

DIRECTIONS
1. Combine the starter, milk, egg yolk, and oil in a medium-size bowl. Combine flour, salt, baking powder, and baking soda in a larger bowl and make a well in the center. Pour the wet ingredients into the well and whisk until fully incorporated.
2. Beat the egg white in a separate bowl until stiff peaks form, then gently fold into the batter.
3. Spoon batter onto greased griddle over medium heat. Cook until bubbles appear on the surface, then flip with a spatula. Remove when browned on the other side.

AMISH FRIENDSHIP BREAD BISCUITS
Makes 24 biscuits

INGREDIENTS

- 1 cup Amish Friendship Bread starter
- ¼ cup oil
- 2 eggs, beaten
- 2 cups flour
- ½ tsp salt
- 2 tsp baking powder
- ½ tsp baking soda
- ¼ stick butter, melted

DIRECTIONS

1. Preheat oven to 350° F.
2. Combine the starter, oil, and eggs in a medium-size bowl. Combine the flour, salt, baking powder, and baking soda in a larger bowl and make a well in the center.
3. Pour the wet ingredients into the well and whisk until fully incorporated and dough begins to pull away from the sides of the bowl.
4. Transfer dough mixture to a lightly floured surface and roll to ½-inch thickness.
5. Using a 3-inch round cookie cutter, cut out biscuits and place on lightly greased cookie sheet.
6. Brush the tops of the biscuits with melted butter. Cover loosely with oiled plastic wrap and let rise for 30 minutes.
7. Bake for 15–20 minutes. Serve immediately.

Quick Tips:

- When omitting cinnamon, you can dust the pans with sugar.
- If you're looking to reduce your cholesterol intake, use egg substitute and reduce the amount of oil by using ⅓ cup oil, ⅓ cup applesauce, and 1 cup flax meal. Also use flax meal to replace up to 2 eggs (1T flaxseed meal plus 3T water per egg) but not if you are also using it as a replacement for the oil as well.
- If you're looking to reduce your sugar intake, use Stevia or other sugar substitute.
- Consider a different flour or mix of flours like rice flour or potato flour (you may need to use a binding agent such as arrowroot powder or xanthum gum to serve as a gluten replacement for nongluten flours).
- You may replace the milk in the recipe with low-fat or nondairy alternatives such as soy milk. For vegan and gluten-free friendship bread starters and recipes, visit us at friend shipbreadkitchen.com.
- Add a topping:
  - Turbinado sugar will give it an extra sweet crunch.
  - Make a streusel by mixing ⅓ cup butter or margarine (softened at room temperature), ½ cup packed brown sugar, ⅔ cup flour, and 2 tsp cinnamon (you can also replace the flour with quick oats).
  - Finely chopped nuts or coconut add texture and a flavor boost.
  - Drizzle with icing by mixing ½ cup butter or margarine (softened at room temperature), 1 tsp vanilla, 1 lb powdered/confectioners' sugar, and adding milk or water until the right drizzling consistency is achieved.
- Starter out of control? You can freeze it to stop the fermenting process. Let it thaw to room temperature (allow 2–3 hours for one cup of starter) before using.

SOME NOTES FROM THE KITCHEN

Amish Friendship Bread and its many variations have been around for more than thirty years. The spirit of the bread is that it is generously shared and passed on. The Web and news media have published numerous friendship bread recipes, all based on the same basic recipe. In truth there is only so much you can do to tweak the basic recipe and any variation thereof. This makes original attribution almost impossible as the bread and its recipe may have predated the Internet as well. As an author who has recipes in her books, both mine and those of others, I'm including a link to the U.S. Copyright Office about the copyright pertaining to recipes for those who would like to learn more about it: http://www.copyright.gov/fls/fl122.html.

SIX DEGREES OF FRIENDSHIP BREAD

In our ad-hoc test kitchen (aka the Friendship Bread Kitchen), we acknowledge that the friendship bread recipes have come to us from others, who in turn got them from others, and that the recipes may have been tweaked or dabbled with, torn apart and rebuilt, gone vegan, gone low cholesterol, gone chocolate mania, and so on. We do our best to attribute whenever possible, and would like to especially thank the wonderful food bloggers and fans of our Facebook page (facebook.com/fbkitchen) who have so generously shared their friendship bread recipes, images, and experiences with us.

For More Information

The Compassionate Friends is an organization committed to providing friendship, understanding, and hope to those who have lost a child (at any age, from any cause) or for those trying to help others going through this life-altering experience. You can learn more about them at www.compassionatefriends.org, or call 877-969-0010.

Open to Hope Foundation is an online resource for people who have experienced loss. They can be found at www.opentohope.com.

For more Amish Friendship Bread recipes or to join our online friendship bread community, visit the book's website at the **Friendship Bread Kitchen,** www.friendshipbreadkitchen.com, or find us on Facebook (www.facebook.com/fbkitchen) or Twitter (www.twitter.com/fbkitchen).

Friendship Bread

DARIEN GEE

A READER'S GUIDE

A Conversation with Darien Gee

Random House: Give us a taste of *Friendship Bread* and some of the characters you created to tell this story. Who was your favorite, who did you connect with the most?

Darien Gee: I have a tenderness for the scenes where Julia Evarts can't get out of bed or where her husband, Mark, is fumbling with a broken token of love. It makes my heart ache when I see Julia's sister, Livvy, going about her life so earnestly but also with so much fragility that I'm worried she might break. I'm grateful that Madeline Davis, owner of the tea salon, gives cellist Hannah Wang de Brisay a book that changes her life. Edie Gallagher sometimes shouldn't speak her mind, but I'm glad (most of the time) that she does. I'm cheering for Connie Colls, from the Avalon Wash and Dry, that she might find her way in the world. I had a lot of fun writing the anecdotal characters, the people from the town of Avalon whose lives were touched by the bread, and I do have to say that Gloria, the psychic, makes me laugh, and I'm charmed by Double A, the biker who bakes. This my round-about, duck-the-question way of saying that, as a mother and author, I don't play favorites—I love them all.

RH: What was your inspiration for the book?

DG: In the spring of 2009 my then eight-year-old daughter brought home a Ziploc bag of Amish Friendship Bread starter. My initial response had been a shake of the head—the starter looked so unappetizing that I couldn't see how it would be worth doing. But as I read through the instructions, I became intrigued, and by the time I tasted the bread, I was hooked. As I was finishing the last piece, I saw a woman in my mind who was reluctantly holding up a bag of the starter, regarding it with a frown. I didn't know where she had gotten the starter but one thing was clear—she was enveloped in sadness, stuck in the day-to-day motions that mimicked life when in fact she hadn't felt alive in years. I knew right then that I wanted to find out more, and I started writing that night.

RH: What is Amish Friendship Bread? Is it really Amish?

DG: Amish Friendship Bread is a cinnamon-sugar cake-like bread made from a sourdough starter that's shared and passed along from friend to friend, neighbor to neighbor, co-worker to co-worker. The first documented appearance of Amish Friendship Bread was in the early 1990s when a Girl Scout troop sent a letter almost identical to the one that circulates today. To my knowledge no one has been able to definitively determine if it originated from the Amish (one of the key ingredients is a box of instant pudding, so I'll let you be the judge). Amish Friendship Bread is less about the actual recipe and more about sharing and community, key principles often associated with the Amish, which is why I think it bears that name.

RH: Tell us about the "Six Degrees of Friendship Bread."

DG: Whenever people tell me they've never heard of Amish Friendship Bread, my response is always, "I bet I can find someone within six degrees of separation [the concept that everyone is six steps away from any other person] who has received the starter or baked the bread." And I always do.

RH: Some people call Amish Friendship Bread a culinary or viral chain letter. Can you tell us about that?

DG: When you receive a bag of starter, the instructions tell you how to care for the starter and then, on Day Ten, divide it and give three bags to three friends, saving one for yourself. Theoretically, if everyone you gave it to did the same thing, after five rounds there would be 1,024 bags of starter floating around out there. After ten rounds, there would be 1,048,576 bags. And after twenty rounds, 1,099,511,627,776 bags (yes, that's over one trillion). It's exponential growth—and on top of that, each bag of starter makes two loaves of bread! Of course not everyone chooses to bake or pass on the starter, but imagine what it would be like if everyone did. And while it is like a chain letter, the good news is that even though the instructions tell you to pass it on, there's no threat or negative consequence if you don't.

RH: As a mother of three children, was it difficult to write about Julia's relationship with her son?

DG: When I first started writing the novel, I didn't know about Josh. When the story started to unfold, I felt a shock and sadness as if I were hearing the news from a friend—I experienced a kind of disbelief, a how-could-this-happen sort of response. I did think about my kids during this time, but as a writer I had to keep writing and follow the story to the end because I wanted to know if Julia would be okay.

RH: Do you think a single act, such as baking for a loved one, can really have the kind of ripple effect you write about in the novel? Is it possible for one person to be able to bring together an entire community like Julia does?

DG: Absolutely. Granted, I am of the "anything is possible" mindset, but I think history has shown that a single person can make a big difference. In the case of Julia, it was never her intention to play the role she did. She just did something that felt good and wanted to share it, as did Madeline and Hannah, and so on and so forth.

RH: Do you still bake friendship bread? What are some of your favorite recipes?

DG: I bake Amish Friendship Bread once or twice a month. I'm always experimenting with new ways to use the starter in recipes, and I have virtual kitchen assistants who help me test and tweak recipes through my website, the Friendship Bread Kitchen (www .friendshipbreadkitchen.com). There are many sweet bread variations (lemon poppyseed, zucchini chocolate chip, butterscotch, and apple spice to name a few), and you can make biscuits and pancakes, too. The cranberry-walnut-flax is one of my favorite recipes for muffins, and we just came up with an amazing recipe for a chocolate cherry almond Amish Friendship Bread biscotti. But the basic recipe that comes with the starter is the simplest and the best.

RH: How do you find the time to write as a mom of three young children whom you homeschool?

DG: I write whenever I can, as often as I can, but I never force it unless I'm on deadline. I've discovered that I'm a better writer because I'm a busy parent—I don't have the luxury of writer's block. When I was single with no kids, I took a whole year off to write, and in the end, even with an agent agreement in hand, I couldn't cross the finish line. My husband, Darrin, is a big reason I'm able to pull it all off. He knows how important writing is to me, and he does everything he can to support me by being with the kids when he's not working or letting me sleep in when I've been writing all night.

RH: What's next?

DG: My next novel is also set in the town of Avalon, Illinois. I believe that scrapbooking and other forms of memory keeping play an important role in keeping special moments alive in us, and the characters in this new novel discover this for themselves as they navigate through the mundane and more challenging aspects of their lives. The heart of the novel is about friendship, of course, but also about how we honor and celebrate the memories and people who've made a difference in our lives. I had a lot of fun writing this book because it helped me reconnect with my creative, crafty side, and also gave me an excuse to start putting some of my own family albums together. Readers will have a chance to get to know some of the more peripheral characters from *Friendship Bread* while meeting new ones, too.

Questions and Topics for Discussion

1. Amish Friendship Bread is the sweet thread that weaves itself throughout the whole story. What are your experiences with the bag of starter, ten-day fermenting process, and the recipes you used to bake the bread?

2. Julia is clearly suffering from depression. What is the cause of her depression and whom does she blame? In what ways does her husband enable her to continue with her destructive emotional pattern? How does this leave him vulnerable?

3. Hannah is a concert cellist who is no longer able to perform due to a back injury and is now living in Avalon. How did she end up moving to Avalon and why does she feel so alone and unhappy? How does she discover a purpose for living in her new life in Avalon?

4. Livvy carries deep pain and guilt that leaks into all aspects of her life. What happened in her past that causes her so much grief? How does that tragedy affect her relationships, self-esteem, and everyday decisions?

5. Throughout the book, we meet many unique and colorful residents of Avalon. What is the common theme of these characters, and of those people, who was your favorite and why?

6. Edie, a very ambitious reporter/writer who follows her boyfriend, Dr. Richard, to the small town of Avalon, is looking for her big break with a story that will get her noticed. What happens that could change her ambitious career plans?

7. Madeline, who owns the teashop and seems like a fairy godmother, reveals that she also has regrets in her life. What are her regrets? How is she trying to redeem herself and make things right? Does this confession change your perception of Madeline? Explain.

8. Hannah, Julia, and Mark all end up in Chicago at the same time. How is this trip a defining moment for each of them?

9. Edie writes an article for the local newspaper about the origin of Amish Friendship Bread in Avalon, singling out one character as the person who started passing around the batter. How does her article affect that person and what kind of chain reaction does it trigger? Does Edie ever discover the real story behind the Amish Friendship Bread?

10. After many days of torrential rains, the local river threatens to flood its banks and although Avalon is spared, the neighboring town of Barrett is not so lucky with many families displaced. How does the gesture to help the needy families of Barrett snowball and serve to unite the residents of Avalon as well?

11. Many relationships were forged, reinforced, and restored throughout the story. How did friendship bread play a part in the mending of those relationships?

12. How do the prologue and the epilogue of *Friendship Bread* bring the story full circle?

Read on for an excerpt from

Memory Keeping

A NOVEL

DARIEN GEE

PUBLISHED BY
BALLANTINE BOOKS

The goat was Connie's idea.

"I'm not so sure about this," Madeline Davis says, frowning. At seventy-five she's trying to make her life simpler, not the other way around. Then again, running a tea salon isn't what most people her age are doing these days. Madeline's days are busy, yes, but she goes to sleep each night happily content, her heart full. And for the past year she's had Connie Colls, her tea salon manager, an unexpected godsend dressed in black with spiky hair, who has also become her friend and housemate.

Now Connie is tearfully looking at her and Madeline feels herself wavering. Connie has never asked for anything before and seeing this young woman about to cry is more than Madeline can bear.

"Well . . ." she says reluctantly. "Maybe for a couple of days until you can find a more suitable home." She watches unhappily as the goat sniffs its way around the garden, then starts chewing on a patch of orange nasturtiums.

"Oh!" Connie wipes her eyes and hurries toward the goat. She waves her hands over the flowers in an attempt to shoo the goat away, but the animal ignores her.

Lord, Madeline knows how this is going to go. She watches as Connie tugs unsuccessfully on the goat's makeshift collar, a frayed rope with a tail that has been chewed through. Well, the good news is that the goat belongs to someone. They just have to find out who.

"I'm going inside," she tells Connie, who's trying to drag the goat into the shade of a walnut tree.

"Thank you, Madeline," Connie says, forcing a bright smile. "She won't be any trouble at all, I promise."

"Hmm. Well, I think she's eating my Double Delights."

Connie turns, stricken. *"No! No roses! Bad goat!"*

Madeline just shakes her head and walks through the back door of the house into her kitchen.

The morning light streams in behind her, a generous sliver of sunshine falling onto the farmer's table that rests in the middle of the kitchen. Fresh loaves of Amish Friendship Bread, scones, and muffins are cooling on wire racks. Two arugula and bacon quiches are in the oven. Her kitchen is fragrant and inviting and Madeline knows her customers find these smells a reassuring comfort. They come to Madeline's Tea Salon for that very reason—the promise of good food and an encouraging smile. A kind word and possibly a joke or two, depending on her mood.

If they're lucky they may get more, like an impromptu performance by Hannah Wang, the young cellist who used to play with the New York Philharmonic and who now resides in Avalon. There's Bettie Shelton, too, with her mobile scrapbooking business. She comes in under the pretense of ordering a pot of Darjeeling tea while she indiscreetly sets up her wares at an adjoining table. On the days Bettie is here even the least crafty Avalonian or unsuspecting tourist is sure to leave with a packet of patterned paper and random embellishments. Madeline remembers what happened last month when a group of men had lunch at the salon, hunched over a table as they ate, speaking in low whispers. It was clear by their body language that they didn't want to be disturbed. Bettie, however, had marched up to them undaunted. Less than a minute later the men found their table littered with colorful ribbons and glittery sequins. Two men bought scrapbooking starter kits, dazed looks on their faces as they handed their money to Bettie. As quickly as she had arrived, Bettie was gone, leaving everyone to wonder what happened while Madeline cleared her table with a chuckle.

The small brass bell over the front door tinkles. A pair of women walk in, smile at Madeline, and choose a table by the window. Madeline knows it's only a matter of time before the tea salon will be bustling with people and laughter.

She selects several tins of the chamomile and rooibos tea blend from the large antique armoire that graces the dining room. She's not sure what came first—discovering so many wonderful finds at garage sales and antique stores and then pondering what to put in them, or knowing that she wanted to sell her own tea blends and looking for an artful way to display them. It was just a small thing to help pass the time in those early months when business was slow, but now it's taken on a life of its own. Connie wants them to open an online store but that's more than Madeline is willing to take on right now. At the moment this balance feels just right, however hectic it may be.

In the kitchen, Connie is at the sink, scrubbing her hands. "Serena took off into the neighbor's yard but she's back now," she says, a look of apologetic guilt on her face when Madeline walks in. "She, uh, kind of ate a few heads of lettuce from their garden."

Madeline raises an eyebrow. "Kind of?"

Connie fakes a cough. "Well, she ate them, but then she threw them back up." Connie wipes her hands on a dishtowel, avoiding eye contact. "I'll call the vet later to see if there's anything special we should be feeding her. Maybe Serena has a delicate stomach."

Goodness. Madeline isn't sure what's more concerning, that Connie has named the goat or that the goat has found its way into Walter Lassiter's vegetable garden. His wife, Dolores, doesn't mind the steady traffic of the tea salon but Walter is always looking for something to complain about. Madeline has a feeling a stray goat may just push him over the edge.

"I'm sure Serena's stomach is just fine," she says, handing Connie the tea. "Do you mind wrapping these? Dora Ponce is putting together a gift basket for the Rotary club auction and I told her we'd make a donation."

"Sure." Connie drapes an apron over her head. "I'll use that pretty paper I picked up at the farmer's market last week. Lucy Pavord is selling her whole stock—she's going to start making birdhouses instead." Connie is about to say more when there's a holler from the dining room. It's followed by the unmistakable sound of porcelain breaking.

"Help!" they hear one of the women shout. "There's a wild beast in here!" Connie hurries to the dining room. There's a stern reprimand and then another exclamation accompanied by the sound of more good china crashing to the floor.

To outsiders Avalon may look like a nondescript Illinois river town, but Madeline knows better. She reaches for the broom and dustpan with a happy sigh then heads to the dining room.

Isabel grasps the hammer and pounds the FOR SALE sign into her front lawn. The earth is hard and unyielding, dry from too much Illinois heat, another long hot August that shows no sign of relief. Maybe she should have watered the lawn first. Maybe she should have hired the kid down the street to do this instead. Maybe she should have called a real estate agent and listed her house properly, instead of trying to do it on her own like so many things these days.

But Isabel doesn't want to wait for people to call her back, to check their schedules, to haggle a fee. To find the garden hose, wherever that is.

Bang bang bang. The sign shakes and shivers.

Last night, when she was the last person wandering the dusky streets after a seven o'clock showing of *The Man from Mars,* Isabel had stopped at Avalon Sunshine Hardware to pick up some laundry detergent. There they were, on clearance, fifteen cans of paint stacked in a pyramid, pointing to the sky. I'll take them all, she told the cashier, handing him a $100 bill. And some of those brushes, too.

She'd declined a drop cloth, spackle, turpentine. Too many things to remember. Just the paint, she'd said. And then she saw it. A sign, bent at the corners, leaning forlornly against the paint cans.

FOR SALE BY OWNER.

She bought that, too. Isabel had everything sent to the house this morning and she met the delivery boy at the door, a hammer already in hand.

Now Isabel steps back to survey her work. The sign is crooked, but it's good enough, and it's clearly visible from the street. She knows her neighbors will be curious, maybe even nervous that she's selling. Avalon is the sort of place where most people come to settle down, where families spend whole lifetimes. Isabel herself married into this small town, Bill having been born and raised here. Buried here, too, almost five years now.

There's a flutter of curtains from the house next door. It's her neighbor Bettie Shelton, the town fussbudget. Isabel knows Bettie had a hand in spreading the news about Bill's departure and then his death two months later, a wrong turn down a one-way street. Casseroles were sprouting on her porch like mushrooms.

"Isabel Kidd!" she hears Bettie holler from inside her house. Bettie's silvery blue hair is still in curlers. She struggles to open the window then settles on rapping the glass so hard Isabel is afraid it might break. The look on Bettie's face is indignant. "What on heaven's earth do you think you're doing?"

Isbael pretends to pick at a speck of dust on the sign.

"Isabel? Do you hear me?"

Isabel gives the sign a halfhearted tap with the hammer.

"ISABEL!"

Exasperated, Isabel scowls and gives the hammer a shake. "Of course I hear you! Who doesn't hear you?" Catty corner from her house, Isabel sees Peggy Lively emerge from her house, dressed in her fuzzy pink bathrobe. "You hear her, don't you, Peggy?"

Peggy just stares at Isabel for a moment before grabbing the morning paper from the walk and hurrying back inside. The door slams shut behind her and Isabel hears the lock sliding into place.

Isabel shoots Bettie an annoyed look and then gives the sign one last pound for good measure. She heads back into the house, knowing that Bettie's prying eyes are watching her retreat.

Inside, Isabel slows when she approaches her living room where the circle of paint cans are laid out like a labyrinth. Putting up the FOR SALE sign was a lot easier, knowing it could be pulled up at anytime, no harm done, a whim put to bed. But this is different. Once done, it can't be undone.

Isabel hesitates, then picks a can at random. She uses a screwdriver to crack it open. It smells new, like a promise, and that's all she needs.

Isabel dips a paint brush into the one-gallon can of Whisper White and puts her first stroke on the wall. It streaks—there's not enough color on the bristles. She dips the brush again and swirls it until it's heavy with paint, then lifts and tries again. This time there's a thick swath of white, smooth and complete. She follows with another stroke, bolder this time.

It goes faster than she thinks, and soon the entire wall is done. It's a blank stare looking back at her, giving away nothing. Isabel leans closer, looking for a hint of the past, but sees nothing other than her own shadow as the tip of her nose bumps against the damp wall. *Ouch.* And then Isabel remembers other white walls.

There, that wasn't so bad, was it?

No, doctor, it wasn't.

Of course he had asked her when she was in a morphine-induced daze, happy to talk to anyone and everyone. Bill wasn't there, didn't even know what had happened. And then, when she was finally ready to find him and tell him, there was the news that he was gone. Dead.

What is it with dentists and their dental assistants? It's an embarrassing cliche that Isabel has to live with. My husband left me for his dental assistant, a woman ten years younger than me. I had a miscarriage, and she had a baby with Bill's blue eyes and his unfortunate big ears.

Isabel had opened the envelope without thinking, had stared at the baby announcement in shock. It was a slap in the face. It was like that woman had to have the final word, had to prove that she still something while Isabel was left with nothing.

So now, at the ripe old age of thirty-eight, Isabel Kidd is alone. No husband, no children. An unsatisfying job as a customer service representative for a corrugated paper company in Rockford, about forty-five minutes away. Some money from Bill's pension. His share of the dental practice went to his partner, Randall Strombauer, a man Isabel never cared for. He's the one who hired the assistant with an eye, Isabel suspects, of having her all to himself. Randall was the single guy while Bill was safely ensconced in a marriage of fifteen years. An open playing field with Randall as the only player. But, of course, things have a way of not working out as planned.

The remaining walls in the living room look shabby and lifeless, dull neighbors to the freshly painted wall. That's how it goes sometimes, she supposes. She could keep it as an accent wall, but she feels for the others. They deserve a fresh start as well. After all, they were all innocent bystanders.

This time she'll do it differently—no need to slap one stroke on after the other. After all, this is her house, her walls. She can do whatever she wants with it.

Isabel dips her brush and begins again.

Yvonne Tate checks the address one last time before shoving the scrap of paper into her pocket. The house in front of her is a sweet bungalow with a white picket fence, sycamore trees lining the street. She opens the gate and goes up the walk, noticing the well-tended lawn and garden. Flower boxes filled with geraniums and impatiens in a summer burst of colors line the windows, butterflies dancing in the garden. It's a sweet home.

Yvonne presses the doorbell and waits. She hears voices inside, a man and a woman arguing, and a second later the door opens.

"May I help you?" The woman is young and pretty, in her late twenties. Her husband stands behind her, about the same age.

"I'm Yvonne Tate. Tate Plumbing. You called about an emergency?"

The couple stares at her. The wife looks past Yvonne for another person, presumably the "real" plumber while the husband just gawks at Yvonne, his mouth slightly open in surprise.

"It's just me," Yvonne tells them good-naturedly. She knows she doesn't look the part. She's slender and athletic, her blond hair pulled back in a ponytail. She has the requisite T-shirt, jeans, and work boots, along with her toolbox, but even with these accouterments and no makeup she is still often mistaken for a model. "We spoke on the phone an hour ago?" she reminds the woman. Yvonne pulls out the piece of paper. "Megan and Billy Newman, right?"

Megan Newman just stares at her. "Yeah, but I thought you were the *receptionist.*"

"I am the receptionist. I'm also the bookkeeper, sales director, and of course, plumber. I'm a one woman show." Yvonne glances at her watch. "Now, why don't you show me the problem?"

Megan doesn't look convinced but her husband is quick to step aside and invite Yvonne in, earning him a glare from his wife.

"How long have you been doing this?" Megan asks, a skeptical look on her face.

"Ten years though I've only been in Avalon about six months. I'm licensed in three states and have a flawless track record." Yvonne takes in the honey colored hardwood floors, the gingham curtains, the slipcovered couch and loveseat. Fresh flowers in glass vases are dotted throughout the house. Wedding pictures are everywhere. "So what's the problem again?" she asks.

Megan and Billy exchange a look. "It's probably easier if we show you," Billy says.

Yvonne follows them into the master bathroom. Once in the bathroom, she lets out a small giggle but quickly composes herself. "Oh," she says. "I see."

Pots and pans are stacked in the bathtub.

"It's just temporary until we figure out what happened in the kitchen," Megan says hurriedly. "We'll show you that later. This is the problem in here." The bathroom sink is new, with two antique faucets, one labeled hot and one labeled cold. Megan turns the knob on the left for the cold water, but water shoots out from the faucet on the right, and vice versa.

"I thought I installed it right," Billy says, scratching his head. "But obviously it's a bit messed up."

"Really, Billy?" his wife says, annoyed. "You *think*?"

"You'll also want to install some shut-off valves," Yvonne says, pointing to the piping below the sink.

"Yeah, I was going to do that next," Billy says, his face red. Megan shoots him a look.

She explains to Yvonne. "I told him we should hire professionals for the plumbing and electrical projects, but no, he had to do it himself. Come on." She motions for Yvonne to follow her.

In the kitchen she opens the doors beneath the sink, revealing a maze of bizarre piping, including a cut-up milk jug attached to the P-trap with zip ties and duct tape. "The kitchen sink leaks so bad that we can't use it at all," Megan says. "Billy rigged up this contraption to catch the water but there's so much we don't even bother using the sink at all. It was supposed to be a temporary thing but we're coming up on three weeks. I can't take it anymore!"

"It's not so bad . . ." Billy begins.

"We're doing our dishes in the *bathtub*, Billy!"

Well, that explains that. "These are pretty easy fixes," Yvonne assures her. She turns to Billy. "Why didn't you just put a bucket underneath, by the way?"

He opens his mouth to respond then scratches his head. "Yeah, that does make better sense," he says.

Yvonne just grins. "I should be able to take care of everything today," she tells them. "If you'd like." She quotes them a price and Megan nods enthusiastically.

"Yes," she says. "Please start right away."

"I thought it would be more expensive," Billy says, surprised. "The company we called quoted us almost double."

Yvonne shrugs. She doesn't worry about the competition, has always had an attitude that there's enough business for everyone. "I'll give you an itemized invoice of the work when I'm done, too."

Megan is humming happily as she goes to the fridge and pulls out a carafe of iced tea and a couple of glasses from a cupboard. She fills the glasses with ice then adds the iced tea. She pushes one of the glasses toward Yvonne. "This is for you," she says. Then she gives her husband a pointed look and picks up her own glass. "I'll be outside."

Billy watches uneasily as Yvonne opens her toolbox. He shoves his hands in his pockets. "She's mad," he says. "I guess I'm a dope for trying to do our own plumbing."

"Not at all," Yvonne assures him. "I think it's great that you tried, Billy." Yvonne is used to coming to the rescue after disastrous DIY plumbing projects—this is nothing. She's all for people learning how to take care of their homes and perform simple home maintenance tasks, but you have to do your homework, have to put in a little more time than just watching a three-minute YouTube video on how to seal your tub. "I'm sure you would have figured it out eventually," she says kindly.

He smiles, grateful, then casts a longing look toward Megan who's leaning back on a lawn chair, her hands shading the sun from her eyes.

"Go join your wife," Yvonne encourages. "She's just ready to have your house in working order. You've been married about a year?"

Billy looks at her in surprise. "Eleven months," he says. "How'd you know?"

Yvonne just gives a nonchalant shrug, digs through her tools for a crescent wrench. Yvonne doesn't tell him what else she thinks, that Megan is clearly nesting. She's seen it in clients before. She's not sure that Billy knows yet, or maybe not even Megan, but Yvonne would bet her bottom dollar that Megan is pregnant.

"She just wants to make your home nice," Yvonne says. "Go on."
Billy grins and then lopes outside after his wife. Yvonne smiles.

Her job isn't dull, that's for sure. She's seen everything in this business—men who try to sweet talk her or aggressively haggle or even intimidate her to get a lower fee. She's been asked out more times than she cares to remember, once by a woman even. She's heard every joke in the book about plumber's crack and whether or not she wears a thong. She's used to it, but it doesn't happen often. Most of her clients are nice, decent people, surprised to find a young woman in this line of work, but supportive nonetheless.

Yvonne loves what she does. It reminds her that things are not always as they seem, that her life is her own, always has been and always will be. Still, it wasn't until ten years ago that Yvonne understood that she needed to step up and actually own it.

It came at a price, of course. On the days where she's feeling lonely or homesick, she battles temptation to pick up the phone, to get on a plane, to look up information she'd be better off not knowing. As difficult as it can be sometimes, Yvonne knows she has to stay the course. It's too painful otherwise.

She looks outside and sees Billy sitting in the chair next to his wife, talking to her. Megan laughs at something he says, and Billy leans over to give his wife a kiss.

It's tender and sweet, yet Yvonne has to look away. She swallows the lump in her throat and gets back to work.

"Here you go." The bartender hefts a plastic bag full of bottle caps onto the bar. There's the sound of metal cascading into a lazy pile as the bag almost tips over, the top unsealed. "Whoa!"

"I got it," Ava says easily, catching the bag in time. The bag is nice and heavy in her hand, and already a couple of bottle caps catch her eye—a navy blue one with a yellow starburst and a red one with white block lettering across the top. Quite a few are bent but that's okay—she wants to practice a few new techniques and they'll do perfectly.

"Great reflexes," the bartender says, grinning. His name is Colin. He unties the apron from around his waist and tosses it into a pile with the dirty towels.

"It's parenthood." Ava gives the bag a shake, delighting in the weight of it. There's easily 200 caps, maybe more. "I've caught many a falling sippy cups in my time."

"In your time?" Colin does a quick appraisal of her and Ava laughs, knowing she looks like a kid herself these days, careless and frayed around the edges. "How old is your son again?" Colin has two boys of his own, in high school.

"Four, going on twenty." Ava reaches for her wallet. "And I'm twenty eight going on fifty."

"I hear that." Colin instantly reddens. "I mean, not that you look like you're going on fifty, because you're obviously not. You don't even look twenty eight." He groans. "Sorry. I just mean I know what it's like to have your hands full."

"It's okay. I know." Ava smiles. "Well, thanks for this. How much do I owe you?"

Colin holds up his hands. "This one's on the house. It's my last day."

"Your last day?"

"Got laid off. A bunch of us did. Restaurant's 'renovating.'" Colin says this sarcastically, with a shake of his head, but then sighs. He gestures to the empty booths and tables around them, even though it's only an hour past lunch time. "They're going bare bones until business picks up. But I found a new job at the Avalon Grill starting tomorrow, so I'll be all right. It's part-time for now, but I hear the full-time guy is a jerk so you never know."

"The Avalon Grill?"

"Yeah. I'll check with my manager, but I'm sure it won't be a problem to put aside some bottle caps for you if you don't mind the driving over to pick them up. It's about an extra fifteen minutes from Barrett."

"Yeah, I know." Ava remembers a pear and blue cheese salad that she used to have for lunch all the time and her stomach rumbles, hungry. "I used to work in Avalon."

Colin writes something on a piece of paper then slides it across the bar toward Ava. "Here's my number. Call me in a couple of weeks and I'll let you know what I have. Or, you know, just call me anytime." His eyes hold hers for a second longer than usual, then he glances away, embarrassed.

Ava doesn't quite remember Colin's marital situation but knows he's either divorced or separated, both of which are already far too complicated for Ava. He's a nice guy and she appreciates his help these past couple of years, putting aside used bottle caps for her and charging no more than a cup of coffee for them, but she can't see beyond that right now. Doesn't want anything beyond that right now.

"Thanks," she says. Her guard is back up, the way it always is when she's around someone who's hitting on her. Awkwardly she slips the piece of paper into her purse and offers her hand. "Well, good luck, Colin."

He shakes it, his cheeks still pink. "You, too, Ava."

In her car, Ava lets out a long breath. She gives the bag a poke, sad that she won't be seeing Colin again, weary at the thought of having to find another source in Barrett for her bottle caps. She knows Colin takes special care not to bend them more than necessary, has actually seen him use a soft cloth over the bottle opener, careful not to scratch the cap. He makes it look easy and effortless and most customers don't even notice that he's taking this extra step, but Ava knows.

She feels herself blinking back tears. She was foolish to let herself get attached, even in this small way. But Colin is really one of the only people she can talk to and he's a decent person, which counts for a lot.

Still, she should know better.

Ava starts her car, the engine reluctantly kicking over, a sign that there's trouble up ahead or at least something that will need attention. A new fuel pump, the starter, a weak battery, who knows. Ava wills the car to last a little longer, begs it, pleads with it. The engine revs and Ava feels a spark of hope that things will be all right.

Then the engine sputters and dies altogether.

Frances Latham gazes at the small black-and-white photograph in her hand. The mop of black hair, the chubby cheeks, the searching dark eyes staring back at her.

"Beautiful," Frances breathes.

The package came yesterday. Reed, her husband, knew it was coming because people started posting on the boards that their referrals had arrived. Pictures were posted with virtual cheers from everyone in the group with the same log-in date from the time their adoption application was accepted by the Chinese government.

But there was envy, too, and anxiety for those who were still waiting. Frances had been ecstatic and then crashed, crying, her emotions bouncing all over the place. Why hadn't they received their referral? What if something was wrong? Reed assured her that everything was fine, but how did he know? How did any of them know? They finally called the agency and the agency confirmed that yes, people were getting their referrals, and the Lathams should receive theirs by the end of the week.

And then Jamie Linde arrived in his UPS truck, a package in hand. Frances could tell by the look on his face that he knew what it was. He didn't seem at all surprised by the hug or the tears, and even offered to take a picture of her holding up the heavy, flat envelope. Frances got Noah, her five year old, to take the picture because she wanted Jamie in it. She had the picture printed the next day and wrote on the back, "Me with our stork, Jamie Linde."

Reed came home immediately and they opened the envelope together. Well, they tried to, at least. The cardboard tab ripped so Reed had to find scissors, and then Frances panicked that they might cut something inside. In the end they used an x-acto knife to carefully slice along one side, wanting to preserve everything as much as possible.

When they saw the picture clipped to the stack of documents, Reed's eyes got wet and Frances gasped. "She's beautiful! Look at her, Reed!" He just nodded and wiped his eyes.

There is still more waiting ahead, but now they know. They know that this little girl is the one that will make their family complete.

Frances closes her eyes, feels the hot tears of joy and relief coming again. They've already made copies of the picture so Reed can take one to work, and each of the older boys wanted one as well. Frances taped copies on the fridge, the bathroom mirrors, the home office, the car. She sent framed copies to her mother and to Reed's parents.

But this one, the original, the one that came from China and taken by someone who had looked this little girl in the eyes, this is the picture Frances holds in her hands.

Mei Ling. Our daughter.

Frances and Reed pored over every detail, put stickies on the pages to send to the agency to get translated, made notes in their notebook of questions and things that needed clarifying. But the bottom line is that they are one step closer to bringing her home.

The phone rings and Frances jumps to answer it. "Hello?" Her voice is breathless.

"Hi, sweetheart." It's Reed, and Frances smiles. He sounds tired, but happy. "How's your day going?"

"Good. Wonderful. Perfect. Do you have to ask?"

Reed laughs, a low baritone that reminds her of her father. Frances wishes that he was alive, that he could meet this little girl, his soon-to-be-granddaughter. "I guess not. I'm just calling to see if you want to take the boys out for dinner. Give you a night off."

"I already have a marinara sauce simmering on the stove," she says. "With meatballs. It's spaghetti night, remember? Tuesday?" Frances is gazing dreamily at Mei Ling's picture and then it hits her. "Wait. You're going to be traveling again, aren't you? Where? When?"

"Arizona. One week. I leave the day after tomorrow."

"Reed . . ."

"Fran, I know. But there's no way around it. And the way I see it,

the more I do now, the easier it'll be when I have to put in my vacation days when we go to China to pick Mei Ling up."

Frances tucks Mei Ling's picture back into a wax paper envelope.
"I wish I knew when that was going to be."

"I know. Me, too."

The timeline is sketchy at best, but now that they've been matched
with Mei Ling, it could be anywhere from six months to a year before
a travel date is set. They have to be ready either way, and even though
there are a few more hoops to jump through, the worst is over.

"So dinner in or out?" Reed asks. "I have to go in a minute—one
more meeting and then I can head home."

"Let's go out," Frances says. She can refrigerate the sauce for another day. At least there won't be any dishes to worry about tonight.

"Did the agency say anything about the medical records yet?"

"No. I sent them an email this morning but I haven't heard back.
I didn't want to call and hound them anymore than I already have."
Frances turns the heat off on the stove.

"I'll call them before I leave the office," Reed says. "See you soon."

"Bye."

Noah, their middle boy, struts into the kitchen. That's his thing
these days—he likes to walk in and command a room. Reed says
Noah is a lot like his uncle, Reed's brother Jason. Too smart for his
own good, Reed often says, and always the center of attention. But
Jason must be doing something right, because he's living in an expensive apartment in Los Angeles, an entertainment lawyer to the stars.

"Mom, Brady won't let me play with the airplane. *My* airplane,
the one I got for Christmas." Noah folds his arms across his chest and
looks cross.

Frances puts away the dry packages of spaghetti. "Can you give
him something else to play with? What about his fire truck?" She
starts clearing the table, readying it for breakfast instead.

"He hates that fire truck. He wants my airplane, but it's mine. I'm
going to hit him."

"Noah." Frances frowns. "We do *not* hit in this family. Got it?"

Noah isn't fazed. "Then I'll lock him in the closet."

Frances is just glad there nobody's here it witness this, especially any of the caseworkers who did the home study for the adoption.

"Noah, you're a big boy. Find something else to play with."

Noah huffs, "Mom!" but turns and stomps back to his room. Frances listens for a yell from Brady, but it doesn't come. In a few minutes they have to go pick up Nick from a friend's house, so they'll have to stop playing anyway.

When the spaghetti sauce is transferred to a container to cool and everything else is washed and put away, Frances grabs her keys and calls to the boys. "Time to get Nick. Everybody in the car!"

When there's no answer, Frances walks down to the boys' room. At some point they'll outgrow this house but for now, Frances likes how cozy it is. All three boys share a room and she likes knowing that at night, they'll all tucked in and together. She's an only child and she always longed for a sibling, always wished she had a brother or a sister to share a room with, to grow up with. Maybe that's why Mei Ling feels so right, so perfect for their family. The boys have one another just like Reed has Jason, but Frances knows that having a little girl is going to change everything for them, and for the better.

Reed teases her that it's just about the fluffy pink dresses and frilly hairbows, but they both know it's much more than that. It's about the softness that comes with having a girl in the home. For Frances, this sweet angel is her long-held wish, her secret hope from the day she married Reed. She always knew she'd have a daughter, and it always surprised her whenever she found out she was having a boy. She wouldn't trade her sons for anything, of course, but always there was the waiting, the expectation. Now it can be put to rest. The daughter she has been waiting for is finally coming.

Frances turns into the boys' room and gasps. Noah and Brady are standing around the remains of a toy airplane, which Noah is proceeding to smash to bits with a plastic baseball bat. Brady is laughing as pieces fly everywhere.

"Noah Tyler Latham! You stop that right now!" Frances hurries forward as Noah takes another swing at the airplane.

"Can't, mom," Noah says. "Airplane crash."

"Airplane crash!" Brady repeats, delighted. He's three. He claps as a plastic shard flies across the room. "Boom!"

"Boom!" Noah roars, and brings the bat down just as Frances tries to grab it. He nails her in the foot and she tumbles toward the beds. "Oh! Sorry, mom."

Frances catches herself, then gives her foot a shake. It stings, but she knows nothing is broken.

"In . . . the . . . car . . . now," she says under her breath. "And then you're cleaning this up when we get home."

"It was Brady's idea," Noah says with a shrug, tossing the bat aside. "Make him do it."

"Brady is *three*." Frances points toward the garage. "GO."

Noah heads out the door with Brady on his heels. Frances stares at the destruction in their wake. She loves her sons, but this supposedly typical boy-behavior is too much. She sees Mei Ling's picture in a frame on the boys' dresser, and feels herself soften once again. Already Frances feels back in balance, no longer outnumbered by all the testosterone in the house.

"You and me," she says, rubbing her foot. She touches the frame gently. "Tea parties and dress up. We'll show these boys how it's done."

DARIEN GEE lives on the Big Island of Hawaii with her husband and their three children. She is currently at work on her next novel. To learn more about Darien and the Friendship Bread Kitchen, visit dariengee.com.

Chat.
Comment.
Connect.

Visit our online book club community at
www.randomhousereaderscircle.com

Chat
Meet fellow book lovers and discuss what you're reading.

Comment
Post reviews of books, ask—and answer—thought-provoking
questions, or give and receive book club ideas.

Connect
Find an author on tour, visit our author blog, or invite one of
our 150 available authors to chat with your group on the phone.

Explore
Also visit our site for discussion questions, excerpts, author
interviews, videos, free books, news on the latest releases,
and more.

Books are better with buddies.
www.RandomHouseReadersCircle.com

RANDOM HOUSE
READER'S CIRCLE
®

THE RANDOM HOUSE PUBLISHING GROUP